D0181048

Rebecca Kertz was first introduced to the Amish when her husband took a job with an Amish construction crew. She enjoyed watching the Amish foreman's children at play and swapping recipes with his wife. Rebecca resides in Delaware with her husband and dog. She has a strong faith in God and feels blessed to have family nearby. Besides writing, she enjoys reading, doing crafts and visiting Lancaster County.

Dana R. Lynn grew up in Illinois. She met her husband at a wedding and told her parents she had met her future husband. Nineteen months later, they were married. Today they live in rural Pennsylvania with their three children, two dogs, one cat, one rabbit, one horse and six chickens. In addition to writing, she works as an educational interpreter for the deaf and is active in several ministries in her church.

REBECCA KERTZ

A Secret Amish Love

&

DANA R. LYNN

Plain Retribution

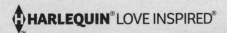

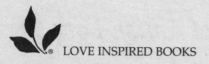

LOVE INSPIRED BOOKS

Recycling programs for this product may not exist in your area.

ISBN-13: 978-1-335-99476-9

A Secret Amish Love and Plain Retribution

Copyright © 2018 by Harlequin Books S.A.

The publisher acknowledges the copyright holders of the individual works as follows:

A Secret Amish Love
Copyright © 2017 by Rebecca Kertz

Plain Retribution
Copyright © 2017 by Dana Roae

www.Harlequin.com

Printed in U.S.A.

CONTENTS

A SECRET AMISH LOVE   7
Rebecca Kertz

PLAIN RETRIBUTION   235
Dana R. Lynn

A SECRET AMISH LOVE

Rebecca Kertz

For my mother-in-law—my other Mom—with love

And now abideth faith, hope, charity,
these three; but the greatest of these is charity.
—1 Corinthians 13:13

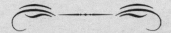

Chapter One

Lancaster County, Pennsylvania

Nell Stoltzfus opened the door to Pierce Veterinary Clinic and gaped as she stepped inside. Pandemonium reigned in the crowded waiting room. Dogs growled and barked as they strained at their leashes. Some owners spoke sharply while others murmured soothingly as they struggled to control their pets.

A cat in a carrier situated on a woman's lap meowed loudly in angry protest of the ear-splitting canine activity. An Amish man sat in the corner of the room with a she-goat. The animal bent her head as she tried to eat a magazine in the rack on the floor near the man's feet. The goat was haltered, and her owner tugged up on the rope lead to keep her from chewing on the glossy pages. The animal bleated loudly as she stubbornly fought to eat.

The goat's noisy discontent joined in the cacophony of human and animal sounds as the unfamiliar Amish man glanced at Nell briefly before returning his attention to his goat.

She searched the room and frowned. Every available seat was taken. There was no sign of Michelle, Dr. Pierce's receptionist, whose job it was to check in patients and, on occasion, bring them into the exam rooms when the veterinary assistant, Janie, was busy.

Nell narrowed her gaze, assessing. On most days, there were usually two or three people in the waiting room. At least, every time she'd brought her dog, Jonas, in, there had been only a few people with their pets waiting.

During her first visit to Pierce Veterinary Clinic, just shy of a month after it opened, she'd sought medical help for Jonas after he was cruelly tossed out of a moving car. The visit had been a memorable one.

She'd met Dr. James Pierce, who'd refused to charge her for taking care of Jonas, requesting instead that she spread word of his clinic to anyone who might benefit from his services. And he'd startled her by offering her a temporary job as his assistant, based on her ability to calm her injured rescue dog who had lain trustingly in her arms.

"You have a natural affinity with animals, Nell," he'd told her during her first visit. During her second and last visit to the clinic, she'd declined but thanked him for his offer, even though she would have liked nothing more than to have the opportunity to learn more about caring for animals since it was her dream to minister to those within her Amish community. But her strong attraction to Dr. Pierce made it wise to keep her distance from him.

Today, Nell had been on her way home after a morning spent with her aunt Katie when she'd decided to stop at the clinic to purchase heartworm medicine for

Jonas. At the veterinarian's suggestion, she had waited to ensure that her dog was fully healed before introducing the medication.

I should go, she thought as she gazed around the room. Clearly, she'd chosen the worst time to come.

She turned to leave, then glanced back when her attention was drawn toward the sound of a door opening and voices. A woman exited from a back room with a tiny kitten.

Nell waited patiently, expecting to glimpse Janie following closely behind. But it wasn't the assistant she saw. It was Dr. Pierce who escorted the woman to the front desk.

Nell watched as he sat at the desk and keyed something into the computer. She heard the deep, indecipherable rumble of his voice as he spoke. The woman handed him a credit card, and Nell continued to watch as Dr. Pierce handled the transaction, then gave the woman a receipt stapled to a paper that she knew would be the animal's health summary.

Nell froze, and her heart beat wildly as Dr. Pierce stood. She sent up a silent prayer that she would remain unnoticed, but she was powerless to move or to keep her gaze from checking for any changes in the man since she last saw him over a month ago.

She released a shuddering breath. The veterinarian was still as handsome as ever, dressed in his white lab coat over a blue shirt and black slacks. His short hair, which was a little longer on the top, was tousled as if he'd recently combed his fingers through the dark brown locks. His features were chiseled, his chin firm. There was sharp intelligence in his dark eyes. She recalled the brightness she'd first noticed in them, and his kindness and compassion when he'd treated Jonas. He had a gentle and sincere smile that warmed her all the way from her head to her toes each time she'd seen him.

A shiver of something pleasurable yet frightening slid down the length of her spine as she realized that she was attracted to him. Dr. Pierce still had the ability to affect her more than any other man since Michael, the man she'd loved and lost.

Nell stiffened and fought to banish the feelings. Dr. Pierce threatened her peace of mind. She drew a steadying breath as she struggled to pull herself together.

James. He'd told her at their first meeting to call him James. She shouldn't. But since that day, every time she saw him she immediately thought of him as James.

She closed her eyes briefly as she shifted farther into the corner of the room to stay unobtrusive. Nell swallowed hard. She didn't want the man to catch sight of her. As the eldest of five Stoltzfus sisters, she was expected to be the first to marry a faithful member of their Amish community. The last thing she needed was to fall for the English veterinarian. Being in James's company was dangerous. Even if he'd had feelings for her, there would have been no way for them to be anything other than polite acquaintances. Not that he felt the same attraction. It was all one-sided—her side.

The woman with the kitten turned to leave. On her way to the door, she walked past Nell, who froze. Nell knew that if she moved even a tiny bit, James might notice her.

Something shifted in his expression, as if alarmed at the number of patients in the waiting room.

Nell waited for him to call back the next patient. As

soon as he left, she would go. She'd return when Michelle was in the office. Jonas could wait another week to start his medicine. Or she could play it safe and go somewhere else and escape the frightening, forbidden feelings she felt any time she was near James.

She sighed. She couldn't go elsewhere. It wouldn't be right after all James had done for Jonas.

Nell remained still but then released a sharp breath when James suddenly saw her. They locked gazes. Surprise and pleasure flashed in the depths of his dark eyes, and she felt an infusion of warmth.

She recognized the panic in his gaze. She sighed. He was lost without his assistant, and she was the only one available who might be able to help.

She had a moment of revelation. *The Lord wants me to stay.*

"Dr. Pierce?" She stepped forward with a tentative smile on her face. Her heart beat rapidly as she remained the focus of his dark gaze. "May I have a word with you?"

"Of course, Nell." He waited for her approach.

"No help today?" she asked softly so that the others within the room couldn't hear their conversation.

He shook his head. "Unfortunately, I'm alone today."

"I'll be happy to help if you'd like."

His eyes brightened as relief swept across his features. "I'd like that. Thank you."

James had never been happier to see Nell Stoltzfus. His receptionist, Michelle, was out sick, and Janie, his assistant, was on vacation, and he was swamped and alone dealing with a crowded waiting room.

As he'd watched Nell push out of the corner and approach, he'd been overcome with an immediate sense of calm. He'd never realized it before, but she had the same effect on him as she'd had on her injured rescue dog when she'd first brought Jonas in.

"Come into the back," he said, aware of the huskiness of his voice. He felt a jolt in his stomach as she smiled and followed him. Nell, a pretty young Amish woman, wore a spring-green dress with matching cape and apron. Her soft brown hair was covered by her white prayer *kapp*. Her nose was pert and perfectly formed, and her mouth was pink with a slight bow to her upper lip. He felt something shift inside him as he became the focus of her beautiful, brown gaze.

"Dr. Pierce, your waiting room seems unusually full." Her softly spoken words jerked him to awareness. She studied him with her head slightly tilted as if she were trying to gauge his thoughts. "I'd like to check your schedule."

They entered the reception area through a door off the hallway, and he showed her where to find the appointment book. "How long can you stay?"

"Through the afternoon." Her shy smile warmed him from the inside out. "May I use your phone?"

"Of course." She would need to get word to her family, he realized, so that they wouldn't worry about her absence. He waited while she made her phone call, trying not to listen as she explained the situation.

"*Ja*, Bob," he heard her say. "*Ja*, that would be *gut*. Thank you. Tell them that I shouldn't be too late." She glanced up to meet his gaze, and James instantly moved away to give her privacy.

He approached after Nell hung up the phone and stood. "Is everything all right?"

"*Ja*, 'tis fine." Her gaze met his, then slid away. He watched her study Michelle's appointment book. Her eyes narrowed. "You definitely don't have this many patients expected today," she murmured with a frown. "I'll have to do some rescheduling."

He started to leave, then turned. "Nell?"

She dragged her eyes away from the page to meet his gaze. *"Ja?"*

"Thank you." He spoke quietly so that no one would overhear him, but he knew immediately that she'd heard.

"You're *willkomm*," she breathed, and then she waved him away as she went back to studying the appointment book.

With a smile on his face, he opened the door to the back room.

"Dr. Pierce?"

He halted and faced her. "Yes?"

"Which exam rooms are available for patients?"

"One, three and four," he told her without hesitation. Then he entered the back of the clinic and went on to exam room two where his next patient waited.

James was examining the ear of a golden retriever when Nell knocked softly before opening the door.

"Dr. Pierce?"

"Yes, Nell?" he inquired without looking up.

"I've put Mrs. Rogan and Boots in exam room one and Mr. Jones with his dog Betsy in three. Mr. Yoder and his goat are in four. I rescheduled three patients for tomorrow because they didn't have appointments and your schedule could handle them then. Mrs. Pettyjohn is here with her poodle. She is your last appointment."

He straightened. "Already?" Amazed, he stared at her.

She gazed at him, her brown eyes filled with uncertainly. "Already?" she echoed.

"Are we really almost finished?" he asked. "Thank you for getting control of the situation so quickly." He looked sheepish. "I've been struggling about how to handle everyone for the last hour and a half." He rubbed his fingers through the dog's coat. "Bailey is going to be fine, Mrs. Martin."

The woman looked relieved as she glanced back and forth between them. "Thank you, Dr. Pierce."

"You're welcome." He turned toward Nell, pleased that she hadn't moved. "Nell, would you mind checking out Mrs. Martin and Bailey?"

"I'd be happy to," she said politely. She turned to the dog's owner. "Mrs. Martin, would you please follow me?"

James caught Nell's gaze as she waited for the woman and her dog to walk past her. He grinned in approval and was relieved to see her answering smile before she quickly followed Mrs. Martin.

Nell came into the back as he exited exam room two. "I forgot to tell you that Mrs. Rogan in exam room one had the next earliest appointment, then Mr. Jones, then Abraham Yoder."

He couldn't keep from studying her face. Nell Stoltzfus was genuinely lovely, with no need for artificial enhancement. He noted her smooth, unblemished skin, her pink lips, the reddish tinge to her cheeks. Since graduating from vet school, he'd had little time for a personal life, especially now that he was working hard to establish his new practice. He didn't know why, but there was something about her that made him long for something more. "Thank you, Nell."

"You're *willkomm*, Dr. Pierce."

He briefly met her gaze. "James, please," he invited. Again.

"James," she said then she blushed. "It was Mrs. Beggs, Mr. Merritt and Mrs. McDaniel whom I re-scheduled."

"I appreciate your help," he told her, meaning it. "I didn't expect Michelle and Janie to both be out today. Janie asked for the week off, and Michelle is home with a stomach bug." He sighed. "I confess that I'm not good at juggling appointments."

Nell looked confused. "Juggling?"

He laughed. "Sorry, I'm not laughing at you but at myself. I don't know how Michelle does her job. She's good at what she does." He studied her thoughtfully, liking what he saw. "Apparently, you're good at it, too."

"At juggling appointments?" She arched her eye-brows.

"Yes." He chuckled, and the smile that came to Nell's pink lips had him mesmerized until he realized that he was staring. He stole one last glance at her as he opened the door to room one.

He heard her *"Ja"* before he closed the door.

The day passed quickly, and soon the last patient had been seen. Nell set aside the appointment book along with the checks, money and credit card transactions for the day. Fortunately, she'd quickly figured out how to use the credit card machine. She'd seen Bob Whittier of Whittier's Store use one often enough to recall how it was done.

She even had the opportunity to assist James with his last patient. Mrs. Pettyjohn's poodle, Roggs, had a lump above his right hind leg. James had determined it to be an abscess following a small injury. He'd asked for her help as he did minor surgery to open the wound.

"Will he be all right?" Nell asked as she handed him supplies and observed his work.

"He'll be fine. It looks as if he got into a rosebush. See this thorn?" He held up a tiny dark object that he'd removed with tweezers. "I'll prescribe an antibiotic for a couple of weeks. He'll have to wear a cone until his follow-up appointment."

Nell had enjoyed her afternoon at the clinic being his assistant. Too much. And she knew it had as much to do with the man as working with animals. Thankfully, the day was over, and after she helped to clean up, she'd be able to leave.

She cleaned the exam room floors with disinfectant. She was quiet as she mopped, her thoughts filled with what she'd seen and heard that day. When she was done, she emptied out the wash water and put away the bucket and mop.

"I'm finished with the floors, Doctor—James," she told him as he came into the reception area where she picked up her purse. "I'll be heading home now."

"Thank you so much for your help today," he said. "I don't know how I would have managed without you." He gazed at her a moment, then frowned. "Why did you come into the office today?"

"My dog, Jonas, is well and old enough to start his heartworm medicine."

"I'll get it for you." James retrieved a box from a cabinet and handed it to her. "Take it. No charge. If you come back tomorrow, I'll have cash for you."

"For what?" She frowned. "For helping out for a few hours? *Nay*, I'll not take your money."

"Nell…"

"*Nay*, James."

"But you'll take the medicine."

She opened her mouth to object but relented when she saw his expression. The man wasn't going to take no for an answer. *"Ja. Danki."* She gasped as she saw the time on the office wall clock. "I've got to go. *Mam* will be holding dinner for me." She hurried toward the door. "*Gut* night, James."

"Good night, Nell," he said softly.

Nell promptly left and ran toward her buggy, which was parked in the back lot several yards away from the building. She unhitched her mare, Daisy, then climbed into her vehicle.

As she reached for the reins, she watched as James headed toward his car. He stood by the driver's side and lifted a hand to wave. She nodded but didn't wave back. As she drove out onto the road, her thoughts turned to her family and most particularly her father, who wouldn't be pleased that she was late for supper.

She spurred Daisy into a quick trot and drove home in record time. As she steered the mare into the barnyard, her sister Leah came out of the house to greet her.

"*Dat*'s been wondering why you're late," Leah said as the two sisters walked toward the house.

"I was helping Dr. Pierce at the veterinary clinic." Nell stiffened. "Didn't Bob Whittier get word to you?"

"About a half hour ago."

"Ach, nay," Nell said with dismay. "I didn't know he'd wait until that late. I called him hours ago."

"He sent word with Joshua Peachy but Joshua got

sidetracked when he saw an accident on the stretch of road between Yoder's General Store and Eli's carriage shop. A truck hit a car and there were children…"

"I'm sorry to hear that. Is everyone all right?"

"Joshua didn't know."

"Is *Dat* angry with me?"

"*Nay*, Joshua told him what happened and why he couldn't get word to us earlier."

"But?"

"But he expected you sooner, and I don't think he was too happy that you stayed to help out James Pierce."

"Leah, you should have seen the waiting room. It was noisy and crowded, and there was no staff to help him. Both Michelle and Janie were out and he was alone. I believe that God wanted me to help him."

Her sister smiled. "Then that's what you tell *Dat*. He can't argue with the Lord."

As she entered the kitchen, Nell saw her other sisters seated at the table with her parents. She nodded to each of them then settled her gaze on her father. *"Dat,"* she said. "I'm sorry I'm late. I didn't expect to be gone so long."

To her surprise, her father nodded but didn't comment.

Nell took her place at the table, and *Dat* led them as they gave thanks to the Lord for their meal. Nell's sister Charlie started a conversation, and all of her sisters joined in as food was passed around.

As she reached for the bowl of mashed potatoes, Nell caught her *dat* studying her with a thoughtful expression. She felt suddenly uneasy. Her father might have seemed unaffected by her lateness, but she could tell that after supper he would want to talk with her, and she had no idea what he was going to say or how she would answer him. The truth was, she had enjoyed her afternoon at Pierce Veterinary Clinic too much to be sorry that she'd decided to stay.

"Tell him what you've just told me," her sister Leah had advised her.

I'll tell him how I felt...that God had wanted me to stay and help James. Dr. James Pierce. She only hoped that *Dat* understood and accepted her decision as the right one.

Chapter Two

James admired the beautiful scenery as he drove his silver Lexus deeper into Lancaster County Amish country. Farmhouses surrounded by acres of corn dotted the landscape. Cows and sheep milled in pastures near Amish residences. Flowers bloomed in riotous color in gardens next to white front porches, while lawns were a splash of verdant green from the summer rains that had showered the earth recently. Familiar dark and solid-colored clothing flapped in the breeze, bringing back memories of James's teenage years living in an Amish community.

Seeing the Amish woman Nell again reminded him that it had been too long since he'd visited his mother and stepfather, so instead of going back to his apartment as he usually did, he turned in the opposite direction, toward the farm where he'd lived from the age of fifteen until he'd left Lancaster County at eighteen to attend college in Ohio.

His stepfather and mother's farm loomed up ahead. The beauty of it nearly stole his breath even while he felt suddenly nervous.

He didn't know why. He knew they both would be glad to see him. It wouldn't matter to them that he'd moved into the area over two months ago and had stopped by only once. He'd set up his practice here because he'd wanted to be closer to his family. Yet, for some reason he'd stayed away.

He drove over the dirt road that led to his stepfather's farmhouse and pulled into the yard near the barn. He didn't see the family buggy. He parked out of the way of the barn door, in case whoever had taken out the vehicle returned.

There was no sign of anyone in the front or side yard as James turned off the engine and climbed out of his car. He paused a moment with the door open to stare at the house that had once been his home.

It had been hard moving into this house after his father had died and his mother had married Adam. It wasn't that he didn't want his mother to be happy. But he'd missed his dad. Grief-stricken, he'd been a terrible son, bitter and angry and difficult to control. But Adam was a kind man, who seemed to understand what James was going through. Because of Adam's understanding, patience and love, James had grown to love and respect his stepfather.

James shut the car door. He was here, and he would wait for everyone's return, not run like the frightened teenage boy he'd been when he'd first moved into Adam Troyer's house. He wandered toward the backyard and saw a woman taking laundry down from the clothesline.

"Mom?" He hurried in her direction.

She stiffened, then with a garment in her hand turned slowly. She was too young to be his mother although the resemblance to her was striking. His eyes widened. "Maggie?"

"Ja, bruder." Her mouth firmed. "You finally decided to pay us a visit."

It had been too long since he'd seen his younger sister. He felt a rush of gladness that quickly turned to hard-hitting guilt.

"You weren't home when I last visited." He regarded her with affection. "It's good to see you, Mags."

"Nobody calls me that but you." She dropped a garment into a wicker clothes basket.

He grinned. "Yes, I know."

Warmth entered her expression. "So you really did move back to Happiness."

"I did—close to two months ago." He held up his hand. "I know. I should have come again sooner. I've been struggling to grow my veterinary practice but…" He sighed. "It's no excuse."

He gazed at his little sister who was now a woman. He regretted missing her teenage years. He hadn't been here for her while she was growing up. He'd left home, driven to follow in his late father's footsteps. He'd attended college in Ohio, then went to Penn Vet for veterinary school. "I'm sorry I wasn't here for you."

She dismissed it with a wave of her hand. "I have a *gut* life. *Mam* and *Dat* are wonderful and Abby—" Her eyes widened. "Have you seen our little sister yet? You won't recognize Abigail, James. She's eighteen now."

Regret overwhelmed him, and James closed his eyes. "I missed too much."

"You're here now," she reminded him softly. She was quiet a moment as she studied him. "You'll have time to see her now."

"And Matt and Rosie?" he asked of his stepsiblings.

Maggie smiled. "They are doing well. You wouldn't recognize them either." She studied him silently. "Matt is nineteen and Rosie's sixteen." She eyed him with curiosity. "Are you happy, James?"

Was he? No one had thought to ask whether or not he was content with his life—not even himself. He should be more than pleased with what he'd accomplished, but was he? He honestly didn't know.

"I enjoy helping animals, and my work reminds me of the time I spent with Dad. But happy? I'm working on it. What about you?"

A tiny smile came to her lips, and her green eyes sparkled. "*Ja,* I'm happy."

He stared at her, intrigued. He grinned. "You're being courted!"

She looked surprised and pleased that after all these years he still could read her so well. "*Ja,*" she confessed. "His name is Joshua Fisher. He's a kind man."

"How old is Joshua Fisher?"

His sister narrowed her gaze at him. "Why?"

He didn't answer her.

She sighed. "He's twenty-one."

"I'm pleased for you, Maggie." Warmth filled him as he studied her. "You like the Amish way of life." Like him, she was raised English until their father died and their mother had brought them from Ohio to live in his grandparents' home in Lancaster County.

Her gaze slid over him. "You didn't seem to mind our Amish life," she reminded him. "Once you'd adjusted."

It was true. He had learned to appreciate the life he'd once rebelled against. The quiet peace that came from working on the farm when he was a boy eventually had soothed his inner turmoil over losing the father whom he'd loved, admired and always wanted to emulate.

"Where's *Mam*?" he said, slipping easily back into Pennsylvania Deitsch, considering how long he'd been away.

Maggie eyed him shrewdly. "In the *haus*." She paused. "*Dat*'s there, too."

"He's done working for the day?" His stepfather was a hardworking man, just like his own father had been. Would Adam scold him for staying away?

James experienced a sudden onset of uneasiness. The man who'd married his mother had been a good father to him, and he'd repaid him by being difficult and mean during those first months…and then he must have hurt Adam, leaving home when he did to follow the path he'd set out for himself away from their Amish village.

"*Ja*, you came at the right time. *Mam* and Abigail are making supper. Will you stay?"

He felt his tension leave him as he acknowledged the truth. *"Ja."* He knew this was an open invitation. It was the Amish way to be hospitable and never turn a single soul away. "Will they be glad to see me?" he murmured. He studied the house. "I guess I'll head inside."

"James!" his sister called as he started toward the house. He stopped and faced her.

Maggie's gaze was filled with warmth and understanding. "'Tis *gut* to see you. Our *eldre* will be happy that you've come. Please, James, don't stay away too long again." She pretended to scowl. "I've missed your ugly face."

James couldn't stop the grin that came with the

lightening of his spirit. "You'll be eager to get rid of me now that I'm living close and can visit frequently."

She shook her head. *"Nay,* I won't." She regarded him with affection. "I'll always be happy to see you, big *bruder."*

They eyed each other with warmth. "I'd better go," he said. "You'll be in soon?"

"A few moments more and I'll be done here."

"I'll see you inside then."

Despite anticipating a warm welcome, James felt his stomach burn as he crossed the yard toward the back door leading into his mother's kitchen. He drew a deep cleansing breath as he rapped on the wooden door frame.

The door swung open within seconds to reveal his stepfather, who blinked rapidly. "James?" Adam greeted softly as if he couldn't believe his eyes.

James offered a tentative smile. *"Hallo, Dat."* He watched with awe as happiness transformed his stepfather's expression.

"Come in!" he invited with a grin as he stepped back to allow him entry. "Your *mudder* will be pleased to see you." He regarded James with affection. "I'm glad you've come back to visit." His eyes brightened as if Adam fought tears. "You look well, *soohn.* Your clinic is doing *gut*?"

James suddenly felt as if a big weight had been lifted off his shoulders as he entered the house. "It's doing better now, *Dat.*" He needed this homecoming. Adam was still the warm, patient and kind man he'd always been, and James was so thankful for him. "It was hard to get started at first. I'm getting more patients, though."

Adam smiled. "I'm happy for you, James. I'm certain that you'll make a success of it." He gestured toward the kitchen table. "Sit, sit. I'll get your *mudder*."

James sat, aware that the house held all the wonderful cooking smells reminiscent of those he'd loved and remembered from his childhood.

Before Adam could leave to find her, his mother entered the kitchen from the front of the house. "I thought I heard voices, husband. Who—" Her eyes widened as they filled with tears of joy. "James!" She beamed at him. "You're back."

James grinned. "*Hallo, Mam*. I'm sorry I haven't been back sooner."

His mother brushed off his apology. "You're here now. That's all that matters." She met her husband's gaze with a pleased, loving smile. "He's come home again," she whispered huskily.

Adam moved to his wife's side and placed a loving hand on her shoulder. His smile for her was warm. "*Ja*, he has." He captured James's gaze. "And he is happy to be here." His stepfather grinned when James nodded. "I know 'tis near suppertime, Ruth, but why don't we have tea first?"

James watched his mother put on the teakettle. He had to stifle the urge to get up and help, knowing that it would upset her if he tried. In her mind, a woman's work was in the house while a man's work was on the farm or at his business. Adam's farm was small but large enough to provide for his family. His stepfather made quality outdoor furniture for a living, and Adam was good at his work.

The teakettle whistled as *Mam* got out cups, saucers and tea bags.

"It's *gut* to be back," James said sincerely. It was good to see his family and the farm.

He made a silent vow that he would return more frequently to spend time with the family he loved and missed, he realized, during the years he'd been away from Happiness, Pennsylvania.

Her father came into the room as Nell was drying the last of the supper dishes. "*Dochter*, when you're done, come out onto the porch. I want to talk with you."

"I'll be right out, *Dat*." She was putting away dishes when her sister pitched in to help. "*Danki*, Ellie." Nell hung up her wet tea towel on the rack when they were done.

"He'll not bite you," Ellie said softly.

Nell flashed her a look. "I didn't think he would."

"Then stop looking scared. *Dat* loves us." Her lips twitching, she teased, "Even you."

"I know, but I'm afraid he's angry that I didn't come right home from Aunt Katie's."

"He's not angry," Ellie assured her.

"Disappointed? Upset?"

"He was worried. Joshua didn't come until it was too late for him not to worry."

"I know. I'm sorry. I didn't know that Bob would send Joshua."

"Nor could you foresee the accident that would keep Joshua from getting to us sooner."

"Then why does he want to talk with me?"

Her sister shrugged. "Only one way to find out."

Nell nodded. "I guess I better go then."

She couldn't regret her afternoon at the clinic. She'd had a taste of what it might have been like if she'd accepted James's job offer as his assistant. She loved animals. She enjoyed spending time with them, caring for them, holding them. After her sister Meg became gravely ill, and Michael—the man she'd loved—had died, her animals had been Nell's only solace.

Working the afternoon at Pierce's Veterinary Clinic, she believed, was God's reward for doing the right thing.

Her father was standing on the front porch gazing at the horizon when Nell joined him.

"Dat?"

"Gut, you're here."

"Dat, if this is about today, I'm sorry that you were worried. I called Bob as soon as I knew that I'd be staying. I didn't know about Joshua and the accident."

"This isn't about today," he said, "although I was worried when you didn't come home."

"I'm sorry."

"You did what you should have. Joshua explained everything." He turned to stare out over the farm. "'Tis about something else. Something I've been meaning to talk with you about."

"What is it, *Dat*?"

"You're twenty-four, Nell. 'Tis time you were thinking of marrying and having a family of your own. Other community women your age are married with children, but you have shown no interest in having a husband. I'm afraid you're spending too much time with your animals."

Nell's heart lurched with fear. He'd talked previously of marriage to her but not negatively about her animals. *"Dat*, I enjoy them." She inhaled sharply. "You want me to get rid of them?"

He faced her. "*Nay*, *Dochter*, I know you care for those critters, and as unusual as that is, I wouldn't insist on taking anything away that gives you such joy. But having a husband and children should be more important. You're getting older, and your chances at marriage are dwindling. You need to find a husband and soon. If not, then I'll have to find one for you."

"How am I supposed to get a husband, *Dat*?" She'd loved Michael and hoped to marry him until he'd died of injuries from an automobile accident.

She knew she was expected to marry. It was the Amish way. But how was she to find a husband?

Chapter Three

Saturday morning found the five Stoltzfus sisters in the kitchen with their mother preparing food for the next day. This Sunday was Visiting Day, and the family would be spending it at the William Mast farm. Nell and her sister Leah were making schnitz pies made from dried apples for the gathering. *Mam* and Ellie were kneading bread that they would bake today and eat with cold cuts tomorrow evening after they returned home. Meg and their youngest sister, Charlie, were cutting watermelon, honeydew melons and cantaloupe for a fresh fruit salad.

"I'm going to Martha's on Monday," Meg announced as she cut fruit and placed it in a ceramic bowl. "We're planning to work on craft items for the Gordonville Mud Sale and Auction."

"What's so special about the Gordonville sale?" Charlie asked.

Ellie smirked. "She's hoping to see Reuben."

Meg blushed. "I don't know that he'll be there."

"But that's your hope," Nell said.

For as long as Nell could remember, Meg had harbored feelings for Reuben Miller, a young man from another Amish church community. She'd met him two years ago at their youth singing, after their cousin Eli had invited Reuben and his sister Rebecca, whom Eli liked at the time, to attend.

Reuben had struck up a conversation with Meg, and Meg immediately had taken a strong liking to him. Although the young man hadn't attended another singing, Meg continued to hold on to the hope that one day they'd meet again and he'd realize that she was the perfect girl for him.

Nell eyed her middle sister. "Meg, if you see Reuben and find out that he's courting someone, what are you going to do?"

Meg's features contorted. "I don't know," she whispered.

"You could be hurt, but still you won't give up…" Leah added.

Meg nodded. "I can't. Not if there is the slightest chance that he doesn't have a sweetheart. I know we spent only a few hours together, but I really liked him," she admitted quietly. "I still do."

"If you want a sweetheart, why not consider Peter Zook?" Nell suggested, anticipating Meg's negative response.

"Peter!" her sister spat. "I don't want Peter Zook's attention."

"Peter's a nice boy," *Mam* said.

"Exactly! He's a boy." She sniffed. "Reuben is a man."

Nell held back a teasing retort. Peter was the same age as Reuben. He was a kind and compassionate young man who'd had the misfortune of falling in love with her sister, who wanted nothing to do with him. In her opinion, Meg could do no better than Peter Zook.

If only she could find someone her age who was kind, like Peter, to marry. An Amish friend she could respect and eventually regard fondly as they built a life together.

"I hope it works out for you, Meg," she said as she squeezed her sister's shoulder gently.

Meg smiled at her. *"Danki."*

"Would you and Martha like help on Monday? I can make pot holders for the sale," their youngest sister offered.

"That would be nice, Charlie," Meg said. *"Danki."*

The day passed quickly with the sisters chatting about many topics while they worked, including their Lapp cousins and who they expected to visit tomorrow at the Mast home.

Sunday morning arrived warm and sunny. At nine o'clock, their father brought the buggy close to the back door. The girls filed out of the house with food and into the buggy. Nell handed them the pies she and Leah had baked before climbing inside herself.

"Dat, Onkel Samuel and *Endie* Katie are coming, *ja?"* Leah asked as *Dat* steered the horse away from the house and onto the paved road.

"Ja, so your *onkel* said," he replied.

"Endie Katie said the same when I saw her the other day."

"Will all of our cousins be coming with their *kinner*? Noah and Rachel, Annie and Jacob, Jedidiah and Sarah?"

"I believe so," *Dat* said.

Nell smiled. She enjoyed spending time with her

male cousins and their spouses. And she was eager to see Ellen, William and Josie's daughter, who had come to her aid and taken her and Jonas to the vet the day Nell had rescued him.

Buggies were parked on the lawn to the left in front of the barn when *Dat* pulled in next to the last vehicle.

Nell got out of the carriage first. Seeing her, Ellen Mast waved and hurried to meet her.

"*Hallo*, Nell! How's Jonas?"

"He's doing wonderfully. His leg is healed, and he's gained weight. I'm about to start him on heartworm medicine."

The young blond woman looked pleased. "I'm so glad. I think it was a *gut* thing that you were the one to rescue him. I'm sure he's happy and well."

Nell beamed. "I'd like to think so." She and Ellen strolled toward the house as the other members of her family slowly followed.

Another gray family carriage parked next to theirs. "Look!" Charlie exclaimed. "'Tis the Adam Troyers!"

"Charlie!" Rosie Troyer called as she exited the vehicle. Abigail climbed out behind her and waved. The eldest sister, Maggie, and their brother Matthew followed and approached Ellen and the Stoltzfus sisters with a smile.

"I didn't expect to see you here," Ellie said with a smile. "I'm glad you could come."

"*Ja*, we thought our oldest *bruder* was coming also, but he was called out on an emergency," Maggie told them.

"*Hallo*, Ellen." Matthew turned to Nell next with a smile. "Nell, 'tis *gut* to see you."

Nell's lips curved. "Matthew."

Adam and Ruth Troyer approached. "Ellen, Nell. 'Tis *gut* to see you both. Ellen," Ruth said, "is your *mudder* inside?"

"*Ja*, I last saw her in the kitchen."

Loud, teasing male voices drew their attention. Nell's Lapp cousins Elijah, Jacob, Noah, Daniel and Joseph hurried out into the yard and gathered on the back lawn. Moments later, they were joined by her friend Ellen's younger brothers, Will and Elam.

Jedidiah came from the direction of the barn. "Found them!" he said, holding up a baseball bat and ball.

"Matthew! You going to play ball with us?" Isaac called.

"*Ja*, I'll play." With another smile in Nell's direction, the young man left to have fun with Nell's cousins.

"Nell, you watch the game and I'll bring your pies inside."

She smiled as she gave her pies to her friend. "*Danki*, Ellen."

Ellen entered the house, leaving her alone with Maggie.

"I didn't know you had another *bruder*, Maggie," Nell admitted, focusing on Maggie's revelation, as the baseball game began.

"*Ja*. He's a doctor and seven years older than me. He left our community when he was eighteen." Maggie's eyes filled with affection. "I've missed him so much. I was able to spend time with him yesterday but still…" She grinned. "Fortunately, he's moved closer to home, and we'll be able to see him more often. I'm sure you'll meet him eventually."

Nell didn't know why, but she felt an odd anticipation as if she were on the urge of learning something significant. "You said your *bruder* was called out on an emergency," she said. "What does he do?"

"He's a veterinarian. He's recently opened a clinic here in Happiness."

The strange sensation settled over Nell. Despite the difference in their last names, could James be Maggie's brother? If the young woman's sibling was a veterinarian, then she doubted that the man was a member of the Amish community. "What's his name?" she asked, although she had a feeling she knew.

"James Pierce." Maggie smiled. "He owns Pierce Veterinary Clinic. Have you heard of him?"

"*Ja*. In fact, 'twas your *bruder* who treated my dog, Jonas, after I found him."

"Then you've met him!" Maggie looked delighted. "Is he a *gut* veterinarian?"

Startled by this new knowledge of James, Nell could only nod at first. "He was wonderful with Jonas. He's a kind and compassionate man." She studied Maggie closely and recognized the family resemblance that she previously hadn't noticed between her and James. "How is he a Pierce and you a Troyer?"

"I am a Pierce." Maggie grinned. "Abigail is, too. But we don't go by the Pierce name. Adam is our stepfather, and he is our *dat* now. We were young when we lost our *vadder*. I was six, and Abigail was just a *bebe*. We lived in Ohio back then. After our *vadder* died, *Mam* moved us to Lancaster County where she was raised. She left Pennsylvania to marry *Dat* and start a life with him in Ohio. *Mam* was heartbroken when *Dat* died. She couldn't stay in Ohio without her husband and decided to return home to Lancaster County."

Maggie's eyes filled with sadness. "I didn't mind. I was too young to care, but James was thirteen and he had a hard time with the move. He loved and admired Dad, and he'd wanted to be a veterinarian like him since he was ten. James used to accompany Dad when he visited farmers to treat their animals. He was devastated by Dad's death, and he became more determined to follow in Dad's footsteps."

Nell felt her heart break for James, who must have suffered greatly after his father's death. "You chose the Amish life, but James chose a different path."

"And he's doing well," Maggie said. "My family is thrilled that he set up his practice in Happiness, because he wanted to be closer to us."

"He missed you," Nell said quietly.

The young woman grinned. "I guess he did. I certainly missed him. I'm glad to have my big *bruder* back."

Nell couldn't get what she'd learned about James and the Troyers out of her mind. It didn't help her churned-up emotions when, later that afternoon, James arrived to spend time with his family.

She recognized his silver car immediately as he drove into the barnyard and parked. Nell watched as he got out of his vehicle, straightened and closed the door. James stood a moment, his gaze searching, no doubt looking for family members. She couldn't move as he crossed the yard to where William Mast and others had set up tables and bench seats. They had enjoyed the midday meal, but there was still a table filled with delicious homemade desserts, including the schnitz pies that she and Leah had baked yesterday morning.

She couldn't tear her gaze away as James headed

to the gathering of young people, including his sisters Maggie and Abigail as well as their stepsiblings, Rosie and Matthew.

Nell found it heartwarming to see that all of his siblings regarded him with the same depth of love and affection. She watched as James spoke briefly to Maggie, who grinned as Abigail, Rosie and Matthew approached him, clearly delighted that he'd handled his emergency then decided to come. She heard the siblings teasing and the ensuing laughter. Maggie said something to James as she gestured in Nell's direction.

James turned and saw her, and Nell froze. Her heart started to beat hard when he broke away from the group to approach her.

"Nell!" Warmed by the sight of her, James smiled as he reached her. "I didn't expect to see you here."

Her lips curved. "I didn't expect to see you here either."

"So you know my family." He didn't know why the knowledge startled him. Not that he was upset. In fact, it was nice to know that before they'd even met, he and Nell had shared an undiscovered connection.

"I've known them a long time. I had no idea that your family is the Troyers." She shifted her gaze to his sister Maggie. "Then I recognized the resemblance between you and Maggie." She smiled. "I've always liked your sister. She's a *gut* friend, and I like her sweetheart, Joshua Fisher, too."

"Joshua is here?" James attempted to pick him out of the gathering.

"*Nay.* He couldn't come today. His *grossmudder* is

ill, and he thought it best to spend time with her and his family."

He was pleased to hear that Nell thought well of the man his sister loved. "He's a good man," he murmured, his gaze on his sister's smiling face.

"*Ja*, and he'll make Maggie a *gut* husband."

James settled his gaze on Nell's pretty, expressive features. "I'm glad you think so. I haven't met him yet, but I trust your judgment."

Nell appeared startled. She blushed as if embarrassed by his praise. "I'm sure you'll meet him soon."

They stood silently for several seconds. James felt comfortable with Nell, and she seemed to have relaxed around him, too.

"Nell."

She met his gaze.

"I was going to stop by your house. I received a phone call from Michelle today. Her stomach virus has spread to her husband and children, and she won't be back for days. Perhaps even a week. Janie isn't due back from vacation for another week. Would you consider working at the clinic next week? I'll pay you a good wage."

She seemed suddenly flustered, but he could tell that she liked the idea. "I'll have to ask my *dat*," she said.

"May I talk with him? I may be able to help ease his mind."

"I don't know…" She glanced toward an area under a shade tree where a group of older Amish men were conversing.

"Are you afraid that he won't like me?"

"*Nay!*" she gasped, her eyes flashing toward his. She softened her tone. "*Nay*. It's not that."

"Then let me speak with him." He frowned. "Unless you don't want the job."

"I wouldn't mind working at the clinic again."

James grinned as he sensed the exact moment when Nell gave him permission to talk with her father.

He immediately knew who her father was when a man looked sharply at Nell and then him. "I'll be right back," James told her as he made his way to the man who'd left the group to approach.

"Sir," James greeted him. "I'm James Pierce. Your daughter helped me last Thursday at my veterinary clinic."

"Arlin Stoltzfus," the man said as he narrowed his gaze to take stock of James, "and I wonder how you know that Nell is my *dochter*."

"A *gut* guess?" James said, slipping into Pennsylvania Deitsch and noting the man's surprise, which was quickly masked by a frown.

"What do you want, James Pierce?"

"A favor," James said. He softened his expression.

"What kind of favor?" The man eyed him with doubt.

"First, would you feel better knowing that I've come to visit my family—the Troyers—and not Nell?"

Something flickered in the man's expression. "You're Adam and Ruth's eldest son."

"*Ja*, I have the *gut* fortune to have their love."

The concern eased from Arlin's expression. "I'm sure you are a *gut* man, James Pierce."

"James," James invited, and Arlin smiled. "But now that I've seen Nell here today, I'd like to ask your permission for Nell to work in the clinic next week."

The man lowered his eyebrows. "Why?"

"I have no staff next week. My receptionist is taking care of her sick family as well as recuperating from illness herself. My assistant is away with her husband and not expected back until a week from tomorrow. I would need her to fill in for one week only."

Arlin glanced toward Nell, who was talking with two young women. "Have you mentioned this to her?"

James shifted uncomfortably. "*Ja*, I wished to know if she was interested before I came to you."

"And she is interested," the man murmured, "which is no surprise, considering how much she loves caring for animals."

Nell glanced in their direction, then quickly looked away, but not before James recognized longing in her expression. She wanted the opportunity to work in the clinic if only for a short time.

Nell's father sighed heavily as he studied his daughter. His expression was light, and there was amusement in his brown eyes as he met James's gaze. "She can work with you. She'll be disappointed if I refuse permission."

James smiled. "And above everything, you want your *dochter*'s happiness." He watched with stunned surprise as Arlin waved at his daughter to join them. Nell approached, looking fearful as she glimpsed her father's stern expression.

"You want to work for him?" he asked sharply.

"*Ja, Dat*, but only if you give permission."

Arlin's expression softened. "He belongs to the Troyers. I give permission," he said, surprising James.

James grinned. "Monday morning, eight o'clock sharp. Can you be there?"

"I can be there," Nell said. She turned toward her father. "I'll have my morning chores done before I go."

"*Ja*, I have no doubt of that," Arlin said.

"Do you need a ride?"

Arlin narrowed his gaze. "She will take the family buggy."

He nodded. *"Danki,"* he said.

"James!"

He glanced over and beamed as his mother approached. "I'm happy you could make it," she said.

He regarded her with affection. "I'm happy I'm here." His gaze flickered over Arlin and Nell who were standing next to him. "My staff is out, and Arlin has agreed to allow Nell to fill in for them next week."

His mother's eyes crinkled up at the corners. "You can rest easily with this one," she told Arlin. "He's a *gut soohn*."

James felt a momentary unease. He didn't feel like a good son. He'd left his family and his community to attend veterinary school and had little contact in the years that followed.

As if sensing his discomfort, his mother squeezed his arm. "He's moved back into the area to be closer to us," she said as she regarded him affectionately.

He did move to Lancaster to be close to his parents for he had missed his family greatly. The tension left him. Despite his past, he was determined that he would be a much better son and brother from this point forward.

Chapter Four

Monday morning, Nell steered her carriage down Old Philadelphia Pike toward Pierce Veterinary Clinic. She viewed the day with excitement. She'd learned a lot from just one day working with James. Imagine what she could learn in the next five!

When the clinic came into view, Nell felt a moment's dread. Learning from James was a benefit of working with the clinic, but working with the man could cause her complications she didn't need in her life. He was handsome and kind, but her attraction to him was wrong and forbidden.

Focus on what Dat *said.* Her father wanted her to marry. He'd find her a husband if she didn't find one on her own.

Nell knew that she just had to remember that although James had an Amish family, he was an *Englisher.* She couldn't allow herself to think of him as anything but her dog's veterinarian—and this week, as her employer.

When she pulled her buggy up to the hitching post in the back, Nell was surprised to see James's silver car parked near the back door. She'd arrived early. It was only seven thirty. She was sure she'd arrive before him and that she'd have to wait for him to show up.

She tied up Daisy, then went to ring the doorbell. Within seconds, the back door opened, revealing James Pierce dressed in a white shirt and jeans.

Nell stared and suddenly felt woozy. She swayed forward and put a hand out to catch herself on the door frame, but James reacted first by grabbing her arm to steady her. Seeing James looking so like Michael, her late beau, had stunned her.

"Nell?" he said with concern. "Are you all right?"

She inhaled deeply. "I'm fine." Like James, Michael, an *Englisher*, had favored button-down shirts and blue jeans. She'd met him in a grocery store before she'd joined the church and still had the option of choosing an English or Amish life. She'd chosen a life with Michael but she'd never had the chance to tell him before he died.

James still held her arm, and she could feel the warmth of his touch on her skin below the short sleeve of her dress. "Are you sure you're all right?"

Nell managed to smile. "I'm well. *Danki*." She bit her lip. "Thank you," she corrected.

James let go and gestured for her to come inside. "Is the day getting warm?"

"A little." But the heat wasn't to blame for her wooziness.

"Come on in. I'll turn up the air conditioner so we'll be comfortable."

The impact of the man on her senses made her feel off-kilter. Nell blushed at her thoughts as she followed him into the procedure area. Fortunately, by the time

James faced her, she had her feelings under control again.

"I'm glad you came," he said. "We have a serious case today. Mrs. Rogan is on her way in with Boots. Her Lab's eaten something—she's not sure what, but she believes he has an intestinal blockage."

"Ach, nay!" Nell breathed. "What will you do? Surgery?"

His handsome features were filled with concern. "I'll do X-rays first to see if I can tell where the blockage is."

"How can I help?"

He studied her intently. "Are you squeamish?"

She shook her head. "I don't think so. Did I seem squeamish yesterday? If you're worried that I'll faint at the sight of Boots's insides, don't be. I was in the room when my *mam* gave birth to Charlie, my youngest sister." She smiled slightly; the memory wasn't the most pleasant. "No one else was home."

He raised his eyebrows. "How old were you?" he asked.

"Nine."

He jerked in surprise. "You were only nine when you helped your mother deliver?"

"Ja." Nell's features softened. "I was scared. I can't say I wasn't, but once Charlie was born, I felt as if God had given us this wonderful new life. Charlie doesn't know that it wasn't the midwife who helped bring her into the world."

"Why not?"

"It's not important. What is important is that she is a healthy, wonderful young woman of fifteen."

She wondered if James was doing the math to realize that she was twenty-four. She saw him frown. Was he thinking that at the age of twenty-four most Amish women had husbands and at least one child, if not more?

"I'm glad you're not squeamish," he said. "Boots will be here any minute, and I'm going to need you by my side."

Even though she knew she shouldn't, Nell liked the sound of his words, of her and James working as a team.

After hearing Nell's story about delivering her youngest sister, James quickly did the math and was relieved to know her age. Then he frowned. Why did he care how old Nell was? It shouldn't matter as long as she did her job, which so far she'd been doing well. He wondered why Nell wasn't married.

Or was she? He'd never thought to ask. To do so now would seem…intrusive. He feared there was a story there, and one he wasn't about to ask her about.

James found he liked the thought of having her at his side while he did the surgery. And why wouldn't he, when after only one day she already had proved her worth?

"I'll be ready," she said. "I'll hand you the instruments you'll need. Maybe you can show me what they are now before Boots arrives? I don't want to hand you the wrong thing."

"Certainly." He moved toward the machine on the counter. There were several packaged sterile instruments in the cabinet above it. "This is an autoclave," he explained, gesturing toward the machine. "I put certain metal instruments in here to sterilize them."

She nodded. "What are those?" she asked of the two packets he'd taken from the cabinet shelf.

James proceeded to tell her what they were—a scalpel and clamps. Then he pulled out a tray of other types and sizes of the same instruments as well as others. "You don't have to be concerned," he said. "I'll pull out everything I need, and then I'll point to the instrument I want on the tray. You don't have to know all the names, although I imagine you'll learn a few as we use them."

He had just finished explaining the tools when he heard a commotion in the front room. "Boots is here," he announced. He was aware that Nell followed closely behind him as he went to greet the concerned woman and her chocolate Lab.

Nell helped him x-ray Boots while the dog's nervous owner sat in the waiting room. It turned out that Boots had swallowed a sock. After James relayed his diagnosis to Mrs. Rogan, he and Nell went to work. He encouraged Mrs. Rogan to go home, but the woman refused to leave until she knew that her dog was out of surgery and in recovery.

"Do you have other patients scheduled this morning?" Nell asked as she watched him put Boots under anesthesia.

"Fortunately, no. Not until this afternoon."

He readied his patient. "May I have a scalpel?" He gestured toward the appropriate instrument. He needn't have bothered because Nell had already picked it up and handed it to him.

He smiled. "Perfect. Thanks."

She inclined her head, and they went back to the serious task at hand. It took just under an hour from the time they sedated the Lab until the time he was moved to recovery.

James went out to talk with Mrs. Rogan with Nell following. "Boots made out fine. We removed the sock, and there's been no permanent injury."

Edith Rogan shuddered out a sigh. "Thank goodness." She visibly relaxed as she glanced from him to Nell standing behind him. "Thank you. Thank you both."

"Boots may have to spend the night here," he said. "I'll keep a close eye on him today. If he does well, then you can take him home this evening. I'll call and let you know."

At that moment, the door opened and Mr. Rogan rushed in. "How is he?" he asked his wife.

"Fine," James said. "The surgery went well, but I'm afraid you may be one sock short."

The man shifted his attention from his wife to James. "You're Dr. Pierce?"

James nodded.

"Thank you, Dr. Pierce. Edith and I have grown very attached to him."

"He's our baby now that our children are married and on their own," Edith said.

"I understand," Nell said softly, surprising James. "I have a dog. I have several animals, in fact, and I would feel awful if anything ever happened to them."

Mr. Rogan studied her with curiosity. "You're Amish."

"I am?" Nell's brown gaze twinkled.

The man laughed. "Sorry. Sometimes I speak before I think."

"Well, you're right, Mr. Rogan. I am a member of

the Amish church and community, and I had the privilege to work with Dr. Pierce during Boots's surgery." She paused. "He's a beautiful dog."

The man smiled. "That he is," he said.

"Edith, it's time for us to leave and let the doctor and his assistant get back to the business of saving lives and making our pets better."

"I'll call you later," James said as the couple headed to the door.

"I'll check on him often," Nell added.

The Rogans left, and suddenly James was alone with Nell. He was proud of the way she'd handled herself with Boots's owners, and he was pleased with how she'd assisted during Boots's surgery.

He glanced at his watch to see how much time he had before his first afternoon appointment.

"A successful surgery calls for a special lunch." He grinned. "Hoagies!"

She laughed. "Hoagies?"

"Sandwiches."

"*Ja*, that sounds *gut*," she said. "But I'll be bringing in lunch for us tomorrow."

"Sounds *gut* to me." James smiled. "We should check on Boots again before I order lunch."

After ensuring that the Lab was doing well, they ate lunch, then went back to work. The rest of the day occurred without any major incidents.

By the end of the afternoon, James was tired. When he glanced at Nell, he saw that she looked exhausted, as well.

"Time to call it quits," he said.

She nodded and reached for the mop and bucket.

He stayed her hand. "We can clean up in the morning." He eyed her with concern. "Are you all right?"

She blinked. "*Ja*, why wouldn't I be?"

"You've been quiet."

"Just thinking."

"About?

"Boots."

James smiled. "He's doing well. I'm glad I called the Rogans. They're happy to come for him. He'll do fine as long as they keep him still, leave his collar on and give him his pain medicine on time."

"And bring him back to see you on Tuesday," Nell added.

"Yes."

"Do you need me to do anything else before I leave?"

James shook his head. "No, go on home." He paused and couldn't help saying, "Be careful driving."

She nodded and left. James was slow to follow, but he watched her through an opening in the window blinds. Once her buggy was no longer visible, he took one last look around the clinic to make sure everything was as it should be, then he left, locking up as he went.

As he slipped onto his car's leather seats, he thought of Nell on the wooden seats in her buggy. He wondered how she'd react if she had the chance to ride in his car. There might be a time that he'd bring her home. He scowled. Probably not, because her time at the clinic was temporary, until Janie came back from vacation.

Nell was a fine assistant, he thought as he put the car in Reverse. She would manage fine until Janie's return.

A dangerous thought entered his mind, but he pushed it firmly aside. He quickly buried a sudden longing for something—or someone—else in his life other than his work, which had been the most important thing to him for some time.

Nell answered the phone when James's receptionist, Michelle, called into the office the next day. "Pierce Veterinary Clinic," she greeted. "How may I help you?"

The woman on the other end sounded dismayed. "Hello? This is Michelle. Who is this?"

"*Hallo*, Michelle. It's Nell. I'm helping James in the office until you or Janie returns."

"That's wonderful, Nell," the woman said. "I was worried about him managing the office alone." The two women chatted for several moments more, catching up, before breaking the connection. Nell went back to work, relieved that Michelle was glad to learn that she was filling in.

"Who was on the phone?" James asked as he came out to the front desk.

"It was Michelle. She and her son are feeling better, but now her husband and two daughters are sick."

"I'm sorry to hear that. Was she surprised that you answered the phone?"

"Surprised but pleased. She's been worried about you." She and Michelle had become friendly since Nell's first visit to the clinic.

James smiled. "I hope you told her to rest, recuperate and take care of her family."

"I did."

"Good."

Nell glanced at the appointment book on the desk. "Boots Rogan is due any minute for his follow-up."

"I want to check to make sure he hasn't bled through his dressing," James said.

Boots's appointment went well, and the owner took him home to continue the dog's recovery.

The afternoon went by quickly, and before they knew it, they'd seen the last appointment. But then an emergency call came in from Abram Peachy, a deacon in Nell's church district. Their mare Buddy had been injured by another horse.

James grabbed his medical bag. "Nell, will you come?"

"*Ja*, of course I'll come." Nell locked the front door and turned off the lights before she hastened through the back door and met James at his car. She hurried toward the passenger side and hesitated, uncomfortable being in such close quarters with James. He was suddenly there by her side, opening the door for her.

Feeling his presence keenly, she quietly thanked him, then slid onto the passenger seat. She ran her fingers over the smooth leather as James turned the ignition. The interior of the car smelled wonderful.

"Which way do I go?" he asked as he glanced her way.

She blushed under his regard and forced her attention ahead. "Take a right out of the parking lot," she told him.

As he followed her directions, Nell was overly aware how close they were in the confines of James's car. Did he feel it too? The attraction between them? Charlotte was waiting outside for them as he drove close to the house. She hurried toward the vehicle as Nell and James climbed out of the car.

Her eyes widened and a look of relief passed over her features as she looked from James to Nell.

"What happened?" Nell asked.

"Something frightened Barney," Charlotte said. "Joshua was getting Buddy out of her stall when Barney reared up and came down hard against her side." She addressed James directly. "She's suffered a large gash. Can you help her?"

"I'll do what I can. Show me where you keep her."

Charlotte led the way, and Nell followed them to the barn where they found Abram near Buddy's stall.

Abram looked relieved to see them. "I put her back in her stall."

James studied the horse. "Good. She's in closed quarters." He addressed Abram. "I may need your help to hold her steady as Nell and I ready her to stitch up the wound."

"She's a gentle soul, but she's hurting bad," Abram said after agreeing to James's request.

Abram's son Nate entered the building. "Can you help us for a minute?" James asked after a quick look in the young man's direction. "Do you have any rope? We'll need to secure it to the rafters and around Buddy to help keep her steady after I give her a sedative."

"Ja," Abram said. "Nate, will you get that length of rope from the tack room?"

Nate immediately obeyed then slipped inside the stall, being careful to skirt the animal until he reached the front right side. *"Dat? You oll recht?"* he asked.

"I'm fine. Be careful, *soohn*," Abram warned as Nate came up on Buddy's opposite side.

James grabbed the rope and with a toss of his arm, he threw one end over the rafter until it fell in equal lengths to the ground. "Nate, could you wrap this around Buddy? Abram, you don't have a wench or pulley, do you?"

The man shook his head. "We'll make do."

He addressed Nell, "Would you get me a syringe and the bottle of anesthetic?"

Nell handed him the bottle and the needle.

He took it without looking at her. She could feel his concern for the animal. She'd seen different sides to the veterinarian over the past week, each more impressive than what she'd seen before.

His face was full of concentration as he inserted the needle. The animal jerked and kicked out, her hoof making contact with James's shin. He grimaced, but that was the only sign that he'd been hurt. Nell worried about him when he continued as if the horse hadn't clipped him.

He stood back. "We'll have to wait a moment or so until the anesthetic takes effect."

His eyes met Nell's. She gazed back at him in sympathy, recognizing pain in his face. She wanted to take a look at his leg and help him, but she remained silent. It was clear that he didn't want his injury to detract from helping Abram's horse.

She felt a rush of something she didn't want to feel. This man clearly loved animals as much as she did.

They waited for tense moments until the horse seemed to quiet. Nell looked at Abram. "It's *oll recht*," she said. She watched as he and Nate released their hold on the horse.

"You might want to leave," James said. "This won't be pleasant to watch."

The two men left, leaving Nell alone with James. He met her gaze. "All set?"

"Ja," she breathed, ready to do whatever he needed.

"Come around to this side. Bring my bag. I'll tell you what I need."

Nell watched while James worked on Buddy. He sutured the mare's wounds, noting how gentle he was with the animal, soothing her with a soft voice.

After twenty minutes, James seemed satisfied that he'd done all he could for the horse.

"Nell, would you please see if you can find a container of antibiotic? I'd like Abram to give her a dose twice a day. He can sprinkle it on her food."

Nell understood when she found the bottle and saw that the antibiotic was actually granules instead of pills.

Soon they were driving away from Abram's farm, heading back toward the clinic. Nell caught James's wince more than once as he drove, but she kept silent. She couldn't offer to drive him since she didn't know how and wouldn't be allowed anyway because of the rules in the *Ordnung*.

James pulled into the parking lot and drove around to the back as usual. She saw him grimace as he climbed out, but she didn't say anything as she followed him inside the building. James went into his office while she went right to work restocking his medical bag with the supplies he'd used at Abram's. When she was done, she entered his office and confronted him.

"You hurt your leg," she said. She swallowed hard. "May I see?"

He gazed at her a long moment, and she felt her face heat, but he finally nodded. Fortunately, the legs of his black slacks were loose. James gingerly pulled up his pants leg.

Nell gasped. His shin was swollen and severely

bruised. She eyed the black-and-blue area with concern. "You should see a doctor," she suggested softly.

"I'll be fine," he said sharply. She didn't take offense for she knew he was hurting.

"I'll get some ice," she said and went into the kitchen.

When she returned, his head was tilted against the chair back, his eyes closed.

"James," she whispered. His eyes flashed open. She held up the ice pack. "For your leg."

"Thank you." He shifted, straightening. His pants had fallen back to cover his injured leg. He tugged up the fabric again, and Nell bent to place the pack on his bruised skin.

"It looks sore," she said with sympathy as she knelt to hold it in place.

James gave her a crooked smile. "A bit."

She shook her head, trying not to be uncomfortable looking up at him from near his feet. "You should go to the emergency room—or a clinic." She rose, and her gaze traveled around the room.

"What are you looking for?" James asked.

"Something to prop your leg up on so you can ice it properly."

"No need." He dropped his pant leg and rose. "It's time to head out. I can ice it at home."

Nell saw him wince as he moved, but she held her tongue. "I'll check the reception area and make sure it's locked up."

"Okay." He waited while she hurried out to the front room to lock up and retrieve her purse from under the desk. She took one last look around, then returned to where James waited near the back door.

"Thanks for your help today."

Nell shrugged. "That's what you pay me for."

A tiny smile formed on his lips. "I guess I do."

They headed outside together. James pulled the door shut behind them and made sure it was secure.

Nell saw that he held the ice pack and was glad. She became conscious of him beside her as she waited for him to turn. "I will see you on Wednesday?" she asked.

He hesitated. "Yes."

"Is anything wrong?" she asked, sensing a shift in his mood.

James opened and closed his mouth, as if to answer but thought better of it. "It's late."

Nell experienced a burning in her stomach. "*Ja.* I should head home." She turned away. Something was definitely bothering the man.

"See you in the morning, Nell."

She paused but didn't look back. She was afraid of what she'd see. "*Ja*, I'll see you then."

Then she hurried toward her buggy, feeling edgy and suddenly eager to be away and at home.

James watched Nell leave, then followed her buggy in his car until their paths split. He continued straight until he reached a small shopping center with a bakery, a candy shop and a small gift shop. He drove around to the back of the building, got out of his car and went in a back entrance that led to his apartment above the bakery.

As he started painfully up the stairs, he caught the scent of rich chocolate. Usually, he'd head into the bakery to buy whatever it was that Mattie Mast was making downstairs. But with his throbbing shin, the only thing he wanted to do right now was put ice on the injury.

The trek up the staircase was slow, and he stopped several times. He breathed a sigh of relief when he finally made it to the top.

His one-bedroom apartment was dark as he entered. He threw his keys onto the kitchen table and went to open a few windows to let in the day's breeze. The delicious scent of baking was stronger upstairs than down.

He refilled his ice bag, then, ignoring his rumbling stomach, he plopped down onto the sofa in his small living room, turned on the TV and shifted to put his feet onto the couch. He carefully set the ice pack that Nell had made on his swollen leg. He gazed at the television, but his thoughts were elsewhere.

It was Tuesday. There was still the rest of the week to get through. Would the pain in his leg let up enough for him to leave his apartment in the morning?

Nell will be there. He would make sure he got to work. She was helping him out, and he needed to be there.

Stretched out on his sofa, he stared at the ceiling with the sound of the television a dull buzz in his ears. The ice felt good against his swollen leg. James closed his eyes, and the day played out in his mind. Nell's calming influence as she worked by his side. Their trip to the Amish farm, treating the mare. Nell's assistance with Abram Peachy and his son Nate. Her calming way with their mare Buddy. His growing friendship with Nell.

He saw Nell clearly in his mind—her soft brown hair, bright brown eyes and warm smile. She'd worn a green dress with black apron today, with a white *kapp*, dark stockings and black shoes. He smiled. He wondered how she'd look at home when she was at ease, barefoot and laughing as she chased children about the yard, with sparkling eyes and her mouth curved upward in amusement.

James wondered how it would feel to spend time with her outside of the office.

His eyes flickered open as shock made him sit up. He was more than a little attracted to Nell Stoltzfus!

James shook his head. He had no right to think about Nell in that way. He scowled. She was a member of an Amish community, a community like the one he'd left of his own free will to choose a different path in life.

He forced his attention back to the television. He began to channel surf to find something—anything— that would consume his interest other than thoughts of Nell Stoltzfus.

Nell's four sisters were in the yard when she returned home.

"We heard what happened!" Charlie said.

"At Abram's," Ellie explained.

"Nate said you were both wonderful. He said you worked efficiently and quietly by the veterinarian's side," Charlie added.

"Was it true that James got kicked by Buddy?" Meg asked.

Nell studied her sisters with amusement. "Do you want me to answer any of you, or would you prefer to provide the answers yourself?"

Leah, the only sister who hadn't spoken yet, laughed. She was the next oldest after Nell. "How did it go?"

"Well," Nell said. "It went well. James sutured Buddy and left her in Abram's care."

"Was it awful?" Charlie asked. "Seeing all that blood?"

"I felt bad for Buddy, but I was *oll recht*. I didn't think much about anything but what I could do to help James."

The sisters walked toward the house as it was nearing suppertime. There would be work in the kitchen as they helped their mother to prepare the meal.

"Only three days more, *ja*?" Leah asked when their sisters had gone ahead into the house.

Nell faced her sister as they stood on the front porch. "*Ja*, in a way I'll be sad to see it end."

"But 'tis for the better that it will." Leah watched her carefully.

"*Ja.*" She leaned against the porch rail. "But until then, I'm learning so much. Things I'll be able to use in helping our friends and neighbors. I know I can't take the place of a veterinarian but I'll be able to handle more than I could before."

Leah regarded her silently. "What's he like?"

"James?"

Her sister nodded. Her golden-blond hair, blue eyes and a warm smile made her the prettiest one of all of the sisters, at least in Nell's eyes. Today, she wore a light blue dress which emphasized her eyes. On her head she wore a matching blue kerchief and she was barefoot. She had come from working in their vegetable garden.

"You saw him at the Masts'," Nell reminded her.

"But seeing him isn't working with him."

For a moment, Nell got lost in her thoughts. "He's a

caring man who's compassionate with animals. He's a *gut* vet. You should have seen him with Buddy. He—" She bit her lip.

"He was injured today," Leah said. "Nate stopped while you were gone. He said Buddy kicked him while he was trying to sedate her."

"*Ja*, but you wouldn't have known it by looking at him afterward. He worked as if nothing was bothering him when his leg must have hurt terribly." Nell had been amazed—not only by his skill but by his attention to Abram's mare.

"You like him."

"I wouldn't work for him if I didn't like and respect him."

"I know that, but I think you feel more for him."

"*Nay*," she denied quickly. "He's *gut* at what he does, and I respect that."

Leah nodded. As they entered the house, Nell wondered if her sister believed her.

She'd felt awful when she saw the extent of James's injury. She'd been startlingly aware of him as she'd pressed the ice pack against his shin. The sudden rush of feeling as she'd held the pack against his masculine leg for those brief moments had frightened her. Caring for him in that way had felt too intimate. She'd risen quickly and searched for a chair or stool to prop up his leg. When James had declared that it was time to go home, she'd been relieved.

"Nell," her mother greeted as she and Leah entered the kitchen. "I heard you had an eventful day."

Nell nodded. "It was more eventful for Abram's mare."

"She's all right?"

"Buddy's fine. James stitched her up as *gut* as new. She'll be in pain for a while, but he left Abram medication for her."

"Gut. Gut," *Mam* said. "Ellie, would you get the potato salad out of the refrigerator? Meg, you carry in the sweet and sour beans. Leah, would you mind getting your father? Supper is almost ready."

"What about me?" Charlie said.

Her mother smiled. "You can set the table with Nell."

Nell went to help her sister. She was home and felt less conflicted in this world she knew so well.

She might have imagined the strange tension between her and James. Tomorrow she'd put things in perspective and realize that the tenseness between them was just a figment of her imagination.

Chapter Five

Wednesday morning, Nell got up extra early to make her favorite contribution of potato salad for Aunt Katie's quilting bee. By the time her mother and siblings had entered the kitchen, she had finished cleaning the dishes she'd used. She automatically started to pull out the ingredients for the cake and pie that she knew that her mother wanted to bring.

"You're up early," Leah said.

"*Ja*, I thought I'd take a look at Buddy this morning before I head to the clinic."

"That's a fine idea," *Mam* said as she came into the room. "I'm sure Abram will appreciate it."

Nell ate breakfast with her family, then stayed long enough to clean up before she got ready to leave. She ran upstairs to get her black shoes. When she was done, she hurried downstairs to the barnyard. She chose to take the family pony cart and hitched up Daisy before she headed toward Abram Peachy's place.

She wondered what time James would arrive at the office this morning. Would she be able to reach him if Buddy suddenly needed additional medical care?

It was six thirty. She knew that Abram and his family most likely would be up and doing morning chores. No doubt Charlotte was already in the kitchen preparing food for this afternoon's quilting gathering.

The weather was lovely. Nell appreciated the colors and scents of summer. A bird chirped as it flew across the road and landed in a tree. The trees and lawns were a lush verdant green, moist with the morning's dew. There was no traffic on the roadway.

Nell steered her horse past Yoder's General Store, where she glimpsed the owner, Margaret Yoder, getting out of her buggy. Margaret made eye contact with her, and Nell lifted a hand in greeting. The woman smiled and waved back.

It wasn't long before she caught sight of Abram's farm ahead. She clicked on her directional signal and slowed Daisy to turn into the barnyard.

Nell saw Abram and Charlotte's eleven-year-old daughter, Rose Ann, as she came out of the house. Nell waved and climbed out of the open buggy and secured her horse.

"Nell!" Rose Ann cried. "Have you come to see Buddy?"

"*Ja*, Rosie. How is she doing?"

The child frowned. "I don't know. *Dat* won't let me near her."

"That's probably for the best. He doesn't want you to get hurt. Buddy's in pain and may kick out or nip you. You had best listen to your *vadder* and wait outside while I check on her."

Nate Peachy came out of the house. "*Gut* morning, Nell. Here to check on our mare?"

"*Ja*, Nate. I was telling your sister that it's best if she stays out here."

Nate smiled at his little sister. "Listen to her, Rose Ann. You know what *Dat* said."

"That I should stay out of the barn until *Dat*, you, Nell or James Pierce tells me I can visit Buddy."

"*Gut* girl," Nate praised. He led Nell into the barn. They eyed the mare silently for a moment before he turned to her. "You need anything?"

"*Nay*, if I do, I'll let you know." Nell smiled as the horse approached. "*Hallo*, Buddy," she greeted softly as the mare poked her head over the top of her stall.

"I'll leave you alone then," Nate murmured.

"*Danki*, Nate."

After Nate had left, Nell returned her attention to the horse.

"How are you feeling today, girl?" She reached toward the mare's head and stroked Buddy between the eyes then down her nose. "Are you in pain?"

She examined the area of the wound, where James had secured a bandage over the laceration. She was relieved to see that there was no blood seeping through the gauze. "Looks like you've not bled through. That's a *gut* thing."

Had James mentioned how long Abram should keep the bandage on? Nell frowned. Longer than one day, she was sure, but for how long? Had Abram given Buddy her medication?

"Did you eat breakfast, Buddy? Did you have your medicine?" She smiled when Buddy butted gently against her hand with her nose. "I'll have to speak with Abram," she told her. "We want you well and happy again." She spoke soothingly to the horse while she stroked her nose and the side of her neck.

She felt someone's presence in the barn before she heard a familiar voice.

"Nell."

"James!" She blinked and stared at him, taken aback by her stark awareness of him. This morning he wore a blue short-sleeved shirt with jeans and sneakers. She swallowed as emotion hit her square in the chest at the sight of him looking so tall, masculine and handsome. "I didn't expect to see you here."

"I see we shared the same thought." His warm smile made her heart race. "Buddy." His soft expression made her feel warm inside. "What made you come?"

"I was worried about her."

He approached, opened the stall and slipped inside. Buddy snorted and shifted uneasily. James set down his medical bag, then turned to the horse.

Nell watched as James spoke to the mare. She was amazed how well the animal responded to his deep, masculine tones.

He placed a calming hand on a spot not far from the wound as he bent low to examine the area around the bandage. "No infection to the surrounding tissue. She looks good." He glanced up at her when Nell remained silent. He searched her features as if he found something interesting in them.

Nell blushed, quickly agreed and glanced toward the horse.

"When does she need her dressing changed?" She kept her gaze on Buddy. The man's unexpected presence made her feel off-kilter.

"We probably should change it now since you're

here and can assist. I'd like a closer look at her sutures." He opened the stall door to invite Nell inside. "Are you up for it?"

"Why wouldn't I be?" Nell asked, excited to learn something new.

The confines of the space seemed smaller than it had when she and James had come to take care of Buddy's injury the previous night.

As she stood by ready to assist, Nell was conscious of the man beside her as he worked. Fortunately, she was able to focus on the task and was ready with whatever he needed. Buddy shifted and snorted in protest as James carefully peeled back the bandage. Nell quickly stroked and spoke to sooth her until the mare settled down.

She watched as James checked the wound. He pressed gently on the surrounding area, and Buddy didn't seemed to mind. He stood back. "It looks great."

Nell silently agreed. She was amazed how well the sutures appeared. James had done an excellent job with them.

"Nell, would you please see if you can find the antiseptic ointment that's in my bag?"

She quickly found the tube and handed it to him along with a fresh dressing. He eyed her with approval as he took them from her.

"Thank you."

Nell nodded. She observed as James spread ointment on a clean square of gauze before he placed it carefully over Buddy's wound. She handed him the roll of surgical tape, and he secured the bandage in place.

James stood. "That should last until we see her next, unless a problem arises."

"I can stop by and check in a day or two," she offered.

He stared at her. "That would be helpful. Thank you."

They gazed at one another for several seconds. Nell felt a fluttering in her stomach. She looked away.

"Are you headed to the clinic next?" she asked as she left the stall with James following closely behind.

He glanced at his watch. "It's early, but I do have paperwork to catch up on." He smiled at her. "You're not due in for another hour."

"Is there something you need done?"

He hesitated. "Nothing that can't wait."

"I don't mind starting early," she said.

Something flickered in the depths of his dark eyes. "I don't want to take advantage, Nell."

"You won't be. If I can help before the clinic opens, I'll be happy to come." Nell headed toward her buggy.

James approached his car, which was parked several yards from her pony cart. "I'll see you there then."

She paused before climbing into her vehicle. "How is your leg?" she asked conversationally. She felt the intensity of his gaze and faced him. She'd seen him grimace when he'd stood after bending to examine Buddy and knew it had to be hurting him.

He didn't respond immediately. "Better today than yesterday."

"Gut." The realization that she had the ability to read him so well alarmed her.

"Nell—"

The ringing of his cell phone stopped his words. Nell waited patiently while James spoke to the person on the other end. When his face darkened, Nell became concerned.

"I'll be there as soon as I can," he said. He glanced at the thick-banded watch on his left wrist. "About ten, fifteen minutes." He listened silently. "Yes." He turned away from Nell, and she heard him issuing concise directions on what the caller should do until he arrived.

Suddenly feeling as if she was intruding on his phone conversation, she moved away to give him privacy.

James finished up his call and approached her with a look of apology. "Emergency," he said. "I guess I won't be doing paperwork this morning." He drew a sharp breath. "Want to come?" He explained about an injured dog that had been found on a man's back patio. "He's severely wounded."

"Ja," she agreed. "I'd like to help."

"It's not far."

Nell felt James's urgency as she left her pony cart and hurried toward his car. "Nate!" she called as she saw Abram's son coming around from the back of the barn. "We have to leave. Animal medical emergency. Is it *oll recht* if I leave my cart?"

"I'll drive it home for you," he offered.

She opened her mouth to object, but James said, "Thank you, Nate. I'll drive Nell home after work today."

Nell slid into the passenger side and buckled her seat belt as James climbed in beside her. He turned to face her in his seat.

"I should have asked you if it's all right if I drive you home," he said.

"'Tis fine," she assured him.

James gazed at her a long moment, nodded and then concentrated on putting the car into gear and driving off Abram's property.

James had visions of the injured canine as he drove toward Fred Moreland's farm. From Fred's description, the dog was covered with blood and in a terrible state. It was the reason he told Fred not to move the animal.

He was conscious of Nell beside him as he drove. Would she be upset by the sight of the injured dog? He frowned. He hoped not. She'd been of tremendous help to him and hoped to keep her working at the clinic for the rest of the week.

Fred waited for him at the end of his front yard as James pulled into the man's driveway and parked close to the house. He got out of the car with his medical bag while Nell climbed out on the other side.

"Where is he?" James asked as Fred approached.

"In the back." The older man looked anxious.

He turned to Nell with concern. "Nell, this could be…"

"I'll be fine, James."

He set his medical kit not far from the little dog. He caught a glimpse of white fur beneath all the dirt and blood. He heard Nell's horrified gasp as she got her first look at the dog, but she didn't say anything as she quickly opened his medical kit and got to work.

"Is he yours?" James asked Fred.

"No. He's a stray. I don't have any barbed wire, but it looks like he got caught up in some. Not sure where."

The animal lay on its side on the concrete patio. He was breathing steadily, which was a good thing. James was prepared for the dog to snap and try to bite when he touched him. "Nell."

"I'm here," she said calmly. "I'll hold him while you give him the injection." She busily prepared the syringe that he would need as he studied her. He could see tears shimmering in her pretty brown eyes.

Nell handed him the syringe and vial of local anesthetic, then she hunkered down by the animal's head and placed her hands on an uninjured area of the small body.

As she touched him, the dog's eyes opened and he looked as if he would struggle to rise, but Nell quickly soothed him with soft words and a gentle stroke. James regarded her a few seconds, amazed by her ability once again, before he found a small area appropriate for the shot. Nell's soft soothing voice continued, and James found that it calmed him as much as it did the injured dog.

"Nell, get me that brown bottle, too, please. I think it will be best to lightly sedate him. It will make things easier for him."

Nell obeyed, and James gave the dog another injection.

"We'll wait a few moments, and then we'll clean him up and take care of his wounds." James eyed the dog, deciding how best to proceed. "Would you please get us a bowl of warm water and an old towel?"

"Certainly," Fred agreed and hurried to do his bidding.

James and Nell were left alone on the man's back patio with the injured animal. "Are you all right?" he asked.

"I'm fine." She hesitated as she studied the dog. "Do you think he got tangled in barbed wire or did someone abuse him?"

James regarded the animal with a frown. "I suspect he was abused."

"Fred?"

"No," he said. "Absolutely not. Fred is one of my clients. He's got a soft touch for all animals. I take care of his cat and dog. It's easy to tell that he loves them. His wife died recently, and his animals give him comfort."

James turned his focus back to the dog and wondered whether or not he should move him. Would it be better to treat him inside?

Before James could decide, Fred returned with an old but clean white enamel basin filled with warm water. He set it, a soft washcloth and towel within James's reach. He had draped a folded blanket over his arm.

"I thought you might want to move him onto this. It's soft and may be more comfortable for him." He dropped down on one knee and unfolded the quilt. "It's okay if it gets wet or dirty. I don't like seeing this little guy on the concrete."

"You found him here?" Nell asked softly.

"Yes. I came out this morning to have my coffee as I often do, when I saw him. That's when I called you, Dr. Pierce. I was afraid to touch or to move him. I didn't want to hurt him, and I didn't know if he'd bite if I tried."

"It was good that you let him be and called me, Fred." James eyed the unfolded blanket in Fred's arms. "You grab an end and we'll spread it out."

With Nell and James's help, Fred folded the quilt into quarters, then spread it over the concrete patio. James and Fred carefully eased the animal from the concrete onto the padded folds.

Nell grabbed the washcloth and dipped it into the warm water. She placed the towel within easy reach and began to clean the area about the animal's neck.

James went to work cleaning the actual wounds with antiseptic cleansing pads. He cleaned a wound on the side of the dog's belly. It looked as if he'd been burned as well as cut.

Nell met his gaze. "He *was* abused."

He nodded as he felt the anger inside him grow.

Fred had gone into the house for more linens. He came out in time to hear Nell's comment. "Someone did this to him?" He looked pale and upset.

"Yes, I'm afraid so." James didn't look up from his task.

"Whoever did this should be in jail," the older man said.

"If he's ever caught, he will be."

"Have you seen much of this before?" Nell asked, her voice sounding shaky.

"Too many times." He carefully washed each wound while Nell cleaned the surrounding areas. "Did you see him walk?" he asked Fred.

"No. He was lying here. I supposed he was able to move well enough to get here."

James went on to check the animal's legs and was upset to find one that appeared to be broken.

"Fred, while he's knocked out, I'm going to take him back to my office. I want to do X-rays. One leg is broken, but until I see the extent of the damage, I won't know the best way to treat him."

"What are you going to do with him then?" Fred eyed the animal with longing. "Do you think I'll be able to keep him?"

"If the leg is bad, I may have to amputate."

He heard Nell's sharp inhalation of breath.

"Doesn't matter to me. Dogs can get by with three legs. I still want him."

"What about Max?" James asked of the man's other dog.

"This one will be fine with him. Max will like the

company. I'll keep them apart until this little guy is well enough."

"If you're going to keep him, maybe you should come up with a name for him."

Fred thought for a moment.

"How about Joseph?" Nell suggested. "You can call him Joey." When Fred looked at her, she explained, "Joseph means 'addition,' and this little guy will be a new addition to your family."

Fred smiled. "I like it. Joey it is. Max and Joey."

Nell nodded, then returned her attention to patting dry the area she'd washed.

"We should move him while he's still sedated," James said. "I've got a small stretcher in the trunk of my car."

"I'll get it," Fred offered, and James handed him the keys.

The man was back in less than a minute. He set the stretcher on the ground, then the three of them took hold of the edges of the blanket and set Joey on the stretcher. James and Fred lifted the stretcher and carried it to the car, setting it carefully on the backseat. Without being told, Nell climbed into the back with Joey.

"I'll give you a call to let you know how he makes out," James said.

"I want him, James," Fred repeated. "No matter what."

James climbed into the front seat and glanced back to see Nell buckled into her seat belt and leaning over Joey while stroking his head tenderly. "Nell." She looked at him. "He'll make it."

"I hope so." She blinked rapidly as if fighting back tears.

James felt the strongest desire to take Nell into his

arms to comfort her. But he ignored it and instead drove back toward the clinic.

He'd been thinking of Nell too much lately. He wasn't sure what to do, but he knew he couldn't risk hurting the young Amish woman who'd worked her way into his affections.

He reminded himself that he just had to make it through the end of the week. Once Michelle and Janie were back in the office, Nell would return to her Amish life and he'd be able to put her out of his mind.

At least, he hoped so.

Chapter Six

Nell felt her throat tighten and her eyes fill with tears as she gently stroked the injured puppy. Who could do such a thing to one of God's poor defenseless creatures?

She looked into the rearview mirror and asked James, "Do you think he'll make it?"

"He will if I can have anything to do with it."

She knew what he meant. James would do all he could, but ultimately the dog's recovery would be in God's hands.

Soon James was pulling into the clinic parking lot. He parked near the door, then got out to help with Jocy.

Nell opened her door. "How are we going to do this?"

James eyed the little dog. "I'll carry him." He bent inside and, using the sides of the blanket, he scooped him up carefully. "Nell, would you get my keys? They're on the front seat."

One look at James's expression had her melting inside. The man was obviously as upset about Joey as she was. Enough that he'd forgotten to grab his keys.

James had straightened with the dog in his arms. "Would you open the door? It's the blue key."

She found the right one and hurried to open the building. She turned on the light and then held the door open for James.

James quickly went to the treatment area. He gently set Joey down on an examination table. "We have to x-ray him. I'm afraid he may have several broken bones—not just a broken leg."

Nell sent up a silent prayer, then whispered, "I hope not."

James checked the dog's heart and breathing with his stethoscope before he moved him over to the platform under the X-ray machine.

"Will he sleep for a while?" Nell asked with concern. She hated the thought that Joey might wake and be in pain. He might get scared and struggle, further injuring himself.

"Yes, long enough. He'll be groggy when he does finally come out of it."

Nell stood by ready to help as James prepared the machine. She helped shift the dog into different positions and then waited while James snapped the photos. Little Joey remained sedated while they worked.

Nell felt her nerves stretch taut as she waited for the results of the X-rays.

"He has a break in his hind leg," James said after reading the films for several long moments.

"Will he be all right?"

"I can't promise, but there is a good chance his leg will heal. We'll have to splint it. Unlike Jonas's injury, this little guy will have his leg bound for several weeks."

He stepped away from the X-ray light panel and moved toward Joey. "There doesn't appear to be any new bleeding, but I'm going to suture the worst of his wounds."

Nell kept her eyes on the little dog. She was feeling emotional. The news that the animal's leg wouldn't need to be amputated had buoyed her spirits, but she still had a hard time accepting that someone could be so cruel to the little dog.

She knew others within her Amish community didn't understand her love for animals. They took good care of their horses, which they needed, and their other farm animals, but they didn't feel the same about dogs or cats. No one within her church community would intentionally hurt an animal, she didn't think. And they'd come to accept that her concern for animals made her a good person to call on when they needed help with them.

Working with James was teaching her how to better help her neighbors and friends…and gave her a sense of purpose.

She settled her gaze on James. His attention was on Joey, his eyes focused on the dog's little body as he meticulously stitched closed one wound before moving to another.

She concentrated on the work so that she could ignore her growing feelings for the man. She gasped, struck anew by how much she liked spending time with James.

James looked up at her, a frown settling on his brow. "Are you all right?"

She managed a smile. "*Ja*, I'm fine." She hesitated as he returned his attention to Joey. "How is he?"

"I think he'll make it, but seeing what was done to

him—" She could feel his anger and understood it despite God's teachings.

"Will he have to spend the night?" she asked.

"I think it would be a good idea."

"I can stay," she offered.

He glanced at her then, his expression soft. "I appreciate it, Nell, but I'll stay. Your family will be worried about you, and I know what to do if something goes wrong."

She felt a sharp tightening in her chest. "Do you expect something to go wrong?"

"I don't know, but better to be safe than sorry." He grabbed a spoon splint and cut it to the correct size before he began to tape it onto Joey's broken leg. He paused to reach into his jeans pocket and pulled out a sheet of paper. "Would you call Fred and let him know?"

"*Ja*, of course." She took the phone number and abruptly left the room. After she told Fred how Joey was doing, she took a minute to compose herself before heading to the treatment area again.

James didn't look up as he continued to stabilize Joey's broken leg. "Did you reach Fred?" he asked.

"*Ja*. He was upset but eager for Joey to get well."

James straightened and turned to face her. A small smile hovered on his lips. "Fred's a good man. Joey will have a good home."

Nell's throat was tight, and she didn't want to break down in front of him. She didn't want for him to believe that she couldn't handle the work. The last thing she wanted was to lose this position.

"Now what?" she asked.

"We'll make him comfortable, and I'll see how he

is when he wakes up. I'll move him into a kennel right now. We'll be able to keep an eye on him while we see patients."

She waited while he gently moved Joey and then headed back out to the front desk area where she pulled out the appointment book and prepared for the day.

It was seven forty-five when she unlocked the door. James's first patient with its owner was already waiting to come in.

The day went quickly because of their full patient schedule and their vigil of Joey. Soon, it was time for Nell to go home. James said that he would take her home, but she felt bad for making him leave Joey for even a few moments.

"I can call someone to drive me," she offered.

James shook his head. "No it's fine. I can take you home."

She waited while he checked on Joey one more time, and then they headed outside. He unlocked his car, then opened her door and waited until she was seated. His kindness made her feel both uncomfortable and somehow cherished.

The interior of the car seemed close, and she was overly conscious of the man beside her as he turned on the ignition, then backed away from the building.

She blinked back tears. What was she going to do? It was wrong to work with James when she had feelings for him. Yet, she couldn't leave the position. It would be unfair to force him to work alone in the practice, especially since she'd promised to help him. And he wasn't the one with the problem. She was.

Nell drew a steadying breath. It would be fine. She wouldn't let on how she felt. She'd finish the job and then get on with her life, taking with her new knowledge of animal care—and a longing for a life with someone she could never have.

James felt Nell's presence keenly as he exited the parking lot. "Which way?"

"Left."

As he drove, he remembered her making a left when she'd departed yesterday.

She was silent as he headed down the road. He flashed her a quick look, wondering how she was feeling. She glanced toward the window but not before he saw her tears.

"Nell." Instinctively, he reached out and captured her hand where it rested on the seat beside her. He felt her stiffen and then look at him with brimming eyes. "He'll be all right."

She blinked rapidly, and he quickly released her hand.

"I'm sorry," she said.

He flashed her a startled glance. "What for?"

"I'm not a *gut* assistant if I cry about a patient, am I?"

"Nell, your compassion, your empathy makes you a great assistant."

"Then you're not disappointed in me?"

"For what?" he said. "For caring?" He paused. "Of course not." He drove past Whittier's Store and Lapp's Carriage Shop.

"Take the next left to get to our farm."

James made the turn and saw a farmhouse up ahead. "Here?" he asked.

"Ja."

Minutes later, he pulled into the barnyard. As he

pulled the car to a stop, four young women exited the house. "Your sisters?"

She nodded as she opened the door and climbed out.

"How's the little dog?" a young redhead asked. "Will he be *oll recht*?"

"We don't know for certain, but we think so."

A dark-haired young woman bent to look inside the car.

"Hello," he said.

"You must be James," she said.

He inclined his head. "I am."

Nell quickly introduced him to her sisters.

"We did what we could for him. I'll know tomorrow morning." He glanced at Nell. "I need to head back."

"Let me know how he does?"

"I will." He gazed at her, interested to see her surrounded by her sisters. "I'll see you in the morning."

"*Ja*, I'll see you then."

James put the vehicle into Reverse and then turned toward the road. He saw that Nell's father and mother had joined her sisters in the yard. He waved at them as he drove off. He would have liked to stay, but he needed to get back to Joey. The last thing he wanted was for the dog to wake up and start to chew on his wounds.

Before he pulled onto the road, he took one last look toward the Stoltzfus residence. Seeing Nell with her family made him feel things he hadn't felt in a long time.

"How was your day at the clinic?" Arlin Stoltzfus asked Nell.

"I'd say *gut*, but we're treating an abused and severely injured dog. Seeing Joey suffer was anything but *gut*, *Dat*."

"Was that why Dr. Pierce left in a hurry?"

"*Ja*. Joey should wake up soon. James needs to be near when he does."

"He's *gut* at what he does," her father said.

"*Ja, Dat,*" Nell said. "He is."

"You have two days left in his employ."

Nell felt a sudden uncomfortable feeling inside. "*Ja*. Tomorrow and Friday—and I'll be done." She sensed someone's curious gaze and turned to see her sister Leah studying her closely.

"He seems like a *gut* man," Ellie said.

"He is," Nell admitted.

"An *Englisher*," *Dat* said as if he had to remind her.

"*Ja*, he is," Nell said, meeting her father's gaze directly. Arlin nodded as if satisfied by what he saw in her expression. "You know his family. You've spoken with him. He is an honorable man." She thought it wise to change the topic of conversation. "How is Jonas? Did he behave today?"

"He always behaves." Charlie's features softened with affection. It seemed that her sister loved the dog almost as much as she. Nell knew she could trust her youngest sister to take good care of him.

"'Tis hard to believe he'd injured his leg," Leah commented.

"I'm thankful that he fully recovered."

The family headed toward the house. "Anyone hungry?" *Mam* asked.

Nell looked at her gratefully. "I am."

"We all are." Ellie glanced back. "Meg? Why are you lagging behind?"

"I'm coming."

Nell waited for Meg to catch up. "Anything wrong?"

Meg shook her head.

"Are you sure?"

Her sister smiled. "*Ja. Danki*, Nell."

"I'll be happy to listen if you need to talk."

"I'll keep that in mind." Meg ran ahead to join Ellie and Charlie who had climbed the front porch after their parents.

She and Leah followed more slowly as the others entered the house.

"Two days more and then you're done working for James," Leah said. She paused. "How do you feel about it?"

Nell shrugged. "Fine. I've learned a lot this week, but I have things here that need to be done."

Leah narrowed her gaze. "Like what?"

"Like care for my animals. 'Tis not fair that my sisters have to do the work."

"We don't mind. Charlie loves taking care of them, especially Jonas." Her sister reached for the handle and pulled open the door. "But I agree that you have something that needs to be done." When Nell met her gaze, she said, "You need to find yourself a husband before *Dat* gets impatient and finds one for you."

Nell experienced an overwhelming sorrow. If Michael hadn't died, they would have been married, and she would have had children by now. She kept her thoughts to herself. None of them knew about Michael and that was a good thing. She had the choice back when she'd met Michael. As a full member of the church, she no longer had the option of falling for an *Englisher*.

She still felt a tightening in her chest for her loss and what might have been had Michael lived.

Chapter Seven

After she'd enjoyed a delicious meal of fried chicken, vegetables and warm bread slathered with butter, Nell stood on the front porch and stared out into the yard. Her thoughts went to little Joey—and James. She had the strongest urge to ride over to the clinic and see how the dog was faring. But she couldn't. Thoughts of Michael made her particularly lonely this evening. It wouldn't be wise to see James, the only man she'd been attracted to since Michael's death.

She climbed down from the porch and crossed the yard to the barn, drawn once again to her animals for solace. James's attempt to comfort her earlier when she'd begun to cry had startled her. The warmth of his fingers covering hers had made feel things she had no right to feel about the *Englisher*.

She had just been upset over Joey, she reasoned. But was that it? She sighed. *Nay*, she'd felt an attraction to him well before they'd treated Joey.

Entering the barn, Nell went to the horses first. She rubbed Daisy between the eyes, then moved to pay similar attention to their other mare, Lily. She ensured each horse had enough water inside the barn and filled the trough in the pasture.

"Do you want to go outside?" she asked the horses when she went back inside. "'Tis a beautiful evening. You can enjoy it for a little while."

Daisy's stall was next to Lily's. She took her out of her stall and released her into the fenced area before she did the same for Lily. Nell felt her lips curve as the two mares galloped into the field. They chased each other in play before they settled down to leisurely munch on pasture grass.

Satisfied that the mares would be fine for a while, Nell stopped back in the barn to visit Ed, their gelding, and her dog, Jonas. Excited to see her, her little dog whimpered and jumped up on his hind legs. When he put his front paws on her skirt, Nell grinned, certain more than ever his leg was completely healed from the injuries he'd received when she witnessed some teenagers throw him out of their moving car.

"Let's not overdo it, Jonas." She gently repositioned Jonas's front paws onto the ground, then knelt next to him. The dog instantly rolled onto his back, exposing his belly. Nell laughed as she wove her fingers through his fur and rubbed.

"Nell?"

"In here!" she called.

Leah stepped into the light. "I thought I'd find you here." She opened the stall door and slipped in to join her. After closing the door carefully behind her, she squatted beside Nell. "Are you *oll recht*?"

"*Ja*, why wouldn't I be?"

Leah's expression turned somber. "What happened earlier?"

"What do you mean?"

"You were upset when James brought you home."

"Joey," Nell said. "What happened to him was heart-breaking."

"I'm sorry," Leah said softly.

Nell felt a clenching in her belly. "Me, too," she said. She continued to stroke Jonas, who clearly loved every moment of her attention. She bit her lip. "*Dat* seemed angry when James brought me home."

"I don't think he was angry. I think he was concerned."

"Why?"

"Because he's an *Englisher*, and he's handsome."

"*Ja*, he is," Nell murmured in agreement.

Leah stared. "Nell, are you falling for him?"

"*Nay,*" Nell said quickly. Too quickly. She had to admit that there was something about him that drew her like a moth to a flame. But she wouldn't give in.

They walked toward the fence to watch the horses. "Are you sure?" Leah asked.

Nell inclined her head.

Her sister sighed. "*Gut.*"

Ellie suddenly joined her sisters at the fence rail. "'Twas a delicious supper, *ja, schweschter*?"

Nell and Leah exchanged amused glances. "*Ja*, it was," Nell agreed.

"Will you bring the dog—Joey—home once he's well?"

Nell shook her head. "*Nay*, the man who found Joey wants him. He lives alone and dotes on his pets. Joey will have a *gut* home with him." She offered a silent prayer that Joey's condition didn't worsen.

"Come inside," Ellie urged. "*Mam* brought out dessert, and she and *Dat* are waiting for you."

"I'm not particularly hungry." But Nell knew her parents would be upset if she didn't return to the table.

"She made carrot cake," Ellie told her. "Your favorite."

"Sounds *gut* to me." Leah grinned.

"I guess I could eat a piece."

"Race you!" Ellie challenged.

The three sisters hurried across the lawn, up the porch and into the house.

James checked on Joey in his kennel several times during the evening. When he saw the little dog was resting comfortably, he relaxed and went to his office to do paperwork. He'd finished what he needed to for the day when he heard the dog whimper.

He hurried toward the treatment area. Mindful of the extent of Joey's injuries, James opened the kennel door and pulled him gently into his arms.

"Who did this to you, little one?" he whispered. He stroked the little dog's head as he moved toward a treatment table. If he ever discovered who it was, he'd call the authorities and have them prosecuted for animal cruelty.

He found some pain medicine and administered it to Joey. "This will make you feel better for a while, little one. I'll stay the night, and if you're better tomorrow, we'll call Fred and he can come for you."

He picked Joey up and held the dog close to his chest. Joey must have sensed that James wouldn't hurt him as the animal burrowed his head closer. James narrowed his gaze as he examined a small wound along the side of his neck. He didn't like the look of it. He grabbed a canister of antiseptic from a cabinet and sprayed it on the wound.

"Don't worry, Joey," he soothed when Joey struggled. "I won't hurt you. I'm here to help." What he wouldn't give to have Nell by his side assisting him. But it was late, and she'd already put in longer than a full day's work.

After setting Joey back in his kennel, James went to the refrigerator in the clinic's kitchenette, searching for some leftover pizza. When he was done eating, he went back to his office to make a few phone calls to check up on his patients. Afterward, he went into a storage closet and pulled out the cot he kept here in case he might need to sleep at the clinic.

He made up the cot, and then wondered what he'd do to fill the remaining hours until bed. He found the paperback book he'd started one afternoon before he'd moved back to Lancaster County and became engrossed in the story. He stopped once to give Joey another dosage of pain medication, then went back to the book.

The next thing he knew, he'd read through half of it, and it was late enough to sleep. He checked on Joey one last time. Satisfied the dog would sleep the night, James lay on his cot and closed his eyes.

Nell arrived for work at seven forty-five the next morning. James had been leaving the back entrance unlocked for her. There was no sign of him in the treatment room when she walked in. She peeked into an exam room but didn't see him. *"Hallo?"*

"I'm up front, Nell!" she heard him call out.

She made her way toward the reception area. As she entered the room, she caught sight of James bent over Michelle's desk, his eyes focused on the computer screen. As if sensing her presence, he looked up.

"Hi." He straightened. "Is it eight already?"

"It's a quarter to." She approached and placed her purse under the desk where she sometimes stashed it. "What are you doing?"

"Updating health records on the computer," he said. "Not my favorite thing to do. Michelle usually does it for me. I did some of them last night but—" He keyed in another entry then stood, looking pleased. "There. I'm all finished. Michelle will be proud."

Nell felt a rush of pleasure upon seeing his grin. Mention of the previous night brought her thoughts back to their patient. "How's Joey doing?"

"He's doing well. In fact, I think I'll give Fred a call later today. I think it will be good for Joey to recover in his new home."

"I'm glad he's doing better."

"Me, too." James frowned. "I wish I knew who did this to him. Whoever it was should be held accountable."

"By whom?"

"Animal cruelty is against the law." He moved out from behind the desk, and Nell took his place.

She opened the appointment book to check on the number of scheduled patients. "There are only three appointments in the book today, and two are reschedules from Friday."

"Only three?" He sounded disappointed.

"We may have another emergency," she said. "Not that we want one," she added quickly, blushing. She knew he was working hard to grow his practice and realized that a schedule like today's wasn't encouraging. "Your first patient doesn't come in until ten."

"We'll check on Joey, then call Fred afterward."

The morning appointments went smoothly. Mrs. Rogan arrived with Boots, and a kitten in a cat carrier. Nell didn't have any experience with cats. She liked them, but they didn't have any on the farm. While they waited for James to finish up with Boots, Nell cradled the kitten in her arms, enjoying the way it purred and cuddled against her.

"She likes you," Mrs. Rogan said with a smile.

"She's sweet."

"Would you like to have one?" the woman asked. "Mimi came from my neighbor's cat's litter. She has three sisters and two brothers. They all need good homes."

Nell thought of how accepting her father had been of all her animals. But she worried if Jonas and a kitten would get along. If not, would *Dat* allow him in the house? She doubted it. She sighed. She really wanted a kitten. "Do Boots and Mimi get along?"

"Oh, my, yes, dear. Mimi even snuggles up to Boots to nap. He seems to enjoy her company."

"I'd like to have one, but I have a dog."

"I'm sure Jonas and a kitten will get along fine," James said. "When a cat is a kitten, it's a great time to introduce the two. Boots here likes Mimi, don't you, boy?" He smiled and rubbed the dog's neck.

"But Jonas lives in the barn," she said. "He does have his own stall. I fixed it up for him."

"I don't doubt that," James said, lending his support. "Nell is a wonderful assistant," he told Mrs. Rogan.

Nell blushed as the woman studied her. "I'm sure she is." She studied her kitten in Nell's arms. "I can bring you a kitten if you'd like. Any particular color?"

"The color doesn't matter."

"I'll pick one out for you then." She beamed at Nell. "Betty—my neighbor—will be so pleased that I've found a home for another kitten."

She checked the woman out at the front desk. "May I help you to your car?"

Mrs. Rogan looked pleased. "Thank you, Nell. You're very kind."

Nell took the kitten's carrier while Mrs. Rogan held on to her purse and Boots's leash. When the woman and her animals were settled in the car, Nell said, "Mrs. Rogan? Would you like to take a few of Dr. Pierce's business cards with you? He hasn't been in our area long. I'm sure he'd appreciate any referrals."

"What an excellent idea, Nell. I'll be happy to pass them to all my animal-loving friends. I've been extremely pleased with Dr. Pierce's care."

Nell hurried inside, grabbed a stack of cards and quickly returned. She handed them to Mrs. Rogan. "Thank you again."

"My pleasure."

Nell felt a sense of accomplishment as the woman drove away. Why hadn't she thought of this sooner? When she'd brought Jonas in originally to be treated for his injuries, James hadn't charged her. He'd asked if she'd spread the word about his practice instead. And she had, but not as much as she could have. James's concern over the number of patients made her realize that she could do more to help grow his practice.

He looked up with a heart-stopping smile. "Mrs. Rogan gone?"

Nell nodded. She hesitated and then asked, "Do you think I'm foolish for wanting a kitten?"

James blinked. "No. Why would you think that? The kitten will have a wonderful home with you"

She felt a rush of warmth. "I'll do my best," she said.

Surprisingly the phone rang moments after Mrs. Rogan left, and James answered it. "We have another appointment for tomorrow afternoon—Betty Desmond, a friend of Mrs. Rogan. Mrs. Rogan must have called her on her cell as she was leaving."

Nell hid a smile. "Did she say who she's bringing in?"

"A litter of kittens. You'll be able to pick out the one you want."

"I'd take all of them if I could. As it is, I'll have some convincing to do at home." But she wasn't worried. Her father was lenient when it came to her and her animals.

Nell turned away. "I'll set things up for tomorrow."

"Thank you, Nell."

She cleaned the exam rooms in preparation for the next day—her last one. There were now seven patients scheduled for tomorrow. Wearing protective gloves, Nell washed instruments, then placed them into the autoclave. She turned on the machine as James had taught her, then went to refill the disposables in the treatment room. One accidentally slipped out from her hand. She reached to retrieve it just as James bent to get it for her. They bumped foreheads as he rose with item in hand.

"Are you all right?" he asked with concern.

Nell felt her heart start to pound at his nearness. They were eye to eye, close enough that she glimpsed tiny golden flecks in his dark eyes.

She swallowed against a suddenly dry throat. "I'm fine," she said, aware of the huskiness in her voice.

James stared at her, a strange look settling on his features. "Nell."

Nell couldn't seem to tear her gaze away. She felt her chest tighten and an odd little tingle run from her nape down the length of her spine.

James's only thought was of how lovely Nell was both inside and out. He couldn't remember the last time he had feelings for a woman. And this one was more than special.

Suddenly he leaned forward and gently placed his lips against hers.

He heard her gasp, but she didn't pull away. His head lifted, and he searched her eyes. She looked thunderstruck and adorable. He bent again and took one last sweet kiss before he pulled abruptly away. "I'm sorry."

She gazed at him, apparently speechless.

"Nell—"

"I have to leave!" she gasped. "I'm sorry, but I won't be in tomorrow."

"Tomorrow is your last day, Nell," he reminded her. James felt a crushing sensation in his chest. "I promise it won't happen again—"

"*Nay*, I can't take the chance."

He studied her flushed cheeks, realized that she was not unaffected by his kiss.

"The office is ready for tomorrow. You should be

fine without me. 'Tis only one day." She turned away and headed toward the front room.

"Nell." He saw her shoulders tense as she faced him. "I'm sorry if I've upset you, but I can't truly say that I regret kissing you."

She blanched, spun, then left in a hurry. He heard the front door open and shut. She had gone. Without saying goodbye.

James closed his eyes. What had he done? He should have known better. She was Amish; he was considered *English*. Their worlds were too different for them to be anything but friends.

He drew a sharp breath as the regret he'd claimed he hadn't felt suddenly filled him. His regret in chasing Nell away.

Chapter Eight

Nell was rattled as she drove home. James's kiss had taken her totally by surprise. She should have pushed him away, and the fact that she hadn't done so scared her. What shocked her the most was that she'd liked his kisses.

It was midafternoon when she steered her buggy into the yard. She knew her family would wonder why she wouldn't be returning to the clinic. It would be easy enough to explain why she was home early this afternoon, for there were no patients scheduled. It made sense to call the day to a close.

But James had seven patients to see tomorrow, and while she felt bad that he would have to manage on his own, she wasn't about to go back. She had to avoid James. Her feelings for him were too powerful. And now that she knew he was attracted to her, too…

To her relief, her family didn't pry into her reasons for not going back to work. Her father seemed pleased that she'd be at home, and for that she was relieved and grateful.

As she washed the dinner dishes alongside her sister

Charlie, she wondered if James had called Fred about Joey. Then she mentally scolded herself. He probably had. Besides, Joey was no longer her concern.

That night as she went to bed, Nell couldn't help but recall the day's events. She sighed. There would be no returning to pick out a kitten. She could only imagine what Mrs. Rogan would think after she learned that Nell no longer worked there.

Moonlight filtered in through the sheer white curtains as Nell lay in bed and stared up at the ceiling. She couldn't stop thinking about James's kiss, his clean male scent with a hint of something. Cologne?

She was lonely. Was that why she'd reacted to James the way she had?

She became overwhelmed with sadness as she thought of Michael and the life she would have shared with him if he hadn't died. If she'd married Michael, she wouldn't be having these feelings about James.

She and Michael probably wouldn't have stayed in Happiness. They might not have moved far, but they would have lived perhaps within Lancaster City, in a small home surrounded by neighboring houses. They would have had children and been happy together...if only Michael hadn't died.

Grief struck her hard, and her eyes filled with tears. *Oh, Michael...*

Lonely and heartbroken, Nell sobbed softly. Unable to control her sorrow, she climbed out of bed and went to look out the window. It was on a night like this that she had left the house to tell Michael that she'd decided to accept his marriage proposal. The moon had been large in the dark sky, the summer air had been warm and balmy, a perfect night for meeting the man she'd loved.

Only Michael hadn't come.

She'd waited for him for over two hours until finally, disappointed, she'd returned home. She'd reached the house and gone upstairs to bed. Then within an hour, her family had been on their way to the hospital after an ambulance had been called for Meg. Her sister had suffered excruciating abdominal pains.

Meg had been admitted to the hospital and spent several days in intensive care. A ruptured appendix had threatened her life.

Overcome with worry for her sister, Nell had attempted to put aside thoughts of Michael. But in those moments when she left Meg's hospital room to go to the cafeteria with her other sisters, Nell had suffered from more than concern.

What if Michael had come to their special spot the next night? What if he'd tried the following nights only to be disappointed when she didn't show?

During the afternoon of Meg's second day in the hospital, Nell had gone downstairs to buy a cup of tea, which she planned to take back to the room. Ellie, Leah and Charlie had gone home with *Mam* and *Dat* to pack a few items for Meg, to see to the animals and to get some sleep.

Mam and *Dat* had appeared to have aged since Meg was first brought in. The doctor had suggested that the family go home to eat properly and get some rest. Meg would need them at their best during her recovery. Nell had volunteered to stay until their return later that evening when she would head home for the night.

Nell had been returning with her tea when she'd

heard loud sounds coming from inside a hospital room on Meg's floor. Without thought, she'd glanced inside and saw a man lying in the hospital bed, hooked up to oxygen and a heart monitor.

She could still recall with startling clarity the awful moment when she'd recognized the patient. The horrible sounds that had come from the heart monitor and oxygen pump had turned her blood to ice.

Michael. It had been her beloved Michael. Her first instinct had been to go to him, but a nurse had stopped her.

"The patient isn't allowed visitors," she'd said.

Nell had wanted to cry out that she wasn't simply a visitor; she was the woman to whom he'd proposed marriage. The agony of seeing him in that bed, knowing that he was fighting for his life, was still painful to recall even after five years.

Her family didn't know about Michael. She and Michael had been meeting secretly as Amish sweethearts often did within her community. Only Michael wasn't Amish. He was an *Englisher*, but at the time, Nell could have left her community without reprisal. She hadn't joined the church yet, so she would have been free to leave.

The next day, after a night at home spent fervently praying, Nell returned to the hospital. She found Michael's bed empty as she passed by his room. Heart pounding hard, she'd asked at the nurses' station what happened to him.

She'd nearly fainted when she'd heard that Michael had died during the night.

In shock, Nell had gotten through each day focusing on her sister. She'd had no time to grieve or accept the fact that Michael was really gone. Afterward, she'd overheard the nurses talking. She learned that Michael's injuries had been sustained in a car accident when his vehicle was struck by a drunk driver's on the night they were to meet. She stared out into the moonlit yard and recalled the way she and Michael had met in a local grocery store. How they'd met up again in the same place on another day. Michael had been handsome and funny, and she'd fallen in love immediately.

After Meg recovered, Nell had decided to join the church. Couples usually joined prior to marrying, but Michael was the only man she'd ever love. There was no reason not to join the Amish church. She had lost Michael but she'd been grateful to the Lord for sparing Meg's life.

Nell turned from the window and went back to bed. And cried until she was so exhausted, she fell asleep.

The next morning, Nell climbed out of bed. She felt groggy from lack of sleep, but she knew she had work to do. She needed to feed and water the animals.

She smiled as she thought of her little dog. Nell was fortunate that her father tolerated her love of animals. After nearly losing her sister Meg, Arlin Stoltzfus had become lenient with all of his daughters.

She slipped out of the house and headed toward the barn. She took care of her pets and the farm animals, then returned to do her house chores. There was laundry to do, dusting to be done, and floors to be swept.

She entered through the kitchen and grabbed the broom from the back room, continuing her day with housework instead of enjoying her last day at the clinic as planned. Her sisters joined in to help, and their happy chatter and teasing helped Nell get through the day.

That afternoon, Nell heard the sound of a buggy as she swept the front porch. She paused to watch as it parked near the house. Matthew Troyer got out of the vehicle.

He waved. "Nell!"

"*Hallo*, Matthew." She smiled, for the young man always appeared to be in good humor.

"I've brought you something." He skirted the vehicle, then bent into the passenger side to pick up a cardboard box.

Curious, Nell set aside her broom and descended the porch steps. "What is it?"

"Come and see."

She approached and peered into the box. "A kitten!" It was a tiny orange tabby. "Where did you—" she began. She blinked back tears as she met his gaze. "James."

"*Ja*, he asked me to bring her to you. Said you were interested in owning a kitten. He thought you might like this one best."

Emotion clogged Nell's throat as she reached in to pick up the cat. "She's beautiful." Cuddling the kitten against her, she glanced at Matthew. "*Danki*, she's... perfect."

He eyed her with fond amusement. "James thought you'd say that."

Warmth infused her belly as she realized how well James knew her. "Please thank him for me."

"You can thank him yourself when you see him."

But would she ever see him again? Only if he came

to a community gathering, which was entirely possible since his family belonged to her church.

Nell glanced back at the house for any sign of her father. She had to break the news to him that she now owned a kitten. "I need to make a place for him in the barn. He can share Jonas's stall."

Matthew blinked. "Wait! There's more." He reached into the back of the buggy for a bag of kitten food, a small scratching post and a small bed. "My *bruder* sent these, as well."

"He didn't have to do that," she said, but it didn't surprise her that he had. James was an extremely considerate man.

"This is James. You've worked with him. This is his way."

"*Ja*, I know."

"Let me carry these into the barn for you."

Nell stroked the tiny cat's head. "*Danki*, Matthew." She was aware of the young man following her as she entered the barn and headed toward her dog's stall. Jonas whimpered and ran toward her as she pulled the door and held it open for Matthew. "You have a new friend, Jonas," she said. "You'll be nice to her, *ja*?"

She hunkered down to allow Jonas to sniff the kitten. She waited with bated breath to see how he would react to his new roommate. Nell grew concerned when Jonas growled and backed away. "Jonas! She won't hurt you. She's just a little thing. Come and meet her."

"He's growling at me, not her," Matthew said as he set the bed near Jonas's and the post in the opposite corner of the stall. "Where do you want her food?"

"You can put it there for now." She gestured toward a table in the back of the stall. "I'll move it later."

Jonas continued to growl, and Nell saw that Matthew was right. The dog was nervous of Matt, not the kitten.

Matthew crouched next to her and held out his hand. "Come. I'll not hurt you. I'm Nell's friend."

Nell flashed him a look, but Matthew was too busy trying to gain her dog's trust to notice her.

"Jonas! Come." The animal gazed at her with trepidation. "'Tis Matthew. He's James's *bruder*. You know James. He took *gut* care of you when you were hurt." She felt a pang in her heart as she mentioned his name.

Matthew didn't move. He waited patiently until finally Jonas inched closer. Although he and James were stepsiblings, they both shared the same patient and compassionate nature. Nell experienced a wave of affection toward Matthew.

The young man didn't speak. He simply stayed in his crouched position with his hand extended toward Jonas.

Finally, Jonas came close enough to sniff his hand then started to lick his fingers. Matthew laughed. "He's a *gut* one, isn't he?" he said with a smile.

"*Ja*, he is. And you were right—he was afraid of you, not this little one."

He regarded her with amusement. "Are you going to keep calling her *little one*, or will you be naming her?"

She made a face at him. "Any suggestions?"

"*Kotz?*"

"I'm not going to call her cat!"

He laughed, and the sound was delightful. "You asked for a suggestion," he reminded her.

"Not a bad one."

Matthew placed his hand over his heart. "You wound me, and I was trying to be helpful."

"Poor Matthew."

He grinned at her. "Nell?"

She set the kitten within distance of Jonas, who didn't seem to be alarmed or angry at its presence. "I think they'll get along."

"Nell." His tone had changed, become serious.

Frowning, she met his gaze. "Is something wrong?"

He shook his head. "I was wondering if you'd be attending the youth singing on Sunday."

"I haven't been to a singing in years."

"Would you consider it?" He paused. "I'd like to take you home afterward."

Her heart skipped a beat. Matthew was handsome and likable, and he would make some lucky girl a wonderful sweetheart. He was nineteen while she was twenty-four. Despite the age difference, she gave serious consideration to having a relationship with him until the fact hit home again that James was his *bruder*.

If Matthew courted her and they became serious with the intention of marriage, then James would be her brother-in-law, and she would have to see him often. She was afraid that her feelings for James would complicate her future, and Matthew would be the one who would ultimately suffer. While she'd suspected Matthew's feelings for her, she'd never thought he would make them known.

"I appreciate the invitation, Matthew," she said gently, because the last thing she wanted to do was hurt this kind young man. "But I think I should stay in. I wouldn't feel comfortable at a singing. I'm sure my younger sisters, Meg, Ellie and Charlie, will be going, but I feel as if the time for singings has passed me by."

Although he hid it well, she could sense his disappointment. "I thought you might like to get out a bit, but I understand."

"Matthew Troyer, you're a nice man and a *gut* friend," she said sincerely.

He gazed at her a long moment before his expression warmed. "Not what I was hoping from you, but I'll take it." He stood. "I should get home. James is staying for supper. 'Tis late. I didn't want to wait until tomorrow to bring your kitten." He brushed off his pants, then extended a hand to help Nell up.

Nell accepted his help and wished that things could be different for them. If she hadn't loved Michael and then met James, she might have given their relationship a chance. She was aware of the warmth of his fingers about hers as he pulled her to her feet. He released her hand immediately and stepped back.

"*Danki*, Matthew."

His smile wasn't as bright as previously. "You're *willkomm*."

Nell accompanied him to his buggy. "Matthew—"

"'Tis fine, Nell." Genuine warmth filled his blue eyes. "At least we are friends, *ja*?"

"Always."

"I'll see you at church service."

"*Danki* for bringing the kitten."

He laughed. "'Twas my pleasure."

As she watched him leave, she realized what Matthew had revealed—that James was at Adam Troyer's residence for supper.

Nell sighed sadly. James had brought the kitten with

him to his parents' house. Apparently, he realized how upset she'd been by their kiss, so he asked Matthew to bring her the kitten.

She closed her eyes as she was overwhelmed. True to form, James remained ever thoughtful of her feelings. What was she going to do about this?

Chapter Nine

"**W**ill you be coming to church service?" *Mam* had asked James last night during Saturday evening's supper. He had come for dinner the night before when his family had convinced him to stay the weekend. Upset over how he'd chased Nell away with his kiss, he'd been in need of some cheering up. And his parents and siblings' love and acceptance of him always made him feel better. So he'd spent last night, and this morning he'd promised to stay another. Therefore, he wasn't surprised when his mother suggested that he attend Sunday services with them.

"*Mam*, I haven't been to church in years," he'd confessed.

"All the more reason to come."

James had gazed at his mother, seen the warmth and love in her brown eyes and smiled. "I'll come."

Sunday morning he went to the barn to see to the animals. As he walked, he glanced down at his garments. On Friday, when he'd been asked to stay, he'd wanted to retrieve his clothing from his apartment. His stepfather had said there was no need. James and he were the same size, and so was Matthew. They owned enough garments to get James through the weekend.

Which is how James found himself wearing Amish clothing for the first time since he'd turned eighteen and left the community. To his surprise, he realized that he felt comfortable in them. It was like putting on a favorite T-shirt. They fit him like a glove and felt good against his skin.

He'd gotten up early and spent longer in the barn than he needed to. But it had felt good spending time with his stepfather's horses and goats. Usually the only animals he saw were sick or in need of medical care, except for the ones that only needed their vaccines and their annual exams.

He'd enjoyed the smell of horse and hay and the sound of the animals shifting in their stalls. The simple joy of just standing and watching kept him longer than he should have been.

But when was the last time he'd spent any amount of time in his stepfather's barn? The moment of peace wouldn't last long, he knew, so he stayed to enjoy it until, conscious of the time, he hurried back to the house. He entered the kitchen just as his mother announced that breakfast was ready. He joined his family at the table and thoroughly enjoyed the home-cooked meal.

"We have to leave for service by eight thirty," Adam said.

"Where is it this week?" Matthew asked.

"The Amos Kings." Adam turned to James. "You've seen the new *schuulhaus*?"

"*Ja*, I know where it is."

"It's on the Samuel Lapp property. The Amos Kings live across the street."

"The large farm?" James murmured. James suspected that the man farmed for a living. Most members of the Amish community had smaller farms that provided food with only minimal cash crops. But he suspected that it was different with Amos King. His farm was larger than most in the area.

"*Ja*, Amos farms more than any of us. Samuel Lapp does some construction work for members of our community. He donated the property, and he with his sons built the *schuul*."

The school hadn't existed when James had lived here as a teenager. Back then, the school had been a small building in need of repair on the opposite side of town. James hadn't attended the school. Since he'd made the decision to become a veterinarian like his late father, his mother and stepfather had allowed him to attend public school.

"Do you have something I can borrow for church?" James asked. Amish dress for church was white shirt with black vest and black pants. He would have looked out of place in his Amish work clothes of a solid shirt, navy tri-blend pants and black suspenders. His mother left the room and returned within seconds. She carried a white shirt, black vest and black dress pants. She extended them to her son.

"I kept them in case you visited and needed them."

James felt his emotions shift as he accepted his former Sunday clothes.

"Danki, Mam," he said thickly. Emotion clogged his throat, making it difficult to swallow.

"Are you certain they will still fit?" Matthew asked.

"Matt."

"He's right, *Dat*. I'm a boy no longer. What if these don't fit?"

"Only one way to find out," Adam said.

James headed upstairs to change. To his amazement, the clothes fit as if tailor-made for him.

His mother smiled when he came downstairs wearing the garments. "I knew they'd fit."

"I don't have a hat," James said.

"Ja, you do," Matthew said. At *Mam*'s insistence, Matthew must have retrieved the black felt hat James had in his youth.

James waited until he and his family were outside before he put it on.

Like the clothes, the hat fit perfectly.

"There you go. You've no worries. You look as Amish as the rest of us," *Mam* said.

James grinned. He couldn't help it. At one time, he'd objected to wearing Amish clothing, but now he appreciated how the simple garments made him feel as if he was a part of something big.

The first person James noticed as Adam steered his buggy onto the Amos King property was Nell Stoltzfus. He experienced a stark feeling of dismay as he saw that she was talking with a young handsome man closer in age to her than he was.

He knew he had no right to be upset. Despite their kiss, Nell and he didn't have a relationship. Given their life circumstances, they never would, but that knowledge didn't make the sight any easier for him.

Matthew jumped out as soon as the vehicle stopped. "Nell!" He hurried in her direction. *"Hallo!"*

James's heart ached as he climbed out more slowly and watched Matthew approach Nell. Unlike him, his brother hadn't hurt Nell or caused her discomfort and embarrassment.

He held out his hand to his sister Maggie. "That's the bishop," she told him as if she could read his mind. "His wife is over there." She gestured toward a chair in the sun. The woman looked frail as if she'd been ill.

"That's his wife?"

"Ja, Catherine. They have a two-year-old son, Nicholas. She's been under the weather recently, and we haven't seen much of her—or him. She must have felt well enough to come. If they leave right after services, then we know that she's not recovered as much as we'd like to think."

James met his sister's gaze. "And you're telling me this because…"

"Nell. I saw your face when you saw her with him, but you've no need to worry." Maggie studied him. "You know that she's a member of the church. Not like me and our siblings but as an adult member. She joined it five years ago, when they moved to Happiness after Meg recuperated from her illness."

"Young people don't normally join the church until right before marriage."

"Ja, that's true. But for some reason, Nell felt compelled to make the commitment. She can no longer leave the church without consequences."

James's stomach burned. "Being shunned by her family and community."

"*Ja*, James. She chose the path of the Lord when she was only nineteen. She'd had no sweetheart or prospects of marriage, but she made the choice anyway."

"I see." It was as bad as James had thought. There wasn't even the hope of a future with Nell, not with his life firmly entrenched in the English world while she lived happily within her Amish community.

"Nell!"

Nell turned and smiled. "*Hallo*, Matthew."

"Bishop John," Matthew greeted.

"Matthew."

"How is your wife?" he asked.

John gestured toward the woman seated in a chair in the backyard. "She wanted to come."

"That's *gut*. She must be feeling better."

The bishop eyed his spouse with concern. "*Ja*, she says she is."

But Nell could read his doubt.

"Where is Nicholas?" Matthew asked.

"Meg has him." She gestured toward the back lawn where the boy walked with her sister. "He's getting big, John. He's two, *ja*?"

"Almost three." The church elder smiled. "He's a *gut* boy. I can't imagine our lives without him."

"'Tis why the Lord blessed you with such a fine *soohn*."

Nell studied the small boy and wondered how difficult it must be for Catherine to care for him when she felt so ill. She had no idea what was wrong with John's wife, but she said a silent prayer that the woman would recover quickly.

"I'm going to check on Catherine," John said.

"If you need anything, please don't hesitate to let me know. I'll do what I can to help."

The bishop gave her a genuine smile. "*Danki*, Nell."

"How is the little one?" Matthew teased after John had left.

"You mean Naomi?"

"You named her!"

"Did you really think that I'd keeping calling her little one—or *kotz*?"

Matthew laughed. "Naomi, I like it."

"Like what?" Maggie said as she approached from behind. "*Hallo*, Nell."

"Maggie!" Nell greeted her with delight. She genuinely liked Maggie Troyer.

"I've brought someone with me." She stepped aside, and Nell found herself face to face with James.

She blushed and looked away. "James. Thank you for Naomi."

"Her kitten," Matthew explained.

A twinkle entered James's dark eyes. "I see. Do you like her?"

Nell stared. "What's not to like?"

His features became unreadable as he looked away.

She immediately regretted her behavior. "How is Joey?"

His face cleared and brightened. "He's doing well. Fred picked him up on Friday. I called to check on him yesterday. Joey's making great strides in his recovery."

"Any idea yet who hurt him?"

Maggie frowned. "Is this the little dog you were telling us about?" she asked her brother.

James nodded.

Matthew scowled. "Surely there is something that can be done."

"I called and reported it to the police. They're keeping an eye out. It's going to be hard because there are no witnesses to the crime."

Ellie approached. "'Tis time for service."

Immediately, everyone headed toward the King barn where benches had been set up in preparation for church. Nell entered and sat in the second row in the women's area. Maggie and Ellie slid in beside her and moments later, they were joined by Maggie's sisters Abigail and Rosie.

Nell watched as James took a seat in the men's area between Matthew and her cousin Eli Lapp. Soon all of the men were seated in one area of the room while the women and children were in another.

The room quieted as Abram Peachy, the church deacon, and Bishop John Fisher, who saw that his wife was comfortably seated next to Nell's aunt Katie Lapp, approached the pulpit area. Preacher Levi Stoltzfus, a distant relative of her father's family, led the service by instructing everyone to open the *Ausbund* and sing the first hymn.

The service progressed throughout the morning as it usually did. Abram spoke to the congregation first, then they sang the second hymn before Levi began to preach. Bishop John had a few words of wisdom for the church community, then the service was declared officially over.

Nell was conscious of James seated across the room. Dressed in Amish Sunday best, he was handsome, his presence a strong reminder of what recently had transpired between them.

Soon, everyone left the barn to enjoy a shared meal provided by the community women. After helping to serve the men, Nell gravitated toward her family with her own plate of food.

"Did you get any of Miriam Zook's pie?" her *mam* asked. Nell shook her head. "You should try it before there's nothing left to taste."

Nell got up from her family's table. "Anyone want something while I'm up?"

"A glass of ice tea," *Dat* said.

She nodded. "Meg? Leah? Do you need anything to drink?"

"We have lemonade," Leah said. "*Danki*, Nell."

As she wandered over to the dessert and drink tables, Nell thought of James and wondered whether or not he'd left. She had her answer as she poured her father a glass of ice tea.

"Nell."

"James!" She nearly dropped the glass, but James quickly reached out to steady it.

"I need to talk with you."

"About what?" she said breathlessly.

"I wanted to apologize about the—"

"Don't say it," she gasped. "Please, James. Not here."

"Then will you understand if I just say that I'm sorry?"

"Ja," she said quickly and tried to dash away.

But James followed her. "Nell."

She sighed as she faced him. *"Ja?"*

"I'm glad you like your kitten. I saw her and thought immediately of you."

"That was kind of you."

"I don't feel kind." He took off his black hat and ran his fingers through his short dark hair. His haircut was the only thing that reminded her that he wasn't Amish. In his current garments, James looked as if he could easily fit into her world. The knowledge that his appearance was just an illusion upset her.

"James, I have to go."

"I miss you, Nell," he said.

"Don't!" She didn't need to hear how much he'd missed her. Or to have to admit the truth that she'd missed him, too. Despite his Amish relatives and appearance, James was an *Englisher*, and she had to get over him. She couldn't allow herself to care.

Nell worked to shove thoughts of James from her mind as she hurried back to her family. The afternoon passed too slowly as she felt the continued tension of James's presence.

"You're quiet," Leah said beside her hours later as they rode home in their father's buggy.

"Just tired."

She felt her sister's intense regard and turned to smile at her reassuringly. To her relief, Leah seemed to accept her explanation. "At least, 'tis Sunday, and we can read or play games if we want."

"Ja." Nell made an effort to pull herself from her dark thoughts. She would enjoy their day of rest and try not to worry about tomorrow and her need to find an Amish husband fast before her father decided to find

one for her. Or she did something she'd forever regret, like giving into her feelings for James.

That night, Nell prayed for God's help in finding a husband, in doing the right thing as a member of her Amish community. She pleaded with the Lord to help her get over the *Englisher* who'd stolen her heart and threatened her future happiness.

Chapter Ten

"You like James," Leah said as she cornered Nell in the barn Monday morning.

"*Ja*, he is a fine veterinarian. I respect him."

"*Nay*, Nell. You *care* for him." She paused. "You love him."

Nell felt a flutter in her chest as her denial got hung up in her throat. "Why would you think such a thing?"

"I saw the way you looked at him."

"What do you mean?" She felt a sharp bolt of terror. "I don't look at him in any certain way."

"And he looks at you in a certain way," Leah said, surprising her. "He cares for you."

But Nell was shaking her head. She didn't need the complication of a forbidden relationship with the *Englisher*.

"Nell, you should think about marrying. Has *Dat* mentioned it to you again?"

Nell brushed a piece of straw off her skirt. "Yesterday after we got home from church. I explained that I've been trying. I considered Matthew Troyer. I know he likes me, and he's a *gut* man, despite the fact that he is too young for me."

"He's not too young. Many of our women marry younger husbands."

"*Ja*, but their young husbands are not *bruders* to a man you are trying to forget."

"Ha!" Leah exclaimed. "So you *are* attracted to James!"

Nell nodded, feeling glum. "I can't help it. And he likes me, which makes it all the more difficult." She sighed. "I care for him, but 'tis hopeless." She put Naomi into her bed and stood. "Do you know *Dat* wanted me to think about marrying Benjamin Yoder? He moved to Happiness recently."

"Isn't he in his sixties?"

"*Ja*, but that isn't the worst of it. Benjamin came here from Indiana." She shuddered just thinking about the man. "I'm sure he's nice but, Leah, he's never been married. Or had children. I can't imagine…" She blushed. "And what if after he marries, he decides he wants to go home to Indiana? His wife would be expected to go with him. I don't want to leave Happiness. This is my home, and my family is here."

"You won't have to marry him. We'll find someone else for you first."

Nell smiled. "We?"

"I'll help you. We don't want to set a precedence of *Dat* choosing our husbands."

"And at twenty-one, you'll be the next *dochter* our *vadder* will want to see married and with children."

Leah inclined her head. "*Ja*. I'll find my own man, and I won't marry for anything other than love."

"And if you take too long and *Dat* wants to interfere?"

"You mean, help me along." Leah grinned. "Then I'll expect you to step in despite the fact that you'll be happily married to your chosen man with your seven children clinging to your apron strings."

"Seven!" Nell couldn't control a snort of laughter. "How long do you think *Dat* will be willing to wait for you? Certainly not long enough for me to give birth to seven *kinner*?"

Her sister shrugged. "Not to worry. 'Tis all just a thought anyway. You'll find your own husband, and I'll find mine."

"Where?"

"Look around. There are a lot of young men in our community."

"Men like Matthew," Nell murmured. "I already told you why I can no longer consider him."

"Because of James."

"Ja." She sighed. "If only I'd met James years ago, before I'd met Michael, then we might have had a chance."

"Michael?" Leah frowned. "Who is Michael?"

James unlocked the clinic Monday morning and went inside. He turned on the computer at the front desk, then slipped into his office to work while he waited for his staff. He made a list of patients he needed to check up on, and just as he finished, he heard the opening of the front door and Michelle's voice.

"Good morning, Dr. Pierce!" she called.

"Good morning, Michelle."

The young woman appeared in his doorway. "You

don't look well. Don't tell me you caught the stomach bug, too?"

"No, I'm fine. Tired but fine."

"I'm sorry that I was out sick so long. I knew with Nell here that you'd be able to manage." She frowned. "Is Nell coming in today?"

He shook his head. "I don't need her now that you and Janie are back." It seemed a lie, telling Michelle that he didn't need Nell. But it was true that he didn't need her in the office. He needed—wanted—her in his personal life.

I shouldn't have kissed her, James thought when Michelle had settled in at the front desk. What on earth had he been thinking?

He hadn't been thinking. He only knew that at that moment he'd been unable to deny his growing feelings for her and he'd desperately needed that kiss.

A longing so sharp and intense that it made him groan and hang his head into his hands gripped him. He had a business to run, a goal to accomplish. It didn't matter how he felt about someone he had no right to love.

He straightened, threw back his chair and went to the window to enjoy the view of the farm across the road. He had done what he'd set out to do—become a veterinarian like his father.

James knew his father had never expected him to follow the same path, despite the fact that James had loved every moment he'd spent at his dad's side while his father had gone out on calls. James enjoyed his job, and he was sure John Pierce would be proud of the man he'd become and the vocation he'd chosen.

But then, did he have moments like this when he'd felt empty inside?

He thought of his siblings. They were so happy and at peace with their lives. They didn't seem to be plagued by the same doubts and unrest that frequently overcame him lately. He felt torn between his chosen life and the life he'd left behind. Spending time with his family gave him a small measure of peace, something he hadn't experienced in a long time.

Suddenly he heard Janie in the treatment room, taking instruments out of the autoclave and putting them within easy reach. They had a full slate of appointments today.

His assistant appeared in his doorway. "Your first patient has arrived. She's new—Mrs. Simmons with her Siberian Husky, Montana. I've put them in room three."

He turned from the window. "Thank you, Janie." He took one last look at the fields of corn that grew thick and lush in the distance before he left his office to see his first patient.

Though everything went smoothly, the day seemed to drag on. James had seen three new patients who told him how pleased they were with his care of their pets. They would tell others about the clinic, each one had promised.

While he knew that was good news, he couldn't seem to get excited about it. His business was growing, which was what he wanted. But then why didn't he feel good or complete? Why did he keep thinking about his family and the life he could have had if he'd stayed within the community? Why couldn't he stop envisioning a different choice which could have given him what he needed and wanted most...a loving relationship with Nell Stoltzfus?

Janie approached him in the treatment room. "Dr. Pierce, I've cleaned the exam room and mopped the floors."

He glanced at her with surprise. His assistant had never cleaned the floors since she'd started work at the clinic. "Thank you, Janie."

"Is there anything else you need?" she asked.

James glanced at his watch. It was already well past closing time. "No, you've done enough, and I appreciate it. Go on home. I'll see you tomorrow."

The girl hesitated as if she had something to say. "Dr. Pierce?"

He looked at her with raised eyebrows. "Yes?"

She shook her head. "I just wanted to thank you for letting me take two weeks' vacation. It meant a lot to me. I know it couldn't have been easy for you while I was gone. Especially with Michelle out sick."

He smiled. "I managed to find some help. But I won't have to worry now that you're back."

"Good night, Dr. Pierce."

"James," he said. "Call me James. We've worked together long enough, don't you agree? Even Michelle calls me James."

Janie grinned. "Good night, James. I'll see you in the morning."

The office was quiet. He enjoyed the silence after hours of tending to his noisy patients. Normally, he'd reflect on his day's work and experience satisfaction. But not today. In fact, he hadn't felt satisfied since the last day Nell had worked at the clinic.

He checked to ensure that the clinic was locked up

before he headed home. The sun was bright in the sky, but it looked like there might be rain in the distance to the east. He would miss the longer daylight hours once fall came. The thought of staying alone in his apartment made him ache.

He felt a tightening in his chest that didn't go away as he reached his apartment and climbed up the stairs. By the time he entered his home, there was a painful lump in his throat and his tired eyes burned.

He threw his keys on the kitchen table, then collapsed onto his sofa. He stared at the ceiling, angry with himself for loving Nell—and for driving her not only out of his office but out of his life.

They could have remained friends if he'd controlled his growing feelings for her. But he'd had to go and kiss her—and ruin their friendship, the only thing he was permitted to have with her.

Four more days of work before the weekend. He had a standing invitation to stay at home. After long years away, he felt compelled to spend as much time on the farm as possible. It wasn't only his mother who was glad whenever he stayed. His stepfather, sisters and stepsiblings were happy to see him, too.

He knew Adam kept busy trying to keep up with his lawn furniture business. His stepfather had added children's swing sets to the list of items he could sell to his customers. If Adam would allow it, he'd like to help with the furniture. He was good with his hands and had learned from his stepfather when he was in high school. He could work with Adam on Saturdays unless he received an emergency call about a patient. He was busy at the clinic during the week and work was not allowed within the Amish community on Sundays.

He envisioned cutting wood, bolting long heavy boards together to form the legs of a swing set. It was something to look forward to—helping Adam with his business and on the farm.

James smiled and closed his eyes. And couldn't block the mental images of Nell that sprang immediately to mind. Only they weren't images of Nell walking away after he'd kissed her.

They were of her walking toward him on their wedding day.

Chapter Eleven

Nell pulled the buggy into the barnyard a little after one in the afternoon. She'd made beds, done the laundry and shopped for her mother. Instead of feeling as if she'd accomplished something, she felt totally out of sorts. Once again, she went to seek comfort from her animals, most particularly Jonas. When she'd returned from the store, she'd put away *Mam*'s groceries, then went directly to the barn.

Jonas greeted her enthusiastically, and she felt her mood lighten as she slipped inside his stall. His happy cries and kisses as she sat down beside him were just what she'd needed. Her fierce longing for a man she couldn't have upset her. She'd never expected to love again, and that she loved James made it hard.

She didn't know how long she sat playing with Jonas, but it must have been some time. Jonas finally exhausted himself and curled up to sleep in her lap. Nell studied him with a smile. Then her eyes filled with tears. It had been Jonas who had first brought her into contact with James Pierce.

Nell lay back against the straw and closed her eyes. It was how her sister Leah found her several minutes later.

"Nell."

She opened one eye. Leah's concerned expression wavered in her narrow vision. She opened her other eye and sat up. "Leah. I'm just having a rest."

Her sister regarded her with worry. "Are you ever going to tell me about Michael?"

Nell had put her sister off after she'd made the mistake of mentioning Michael's name. She'd had no intention of ever telling her family about him. Michael was dead, and there didn't seem to be any reason to resurrect her feelings for him—and her grief.

Jonas stirred in Nell's lap as Leah slipped inside and knelt in the stall beside her. "He's a *gut* dog." She reached to stroke the dog's fur.

Nell smiled. "He gives me comfort."

Leah looked at her. "Why did you need comfort? Because of Michael?"

Nell stiffened. "Leah…"

"You should just tell me. I won't tell anyone if you don't want me to." Leah studied her with compassion. "What happened, Nell?"

Nell felt her face heat up.

"Nell—"

"James kissed me."

"What?"

"He kissed me. He didn't grab or hurt me. It was an innocent kiss that happened after we accidentally bumped heads."

"Nell," Leah whispered.

"*Ja*, I know. That's why I didn't go back to work for him at the clinic."

Leah eyed her with sympathy. "Although you loved the job."

"I only had one day left. Why should I risk it?"

As Leah remained quietly beside her, Nell finally gave in to the urge to tell her about Michael. "Leah, I've kept something from you and our family. It happened right before and then during the time Meg was ill."

Leah shifted to sit. "Michael?"

"Ja," Nell said. "He was an *Englisher.* I fell in love with him and we used to meet each night in secret. Our meetings were innocent, but he was handsome and kind, and I loved him."

Leah gazed at her with confusion. "Michael left you?"

"Not exactly. One night he asked me to marry him. I told him I would think about it, although I knew what I was going to tell him the next day. That I would leave the community to be his wife."

Her sister frowned. "I don't understand."

"That night I waited for Michael, and he didn't show—it was the night that Meg became ill. I went to our special spot, ready to give him my answer. I knew he loved me, and when he didn't come, I thought he'd been detained for some reason. I waited for hours, then finally I went home. I went right to my room and cried and prayed and hoped that I hadn't been a fool for loving him."

Tears filled Nell's eyes, and she couldn't hold back a sob. "Then Meg got sick, and we all went to the hospital. I couldn't think about Michael, Meg needed me— she needed all of us."

"You were the strong one, and *Mam* and *Dat* needed

you, too," Leah murmured, her blue eyes filled with emotion.

"The next day I was coming back to Meg's room after getting tea from the cafeteria, I heard a terrible loud beeping. It was in a room on the same floor as Meg's. I looked inside as I walked past and that's when I saw him. It was Michael, hooked up to life support.

"At first, I felt faint, but then I wanted to run to him. I needed to scream and cry and beg him to get better. I started into the room, but his nurse stopped me. She told me that I was in the wrong room, that Meg was in another. She said that this particular patient—Michael— wasn't allowed visitors." Nell wiped away tears. "The nurse looked at me and saw Amish. No one would have believed me if I'd told them we were in love."

She felt Leah's touch on her arm. "What happened to him?"

Nell's eyes filled with tears as she was overcome by her memories of that day. "I later learned that he'd been in a car accident. He was driving to meet me when a drunk driver struck him." She stood and turned away as her tears trailed down her cheeks.

She hugged herself with her arms. "Michael died from his injuries the next day. I wanted to rail against God, but in the end I put myself into His hands instead. I prayed for Meg to get well. I had already lost Michael, and I couldn't let myself grieve. I knew I'd fall apart and completely lose it. The only thing I could do was to pray for Meg's recovery."

Nell offered Leah a sad smile as she continued, "When Meg got better, I was so relieved. I'd made a promise to God, and I kept it. I joined the Amish church less than three months later."

Leah drew a sharp breath. "That's why you didn't wait until marriage. You'd lost the only man you'd ever love—or so you thought, and you thanked the Lord for Meg's recovery by fulfilling your promise to Him."

"Ja," Nell whispered. Her tears trickled unchecked. With a cry of sympathy, Leah hugged her. "Leah, you can't tell anyone. Please. You can't tell *Dat* or *Mam* or our sisters. Meg especially must never know."

Leah opened her mouth to object.

"Please, Leah."

"I promise that I won't tell them, but only if they don't ask. If one of them learns the truth, I won't lie."

She released a sharp breath. Nell was sure that after all of this time no one would find out. *"Danki."*

"But now you're in love with the *English* veterinarian. But this time the choice of whether or not to leave is no longer yours."

Nell inclined her head. *"Ja,* 'tis not."

"You've joined the church, and there is no obvious way for you and him to be together."

"Ja."

Leah stood abruptly, held out her hand and pulled Nell to her feet. "You've done the right thing. Avoiding him."

"But it still hurts."

"I know," Leah said. "Come. Let's go into the *haus*. It's near suppertime, and you must be famished."

Nell stared at her sister. She had no idea that by simply telling Leah about Michael she'd feel a lightening of her burden. "I *am* hungry."

Leah grinned. "Let's hurry in before our younger sisters decide to eat everything and leave us nothing."

When they entered the kitchen, it was to find their

other three sisters and their mother working together to prepare a meal.

"Nell, I wondered where you'd gone to," *Mam* said. "*Danki* for doing the wash and all the housework."

"I didn't mind. I like being busy."

Her brow furrowing, *Mam* glanced her way. If she'd noticed Nell's red-rimmed eyes, she didn't mention it. "How's your kitten, Naomi?"

"She's fine. *Dat* was *gut* about allowing me to keep her."

"Because he knows that you won't leave her care to your sisters, and you prefer to take care of her yourself."

Dat came in when the meal was ready. He gave the prayer of thanks. Conversation during dinner was loud and filled with feminine laughter. Nell smiled at Ellie as she regaled them with a story about the one family she cleaned for. Meg offered comments on how Ellie should handle the husband the next time he left food on dirty dishes on his night table.

Nell became aware of her father's gaze as Charlie joined in with the outrageous solution of putting the food in the man's bed and the dishes in his bathtub. As her father watched her, she saw something in his eyes that gave her concern.

"I'll lose my job if I do that." Ellie laughed.

"Husband," *Mam* addressed him. "Chocolate cake for dessert?"

Dat nodded to *Mam*, a soft expression on his face.

Once the leftover fried chicken was put away, *Mam* brought out the cake and sliced each of them a nice-sized piece. When they were done with dessert, Nell and her sister Leah rose to clear the supper dishes while Charlie and Meg filled up the sink basin and started to wash. With five daughters in the house, there was always plenty of help, so when her father beckoned to her, Nell did whatever any good daughter would do. She handed Ellie her dish towel and followed him out into the other room.

She felt edgy as she waited for her father to speak. She had a feeling she knew what he wanted to talk about.

"Have you given it any thought?"

"*It?*"

"Marriage. A husband." Her father studied her thoughtfully.

She relaxed and smiled. "*Ja, Dat*. I haven't found the man I want to marry yet, but I will. I just need a little more time."

Dat sighed. "You can have more time, but not too much." Then he hesitated as if he had something else on his mind. "Nell, I know how much you enjoy your animals. You've got a certain way with them, everyone says so. But you have to face the fact that your husband might not care for them as you do."

Nell gazed at him with a little smile on her lips. "Then I'll find a man who does love animals as much as I do."

He narrowed his gaze. "You're asking a lot of the man who hasn't married you yet."

"I'll find the right man, and he'll understand how I feel."

"You need to find him quickly, *dochter*."

"How can I rush this? I'll not marry for anything but love."

Her father's jaw tightened. "Are you disrespecting me with your tone, girl? I'm still your *vadder*."

She sighed. "*Dat*, I mean no disrespect. But this isn't easy for me. I thought I might be a *schuul* teacher until I meet a man I can love and who loves me, too."

"'Tis past the time to be thinking about becoming a *schuul* teacher. 'Tis time you took a husband."

"You think I have nothing to offer the *kinner*?" she asked softly. She was hurt by his dismissal of her skills. Was she that old that all he could think of was marrying her off?

"You could still marry Benjamin Yoder. He's single and never been married."

"*Nay!* I'll not marry a man older than my own *vadder*!"

Her father swallowed. "In truth, I don't want that for you either."

"I didn't think you wanted me to be unhappy."

His lips firmed. "Of course, I want your happiness. 'Tis my fondest hope that all of my girls will be happy in marriage, but time is passing you by, Nell. You have to take your chance soon."

Tears filled her eyes, and she tried to blink them away. She thought of Michael and then James. She could love James, marry him if he were a member of the Amish community. James loved animals as much as she did. Her heart ached, for she knew she would never have a life with him.

"Nell…" Her father's expression softened. "Know this. I do want you to be happy."

"*Ja*, I know."

"You deserve to have a husband, a family. You'll make a wonderful *mudder*."

"*Dat*, I'll try harder to find someone I can love. But *please* don't arrange a husband for me. I can't…*please*."

He nodded. "You will be open-minded? Give up this notion of being a *schuul* teacher?"

"Ja, Dat."

The man looked relieved. *"Gut."* He smiled. "How is Jonas?" he said, quickly changing the subject. The little dog had worked his way into her father's heart, it seemed.

"He's doing well. Have you been to visit him?"

A slight tide of red crept into her father's cheeks. "This morning."

"He's a wonderful pet." Nell gazed at her father with fascination. "And Naomi? Have you visited with her, too?"

He looked embarrassed. "Neither one works or provides a service," her father pointed out.

"Ja, they do. They give unconditional love."

Her father laughed. "That they do, so I guess that is something."

Friday morning, James woke up with a stiff neck, a sore back and with the television murmuring softly. He must have finally fallen asleep on the sofa and left it on. Unable to sleep for hours last night, he'd alternately stared at the ceiling and the TV.

He couldn't get Nell out of his mind. How could he have been so foolish to give into his feelings? If he had controlled himself, he might have been able to spend more time with her.

He glanced at the clock on the cable box: 6:45 a.m. He had to get moving, or he'd be late for work. He sat up quickly and groaned at his aching muscles. There were consequences for sleeping on his old sofa five nights in a row. He'd fallen asleep to the noise from the

TV, so tired each night that he'd been unable to find the strength to go to bed.

He grabbed the remote and turned off the TV. For a moment, his apartment was blissfully silent. He closed his eyes and drank the quiet in.

But then his thoughts filled with Nell again, and his brain buzzed with regret. James stood and headed to get ready for work. The only bright side was that it was the weekend, and he'd be spending it with his family. And there was a possibility that he might see Nell again on Sunday.

When he saw her, he vowed, he wouldn't joke or smile or cause her discomfort. He would be polite so that she didn't feel threatened. He wanted her in his life, even if only from a distance.

"James?" Janie poked her head into his office where he'd sat down between appointments. "Your next patient is here."

"Who is it?"

"Mrs. Becker and her dog Melly."

"Thank you. Would you please put them in exam room two?"

She nodded and left. James sat a moment longer.

The day went by quickly, for he had enough patients to keep him busy. He'd seen a record number of patients this week.

Janie was cheerful and clearly happy to be back at work in the clinic, but she wasn't Nell. Still, the tech's mood became infectious, and there were moments during that day that he smiled and laughed. Maybe he could do this after all, James thought. Maybe he could get past his feelings for Nell even if he couldn't ever forget her.

But then right before closing, Nell came to his office.

"Hi," he heard Janie say. "Welcome to Pierce Veterinary Clinic. Oh, poor baby, is this the little one who needs medical attention?"

He became alert as he heard Nell's voice, but he couldn't make out her words. He waited patiently for his assistant to come for him, although he was eager to see Nell and help.

"Come on back to exam room one," he heard Janie say. "You'll find it on the left as you go down the hall."

James had to smile. Nell knew exactly where the exam room was, where everything was in the clinic, but he doubted that Nell would say anything about having worked here while Janie was on vacation.

Janie entered his office. "You've a patient in exam room one. A little dog with a bee sting."

James was instantly concerned. Jonas got stung? He hurried into the exam room, where he found Nell with Jonas in her lap. She was hugging her pet against her. The dog was whimpering, and Nell was doing her best to soothe and comfort him. She must have sensed his presence because she looked up, happy to see him.

"James!" She rose quickly, mindful of her dog. "Jonas got stung by a bee. I put vinegar on it. I didn't know what else to do."

"You did good, Nell," he said quietly. "Vinegar helps draw out the toxin." He softened his expression as he held out his arms.

Nell didn't hesitate to hand him Jonas, and James experienced a deep sense of joy that she trusted him.

"Let's see, Jonas," he murmured as he placed him on the metal exam table in the room. "What have you done to yourself?" He examined his little swollen nose.

He heard Nell sniff, glanced over and saw her tears. "I only let him outside for a moment," she told him, "and I kept him on his leash."

"Nell," he said kindly, "dogs get into things. If they didn't, there wouldn't be a need for veterinarians like me." He used a magnifying glass to study the dog's nose more closely. "Ah, I see the stinger."

He reached into his pants pocket for his wallet. He flipped open the billfold and removed out a credit card.

He leaned close and scraped across the tip of Jonas's nose with the edge of the plastic card. "Got it!" he exclaimed. He displayed the tiny black object on his thumb. "Bee stinger." He smiled. "He should recover quickly." He handed her a tube of ointment. "For the itch," he said. "He's liable to keep scratching at his nose before it heals completely." He opened a bottle and shook out a pink pill. "Benadryl. And make sure you use the plastic collar I'm going to give you. He will try anything to get at his nose."

Nell nodded, and he knew that she recognized the bottle from her time working here. "I'll give him a Benadryl now. It doesn't appear that he's allergic, but I'll send you home with the liquid form anyway. It may help with some minor reactions. If his nose starts to swell or he becomes lethargic on the Benadryl, please bring him back. Better yet, call me immediately." He jotted his number on a Post-it note. "It's my cell phone. Don't wait if there's a change in him. All right?" He locked gazes with her.

"Ja," she promised, and he felt something tight ease within his chest.

Janie called out that she was finished for the day and was getting ready to lock up. He went to the door with Jonas in his arms to acknowledge his assistant's departure. "We'll be leaving in a minute. Good night, Janie. See you on Monday."

"James, *danki* for seeing him at such short notice," Nell said as he brought Jonas back to the table.

"Always," he said as he grabbed a collar from a cabinet and handed it to her. "Whenever you have a problem with Jonas or Naomi or any of your animals, come right in. You don't have to call. You don't need an appointment. Just come."

He saw her mouth open and close as she tried to process what he'd said. He watched her physically gather her composure. *"Danki."*

He glanced down at Jonas and smiled. "Back to your *mam*," he murmured as he lifted the little dog and placed him into Nell's waiting arms. His arm brushed Nell's, and for a moment, their eyes locked and tension arced between them.

He headed toward the door, waiting for her to follow him. "If he is still bothered by the sting, try using a cold pack on his nose. You can use ice in a plastic bag. Put it on his nose for short time intervals—about ten minutes on and fifteen off." He opened the door. "Make sure it's not too cold for him. If it is, wrap the bag in a dish towel."

He gestured for Nell to precede him into the front reception area. "Take care of yourself, Nell—and Jonas."

"James, I need to pay you."

"Not necessary." His tone was insistent but gentle. "I still owe you for your help here in the office."

Nell sighed. "I… *Danki*."

He smiled and waited while she went out the door. Then he quickly closed it behind her before he called out to her or did something that he would regret. Like kiss her or hug her.

When she was gone, James locked up the office and drove to his family farm. Fifteen minutes later, he took a duffel bag from his trunk and headed toward the house. He entered through the kitchen.

"Hallo, Mam."

"James!" she gasped with pleasure. "It's late. I thought you'd changed your mind about spending the weekend."

"Not a chance. I had a late appointment." After setting his bag by the door, he pulled out a kitchen chair and sat down.

Her brow creased with concern. "Everything *oll recht*?"

"Dog with a bee sting. I was able to get out the stinger. I was concerned because he got stung on the nose, but I believe he'll be fine."

His mother looked relieved, and something startling occurred to him. "*Mam*, how many times did Dad talk with you about his patients?"

Mam smiled. "Quite a few. He needed to talk, and I liked listening to him." She opened a cabinet door and pulled out two cups. "Coffee or tea?"

"Tea, please." He'd always found comfort in tea whenever he was sick or wanted to remember his time at home. His mother didn't say anything as she put on the kettle and took cookies out of the pantry. She set them within James's reach and then fixed their tea.

"What about dinner?" James asked.

"There's time. I was going to have tea myself," she assured him as she sat down across from him.

She prepared her tea the way she liked it, took a sip, then looked at him.

"Tell me what's wrong." Her warm brown eyes held concern.

"Nothing that can be fixed." He swallowed hard. "But I feel better now that I'm here."

Her expression grew soft. "James, this will always be your home. I love that you enjoy being here. Come whenever you want. You don't have to ask first."

James realized he'd said the same thing to Nell about the office. And he'd meant it. He smiled at his mother as a huge burden was lifted from his shoulders. *"Danki."*

He glanced toward the kitchen window as they finished their tea. "I parked behind the barn."

"Don't want anyone to know you're here, *ja*?" *Mam* teased.

"It doesn't seem right to park a car in your driveway."

She shook her head but a smile played about her mouth. "'Tis fine. You can park it wherever makes you feel better."

James reached out to clasp his mother's hand. "I love you, *Mam*," he said.

"I love you, *soohn*. I wish I could help with whatever is bothering you."

"You already have, *Mam*," he whispered.

"You'll be staying in Matt's room again," *Mam* said as he stood and retrieved his duffel.

He didn't mind. He and Matthew had become close since he'd moved back to Happiness. His brother seemed to enjoy his weekly visits almost as much as he enjoyed staying the weekends in his parents' house.

He carried his belongings upstairs and into Matthew's room which had two single beds. He put the duffel bag on the bed he'd been given the last time, then moved to look through the window at the farm fields below.

The crops Adam had planted were green and thriving. James smiled. He enjoyed the view. It brought back childhood memories of living in Ohio with his parents and of his home here in Pennsylvania with his mother and stepfather.

"Come downstairs after you get settled," *Mam* called up. "You can keep me company while I make dinner. *Dat* and Matt are at your *onkel* Aaron's. Maggie, Abigail and Rosie have gone to the store but will be home soon. They'd planned to stop to see the Stoltzfus girls on their way back."

James felt a jolt. He wasn't surprised that his sisters knew the Stoltzfus girls. They belonged to the same Amish church community. But he hadn't realized that the girls were friendly.

Seeing Nell in his office this afternoon, knowing that she'd come to him for help, warmed him. He couldn't have Nell Stoltzfus as his sweetheart, but perhaps there was still hope that they could be friends.

His stepfather and brother arrived home an hour later, surprised to discover that James had gone to the barn to check on the animals.

"James!" Adam exclaimed. "*Gut* to see you again, *soohn*." He grinned. "Can't manage to stay away from us, *ja*?"

"*Ja,*" James said soberly. "I enjoy spending the weekends with you." He swallowed. "If it's not too much trouble."

"You can stay every weekend—and every weekday if you'd like. We love having you here." He narrowed his gaze. "Where is your car?"

"Behind the barn." James spied his stepbrother, Matthew behind his father. "Matt, I hope you don't mind sharing again."

Matthew grinned. "I don't mind as long as you keep to your own side of the room."

James grinned. "You always know how to put me in my place, little *bruder.*"

"As you know how to put me in mine, big *bruder,*" he teased.

"Our animals *oll recht*?" Adam asked.

"They are fine." He met Adam's gaze. "They look well fed and healthy." He paused. "Are you having any problems with any of them?" Adam shook his head. *"Gut."*

"We're going inside," his stepfather said. "Coming?"

"Ja, Mam has a *gut* supper simmering on the stove. Chicken potpie." James regarded his brother with amusement. "You staying behind?"

"And have you eat my share of supper?" Matthew smiled. *"Nay."*

"You don't seem upset to have a roommate again," he told Matthew as they followed their father toward the house.

Matthew shrugged. "I've gotten used to you."

"Ja?" James smiled.

"You grew on me. It seems I've missed my older *bruder,*" he confessed.

"Danki, Matt," James said softly. "I've missed you, too."

"Are you hungry?"

"Starved." James stared at his brother's garments.

"I've brought my own clothes, but may I borrow some of yours?"

"Missing our suspenders, are you?" Adam teased. He turned to his other son. "Matthew, do you think you could find some clothes for your *bruder*?"

Matthew sighed. "If I must." But then he grinned. "I'm sure I have a few things that will fit him despite the fact that he's an old man now."

"Don't be smart, youngster," James said with a laugh. "I'm not an old man, and you know it."

James changed into the Amish garments that Matthew got out for him. He was standing with his brother by the pasture fence when his sisters arrived home with their purchases and news from Whittier's Store.

"Did you see Nell and Charlie?" Matthew asked.

"*Nay*, we didn't have time to stop. We saw Daniel and Isaac Lapp, and we got to talking with them. I wanted to give Leah some quilting fabric. I'll have to bring it with us tomorrow." Maggie glanced at her older brother. "Nice to see you at home again, *bruder*."

"Nice to be home again, Mags."

His sister growled playfully at his use of the *English* nickname.

"Supper!" their mother called.

"We'd best hurry. She may be needing help before we sit down to eat," Maggie said.

The sisters rushed on ahead of them, and the men followed. James felt an infusion of good humor. It was good to be home.

Nell's sisters were laughing. The five of them were in their family buggy taking a drive to visit their cousins. Aunt Katie and Uncle Samuel would be hosting

Visiting Sunday, and the girls wanted to help out in any way they could. With seven sons, more than half of whom were married, and Hannah, her eight-year-old daughter, Aunt Katie had less help than their *mam* did in the Stoltzfus house. Nell knew that Katie's daughters-in-law had offered to come, but they had children to take care of, and Katie thought it best if they stayed with her grandchildren. It was only natural for the Stoltzfus sisters, Katie's nieces, to help out instead.

Nell, who sat in the front passenger seat while Leah steered the horse, heard laughter from her sisters in the seat behind them. She glanced back. "Charlie, I don't know why you insisted on bringing Jonas. You don't have to watch him. His nose is fine. What will we do with him while we work?"

"I brought his kennel," Charlie said with a chuckle. "Stop, Jonas!"

"Nell, he's trying to give puppy kisses," Meg said with laughter.

"Trying and succeeding," Ellie said. "I just got licked in the face."

"Eww!" Meg said, and she roared with delight when she received a doggy kiss of her own.

"Look!" Charlie reached over Nell's shoulder to point to a farmhouse on the right. "There's Matthew Troyer. He's waving to us."

Nell glanced over with a smile that promptly froze on her face when she saw the man standing beside Matthew. She knew immediately who wore the Amish solid shirt and tri-blend denim pants with black suspenders. It was James. "Who's with him?" Ellie asked. Her voice held interest.

"You've met him," Meg said.

A car came up from behind them, and Leah slowed the buggy, steering it closer to the side of the road.

"'Tis Matthew's *bruder*, and he's someone too old for you," Charlie told her.

"Ha! As if any eligible man in our community is too old for me," Ellie said. "He may be too old for you, Charlie, but not for me."

Nell couldn't keep her eyes from James. Her heart thumped hard as she recalled her time with Jonas in his office yesterday afternoon. He'd been kind and patient... and too professional.

Matthew leaned in to say something to his companion, and James turned, giving Nell a full view of his handsome features. The shock of her continued attraction to him hit her hard. It didn't matter if he'd been professional and friendly. As she met his gaze, she immediately recalled their kiss.

As if sensing Nell's disquiet, Leah looked over and frowned.

"James," Nell murmured. She gestured toward the man in Amish dress, and her sister's eyes widened.

Matthew waved at them to pull into the driveway. She and Leah exchanged glances. They had come for fabric. She could get it from Maggie and then leave immediately. Nell felt her pulse race as Leah turned on the blinker, then pulled onto the Troyers' dirt driveway.

"*Hallo*, Nell," Matthew greeted with a smile.

"Matthew," she greeted pleasantly. She flashed James a look. "James."

"Where are you headed?" the younger brother asked.

"Aunt Katie's," Leah said. "But Maggie has some fabric that she was going to drop off today if she had the time."

"I'll get her for you," Matthew offered, drawing Nell's attention. She looked away as he entered the house, leaving the sisters alone with James.

"Will you be coming to visit at the Lapps tomorrow?" Charlie asked from the backseat.

"I don't know yet," James said.

Nell locked gazes with him. "You should come," she urged and was rewarded by his look of surprise.

"I'll consider it if my family goes," he said.

Nell blushed and was unable to look away.

Matthew exited the house with his sister.

"Sorry we didn't stop by this afternoon," Maggie said as she handed Nell a plastic bag.

"We could have gotten them from you tomorrow, but since we were on our way to Aunt Katie's anyway…"

After their initial eye contact, James seemed to be avoiding Nell's gaze.

There was no logical reason why she should feel hurt, Nell realized. Unless it was because, wrong or right, she wanted his attention.

"We should go—" Leah began.

Nell took the hint. "*Ja*, we need to go. It was *gut* to see you," she said. She started to turn away until James called out to her.

"Nell?"

She froze then glanced back.

"May I speak with you a moment?"

She nodded and followed him to where they could talk privately. "Is something wrong?"

James gazed at her warmly, his intense focus making her wish for things she couldn't have. He didn't say anything for a long moment, as if he were happy just to have her attention.

"James?"

His gaze dropped briefly to her mouth. "How's Jonas?" he asked.

She swallowed hard. "He's fine. Doing well. *Danki.*"

"Nell, I miss you."

"James, we can't do this. *I* can't do this."

"What exactly is this?" he asked quietly. "The fact that we like each other but shouldn't?"

"*Ja*, we shouldn't," she said and started to turn.

He captured her arm. "Nell, I'm sorry. I know I have no right to ask anything of you, but please…consider us being friends if we can't be anything more."

"I don't know if I can," she whispered.

"Can't be friends?"

"'Tis too risky. I want more, but it will never happen. So I'm sorry, James, but we can't be friends. Ever." With that last remark, Nell hurried back to the buggy where her sisters were chatting with Maggie and Matthew while they waited. Nell saw that their sister Abigail had joined them.

"*Hallo*, Abigail," she greeted, then she leaned into her sister and said, "Leah, we have to go. *Now.*"

"Matthew, it was nice to see you," Nell said with a smile. "Nice to see you again, James," she said politely. She drew on all of her skills to hide the fact that she remembered his kiss and how much she'd enjoyed it. "Enjoy your time with your family."

James looked at her. "I will. *Danki*, Nell."

Leah climbed into the front seat of the carriage while Nell got in on the passenger side.

"Have a *gut* evening," Leah said.

"Bye, Nell," Matthew said. "I hope to see you at the Lapps' tomorrow."

Nell nodded. She had no choice but to go. Would James be there, as well?

Her glance slid over him briefly before she stared ahead as Leah steered their buggy toward Aunt Katie's. She shouldn't want him there, but she did. Nell closed her eyes. She was a fool for loving him. But she couldn't seem to help herself.

She needed to find an Amish husband…soon.

Chapter Twelve

Katie Lapp came out of the house as Leah steered the family buggy into the barnyard and parked. Nell climbed out and waited for Leah while their sisters ran toward the Lapp farmhouse.

"We've come to help, *Endie* Katie," Charlie cried.

"Wunderbor, g'schwischder dochter." Wonderful, *niece*, they heard their aunt exclaim. "I'm so glad you could come—all of you! Come inside!"

Leah hitched up the horse before she turned to Nell. "What are you thinking?"

Nell frowned. "I'm wondering why I can't forget him. He makes it hard, staying with his Amish family, dressing like them."

"He's still an *Englisher*, don't forget. He made the choice to leave our way of life." Leah fell into step beside her as they slowly made their way to the house.

"I know."

"But you still love him."

Nell met her sister's gaze with tears in her eyes. *"Ja."* *Why doesn't he wear jeans?* Nell thought. He could have worn jeans, and she'd be unable to forget that he was *English* and unavailable to her. But would it have helped even to see him like that?

Nay, she thought. James in jeans was just as devastating to her peace of mind. Although seeing James in Amish clothes gave her a fierce longing for something she could never have.

Nell preceded Leah into Katie Lapp's house. "*Endie* Katie. Where would you like us to start?"

"Charlie and Hannah are in the kitchen. It would be helpful if you could work in the great room?"

"We'll start there then," Leah said.

Grabbing cleaning supplies and a broom, the sisters entered the large great room, where the family often gathered for late evening and Sunday leisure time.

"What are you going to do about your feelings for him?" Leah asked as she dusted the furniture.

"What can I do? 'Tis not like it matters one way or another how I feel. I have to marry within the Amish faith." Nell swept the floor with long, even strokes of the corn broom.

"You're upset," her sister pointed out. "And hurt. I don't know how to help you."

Nell blinked to clear her vision. There was suddenly a lump in her throat. "No one can help me."

"Matthew cares for you," Leah said. "You could still marry him."

"*Nay!* He'll still be James's *bruder*. And it will seem as I'm deliberately trying to hurt him."

"Matthew?"

"*Nay*, James."

"If he's staying the weekend, James may come visiting tomorrow."

"I know." Nell felt a burning in her stomach. Odds were that he'd come.

"There will be plenty of opportunities to have a word with him and clear the air." Leah paused in her dusting and touched her arm to draw her gaze. "You could check on *Onkel* Samuel's farm animals. 'Tis possible he'll follow you."

It was true. He might follow her because of the nature of his profession. "And if he does, what am I supposed to say to him that I haven't already said?"

"You'll think of something."

"You're not afraid I'll do something terrible, like run away and marry him?"

Her sister's blue eyes widened. "You're not actually considering it, are you?"

Nell's face heated. *"Nay."*

"Then we have nothing to worry about. Just tell him to leave you alone and be done with it."

Nell doubted that it would be so easy. She loved James too much to be cruel. But being cruel might be the only way for him to get on with his life without her.

James liked working side by side with Adam and Matthew. The manual labor on the farm felt good, and it gave him an outlet for the frustration of struggling to make a success of his practice. He also enjoyed helping Adam in his small furniture shop attached to the barn.

The only concession he allowed himself during these weekends was to keep his cell phone with him.

He needed to take calls in the event of an emergency. Fortunately, there had been no such calls.

His thoughts focused on Nell as they did often during each day. The image of the young Amish woman constantly hovered in his mind. He'd seen her this afternoon, and he missed her already.

He sighed. There was no chance for them. Why couldn't he put her out of his mind?

Then there was Matthew. It was clear that his younger brother had feelings for Nell. It would be acceptable for Matthew and Nell to have a life together. Acceptable to the community, but not to him.

He heard a bell from the direction of the house.

"Dinnertime," Adam announced, glancing toward his sons who were fixing the fencing on the far side of the property.

"Thanks be to *Gott*. I'm as hungry as a bear." Matthew straightened and leaned on his shovel. The two brothers had just replaced a rotten fencepost.

"You're always hungry," *Dat* said.

"How do you know about a bear's appetite?" James teased. "They hibernate through the winter and don't eat while they're sleeping in their den."

"The animal expert," Matthew groused, but the grin on his face told James that he was teasing back.

"Wonder what *Mam*'s fixed for supper?"

"More than you eat on your own, James, I'm certain."

James stretched, reaching over his head until he experienced the sharp pull of his arm muscles. He felt good, better than he had in a long time.

"Thanks—I mean, *danki* for allowing me to stay the

weekend again," James said, regarding the two men beside him with warmth.

"Come every weekend. I'm always happy to share the work," Matthew joked.

Adam gazed at him with affection. "We enjoy having you, *soohn*."

The dinner bell resounded again, and the three men started toward the house.

"You want to see my place?" James asked his brother. "I live over Mattie Mast's Bakery."

"You do?" Matthew's eyes had widened. "Must smell *gut* in your *haus*."

"Most days. Monday through Saturday, it's a sure bet. I particularly like Tuesday's when Mattie makes her special chocolate cake."

"*Mam* made a chocolate cake this morning," Matthew said.

"She did?" The thought made his mouth water.

"She said something about it being your favorite," Adam interjected.

James suddenly felt emotional. "It is."

Adam regarded him with a knowing look.

Matthew, on the hand, appeared puzzled. "*Ja*. Why are you surprised?"

"I haven't been home much these last years." James paused. "I haven't been the best son."

"You're a fine *soohn*, James, and don't you forget it. As for not coming to visit much, you're home now, and you moved to Lancaster County to be closer to us, *ja*?" Adam said.

James nodded.

"Then stop fretting. Be welcome. Come and stay

anytime you want. Move in if you'd prefer. We love having you here." He hesitated.

"Thank you, *Dat*," he said softly.

"Let's eat," Matthew rumbled. "I'm as hungry as a b-boar!"

James laughed, and Adam joined in. Matthew glanced at each of them sheepishly until he began to giggle himself.

They could smell *Mam*'s cooking through the kitchen window. It was a warm day. In sweltering temperatures, the shades would be drawn and windows might be open or closed depending on whether or not there was a breeze.

James entered the house, stepping into the kitchen behind Adam and Matt. One look at the table laden with an Amish feast made everything worth it. He had missed such meals with his family. From the pleased look on her face as she noted his happiness, his mother had missed having him home, too.

Sunday morning Nell woke up early. The rest of the family was sleeping in. Since it was Visiting Day, they didn't have to be at the Lapps' until nine thirty or ten o'clock. She slipped downstairs, taking extra care to be quiet, and went into the barn to feed and water the animals.

Nell heard Jonas's excited barks. She hurried to his stall with a smile.

"*Hallo*, little one. Would you like to go outside?" She snapped on his leash and led him out of the barn. She walked about the property for a while, then took him back inside. Her gaze settled on Naomi's bed, and Nell was overwhelmed with sudden tears. James had known just what she would want—something for her new cat.

She crouched down and picked up Naomi. She was so tiny. The kitten was eating well, no doubt because James knew exactly what her cat would need. She grabbed a little toy, held it to Naomi's mouth. The kitten batted at the stuffed mouse playfully.

Nell put her down and watched for several moments, feeling a longing so intense that it nearly stole her breath. James. Why did she have to fall in love with an *Englisher*?

Nell was sure that Leah was correct. James was an *Englisher* with a stepfather, mother and siblings who were Amish.

She knew that she would have to talk with him, no matter how hard it would be to listen, and to step back after they'd parted friends.

She didn't want to be friends with James, but it was her only option. She poured dog food into Jonas's bowl and refilled his water dish.

James and she had a lot in common. They both loved animals. They enjoyed each other's company and got along well. But the most vital thing that was different about them was their chosen way of life.

Nell had chosen God's way through the Amish church, while James had made the choice to leave the community and become a veterinarian, with a life with TV, radio, cars and computers. She couldn't help the small smile that formed on her lips. *Maybe not computers.* He didn't like using the one in the office. He left that up to Michelle to handle.

I'm sorry. His words came back to haunt her. What

exactly had he been apologizing for? She'd thought it had been because of the kiss, but what if it was more?

Her mind replayed every day since her first meeting with James. From his tender care of Jonas, his compassion and concern for Joey, his patience and intensity while caring for Buddy and the other animals he treated in and outside of the practice. She sat, stroking Jonas, watching Naomi play, giving equal attention to both her beloved pets.

"Nell!"

"In here, Charlie!"

"We made breakfast. How long have you been out here?"

Nell shrugged. "What time is it?"

"Nine thirty."

She felt a jolt. "It is?" How had three hours passed so quickly? Had she been so wrapped up in her thoughts of James and what she was going to say to him that the minutes had flown by?

"*Ja*, come and eat. *Mam* and *Dat* will want to be heading to Aunt Katie's soon. There are muffins and pancakes, ham and bacon—and cereal if you want it."

"I'll be right there." Nell pushed to her feet. "Bye, little ones," she whispered.

Charlie waited for her outside the barn. "Who do you think will come visiting at *Endie* Katie's today?"

"I have no idea. The Kings and the Hershbergers, most likely."

"And the Masts and Troyers."

"And all their children and spouses and their grand-children," Nell added.

"I wonder if the boys will play *der beesballe*."

"What else will they do on a nice summer's day?"

"*Ja*, they'll play baseball, and I'll get to watch." A mischievous look entered Charlie's expression. "Maybe I'll convince them to let me play."

Nell laughed and hugged her sister before they climbed up the front porch. "I have no doubt you'll be playing baseball today. You are *gut* at convincing people to do what you want."

Charlie paused and frowned. "Is that a bad thing?"

"*Nay*, sister, 'tis a *gut* thing," Nell said as they entered the house.

He wasn't here. The Troyers had arrived an hour ago, and there was no sign of James. Nell stood at the fence railing and overlooked her uncle's pasture.

I should have stayed and talked longer with him at the Troyers' yesterday.

But she hadn't. She'd become upset at seeing him there, at him being Matthew's brother, that she'd been eager to get away. And just when she'd made up her mind to tell him to leave her alone, he didn't show.

Nell heard laughter behind her. Elijah, Jacob, Jedidiah, Noah and Daniel, Aunt Katie and Uncle Samuel's sons, were playing baseball. Isaac, another son, stood near the house talking with Ellen Mast, the girl who'd loved him forever.

Ellen was a good friend, and Nell hoped that her cousin saw her in the right light—and soon. It was obvious to her that Isaac had similar feelings for Ellen but was, for some reason, holding back. She wondered if it had something to do with the trouble he'd gotten into two years back. Nell had never believed that Isaac had been responsible for the vandalism at Whittier's Store—none of them did. But Isaac had never defended himself or confessed the truth, and so he suffered because of it.

Her gaze followed the horses in the pasture. The mares were running through the open space, beings of pure beauty in energy and form. Closer to the fence, goats munched contentedly on the grass. To the left were the Lapps' two Jersey milk cows.

She heard hens clucking from a pen near the barn. She smiled, wishing she'd brought Jonas. Naomi was too little to expose to curious eyes and small hands.

"Nell."

She stiffened. Why was she imagining his voice? It hurt that she was so caught up in her feelings for him that she pictured him everywhere.

"Nell, I have to talk with you." His touch on her arm convinced her that the voice was real.

She turned, locked gazes with him. There was a depth of emotion in his dark eyes that quickly vanished as they stared at one another.

A quick study of him revealed that he'd changed clothes. Gone were the Amish garments he'd worn yesterday. Today he was back to wearing jeans and a blue button-down, short-sleeved shirt.

"What are you doing here?" she demanded, all thoughts of her desire to talk with him gone in the reality of his presence.

"I was on my way home, but I wanted to talk with you first."

"Why?"

"To explain about my family."

"What?" She bit her lip and blinked rapidly. Why did being near him upset her so much? "I know about your family. Your sister told me."

"I'd like to tell you why I kept the Pierce name." He leaned against the fence rail beside her, his tall form seeming bigger and more present than ever before.

"James." She gestured to the gathering in the yard behind them.

He didn't seem to care that someone might be watching, listening. "My mother was raised in an Amish household. When she met and fell in love with my father, John Pierce, she made the choice to leave her community and marry him. They moved to Ohio where my dad set up his veterinary practice. They were happy. I was born a year and a half later, and years later, my sister Maggie was born."

"Maggie Troyer."

"Except she was Maggie Pierce. Then Abigail came into our lives. When she was just a small child, my father died when he was on a vet call. He'd had a massive heart attack. He was forty."

"I'm sorry." She gazed at him with sympathy. She could see that the loss still deeply affected him after all these years. "How old were you?"

"Thirteen."

"A time when a boy needs his father."

"During the weekend, I used to accompany him on calls. I was sick that Saturday and couldn't go. I had a cold. He told me to stay home." He paused, closed his eyes then opened them. "I should have gone. I might have been able to do something."

"Nay!" Nell cried. "What could you have done?"

"Called the ambulance. Something."

She drew a deep breath as she fought the urge to pull him into her arms and offer comfort. "Didn't someone call the ambulance?"

"The homeowner. But Dad was in the barn tending to a cow when he keeled over. By the time the man found him, it was too late."

"I'm so sorry," she said softly, reaching to touch his arm. "That must have been difficult." She no longer cared that they were standing in full view of everyone near the fence. Her concern was only for James. "Then your *mam* came home to Pennsylvania with you, didn't she?"

"Yes, she was suffering, grieving. I didn't want to leave Ohio. It had been my home. My father was buried there. I'd gone to school there, and my friends were there, but I didn't say a word. Mom was hurting so badly. I understood her need to be with family. But to leave the English world to live with my Amish grandparents was more than I could handle. I was a sullen, angry teenager, and I didn't make things easy for anyone once we'd moved back. Suddenly, not only had I lost my dad but also my life and my identity."

Nell studied him. He stared at the animals in the pasture, and she watched as, miraculously, a small smile came to his mouth.

"This view reminds me of one at my grandfather's. *Grossvadder* was a kind and patient man." He closed his eyes, shuddered. "I still miss him—both of them. My grandfather and grandmother."

He opened his eyes and fixed her with his dark gaze. "One day, I became so overwhelmed with grief that I broke down and cried. I sobbed as if I was a baby and I'd lost sight of my mother. *Grossvadder* saw me crying and nodded as if I had done the right thing to break down. He'd moved on without a word, but I could read his thoughts even as I cried. Afterward, we talked. He said it was good to be strong, but that it is a stronger man who allowed himself to cry and to heal. He taught me about God and love, and because of him, I learned to settle and enjoy my life at the farm until Adam's wife died. *Mam* took my sisters with her every day so that she could take care of Adam's two children while he grieved. Matthew was three and Rosie was a newborn. Adam's wife, Mary, died after giving birth to her."

Nell knew what it was like to lose someone you loved. Lately she'd seemed to be moving past her grief until she mostly thought of Michael with simple affection. Only on occasion did the pain rear up and strike her when she least expected it.

"You didn't like your *mudder* helping Adam?"

James shook his head as he faced her and he met her gaze head-on. "I didn't mind that. I minded that she and Adam later fell in love and married. I felt as if their love was a betrayal to my father. It was wrong, but I was fifteen—what did I know about love? I'd had a girlfriend in high school—but it wasn't anything serious and our relationship didn't last. When Dad died, I made a vow to honor him by following in his footsteps. I would become a vet. I'd always thought I wanted to be one anyway, but my goal became more of an obsession after losing Dad."

He glanced back toward the yard and stared at her

cousins playing baseball. His lips curved. "I used to play baseball in Little League and in school. I loved it."

He drew a sharp breath, then released it. "I attended public, not Amish, school. By the time we moved here, I was already finished with eighth grade. *Grossvadder* approved of me continuing at the closest high school. Mom understood. She had loved my father. I'd known that. I'd seen and felt their love. Mom knew that continuing my education was the only way I could become the vet I was determined to be."

"And you did," Nell said with warmth. She paused. "What happened after your *mudder* married Adam?"

"We moved to live with him, of course, and I became a nightmare. I acted terribly toward Adam. I was difficult, and I rebelled the only way I knew how by being cold, unfeeling and nasty to him."

Nell saw regret settle between his brows. This James she was learning about was even more appealing and more attractive to her. She bucked herself up with the reminder that the most they could ever be was friends—and that it would be wiser for her to keep her distance from him.

"I take it things eventually changed between you and Adam."

James flashed her a grin. "No thanks to me. I give Adam all the credit. The only time I ever behaved was at school. I studied hard because I was determined to get into a good college."

Nell was curious. "How did Adam change your relationship?"

"One day he'd had enough. It was late during my sophomore year. He took me aside, and we had a talk.

Well, he talked, and I listened. He told me that he loved my mother and my sisters and that he loved me no matter how difficult I acted toward him. That his love won't stop because I wanted it to. He said that he wouldn't replace my dad and that he didn't want to. A dad's place in a son's life is important. He simply wanted to be my friend and to be there whenever I needed him."

"Oh, James... Adam is a *gut* man."

James blinked, his eyes suspiciously moist. "Yes, he is. He then told me that I needed to be a man, not a boy."

Nell raised her eyebrows, hurting for the boy he'd been and the man he was. "I doubted that went over well."

"Actually, it did. I understood what he was saying. I realized that God had given me Adam after He'd taken my father."

"James..."

"I'm not angry with God, Nell, but I do think that He took Dad home for reasons of His own."

"Matthew and Rosie might believe it's because they needed a *mudder*—your *mam*."

He smiled. "She loves them like her own." He slipped his hands into his front jeans pockets. Suddenly, he seemed uncomfortable as if he might have revealed too much of himself. "Adam became a father to me, and I let him. He's never been anything but fair and understanding, even when I chose to leave the community to attend Ohio State, my father's alma mater. And later when I left for Penn Vet—the University of Pennsylvania's Veterinary School. Even when I stayed in the Philadelphia area afterward and worked for six years in an animal hospital there."

"But then you decided to move back to Lancaster County."

"To be closer to my family," James said. "I realized that I was working all the time. I wasn't really living. My father would have hated that. He loved being a vet, but he loved his family more." He removed a hand from his pocket to run fingers through his dark hair. "I missed *Mam*, *Dat*, Maggie, Abby, Matt and Rosie."

She held back a smile as she noted how he'd slipped into his former Amish life pattern with the Pennsylvania Deitsch names for his mother and father.

"So now you know."

Nell didn't know how to respond. Why had she chosen to believe ill of this wonderful, kind man? Because she didn't want to have these warm and affectionate feelings for him.

"I should go," he said as he straightened away from the fence and faced the yard. "Work tomorrow." His brow furrowed. "I'll miss you, Nell. You were the best assistant a man could have."

Emotion rose as a knot in her throat. "I'm sure Janie is better," she said hoarsely.

"I doubt it." He looked up and apparently saw something that made him separate himself from her not only emotionally but physically, too. He drew back a few feet from her. "Matt," he greeted.

Nell smiled at James's brother. "*Hallo*, Matt. Tired of playing baseball?"

"*Nay.*" He glanced from her to James and back. "Did you like working for my *bruder*?"

"Ja," Nell said, "I learned a lot from him. You know how I love caring for animals."

"I do." Matthew's expression had turned soft.

"I need to go," James said.

"I'll walk you to your car," Matthew offered.

"You just want to take another close look."

Matthew laughed. "Maybe."

James turned to Nell. "Goodbye, Nell. Thanks again for filling in at the clinic when I needed you."

"Thank you for Naomi and taking care of Jonas when he needed you."

"You're *willkomm*." James gave her a sad smile.

Then Nell watched him walk away, and her heart ached for what she couldn't have and what her life would never be.

Chapter Thirteen

It was late. Darkness had settled over the land. Nell had brought in the horses when she heard a car rumble down the driveway. James. He came to mind immediately. She closed the back barn door and hurried through the building to meet him out front. But it wasn't James who was getting out of his car. It was their *English* neighbor, Rick Martin.

"Nell," he said soberly when he caught sight of her. "I have bad news. Catherine Fisher was rushed to the hospital a few minutes ago."

"Ach, nay!" she breathed. "And Bishop John?"

"He went with her to the hospital. I've brought their son, Nicholas. Catherine asked if you would watch him."

Nell swallowed. "She mentioned me?"

"Yes, by name." Rick opened the back door of the car. The little two-year-old lay on the backseat. Curled up in sleep, the boy looked like a little angel. "He doesn't know what happened. He was upstairs napping when Catherine collapsed."

"I'm sorry," she murmured. She reached inside the

car and lifted baby Nick into her arms. He cuddled against her, and she sighed. "Thank you for bringing him, Rick."

"I'll find out how she is and let you know."

Nell nodded. "I'm going to bring him inside and put him to bed before he wakes up."

She turned toward the house with the bishop's son in her arms. She didn't wait for Rick to leave as she entered the house. As she headed toward the stairs, she met her mother.

"Nell."

"'Tis Nicholas Fisher, *Mam*." Nell shifted to bring the child closer. "Catherine is in the hospital. John went with her. Rick brought him. Before the ambulance took her away, Catherine asked that I watch him."

Her mother's expression softened as she studied the sleeping child in Nell's arms. "You'll put him in your room?"

"Ja," Nell said. She eyed the child in her arms with warmth. "I wonder why Catherine asked for me?"

"Everyone has seen how you are with their animals, Nell. If you have enough love and compassion for animals, imagine how much you have for a little boy?"

She widened her eyes. "You think that's why?"

"I do." *Mam* smiled. "You're a kind and loving woman, and everyone sees it."

Nell started up the stairs then stopped. *"Mam?"*

"Ja, Nell?"

"What if someone loves the wrong person? Someone who isn't right for her?"

Her mother looked at her with love and understanding. "Does this someone recognize that it's best to avoid the wrong man?"

She nodded.

"Then you have your answer, Nell. Although God the Father might not disagree. The Lord wishes us to love all men."

Her heart was heavy as Nell climbed the stairs with the small boy in her arms. She felt terrible for Catherine and John. She was worried about little Nick, who would awaken in the morning looking for his mother.

With Nicholas in one arm, she pulled back the top layers on her bed. She laid the boy gently on the mattress and covered him with the sheet and quilt. Then she pulled up the chair that she'd kept in the corner of her room and sat—and she watched him until exhausted, she climbed onto the double bed next to him. She offered up a silent prayer that Nicholas would have his mother and father home by tomorrow morning. With that good thought, Nell was able to close her eyes and sleep.

"Catherine Fisher died during the night," *Mam* told James and his siblings at breakfast on Sunday morning. "John was by her side."

"When did you hear this?" Adam asked.

"Just a few minutes ago. Nell's *mudder* stopped by. It seems that Catherine's last words were that Nell take care of their little son, Nicholas, while she was in the hospital. She didn't realize that she wouldn't be coming home again."

James's thoughts went immediately to Nell. "Where is Nicholas now?"

"He's still with Nell. John's still at the hospital, making the final arrangements for his wife."

"What's going to happen now?" Matthew reached for a muffin and put it on his plate.

"Nicholas no longer has his mother. John will need to marry again and quickly for the sake of his son."

"Who would want to marry a grieving widower with a young child?" James really wanted to know.

"Nell might," *Mam* said. "She's single and well past the age of marrying. It would be a *gut* arrangement for the both of them."

"Nay!" James exclaimed. When his mother stared, he blushed and looked away. "It makes no sense for them to rush into marriage. I know too many people who married in haste and then suffered afterward."

"But these people you know—they weren't of the Amish faith, were they?"

James shook his head. "No. But why would that make a difference?"

"It's not unusual for a man to take a wife simply for the sake of his motherless child. The couple will find love and respect with the passage of time," Adam explained.

Feeling a hot burning in his gut at the thought of Nell marrying another man, James couldn't let it go. "And if John…"

"Bishop John," his mother said.

"And if the bishop doesn't accept his new wife as someone he could love? What will that mean for the woman?" For Nell, he thought.

Adam looked sorrowful. "Only the Lord knows the answer to that question, James."

James looked from his stepfather to his mother. *"Dat,* you didn't," he reminded. "It wasn't until you fell in love with *Mam* that you asked her to marry you."

"*Ja*, 'tis true. I couldn't at first. I was grieving too much, but then your mother entered my heart like sunshine on a dark, stormy day. It was then that I asked her to marry me. I'd had an inkling that she had similar feelings for me."

"How?" James asked. "How did you know her feelings?"

Adam gazed at his wife with soft eyes. "She told me."

"She *what*?" It was Matthew who had spoken.

Mam laughed. "Not in words, *soohn*," she assured Matt, "but in looks and my caring for you and your sister."

Matthew joined in her laughter. "It would be fine if you'd told him, *Mam*, right off."

"Right for you," James said with good humor. "I would have been a nightmare worse than I already was if you'd married right after Mary died."

"I would have been right with you," Matthew admitted with a grim smile.

"Is there anything we can do?" Maggie asked. She'd been listening quietly up until now. "Nell may need some of Nicholas's things. We could get them for her."

"I'll go with you," Abigail offered.

"James?" Rosie said. "You know Nell. Maybe she'd like you to bring her little Nick's things?"

He looked at his stepsister and sisters. "I don't know—"

"That's a fine idea, James. You have a car. You can drive over to the bishop's house and gather what Nell will need."

"I could get there faster," James agreed. "What if John isn't home? How will we get in?"

"The bishop doesn't lock his house," Maggie said.

"He trusts that God will protect his family and his home."

James frowned as he stood. God hadn't kept the man's wife from death's door. Not that he thought less of God. Life and death were simply the way of a person's existence. "Rosie, it was your idea. Would you like to come with me?"

Rosie stood and carried her breakfast dishes to the sink. *"Mam—"*

"Go, *dochter*. James needs your help as much as Nell is going to need his."

Leah sneaked into Nell's room where Nell lay awake next to the bishop's sleeping child. She motioned for her sister to step outside.

Nell frowned as she stood in the hallway.

"Nell, Catherine is dead." Leah flashed a look of concern toward the boy in Nell's bed. "She died during the night. There was something wrong with her heart."

"John—"

"Is devastated. He'll not be thinking of his son at a time like this. It could be the reason why Catherine asked you to care for him…because she knew she wouldn't be coming back."

Nell's eyes filled with tears. "But why me?" She drew a shuddering breath. "What am I going to tell that little boy? Nicholas, your *mam* is dead, but it's okay because she is with the Lord?" She lifted a hand to brush back an escaped tendril of soft brown hair. "He'll never understand that. He's too young to know about God and death…and losing his *mudder*."

"Get dressed," Leah said. "We need to figure out a way to get more of Nicholas's things."

"*Ja*, Rick only brought Nicholas. He had no clothes, no diapers." Nell grimaced with wry humor as she glanced toward her bed. "I'm going to need clean sheets, I think."

Leah chuckled. "A wet bed is the least of your worries." She moved into the room. "I'll sit with him. *Dat* wants to see you. He's waiting for you downstairs."

Nell raised her eyebrows. "What could he possibly want—" Her eyes widened. "*Nay,* surely he won't suggest that I step in and marry John?"

"Only one way to find out."

"Fine. Let me change clothes, and I'll go down to see what he has to say."

"Remain calm," her sister instructed. "Don't lose your temper. If you stay calm, you'll retain the upper hand."

Dressed and ready to face her father, Nell went downstairs, pleased that Nicholas continued to sleep for now.

Arlin Stoltzfus was at the kitchen table. Her sisters and mother were absent. Having no one in the room was a sure sign that her father had something serious to say to her.

"*Dat?*" She entered the room as if she wasn't concerned with what he might say. She poured herself a cup of tea and then held up the teakettle. "Would you like some?"

Her father shook his head. "*Nay,* I've had my morning coffee. Sit down, Nell."

Nell sat, pretending an indifference that she was far from feeling. "Doughnuts! I love doughnuts. And there are powdered and chocolate glazed. I'll have one of each!" She knew she was rambling, but she couldn't seem to stop herself.

"Nell."

"Ja, Dat?"

"We need to talk about Nicholas—and John."

"Nicholas is still sleeping, poor *boo*." She took a small bite of her powdered doughnut, chewed and swallowed. "I imagine John is devastated over losing Catherine. And Nicholas—how is he going to react when he learns that his *mudder* isn't coming home to him?"

"Nicholas will be fine once he gets another *mudder*."

Nell stared at him. "Another *mudder*? No one can replace his *mudder*."

"He can, if you marry John."

"Dat, the man just lost his wife. The last thing he'll want is to marry me—a stranger. I'll be happy to care for Nicholas until he has his time to grieve, but to even suggest that he marry so quickly…"

"You *will* marry him."

"I—*what*?"

"This is your opportunity for marriage. John is a fine man. He'll make you a *gut* husband. Nicholas is a sweet little *boo* who needs a mother."

Nell gazed at her father in shock. *"Dat*, surely you don't believe that God wants me to be Nicholas's mother?"

"There are many young women within our community, *dochter*. If God didn't want this, then why did Catherine specifically ask for you?"

"Dat," she whispered. *"Nay."* But what if the Lord did want this for her? What if this was the answer to her prayers regarding her forbidden love of James? If she married John, then she would have to get on with

her life without James. It was something to think about. "I'll consider it, *Dat*."

Her father looked pleased. "Do that, but do it quickly. John is a practical man. He will want to marry again soon for the sake of his *soohn*."

Nell opened her mouth to object. She didn't believe for one second that John would be in a hurry to marry. Not when he was still grieving over the loss of his beloved Catherine.

With Rosie's help, James entered John Fisher's house and found clothes, a blanket and a basket of clean cloth diapers for Nicholas. They left as quickly as they'd come, and James drove right to the Stoltzfus farm so that he could hand over the boy's belongings to Nell.

His heart was pounding hard as he drove up to the Arlin Stoltzfus residence. Rosie opened her car door first and reached into the back for the basket of diapers. James carried the rest of the items—the boy's nightgown, some socks, shoes, little shirt and pants—and cute little straw and black felt hats.

His sister waited for him to join her before they climbed the steps to the large white house. James glanced at his sister and nodded. Rosie raised her hand and rapped her closed fist on the doorframe.

The screen door opened immediately, and James found himself face to face with Nell's sister Leah. "I—we've—" he said, including his younger stepsister, "picked up a few of Nicholas's things from the house."

Leah glanced from him to his sister. Rosie held up the wicker basket. "I have clean diapers."

"I brought his blanket and his garments—and his

hats." James smiled as he studied the hats that lay on the pile of clothing in his arms.

"That was kind of you," Leah finally said. She opened the screen door and stepped aside. "Come in. Please."

James followed Rosie into the house.

"You must have gone early," Nell's sister said.

"As soon as we heard," he admitted.

"Let me get Nell. You may take a seat if you'd like. There are doughnuts on the table and fresh coffee on the stove."

"Thank you." James exchanged glances with Rosie, then together they set the items they carried close by and sat down.

Nell came into the room less than a minute later. "James! Rosie, Leah said you brought Nick's clothes."

James stood as she walked into the room. "Yes, we thought you could use them, considering what happened."

The young Amish woman's eyes filled with tears. "He's going to need them."

"*Mam* said that Catherine asked for you to take care of him."

"*Ja*, I was surprised. I didn't know Catherine that well." She bit her lip, looked away. "*Dat* believes God has a plan."

"What kind of plan?" James asked. He had a bad feeling about Arlin's belief in a plan that somehow involved Nell with the bishop's son.

Nell shook her head. "It doesn't matter."

"Nell," he began. "Can I do anything for you? Something? *Please*, I want to help."

He saw her swallow hard. "You've already done a lot by getting Nicholas's things for him," she said.

"Nell!" Leah called. "He's waking up!"

"I'm sorry," Nell whispered. "I have to go to him." Her gaze went to Rosie but settled longer on James. *"Danki."* She blinked back tears. It was as if she were saying goodbye. To him.

They didn't stay for doughnuts and coffee. James drove back to the house with his sister.

"What do you think Nell meant when she said that her *vadder* thinks that God has a plan?" Rosie asked, breaking the silence in the car.

"I don't know." But then he realized that he did. Arlin Stoltzfus had been wanting his daughter to marry, and with Catherine's death, Bishop John would be seeking a mother for his child.

No! James thought. He couldn't allow her to marry John Fisher. John would never love Nell like he did. But what could he do?

He was powerless to stop them from marrying. An *Englisher*, he had no right to marry Nell or to stop her from heeding her father's wishes.

Chapter Fourteen

Her *dat* was right. Bishop John was grieving but he would marry again for the sake of his young son. Nell herself was exhausted. She'd gotten little sleep since her *dat* had made the suggestion that she become John's new bride. And while it was true that she'd not found a man to marry on her own, Nell knew that she'd never find the love she'd once hoped to find in marriage. Not when she loved James, who could never be her husband.

Little Nicholas had taken to Nell as if she was the one who'd given him birth. Nell found out the reason why after learning just how ill Catherine had been since giving birth to her son. She'd been unable to take care of him except for short periods of time. Nicholas had spent time in several different neighboring households who cared for the little boy while Catherine had attempted to rest and recover. Only she never had.

The night she realized that she would soon become John Fisher's wife, Nell dreamed of Meg's hospital stay, of going for tea and hearing the beeping of life-support machines…and looking into a room and getting the shock of her life. Only it wasn't Michael in the room in her dream. The man in her dream was James, and when she saw him hooked up to machines, Nell cried out and fell to her knees. *"Nay! Nay!"* she screamed.

She woke, gasping for air, her heart pounding hard with the sudden concern that something had happened to her beloved James. She might not be able to have a life with him, but that didn't mean that she wouldn't think of him, worry about him, every single day for the rest of her life. Whether she was the bishop's wife or not.

Nell recalled little Nicholas and wondered if her screams had frightened him. She looked next to her to the empty space and remembered that Leah had taken him to sleep with her for the night. Nell had suffered from lack of sleep since learning of the child's mother's death. Leah had suggested that if Nicholas was with her, Nell might be able to rest without worry and with the possibility of sleeping late.

She rose and went downstairs. Her head hurt. Her heart ached. She didn't know how she was going to go through with the wedding. Because of Nicholas's age, *Dat* thought she and John should marry quickly. Nell wanted to wait until November, after the harvest, when it was wedding time.

"There is no reason to wait, Nell," her father had said time and again. "John's a widower. Widowers don't have to wait until the month of weddings."

"I want to wait," Nell insisted. "Unlike John, I have never been married. Don't I deserve a wedding like the other young women in our community."

"Nicholas needs you."

"I need the time. I'm happy to care for Nicholas before the wedding. There is no reason to wait for that."

And so her father had relented. Even John, Nell realized, seemed relieved. What kind of future would they have if both of them married only for the sake of a child?

An unhappy one, Nell thought, but then she didn't expect to be happy without James Pierce in her life.

The number of appointments had increased in Pierce Veterinary Clinic. James tried not to think of Nell's upcoming marriage to the bishop as he kept himself busy seeing patients during the week and worked hard in Adam's furniture store on Saturdays.

He was amazed at the change in his business. He'd gone from worrying about his finances to raking in money. He should be glad. It was what he'd always wanted, but he realized that he was never going to feel successful. Because he was missing something—someone—vital in his life. *Nell.*

Two weeks had passed since he'd given her the child's belongings he'd retrieved from the bishop's house. He wondered if she was happy. Was she looking forward to her marriage? Did she love the thought of becoming Nicholas's mother for real?

He wondered how her dog, Jonas, was faring. If she had been one of his *English* clients, he would have called and found out if Jonas had suffered any ill effects from his bee sting. He could have stopped by the house and visited Naomi, seeing if there was anything Nell needed in the way of shots or food or cat toys.

"Last patient before the weekend, Dr. Pierce," Janie said as she entered the back room. "Exam room four."

"Thank you, Janie."

The last patient was a simple checkup with shots. He was tired when the day ended.

He came out to the front desk to hand Michelle the last patient's summary.

His receptionist eyed him intently. "Have you heard from Nell?"

He shook his head. "No. She's busy taking care of Nicholas Fisher. She's going to marry the boy's father."

"And you're going to just let her?"

"What else am I supposed to do? She belongs to the church. I'm considered an *Englisher*, and she can't marry me without serious consequences."

A small smile curved Michelle's lips. "So you've thought of marrying her," she said with satisfaction. "You love her." She shut down the computer and stood. "You should talk with her. Tell her how you feel."

He frowned. "You're awfully bossy lately." He sighed. "I appreciate the thought, but it won't help. I wouldn't hurt her with my love. If she marries me, she'll be shunned by her family and friends."

"If you were an *Englisher*."

He stared at her, puzzled. "I am *English*."

"But your family isn't."

"Yes, but…"

"Think about it, Dr. Pierce." She picked up her purse and went to the door. "I'm going home. I'll see you on Monday."

He couldn't help smiling at Michelle's attempts to throw him into Nell's path as he locked up and left. Even though there was no hope of that happening. Still, he drove out of the parking lot in the direction of the Stoltzfus residence. It wouldn't hurt to check on Jonas and Naomi…and to see Nell one last time before she became another man's wife.

"Hello! Is Nell home?"

Startled, Nell dropped a garment and spun. "James!"

"Nell, I didn't realize it was you. You look different with your kerchief." He smiled. "I hope you don't mind, but I stopped by to check on Jonas and Naomi."

"That's kind of you." She felt self-conscious in his presence. Wearing her work garments and taking down clothes didn't make her feel any less conspicuous and dowdy.

"Come and I'll show you where I keep them." She waved to her sister Ellie who was leaving the barn. Nell approached her, aware that James followed. "Ellie, would you please finish taking down the clothes?"

Ellie glanced from Nell to James and back. "*Ja*, I'll be happy to." She smiled. "Come to see her animals, I take it."

"I haven't seen Jonas since his bee sting, and Nell hasn't brought Naomi into the office yet."

Ellie met Nell's gaze. "I didn't feed either one. Wasn't sure if you wanted me to."

"That's fine, Ellie," Nell said. "I'll feed them. *Danki*."

She was overly conscious of the man beside her as they walked into the barn. "I did what I could to make them comfortable."

"Stop fretting, Nell. You love them. I know they're well cared for."

She stopped, looked at him and was shocked to see sincerity in his dark gaze…a small upward curve to his masculine mouth.

Nell heard Jonas's excitement as they drew close to his stall. He always seemed to know when she came to visit him. He'd bark and whimper and rise up on his hind legs as soon as he saw her.

"Jonas!" she crooned as she opened the stall door and went in. James followed behind her. "Guess who's here, buddy? 'Tis James."

"Hey, Jonas," he said softly. "May I examine you?" He bent and sat on the straw.

To Nell's delight, Jonas immediately crawled to James. He curled onto James's lap and looked up at him with big brown eyes. "How's your nose?" James bent and examined the injured area. "It looks good. All healed, huh?"

"*Ja*. He's suffered no ill aftereffects."

"Good." James smiled. "I brought you an EpiPen to keep on hand in case it ever happens again. I know Jonas wasn't allergic, but that could change if he gets stung again. Also, if he ever gets stung in his mouth, don't wait, Nell. Bring him in immediately. Okay?"

"I will," she promised, frightened by the thought. "I've kept him away from our flower beds."

James looked approving. "Unfortunately, you can't always avoid bee stings. Sometimes bees show up when you least expect them. Oh, and, Nell?"

She met his gaze. *"Ja?"*

"The same goes for hornets or wasps. Hornets and wasps will keep stinging. A bee loses its stinger, but they don't."

"I've never been stung," she admitted.

"I have, and it hurts terribly. Putting vinegar on it was the right thing to do. Remember that remedy if it happens to you or to Nicholas."

Tension rose between them at the mention of Nicholas.

Nell's kitten, Naomi, woke up and clambered over to James's side, easing the strain of the moment. She tried to crawl onto his lap beside Jonas. Nell saw that James looked surprised when Jonas allowed it. He shifted a tiny bit so that the kitten could snuggle against both of them.

Drawn to be included, Nell sat next to James. She could feel the heat of his skin when his hand accidentally brushed her as he moved Naomi into a different position.

"I'll take her," Nell said.

He handed her the kitten, his eyes never leaving hers. She experienced a flutter in her chest as she carefully took Naomi and held the cat to her cheek. "I love how she purrs."

"Like a motorboat," James agreed. "A soft one."

James gazed at the woman before him and experienced a painful lurch in his chest. He cared so much for her that it was a physical ache in his gut. The thought of her married to another man agonized him.

He realized that he should leave, but still he lingered. He shifted Jonas a little and reached for his medical bag. He quickly found what he was searching for and handed it to her.

"The EpiPen."

Nell looked at the pen, then accepted it. "How would I use it?"

He showed her how it worked. Then he placed Jonas carefully in his bed and stroked him one last time before he pushed to his feet. "I should go."

He had plans to be with family again this weekend. Nell surely had plans with the bishop and his son.

She set Naomi down and started to rise. James held out his hand and after a brief hesitation, she accepted his help. He released her hand as soon as she stood. He stepped back.

"Remember you don't need to call first if either of them is having an issue."

She murmured her agreement, and he followed her as she led the way out.

Emotion got ahold of him, and he stopped. "Nell."

She halted and turned. *"Ja?"*

"I—I care about you." He tried to gauge her reaction. "A lot." He heard her intake of breath, the way she released it shakily. "I know that you're going to marry the bishop, but—"

"James—"

"I know."

She seemed to struggle with her thoughts. "I care for you, too. But you know it won't work. I'm a member of the Amish church. I joined years ago. I can't leave, or I'll lose my family."

"I know," he whispered. "I won't say any more. I won't tell you how I wish you were mine."

"'Tis better this way. With you, I'd be shunned."

He felt a sharp pain. "I know. I'd never want that for you." He stiffened his spine, lifted his head and managed a smile. "I should go."

She nodded, turned, and continued on. James gazed at her nape beneath her kerchief and the back of her pretty spring green dress and tried not to feel devastated. Why did he have to fall in love with someone he couldn't have?

Always polite, Nell walked him to his car, and waited while he got in and turned the engine.

"Take care, Nell. Please don't let what I said stop you from seeking my veterinary services. I just had to say it one time. I won't make you uncomfortable again."

"Goodbye, James."

"Have a happy marriage, Nell."

He shifted into Reverse, backed up a few feet and made the turn toward the road. He pulled onto the pavement and saw the car too late to avoid it. The impact jerked him forward painfully, then forcefully bounced him back against the seat. And then he felt nothing.

Chapter Fifteen

Nell watched James drive away with a sinking heart. She knew he was upset. She would be marrying John, and there was nothing either of them could do but accept it.

She saw the flash of his car's right blinker, watched as his dark head swiveled as he checked both ways before he pulled out onto the road. She turned away, unable to watch the final moments of his departure. Then she heard a high-pitched squeal of tires, followed by a loud crash.

Nell took off running. There was the sound of a skid, then she saw the blur of a white vehicle as it whizzed past. Gasping, she reached the street and saw James slumped over the steering wheel of his Lexus.

As she ran forward, she glimpsed the pushed-in left front of his car, the tangle of broken fiberglass, metal and glass. She realized that James was sandwiched between his seat and the air bag. And she screamed.

"James!" Frantic, she ran to his driver's side. "James! James!"

"I'm all right," he muttered.

"*Nay*, don't move! You'll hurt yourself!"

"Nell! We thought we'd heard something!" Leah and her other sisters rushed to help.

"We need someone to call 911! We need to call 911!" Nell was beside herself as hysteria threatened to overwhelm. "How do we get to a phone?" The closest phone booth was down the road. "James needs help now! What do we do? What can *I* do?"

"I have a cell phone," Ellie said, pulling it from beneath her apron.

Nell stared, hoping she wasn't imagining things. "You have a cell phone?"

"What?" Ellie said defensively. "I clean for *English* families. They have to be able to reach me. The bishop approved it." She tugged on a pocket sewn to the underside of her apron.

"Thanks be to *Gott!*" Nell exclaimed. She didn't care that the phone and Ellie's pocket were deviations from the *Ordnung*. Pockets were fancy, but Nell didn't care. She was too happy, so very happy that her sister possessed both.

"Please, Ellie," she whispered. "Call 911." Close to James's window, she leaned in, mindful of the glass. "We've called for help."

James was barely able to nod. The air bag had deflated and finally she could see him. "Nell," he murmured.

"Don't talk. Don't move! Please, James!" She sounded high-strung, but she didn't care. This was James, the man she loved. Her recent nightmare about him in a hospital room came back to taunt and scare her.

Please let him be all right, she prayed. *Please, Lord. He's a* gut *man. Please help him. Please help me.*

It wasn't long before the ambulance arrived along with a local police officer. The EMT examined James, and as a precaution, the man used a brace to secure James's neck. Nell had to stifle a cry at the sight of it. She didn't want to upset James, who already had suffered enough.

The men carefully extracted him from the vehicle. They placed James gently on a stretcher, watchful of his condition and any unknown injuries.

The officer questioned Nell. "Did you see what happened?"

"I didn't see the accident. I saw James look both ways before he pulled onto the road. I turned to go back inside when I heard the sound of the impact, then of another car speeding away."

"Sounds like a hit and run," the officer said.

"Is James all right?" Nell asked anxiously.

"They'll be transporting him to the hospital to make sure," the technician said. "Things could have been worse."

Ja, he could have died. Nell couldn't keep her gaze off James who lay on the stretcher, looking frightfully vulnerable. She addressed the EMT. "May I talk with him a moment before you take him?"

"Not for long. We need to transport him—and the sooner the better."

Nell flashed her sisters a look. "Go," Leah said. "You don't have much time."

She was trembling as she approached the stretcher. "James," she whispered. "Are you *oll recht*?"

"I'll be fine, Nell."

"Your nose is swollen. You're going to have two

black eyes." But she still thought of him as the most handsome man she'd ever known.

"The air bag," he breathed with a weak smile. He closed his eyes and exhaled.

"May I call the hospital to see how you are doing?" she asked, feeling suddenly shy.

He opened his eyes and focused his dark gaze on her. "Yes, if you want to."

"Do you want me to tell your family?"

He gazed at her with pain-filled dark eyes. "Yes, please. They'll be worried when I don't show. I planned to spend the weekend with them again."

"I'll go to them as soon as you leave," she promised, glad that she could be of help. "What about Michelle? Would you like me to call her, too?"

"No need. I'll give her a call if needed. I hope that I'll be examined and then released in a few hours."

Nell nodded, but she sincerely doubted that James would be staying anywhere but the hospital for a while.

"Time for him to go, miss," the technician said.

Nell stepped away, but she couldn't stop looking at him, caring…loving him. She shed silent tears. It didn't matter if she shouldn't care or love him. The only thing that mattered—and hurt—was that when he was well again, she would no longer have an excuse to see or talk with him. Her tears fell harder.

Her sisters joined her, standing around to offer her comfort as Nell watched the ambulance workers pick up James's stretcher and load it into the back of the vehicle.

Nell wiped away her tears and hurried forward. She needed to see him one last time. "James!"

"Nell." He gave her a genuine smile. "Don't worry."

She swallowed hard as she fought unsuccessfully to stop crying.

"Nell," he groaned.

She blinked, managed a grin. "I will talk with you soon."

And then they took him away. Nell stood a moment and as the ambulance drove away, her tears fell, streaking silently down her cheeks.

Leah slipped an arm around her waist. Ellie hugged her shoulders. Charlie stared a moment at the disappearing vehicle before she turned to Nell. "Let's get going. You need to tell the Troyers what happened."

Nell strove for control, drew herself up. "Will you take care of Nicholas for me?" she asked Leah. She heard a sound behind her and saw that Meg had readied the carriage.

"We'll go with you. I'll tell *Mam*. She'll be happy to watch him."

"All of you want to go?"

"I'm happy to watch Nick, but what will the Troyers think if all five of you drop in to give them the news?" *Mam* said, coming up from behind.

Blushing, concerned with how things might look to her parents, Nell said, "It might cause them more worry."

"Leah, Ellie, you go with Nell," *Dat* said. "Meg, you can help with Nicholas. Charlie, you can help your *mudder* with supper." His gaze was shrewd as he studied Nell. "He will be fine, Nell, but we will pray for him."

"Danki, Dat."

Within minutes, Nell and Ellie were in the family

buggy as Leah drove at kicked-up speed toward the Troyers'.

Nell was still shaking. She stared ahead with her hands clenched in her lap. All three sisters were in the front seat. Ellie placed her hand over Nell's.

Nell blinked and turned her hand to squeeze Ellie's. "I'm glad you're coming," she admitted.

"We're sisters, and we are always here for you."

Nell thought that she might need her sisters more than ever in the coming weeks and months. During James's recovery. During her marriage—if she could go through with it—to John Fisher.

"Nell!" Matthew Troyer greeted them as they pulled into the yard.

Nell climbed down from the buggy with her sisters following. "Are your *eldres* home?"

He nodded. "What's wrong? Has something happened?"

"I'd like to tell all of you," she said quietly, but then she relented. "James was in an automobile accident." Her voice broke on the last word.

His face blanched. "Come inside."

They hurried toward the house while Nell's sisters waited outside.

"Mam! Dat!" he called as they entered the main hall.

"In the kitchen, Matthew!" his mother responded.

They entered the room to find the family getting ready to sit down to supper.

"Nell," Ruth greeted warmly.

Nell was unable to manage a smile. "I'm afraid that I have serious news. James was in an automobile accident this evening. He's in the hospital. He spoke with me before the ambulance took him. I think he'll be all right."

"Nay," his mother whispered as she rose, swaying. Adam immediately got up and put his arm around her.

Nell heard his sisters cry out, and she felt for them. She loved James, too, and knew it hurt to hear such terrible news.

A knock on the back door heralded her sister Ellie. Matthew opened it and invited her in. "I called Rick Martin," she said with the cell phone still in her hands. "He's on his way. He'll take you to the hospital."

"Danki," Ruth and Adam said at the same time.

The whole family was obviously devastated by the news.

"What happened?" Adam asked.

Nell explained that James had stopped in to check on Jonas and Naomi. "He told me before he left that he planned to spend the weekend with you."

"Ja," Matthew said. "He likes to visit on weekends and help with the farm work." He blinked rapidly, then drew himself up. "We like having him."

"We just got him back," his sister Maggie cried. "We can't lose him now."

Nell inhaled sharply. She didn't want to think about James dying, she didn't want to think about anything except for him to be walking through that door and awarding her his wonderful smile.

Impulsively, Nell reached out and gently squeezed his sister Maggie's hand.

Rick Martin arrived, and Nell watched as the Troyers piled into the car and left.

Nell returned to the buggy with her sisters. Ellie and Leah gave her a hug.

"He'll be *oll recht*," Ellie said.

"I hope so." Nell climbed into the buggy. She closed her eyes and offered up another silent prayer. *Please, Lord, allow James to heal. Please let him be well.*

At home, Nell and her sisters got out of the carriage and went into the house.

"How are the Troyers?" *Mam* asked as they came inside.

"Understandably upset," Leah said.

Nell wasn't hungry, but she knew her parents would worry if she didn't eat.

"Dinner is ready," Meg declared.

Nell sat at the table with her family, but the sick feeling in her stomach made it difficult to eat.

James had a doozy of a headache. His nose hurt, and his face, shoulders and chest felt like they had been beaten with a piece of wood. But all in all, considering what could have happened, James felt fortunate. He was alive and eventually would heal. Unless there was some injury the doctors hadn't discovered yet. Soon he would know.

He thought back to the moment of impact. A white sedan had been speeding in the opposite direction when James had made the right turn. For some reason he couldn't begin to fathom, the car crossed into his side of the road, only pulling back at the last second, crashing into the driver's side of his Lexus. If it wasn't for the air bag deployment, he figured he'd have been hurt a lot worse.

What had shocked him, however, was that the driver of the car had taken off. He'd been stunned and unaware of himself for a moment, but that lasted only several seconds. The next thing he heard was Nell's scream.

"Mr. Pierce," a nurse said as she entered his emergency room cubicle. "Your family is here."

"Are they allowed back?"

"Not all at the same time. Who would you like to see first?"

He immediately thought of Nell, but of course she wouldn't be with them. Would she?

"I'd like to see Adam please. Adam Troyer, my father."

The nurse left and moments later returned with Adam.

Adam came to the side of the bed, his expression worried, his brow creased with concern. "James, *soohn*, are you *oll recht*?"

"I'll live. I'm waiting for them to take me to X-ray." He managed a smile for the man who'd had nothing but love and patience for an angry teenager. "Is *Mam* ok?"

"She's worried as we all are. She'll come in next." He gazed at James, no doubt noting his swollen face, cut forehead and bruised nose and black eyes. "When your *mudder* sees you..." Adam began.

"*Ja*, I know." James shifted slightly and grimaced. "I needed to see you first so that you can prepare her."

"I will. I'm glad to see you awake and talking. We imagined the worst when we heard the news from Nell."

"Is she all right?" James asked quickly.

"Shaken up, but she gave us the message. Tried to ease our fears, but that's hard to do when you envision your *soohn* in a car crash, hurt, unconscious. Bleeding."

"I'm sorry, *Dat*."

Adam waved his apology aside. "You did nothing wrong." He paused. "Nell…she must care for you a great deal."

"She does?" James asked with hope. But his hope died a quick death. Nell was going to marry the bishop.

"How do you feel about her?" Adam asked.

"I…" He looked away, stared at the curtain surrounding his hospital bed.

"You love her."

"Which is why I should stay away from her. Nell is a member of the church. There can be no future together for us." Although he'd like nothing more.

"What makes you think you can't have a future with her? You have the power to change your situation. Nell doesn't. You could come home, join the church and marry Nell."

For a moment, an idea that Michelle had given him appealed. "I can't." He sighed. "I spent all of my dad's money to become a veterinarian. I wanted to follow in his footsteps."

Adam pulled a chair closer to the bed and sat down. "And you went to school, worked hard, became a veterinarian and from what I hear from others, you are a *gut* one."

"Business is picking up."

"But why does having one thing negate having another? Members of our Amish community need basic veterinary care for their animals. It would be a simpler life, 'tis true. You wouldn't have your fancy car."

"The totaled car?" James commented with amusement.

Adam's lips twitched. "*Ja*. But James, I may be wrong, but you seem happier and more at peace when you stay at the farm. 'Tis almost as if you've missed the life."

James didn't say anything as thoughts ran through his mind. "I am happier there." He grew silent as realization dawned. "I do miss it."

"So? Why can't you return to the Amish life and still be a veterinarian? You'd be more of a country vet than a city one. It would be different, but it would be just as rewarding."

"It's something to think about," James agreed. Life in the Amish community with Nell as his wife? It sounded like the closest to heaven that a man could ever come to. If he still had a chance and Nell chose not to marry John.

Adam stood. "Your mother will be fretting. I'm going to leave and tell her to come in."

"Danki, Dat."

Adam placed a gentle hand on his shoulder. "We can talk later."

"You won't tell *Mam*? Or anyone about my feelings for Nell?"

"For now. But if I were you, I'd talk about them with your *mudder*. She loves you and can offer a woman's side of things."

James nodded. He watched the curtain close behind Adam. Moments later, it opened again, and his mother walked in.

Nell didn't feel well. The food she ate settled like a lump in her belly. She knew she wasn't good company and that she should be spending more time with Nicholas. While her family moved to the great room after cleaning up after supper, Nell put Nicholas to bed, then went to sit on the front porch. The day lengthened, and darkness fell.

Was James all right? How was his family? The worry about James consumed her to the point where she felt physically ill. She loved him. He was an *Englisher*, and she had no right. He had obviously made the choice to leave the community and she couldn't ask him to change. She thought he had some affection for her. But love? His loving her would only complicate matters.

Nell heard the sound of a buggy—the clip-clop of a horse and the noise of metal wheels rolling over gravel before she saw the lights of the vehicle. As the carriage drew closer and stopped, she saw a flashlight flare, and someone stepped out, illuminated by the golden glow. It was James's sister Maggie. She realized that James's family was in the buggy behind her.

Nell felt instant alarm. "Is James *oll recht*?"

Maggie smiled. "He'll be fine, Nell." She approached and placed her hand on Nell's arm. "*Danki* for all you did for him."

Nell exhaled with relief. "Is he home?"

"*Nay*. He's still in the hospital. They want to keep him overnight and maybe one more day. He's battered and bruised, and he broke his collarbone. He won't be working at the clinic for a while, I'm afraid."

"*Ach, nay!*" Nell couldn't imagine James not working at the clinic for any length of time. Recalling how much being a veterinarian meant to him, she knew it would upset him to stay away.

"*Danki* for stopping by and telling me." It was late. His family didn't have to go to the trouble of letting her know, but she greatly appreciated it. She wondered if she would have been able to sleep if she didn't.

"We didn't just stop for that," James's sister said. "James wants you to use this until he gets out of the hospital."

It was his cell phone. Maggie extended it toward her, and Nell accepted it, her mind reeling from his thoughtful concern for her.

Maggie smiled. "He'll call you. Said he wants to talk with you himself."

She swallowed hard. "That's kind of him."

The other young woman nodded. "I should go."

Nell walked her to the buggy and the rest of the family who had remained inside. "I'm glad that James will be *oll recht*," she told them.

"We are, too," his *mam* said, echoed by Adam and his other siblings.

"*Danki* for what you did," Matthew said quietly.

"I did what I needed—wanted—to do. No thanks necessary."

Once Maggie was settled in the vehicle, Nell stepped back, clutching James's cell phone against her.

"Nell!" Maggie called as the buggy moved. "James said you can charge the phone at the clinic."

Nell hadn't thought about the phone battery dying. What if there wasn't enough charge left to answer James's phone call?

The Troyer family left, and Nell went back to the house. She entered the great room. "I think I'll head up to bed. Nicholas hasn't woken up, has he?"

"*Nay*," her mother said. "He's sleeping soundly." She smiled. "*Gut* night, Nell."

Her siblings echoed her mother's good-night. Her

father eyed her carefully. If he noticed the cell phone in her hands, he didn't comment. "Sleep well, *dochter.* You did well today."

Blinking back tears, Nell murmured good-night, then quickly spun and headed toward the stairs. James's phone felt warm to the touch. It felt like she was holding his hand. She sighed, feeling close to him. She couldn't believe he'd sent her his cell phone.

After reaching the top landing, Nell walked the short distance down the hall to her bedroom. She looked inside, but didn't see Nicholas. She paused. Did Leah put him in her bed again?

She checked and found him sound asleep just as her mother had said. She was surprised to see that someone had brought in a crib for him. Why they'd put it in with Leah, she had no idea. She would ask them in the morning, not tonight. Not when she was expecting James to call at some point.

She hit a button on the phone, saw the face light up and was relieved to discover that the phone was fully charged. She set it carefully on her night table. James would probably call her tomorrow. She could rest easy tonight at least. She looked forward to talking with him. Just to assure herself that he is all right, she thought.

A short while later, Nell fell asleep and slept through the night until the soft ringtone of the cell phone next to her bed woke her the next morning.

Chapter Sixteen

"James?"

"Yes, Nell."

Nell closed her eyes. The sound of his deep familiar voice moved her through an ever-changing realm of emotion. "How are you feeling?"

His slight chuckle quickly died. "Like I've been run over by a truck."

She inhaled sharply. "I'm sorry."

"What for?" His genuine puzzlement filtered through the phone connection. "You have nothing to be sorry about." He paused. "Thank you for coming to my rescue."

"I didn't do much."

"Nonsense. You did a lot. You got me help. Told my family. Cared."

Nell's heart started to thump hard. "I did what anyone would do." But it was more. She loved him, but she shouldn't. Still she couldn't hang up the phone.

A few seconds of silence. "Maggie said that you'll be staying another day in the hospital."

"Yes. Unless they decide to release me sooner. I

have some bruising they are concerned about…and my head. I think once they see I'm all right, the doctor will allow me to leave."

Nell couldn't forget the awful image of him trapped in his car behind the airbag. Her mind switched to her awful dream, and she gave a little sob.

"Nell? What's wrong?"

"You were in a car accident."

"I know, sweetheart. Believe me, I know."

He said it with such dry humor that Nell couldn't help but laugh. She missed this man. How was she going to live without him? His endearment warmed her as much as it frightened her. She had to believe that it was his condition and pain medication.

"*Danki* for giving me the use of your cell phone. I was worried about you. 'Tis *gut* to hear your voice."

He didn't immediately reply, and a tense awareness sprang up between them. "I feel the same. It's good to hear your voice. It's not the same in the office without you." She heard him draw a breath. "I miss you."

"James—"

"Nell, it's okay. We're just talking."

He was right. "*Ja*, just talking," she agreed. "Maggie said you won't be able to work in the clinic for a while. What will you do?"

"I'm going to call an old college buddy of mine. We both attended Penn Vet, and we both took our first jobs at the same animal hospital after graduation. I left the practice, but he still works there. I'm hoping that he'll be able to get away for a time and fill in for me."

And if he doesn't, Nell wondered, *then what will you do?*

"If it doesn't work with Andrew—that's his name,

Andrew Brighton. He's English." He chuckled. "To you, we're all English, but Drew is truly an Englishman. He's from Great Britain."

"He has an accent?" she asked, and her lips curved into a reluctant smile.

"You like men with accents?" He made a growl of displeasure. "Ignore me. I'm hurting, and it's almost time for my pain pill."

"I should let you go."

"Yeah. The nurse is here to take my vitals." A voice asked him something on the other end of the line, and Nell heard James mumble something in reply. She wished she could see him. It was reassuring to hear his voice, but she wanted to see him so she could gauge with her own eyes how he was faring.

"Nell, are you still there?"

"*Ja*, I'm still here."

"May I call you again?"

How could she say no? *"Ja."*

"I'll call you after lunch—about one?"

"I'll be here." She should remind him about Nicholas, that the little boy might need her, but she didn't.

"Have a good morning, Nell."

"Feel better, James."

"I already am…after talking with you."

And with that, he hung up.

Nell stared at the phone, wondering what she was doing—what they were doing. She was going to marry the bishop! She shouldn't be talking with James. It was wrong. Just as wrong as it was to love James.

She tried but couldn't convince herself to return James's phone to Maggie. No, she needed—enjoyed—talking with him too much.

One o'clock came and went, and Nell grew worried. What if James's condition had taken a turn for the worse?

She started to panic. She flipped open the phone, pressed some buttons. She read the word *Recents* on the screen. She saw the time next to the number. Was that his hospital room telephone number?

She was behind the barn in the pasture. Leah was in the house with Nicholas. *Mam* and her other sisters had gone into town. Her father was at Aunt Katie's with Uncle Samuel. He had said he wanted to ask her uncle about adding on to the house.

Dare she call that number? She was concerned. If he didn't call soon, she would call the hospital…

The phone vibrated in her hands as she heard the familiar ringtone. She didn't know what the tune was. The only music the *Ordnung* permitted was the hymns from the *Ausbund* that they sang during church services.

The music continued, and Nell broke away from her thoughts to answer.

"Nell? Are you there?"

"*Ja*, James. Are you *oll recht*? I was worried."

"I'm sorry. I know it's later than one, but the doctor was in my room, and I couldn't call."

She experienced a knot in her belly. She had a mental image of him in bed, ill, sore, hurting. She closed her eyes, tightened her grip on the cell phone.

"What did the doctor say?"

"That I'm doing well. I'm being released this afternoon."

"You're going home?"

"Not to my apartment. I live over Mattie Mast's Bakery. The doctor wants me to avoid stairs."

Where would he stay? "You'll be staying with your family," she guessed. It made sense. He'd be comfortable, cared for, and he already enjoyed his weekends there.

"Yes, I'll stay with my mother and Adam. I've called Rick Martin. He's going to come for me when the paperwork for my release is ready."

She heard movement as if he were shifting the phone. "Will you come see me?" he asked.

Dare she?

"You can bring me back my cell phone."

"When?" she asked as she felt her face heat. Fortunately, he couldn't read her thoughts or see her blush.

"I'll borrow Rick's cell to call you once I get to the farmhouse."

Silence reigned between them for several seconds, which seemed longer. "Nell? Will you come?"

"*Ja*, I'll come." She could sense his relief that she would be visiting. "I know that you're eager to get your phone back."

"No, Nell. I'm eager to see you."

"The nurse will go over your instructions, then you'll be able to leave," Dr. Mark Keller said.

"Thanks, Doc."

The man smiled. "I'm glad it was nothing serious, James. It does upset me to think that I'll need to find another vet. I like you and so does Fifi." He grimaced as he said the name. "Frankly, I'm not particularly happy with my wife's name choice for our miniature French poodle."

James grinned. "Maybe you can tell her that it's too common for French poodles, that yours is special, and she needs to come up with a name that is unique."

Dressed in green scrubs after having been on call for most of the night, the man looked like the competent and confident surgeon and internist that he was. However, his expression lacked confidence as he talked about dealing with his wife about their dog. "Any suggestions?"

James gave it some thought. "None that immediately come to mind." He grinned. "Check the internet. Find some fancy French name."

The Kellers had come into his office a while ago with their miniature poodle that was just old enough to be taken from its mother. They had brought her to him straight from where they'd gotten her. This was their first puppy.

"The internet." The doctor laughed. "I'll do that."

James felt dizzy as he swung his legs off the side of the bed.

"Remember to take it easy. Don't go into the office for any reason for at least two weeks." He paused. "You have a broken collarbone," he reminded him.

James sighed. "I know."

"It will be longer before you can see patients—about six weeks. What will you do?"

"I called a friend of mine to cover for me."

"Is he good?"

"Yes, he's good," James assured him. "We went to school together, worked in the same practice outside Philly."

The doctor looked relieved. "Maybe we'll get lucky and won't need a vet before your return to work." He looked over his shoulder at someone James couldn't see. "There is an officer here to speak with you. Says he found the hit-and-run driver."

James closed his eyes as another wave of dizziness swept over him. "Okay. Send him in."

"James—or should I say, Dr. Pierce?"

"James is fine." He managed a smile. "I'm your patient. You're not mine."

The doctor's mouth curved briefly in response. "Do you need another pain pill?"

"No, I already feel as weak as a baby lamb."

"Nevertheless, I'll send a prescription home with you. Given where you're going, I'll also have it filled in the hospital pharmacy. I'll ask the nurse to wait until it's filled before releasing you."

"Thanks." James stopped the doctor as he started to leave. "What about *Abella*?"

The man looked thoughtful, then his features brightened. "I like it. Now I just have to convince my wife."

Dr. Keller left, and the police officer entered the room. "Mr. Pierce," he greeted. "I'm Officer Todd Matheson. We found the person who hit you…"

James was told it was a teenager. A seventeen-year-old girl. James experienced a myriad of emotions as he listened to what Officer Matheson was telling him.

"She saw a rabbit on the road. She swerved to avoid hitting it."

James could understand the quick reflex that would have someone trying to preserve an animal's life. Who would understand better than he about valuing an animal?

"What will happen to her?" James asked. "You won't press charges, will you?"

"It's complicated. She did surrender herself at the station." James was surprised to see concern flicker across the officer's features. "I think there's more to it," the man said. "She was sobbing, crying hysterically, when she came in. She kept saying, 'Don't tell them. Please don't tell them.'"

"Who?" James asked.

"Apparently, she's in the foster care system. She didn't want her foster parents to know. It was almost as if she is terrified of them."

James frowned. "Does she have reason to be?"

"She was driving their car. Maybe she was afraid she'd get in trouble."

"Do you believe that?"

Officer Matheson shook his head. He looked quite intimidating in his police uniform, but there was something about him that told James the man was more compassionate and caring than most.

"Can you find out?" James hated the thought that a young girl had made one mistake that could make her life more miserable than it already was.

"I'm certainly going to try."

Later, as he sat buckled carefully into the passenger seat of Rick's car, James thought about the girl who had hit him and run. His mind naturally veered to Nell. What if it had been Nell who was the seventeen-year-old driver? Of course, she'd had a much better upbringing than Sophie Bennett apparently had. And she was Amish and would never get behind the wheel of a car. *Sophie.* That was the girl's name.

"You feeling all right?" Rick asked.

"Sorry. Preoccupied with what I learned today." He saw the man's curiosity and decided to satisfy it. Rick

Martin had been a godsend to his family. Telling him about Sophie was the least he could do.

"The police found the hit-and-run driver." James went on to tell him about the girl, the officer's suspicions and James's own concern for a teenager he'd never met.

"I hope they go easy on her," Rick said. "Sounds like they might need to find her a safe home with loving foster parents who will take good care of her."

"Yeah." James couldn't agree more.

A few minutes later, Rick pulled the car into the Troyers' driveway and drove close to the house.

"Thanks, Rick." James reached gingerly into his front pocket, trying not to wince at the ensuing pain. He pulled out a few bills that he'd taken from his wallet earlier. He'd put his wallet in the bag with his medication and paperwork.

"No." Rick placed a hand on his arm to stop him. "No payment. I won't take it. You helped our guinea pig, Tilly. Our daughter was beside herself until you took a look at her." He continued, "You wouldn't let us pay. Said it was nothing. But it was something to Jill and to me. So, no, I will not take your money—ever."

"Rick—"

"Ever, Doc. Or you or your family won't get another ride from me."

James stared at him in shock. Then he saw the tiny grin that hovered over Rick's lips. "Oh, I get it." He smiled. "Thanks."

"You're welcome."

"Does this mean that I can borrow your cell phone if I need it?"

He handed James his phone. "What happened to yours?"

"A friend has it."

James quickly made the call, was glad when Nell picked up after the first ring. "I'm home," he said. "Just arrived."

"How are you feeling?" Nell asked with concern.

"Fine."

"When do you want me to visit?"

"Now?"

"I'll be there soon."

"Okay. I'll see you soon."

James ended the call and handed Rick back his phone, grateful when the man didn't ask him who he'd been calling. "Thanks."

"The phone call will cost you," the man joked.

James laughed. The door to the Troyer house opened, and every member of his family came hurrying to see him.

"Gang's all here."

"Nice gang," Rick commented.

James agreed. "Yes, the best."

The door opened, and Adam reached in to help him rise. His mother and sisters fussed over him while Matthew stayed behind a few moments, apparently to discuss something with Rick.

Once inside the house, with his mother on one side and his stepfather on the other, James was escorted to the great room where he was lowered into a comfortable easy chair.

"We've set up a bed in the sewing room for you. You'll have plenty of space. We didn't want you to go up and down the stairs. This way you'll be comfortable, and we'll be close if you need us."

"Danki, Mam. Dat." His gaze swept over his siblings, including Matthew who was carrying the plastic bag from the hospital. "All of you."

"You look pale," Maggie said. "Do you have your medicine?"

"It's in here," Matthew said as he approached and handed it to *Mam.*

His family all stood around him, making him feel slightly uncomfortable. He stared back at them. "What?" he finally asked.

"Your poor face."

"It's bad?"

"Could be worse," Matthew said.

They all laughed, and the tension that had crept into the room dispelled.

"Tea!" *Mam* exclaimed.

"Mam?" James called her back. "Make enough for one more?"

She gave him a curious look.

"Nell is coming. She likes tea, I think." He tried to keep his thoughts private and quickly said, "She's bringing back my cell phone."

Mam nodded, and she along with his sisters headed toward the kitchen while discussing what food they'd serve once Nell got there.

She came within the hour. James heard her voice as she entered through the kitchen. He suddenly felt like a nervous schoolboy. Ever since he'd talked about her with Adam, he couldn't get the possibility of her in his life out of his mind.

Dr. Drew Brighton would start on Monday. Much to

James's delight, when he'd talked with his friend this morning, he'd learned that Drew was tired of his job at the animal hospital. He'd grown up in a rural area, and the city life was starting to get to him. "I'd love a chance to help you out," the man had said in his thick British accent.

And that got James to thinking. He wouldn't mention it to anyone. Not until he knew if it would work or not.

Nell walked into the room, stealing his attention immediately. She was a vision of loveliness in her purple dress and black apron and prayer *kapp*. He gazed at her as she approached, holding his cell phone. She seemed shy. He heard her inhale sharply as she drew near.

"James," she gasped, "your injuries!"

"I look like a bit of a monster, don't I?"

"*Nay*, not that." She took a chair next to his. His family, James noted, had thankfully made themselves scarce. "I'm sorry for your pain."

He regarded her with affection. "I'm fine."

"You don't look it!"

"You sound as if you care," he teased. He saw something in her expression that gave him pause.

"I care. We're friends, *ja*?" She stared at him, looked away. "Have you forgotten about John?"

"How could I forget?" he said. "Although I'd like nothing more."

Nell was more than a friend, and he figured she knew it. But for now, she believed that she would be marrying the bishop, unless he could figure out a way to convince her otherwise.

"*Mam*'s making tea. Will you stay for a cup?" he asked.

She nodded and happened to glance down at the

phone in her hands. "Here." She extended it to him. *"Danki."*

He accepted it and placed it on a nearby table. "You figured out how to work it easily enough." He should be thanking her for letting him call her. She could have refused the phone, and he would have had no way to talk with her. It was her voice that brightened his day, made the pain of his injuries more bearable. *Nell soothes me as she does the animals.* His lips twisted. What did that say about him?

"Ja, it took some learning, but it wasn't as hard as I thought. It's not what they call a smartphone, is it?"

He shook his head, unable to pull his gaze from her face. "No. It's just a flip phone. I don't like fancy technology. It's wasted on me." He loved the color of her hair…her warm brown eyes. The warmth of her smile when she was amused. The rich vibrancy of her laughter… He sighed, glanced away.

She chuckled. "Like your office computer." Her brow furrowed. "What's wrong?"

"Nothing. Everything's fine." He returned his focus to her with a smile, drinking in the sight of her as a thirsty man longs for a glass of cold water.

She stayed just long enough to finish her tea and have a piece of cake. It seemed like she'd just arrived when she stood and said she had to leave.

"Stop by again, Nell," Maggie invited.

His sister Abigail had collected the dishes and stood with a pile in her hands. *"Ja*, Nell, come see us." James's mother, Ruth, and sister Rosie echoed his other sisters' sentiment.

James watched Nell interact with his family. They

liked her, a genuine like and respect that told James that Nell could easily become a member of the family.

Nell turned her attention his way. "Take care of yourself, James," she said. "Feel better soon."

"Will you come see me?"

"I don't know." She blinked, looked away, then glanced back. "I will if I can."

The fact that he couldn't get her to agree worried him. What if he was wrong about Nell's feelings for him? What if she wanted to marry John and be a mother to his son, Nicholas? He watched helplessly as she paused in the archway as she was leaving and met his gaze.

And then he held on to hope. Joy filled his chest, stealing his breath as he saw a longing that mirrored his own. If he could have risen without aid, he would have gone to her. For now, he could only keep his feelings to himself and watch her leave, until he knew whether or not all would go according to plan.

Chapter Seventeen

James had called Michelle and Janie after he'd confirmed with Drew that his friend would cover for him while he was recuperating. Michelle had been extremely upset to learn about his accident. When she'd asked how it happened, he told her that someone hit him on the road near Arlin Stoltzfus's place.

"I'm glad Nell was there for you," she'd said softly.

Janie was more matter of fact about his injuries. "I'll help Dr. Brighton get situated in the office." Then she'd wished him a quick recovery.

Midmorning on Monday, James called the office to speak with Drew. "How are things going?" he asked.

"Fine. You've got a busy practice," Drew said. "I never imagined you were this successful."

"Ha! Didn't think I had it in me, huh?" James couldn't bring himself to confess how hard things had been before they'd suddenly got better. "Does it bother you to be working in a successful practice?"

Drew snorted. "No, not at all. In fact, I'm enjoying myself." He hesitated. "Take all the time you need."

"I will." James had a sudden thought. "Drew, stop by the house on your way home tomorrow, will you?"

"Be happy to. Haven't seen you in a while. I'd like to get a glimpse of how ugly you've gotten with that banged-up face."

Drew had been staying at James's apartment since Sunday night. The arrangement worked well for both of them. It was nice to know that someone he trusted would be living in his apartment while he stayed with his mother and Adam.

"Funny," James said with a laugh.

As he closed his cell phone, he got more comfortable in the chair and shut his eyes. He must have dozed, because the next thing he know it was late afternoon.

He blinked and focused as someone came into the room.

"*Gut*, you're awake. You've skipped lunch. I'll make you a snack."

"*Mam*," he said as she turned to go back into the kitchen. "I've asked my friend Drew to stop by."

"The one who is running the practice while you're recovering?"

"Yes."

"Does he like tea or coffee?"

James chuckled. "The man's a Brit—from England. He's a tea man all the way."

His mother eyed him with amusement. "Will he be happy with zucchini cakes and lemon squares with his tea, or do I need to pull out my recipe for scones?"

"I'm sure whatever you have will be fine."

Just before suppertime, Drew appeared and stared down at him aghast. "You look like a Sasquatch attacked you, James."

"Sasquatch?"

"The huge, hairy caveman people say they've seen living in the woods. You look dreadful."

"Thanks, Drew. I appreciate the sentiment."

The British man grinned. "All right, that might have sounded a bit dramatic."

"You think?"

"But seriously, James, you look awful."

"So I'm told." He studied his old friend and realized that he missed Drew's dry sense of humor and quick wit. "I've got a proposition for you."

Drew folded his long body into a nearby chair. "Do tell."

And so James did.

Drew cocked his head as he listened. "Seriously?" he asked. "Wow, I never thought this of you."

"When you know, you know." James stared at him. "Do we have a deal?"

Drew smiled slowly and stuck out his hand. James grabbed it and they shook it twice, then again. "Deal."

James beamed, feeling hopeful for the first time in his life.

Nell steered her buggy into the clinic parking lot and to the back of the building. A black SUV was parked in James's spot. For a minute she stared, recalling the wonderful times she had working with James, learning about the man, falling in love with him.

But now it was over, and she'd never again have a reason to spend time with him. She would consent to marry John as soon as possible. She would only allow herself one more visit this afternoon to see how he was faring.

With a silent sob, she got out, hitched up her horse then circled the building to enter through the front door.

Michelle sat in her usual spot behind the desk. "Nell!" Her eyes widened with delight as Nell approached.

"Lunch?" Nell asked of the girl she'd gotten to know since she'd first brought Jonas to the clinic. The two women had shared an instant connection.

"Definitely!" The other woman stood. "Janie just showed in the last patient. I'll tell Drew that I'm leaving and ask Janie to handle the last check-out."

Nell sat while Michelle went into the back room. The woman returned within minutes and smiled. "Last patient is almost done. Do you mind waiting?" She lowered her voice. "I'd rather check out the last one myself since it's so close."

"I'll be happy to wait."

Michelle grinned.

Nell picked up a dog magazine and leafed through it. She looked up when she heard voices and watched as a tall, handsome blond man in a lab coat escorted a woman with a cat carrier to the front desk. Nell felt a jolt. She recognized the cat owner.

"You have nothing to be alarmed about, Mrs. Rogan. Your kitten will be fine. I suggest you keep her away from Boots for a while…or at least Boots's food." The man was obviously British. His richly accented tone was pleasing to her ear. *James's friend Andrew Brighton.*

"I will," Edith Rogan promised. The older woman turned, saw her sitting in the waiting room. "Nell!" she greeted with obvious delight. "How are you?"

"I'm well, Mrs. Rogan."

"I miss seeing you in the office."

Nell smiled. "I enjoyed working here."

"Why are you here? Is something wrong with kitty?" Mrs. Rogan asked.

"Nope," Michelle piped up before Nell could answer. "She's my lunch date."

"Naomi is wonderful," Nell assured.

Mrs. Rogan looked pleased. "Enjoy your lunch, Nell. It was nice seeing you again."

"You, too, Mrs. Rogan."

Nell rose as the woman went to the door. Mrs. Rogan halted and turned. "I was sorry to learn what happened to Dr. Pierce."

"*Ja*, it was terrible."

"He doing all right?"

"He'll be fine. I thought I'd stop by and visit with him later today."

"You give him my regards."

"I will, Mrs. Rogan. Thank you."

"Aren't you going to introduce us?" a rich British voice asked.

Nell turned and met the man's curious gaze.

"This is Nell Stoltzfus," Michelle said. "Nell, Dr. Andrew Brighton."

"It's nice to meet you, Nell," he said with gray eyes that regarded her warmly.

She felt her face heat. "Nice to meet you, too."

Michelle watched the exchange with amusement. "We're going to go, Drew. I'll be back in an hour."

"Take as long as you like," Drew said, withdrawing his gaze from Nell.

"I'll take the rest of the day," Michelle teased.

"Better not," the man quipped. "It seems Nell here has plans for the afternoon."

Michelle grabbed her arm and escorted her to the front door. "Come on, Nell. Don't let this Brit embarrass you."

"Embarrass her!" he exclaimed. "That wasn't my intention!"

Michelle grinned as she shut the door, blocking out his words. "He is just too easy to tease!"

Nell laughed. "You are terrible."

"I know. Don't you love it!" She pulled Nell toward her car. "No offense, but I'm driving."

"Where are we going?"

"I know a little place," Michelle said.

Ten minutes later, they were seated in Katie's Kitchen in Ronks, sipping on fresh-brewed ice tea and enjoying their delicious yeast rolls with the restaurant's signature peanut butter spread. Nell had been there before and enjoyed their food.

"So you're going to see James today," Michelle said after the two had caught up on news of their families.

"*Ja.* I haven't seen him since the day after it happened."

"You visited him in the hospital."

Nell shook her head. "*Nay.* At his family farm where he's recovering." She took a sip of her ice tea. "Have you heard from him?"

Michelle finished chewing a bite of roll before answering. "Yesterday. He called to speak with Drew." She smiled. "He sounded good. Said he was feeling better."

"He was really hurt, Michelle. His face…" Nell blanched as she recalled the accident.

The other woman reached across the table to squeeze Nell's hand. "You were there. It must have been awful."

Nell released a sharp breath. "You have no idea." She shifted uncomfortably when Michelle's gaze sharpened.

"Dr. Brighton is working out?" Nell said, changing the subject.

"Oh, yes. He is wonderful. He's like James in many ways. Both are kind and compassionate men with a deep love for animals."

Nell smiled. "I'm glad James was able to call on someone to help so quickly."

"Yes. You won't believe how busy we've become!"

Nell was glad. She'd done all she could to help James build his practice, handing out his business cards, getting others to hand out cards and recommend the clinic…spreading the word throughout her Amish community.

All too soon, Michelle's lunch hour was up, and they were heading back to the clinic.

"We'll have to do this again," Michelle said with warmth as she pulled into the lot and parked. The women got out and met in front of the vehicle.

"*Ja*, I'd like that."

Michelle encircled her with her arms. "Great to see you. Take care of yourself."

"I will. You too."

Michelle went inside, and Nell suddenly experienced nervous excitement as she unhitched Daisy and climbed into her buggy. It was time to see James. She both yearned for and dreaded the visit.

Last time. Soon, James would be well and back to work, and except for the rare occasion when she might need to call on him for her animals' medical care, she wouldn't have much opportunity to see him.

Losing Michael had been devastating, because Michael had died while he'd been on his way to her. But losing James would be different. She was older now, and she'd had a chance to mourn Michael's death.

When she left James this afternoon, she knew she would feel destroyed. She was glad that James would be out there in the world, doing what he loved to do. It was her only comfort. But him being so close yet out of reach was going to hurt her like nothing else ever had.

James was still sore but feeling better. He knew his face was black-and-blue. His sister had used his battered looks to coerce him into staying put in the chair. But he could no longer remain inactive. He knew he looked terrible, but thanks to ice and time to heal, the swelling around his nose had gone down. The ache in his muscles had become bearable with no need of medication to help him with the pain.

He knew he'd been given orders to rest for the next two weeks, but he was going crazy. Maybe if he just went outside for a little while. Surely, he could sit on the front porch and read or something. Anywhere but the inside of the house which he loved but had had enough of for now.

He stood and went into the kitchen. His mother and sister Abigail were at the table, snapping green beans they had picked from their vegetable garden.

"You should have called out if you needed something," *Mam* said.

"I had to move. Seems like I've been sitting in that chair for months."

His sister smirked. "James, 'tis only been five days."

He sighed. "I know. I'm not used to the inactivity. I want to be outside helping *Dat* and Matt."

"We can't allow you to do that."

The kitchen windows were open, and a light breeze blew into the house helping with the heat.

"'Tis a while before supper. Do you want something to eat?"

"If I eat any more, I'll gain ten pounds."

His sister ran her gaze the length of his lean form. "Doubt it."

Her dry tone made James smile. "I'll have an ice tea." When his sister started to rise, he said, "I can get it."

He saw his mother put a hand on his sister's arm as if to stop her from objecting. James moved stiffly to the refrigerator where he took out the pitcher. He shifted more slowly closer to the cabinet where the glasses where kept. "Do either of you want a glass of tea?"

"I'll have a glass," Abigail said strangely. James flashed her a glance and saw an amused look on her pretty face. She looked so much like their mother, but her hair was blond while his mother's hair was a sandy brown.

"In the cabinet," James teased, filling his own glass before setting down the pitcher. He felt slightly unsteady as he moved toward the table and pulled out a chair.

"If you sit here, we'll put you to work."

By this time, James was feeling awful. "I think I'll go sit in the other room."

"Don't spill that tea," Abigail taunted with a laugh.

"Brat!" James chuckled as he carefully returned to the great room and took a seat.

A window on the one side of the room was open and faced the driveway. James sat and closed his eyes while wondering what Nell was doing. She had said she would visit again, but it had been four days since he last saw her and he missed her like crazy.

He heard the sound of buggy wheels as a vehicle came down the driveway. *Dat* and Matthew must be back after going to the store to pick up chicken feed and a few other supplies.

He leaned back, closed his eyes. He heard the kitchen screen door slam shut, but he didn't move. Then he sensed someone enter the great room and stare at him. And he knew immediately that it wasn't his father or Matthew.

His eyes flickered open and he thought he was imagining things because he'd wanted so badly to see her. "Nell."

She hesitated in the doorway between the hall and the great room. "James."

"Come in and sit." Then it occurred to him that she might have come for some other reason than to see him. He frowned. "If you have other business and don't have time…"

She came forward and took the chair across from him. "I came to see you."

He couldn't help the grin that burst across his lips. "I'm glad. I've been wanting to see you. Talk with you."

She looked surprised. "You were?"

He picked up his glass. "Would you like some ice tea?"

"That would be nice."

"Abigail!" he shouted. He met Nell's beautiful brown gaze with an amused smile.

"Already got it, *bruder*," Abigail said curtly as she handed Nell a glass. "I don't mind waiting on her."

His sister stayed in the room and hovered.

"Abigail, *danki*. Now please leave us to visit alone," James told her. "I don't need you hovering."

With a sigh of exasperation, his sister left. Nell had a strange look on her face as she stared at him.

"I'm sorry," he said, worrying what Nell was thinking.

"I'm not."

"What?"

"You and your sister…you're just like me and mine."

He released a sigh of relief. "I love her."

"I can tell."

"I love you."

She froze. "What?"

"I said I love you."

She seemed shaken as she looked away. "James, you shouldn't say that. You know I'm marrying John."

"My friend Drew is joining the practice. He's staying."

Nell looked confused. "That's nice. I heard that business is up. You'll need his help."

"Thanks to you." He had learned recently just how much Nell had worked to grow Pierce Veterinary Clinic.

She blushed, looked away.

"Drew is going to be working at the clinic while I work from home."

Nell arched her eyebrows. "You're going to work out of your apartment?"

James gazed at her, watching every nuance of her expression, hoping for a glimpse of her thoughts, something that told him she cared for him more than as a friend. He had told her he loved her, but she hadn't reciprocated. Or did she brush off his feelings because she was Amish and he was English and she was afraid to acknowledge them?

"For a while I'll be living here. *Mam* and *Dat* assured me that it would be all right. Matthew doesn't mind sharing his room for a while." James reflected how his relationship with Matthew had greatly improved since he'd begun to spend time at home.

"You're going to be living here," Nell said. "Why?"

"I'm rejoining the community. I plan to join the church come November."

Nell's mouth opened and closed as if she didn't know what to say.

"I don't understand…"

"If you'd listened to what I said, really listened, you'd know."

Nell stared at the man she loved, unsure of what he was saying. She was afraid to hope, afraid to love, but at the same time, she was terrified of no longer having him in her life.

Now he was telling her that he'd be moving back to the Amish community. Had she only imagined that part because she'd wished for it?

"Nell." He rose from his chair, crossed the distance between them and sat down next to her.

She met his gaze with longing and hope…and everything she was afraid he'd see in her expression. "Why are you telling me this?"

He took hold of her hand, capturing it between his larger ones. His dark eyes held a sudden intensity that stole her breath. He looked vulnerable with his twin black eyes and bruised face, but she could feel his strength. Dressed in a solid maroon shirt and tri-blend pants held up by black suspenders, James looked as if he had always been Amish, that he'd never left the community. He'd shaved recently, and his firm chin was smooth and drew her attention. What would he look like in a beard as a married man? She gasped as hope reared up, enthralling her.

"James—"

"I love you, Nell. I want to marry you if you'll have me. Will you forget John and become my wife?"

"But, James, you've been *English* for so long."

"That's true. I worked hard to be what I thought my father wanted for me. I went to school, became a vet-erinarian, worked near a city…and opened a practice here. But you know all that."

Her heart was pounding hard. James was offering her most secret desire—to be his wife, to live with him, have his children…to love him until their lives ended.

"I haven't been happy, Nell, in the *English* world. Not until you stepped through the door of my clinic with Jonas in your arms. You calmed me like you did him. I knew I had to get to know you. I figured right then that I wanted you somehow in my life."

He was running his fingers gently over the back of her hand. His caress tingled and thrilled her.

"Nell," he went on. "I'm happiest here in the com-munity. When I told Adam about my feelings for you—"

She felt a jolt. "You talked with Adam about me?"

His features were apologetic. "I needed his advice. I loved you and thought I didn't have a hope of having you in my life. Adam told me that above everything else, my father wanted me to be happy." He paused, and his hand cupped her face. "That I could easily be a country veterinarian working in our community." He drew a deep breath, released it slowly. "You make me happy. I love you. Please allow me to love you. Marry me."

Tears trickled down her cheeks as she gazed at him. "I said that I'd marry John."

"Does John really want to marry you because you're you? Or because he needs a mother for Nicholas?"

"He wants a mother for Nicholas," she admitted.

"Then it doesn't have to be you. Another woman will do."

She recognized love in his dark eyes. "I'm afraid."

He jerked. "Of me?"

"*Nay.* Of backing out of marrying John, of telling my father of my true feelings." She blinked back tears. "But most of all—what if you aren't happy with being Amish? I want you to be happy," she sobbed. "I don't want you to ever regret the choice you made. I don't want you to be sorry that you married me."

"Sweetheart." He wiped away her tears with his fingers. "I will never regret marrying you. Don't you understand? I love you—so much. Not having you in my life will kill me. You mean that much to me."

"I do?"

He nodded.

"Oh, James, I love you so much it scares me."

"Then you'll marry me?"

"I want to—"

"But?"

"We can wait. I need to know if you change your mind."

"Never! I will never change my mind." He drew her closer. "Nell, let me court you. We have until November before we can marry. Let me prove to you that this life—and you—are what I want more than anything in the world. So, Nell, sweetheart, may I court you?"

Basking in the radiance of his love, Nell felt warm and tingly…and so much in love. *"Ja."*

James groaned, and suddenly he was kissing her, a gentle kiss that made her feel special. He pulled back, his eyes glowing, his mouth curved in a tender smile. "I'm afraid it may be weeks before I can court you properly."

"I can wait."

"But you'll come visit me."

"Ja, James, I'll come," she promised. "Every day."

"And you don't love John."

"Nay, I love you. Always have. Always will.

"And you're going to marry me, not him."

"Ja, I'm going to marry the man I love."

She watched as his eyes closed as she heard him murmur, "Thanks be to *Gott.*"

And Nell had never felt happier. She loved this man, and she would pray every day that God would bless their marriage.

Epilogue

Summer slid into autumn, the months flying by so quickly that Nell wondered where the time had gone. As promised, James had moved all of his things into the Troyer farmhouse. Nell visited him every day while he healed, and afterward, the man spent every moment that they were together proving how much he loved and valued her.

It had been difficult for her to tell her father that she wouldn't be marrying the bishop. Telling the bishop himself had been easier, for as she'd thought, he wasn't done grieving for Catherine. He wasn't ready to marry again.

As for Nicholas, there were plenty of community women who were happy to help with the little boy's care. But as time went by, John kept the boy close with him more often than not.

The fall harvest had come and gone. James had purchased a small piece of property, and the community had worked during the last months building a home for the soon-to-be-married couple.

The house was perfect, at least to Nell. There was a

room for James's satellite veterinary office and plenty of space for the children she and James both hoped to have one day. James asked her to be his veterinary assistant. Nell quickly accepted the position.

Dr. Andrew Brighton was doing well at the clinic. Since Drew would be the only one working in that office, James had insisted that the clinic be renamed to Brighton Animal Hospital, but Drew had disagreed. The friends had compromised by adding Drew's name first to its current name, making it Brighton-Pierce Veterinary Clinic.

Their wedding banns were read in church. James had fit right back into the community, and each passing day had convinced Nell that he truly was happy and belonged.

The morning of their wedding finally arrived. Her parents' house had been transformed to allow for the wedding feast, and the wedding ceremony was at Aunt Katie and Uncle Samuel's.

After riding together while holding hands, Nell and James arrived at the Lapp farm, eager for the services, the ceremony, that would join them as man and wife.

Afterward, they got into the buggy driven by their attendants—Nell's sister Leah and James's brother, Matthew. Leah and Matthew were chatting about the ceremony, the day and celebration to come.

James leaned closed to Nell, his breath a soft whisper in her ear. "I love you, wife."

Nell smiled as she regarded him with love. "I'll love you forever, husband."

And then her husband of less than an hour leaned close and gave her a tender kiss that stole her breath, her heart—and bound her to him forever. James's head lifted; his dark eyes glowed. His face had healed, and he looked as if he'd never suffered in the accident. Her new husband was easily the most wonderful and handsome man Nell had ever laid eyes on.

She had everything she'd ever wanted—James, the man who loved her, her life's partner. *Thank You, dear Lord, for blessing us with Your love.*

* * * * *

If you loved this story,
check out the books in the author's
previous miniseries
LANCASTER COUNTY WEDDINGS:
NOAH'S SWEETHEART
JEDIDIAH'S BRIDE
A WIFE FOR JACOB
ELIJAH AND THE WIDOW
LOVING ISAAC

Available now from Love Inspired!

Find more great reads at www.LoveInspired.com

PLAIN RETRIBUTION

Dana R. Lynn

This book is dedicated to my family, who supported me through all the craziness. Love you. And to my Lord, in awe of His many blessings.

Acknowledgments:

Thank you so much to everyone who helped with this book. To my friends in the Deaf community, thank you for helping me to get into my heroine's head and understand her better. To Shelley Shepard Gray, thanks for sharing your experience and love of the Amish community. It made such a difference! To my critique partners and friends, thank you for reading and pointing out problems, lending a shoulder to cry on, or just sharing a cup of coffee and letting me vent.

Thanks to my editor, Elizabeth Mazer, and Love Inspired Books for all the hard work and support. You are amazing and I am so grateful for the opportunity to work with you.

A special thanks to my agent, Tamela Hancock Murray. Even though you are not the agent of record for this book, your advice and friendship have been invaluable.

Special thanks to my late agent, Mary Sue Seymour, a wonderful mentor and friend.

What shall we then say to these things?
If God be for us, who can be against us?
—*Romans* 8:31

Chapter One

She hated this time of night.

Rebecca Miller stepped outside and shut the shop's door behind her, taking care to lock it. The air was thick with the smell of wood smoke from the houses nearby. She rubbed her arms to ward off a chill—not all of it from the cool fall air. The hair on the back of her neck prickled. Was she being watched? Holding the key out in front of her like a weapon, she peered into the darkness. Nothing. Her brother Levi would have cautioned her against letting her imagination run wild. Her Amish mother would chide her for her lack of faith in the Lord's protection. Well, she had faith. But she had also learned the hard way that having faith did not prevent horrible things from happening. And she had the scars, mentally and physically, to prove it.

Her breathing quickened. She forced herself to breathe slowly. In. Out. In. Out. Better. Was she panting? Could anyone hear it? Levi had told her that hearing people could hear the sound of her rapid breaths when she was frightened. How accurate that was, she didn't know. She'd never heard breathing, or any other sound, in her entire life. Rebecca had been profoundly deaf since she had been born into her large Amish family. They hadn't put hearing aids on her. When she had left her Amish community instead of being baptized at seventeen, she had tried them, but didn't notice any difference. Now at twenty-five, she had no interest in trying them again.

She rarely allowed her deafness to hold her back, having spent years striving for independence in the hearing world, but sometimes she felt the lack of hearing keenly. Like now, knowing if someone was stepping closer to her, she'd never hear them coming.

She wondered again what had possessed her to agree—for the first time since she'd taken the job—to close by herself the bookstore she worked in. Every other time she'd worked this late, she'd had someone else closing with her. Granted, it was only a little after eight thirty in the evening, but in October, it was so dark out that it might as well have been ten o'clock at night. She shivered. Whether from cold or apprehension, she wasn't sure.

Sucking in a deep breath for fortification, she started across the empty alley to where her car was parked. Maybe she should have taken her best friend Jess's offer to let her husband, Seth, drive her home when he had finished his work shift. She could have waited inside the locked store until he came, and they could have retrieved her car tomorrow. Not wanting to put them out, she'd refused. Now she wished she'd accepted.

No. She shook her head. It was time she took care of herself and got over her fear of the dark.

In her periphery, a shadow moved. She flinched.

You're being ridiculous, she signed in her head. No one was there.

Her heart continued to thud inside her chest. Memories of the past started to cloud her thoughts. What if someone was out there, like before? Only, this time, she was alone. Of course, having people with her hadn't been enough to protect her back then.

Please, Lord, be my shield.

Holding her hand out, she pressed the key fob to unlock the car door. The headlights blinked, then remained on. In the sudden light, she saw her hand was shaking. She hated the fear that crawled inside her. The fear that kept her from going about her life like anyone else. Instead, she was constantly looking over her shoulder.

Just a few more feet, and she would be safe inside her car. She quickened her pace and practically threw herself into the car, then slammed the door behind her. Leaning back against the headrest, she let out a slow breath and felt her heart pounding inside her chest.

Remaining where she was, she flicked her gaze to the rearview mirror. And froze.

Cold, dark eyes glittered at her from beneath a dark ski mask. Someone was in her car!

Whipping around, she came face-to-face with a nightmare. The intruder shot forward and grabbed her by the neck and yanked her back against the headrest, trying to choke her. She couldn't breathe! Lungs burning, the keys fell from her hand as she twisted and turned, trying to break her attacker's hold. Both of her hands latched on to the arm around her throat. She tugged and pulled with all her might, but to no avail. Her eyes seemed hyperfocused, zooming in on every detail as adrenaline coursed through her system. She saw every hair on the arm that tightened around her throat, noted the sharp lines of the tattoo on his wrist. She struggled against her attacker's grip, but he wouldn't budge. Her knee banged against the steering wheel. She barely noticed it.

The alley was empty. There was no use hoping anyone would see her.

The man's grip tightened. Rebecca clawed at his arm as hard as she could, feeling several fingernails break off. Lifting one hand, she shoved it back into the attacker's face, stabbing her thumb into one dark eye.

The black-masked figure reared back and rubbed his injured eye.

She was free! But she wasn't safe. Not yet.

Before the villain could recover, Rebecca fumbled for the door latch and tumbled out of the car. Gaining her feet, she bolted.

Out into the alley and toward Main Street, she ran as fast as her long legs would carry her.

As she approached the end of the alley, the glow from the streetlights cast shadows on the buildings she raced past. The attacker's shadow loomed too close. And it was getting closer. Her attacker was only a few feet behind her! Leaning forward, she pushed herself harder.

A hand slid down her hair. She felt a few strands catch, rip out of her scalp. The pain was instant, but it wasn't enough to stop her. She kept running, even as her eyes watered.

She opened her mouth. She screamed. Whether it was loud enough for anyone to hear, she had no idea. But her throat was raw. And her energy was waning.

Almost there.

Her attacker grabbed her from behind and threw her to the ground. Rebecca skidded onto the ground. Gravel scraped across her palms, and she ripped her skirt.

She flipped herself over to a sitting position so she could see her assailant. As he rushed toward her again, she scooped up a handful of dirt and gravel and flung it at the disguised figure with all her might. Her aim was true.

There was a brief moment of satisfaction as he covered his eyes with his gloved hands. But she knew this wouldn't hold him off for long, so she didn't hang around to gloat. She jumped to her feet and ran out into the street.

And right into the path of a moving car.

The car veered slightly to the side and came to a sudden halt inches from hitting her.

Praise the Lord. She sent up an earnest prayer. It was a police car. She had almost been run down by one of LaMar Pond's finest. And now she had an officer to protect her from the attacker, who had to be closing in on her by now.

Shooting a panicked glance over her shoulder, she exhaled in relief when she saw her attacker had fled.

The police car door opened and a tall officer jumped from the vehicle and rushed to her side. He pulled her off the street and onto the sidewalk, under a streetlight. For the first time, she took note of his familiar features. Warm blue eyes, blond hair that tended to get shaggy. Miles Olsen. She sighed in relief. She had met the young officer last spring when Jess had been in danger. Not only was he a policeman, but he was also the only one in LaMar Pond who could sign.

"Rebecca! I almost hit you. What's wrong?" Miles signed to her in fluent ASL.

"You didn't see him?" she signed back.

He immediately straightened and peered into the alley she had just exited. "Was someone bothering you?"

"He attacked me. He was waiting in my car. I didn't notice until I'd already gotten in…"

She couldn't go on. The trembling started inside and worked itself outward until she was shaking so hard she could barely stand up.

A strong arm wrapped around her shoulder and led her back to the police car. Miles ushered her into the passenger side of the car then reached past her to flip on the hazard lights and grab a flashlight. He switched on the light and shone it back down the alley. Which, as far as she could see, was empty.

Activating the radio hooked to his shoulder, he said something into it. "I called for backup. It should be here soon," he signed to her when he finished. "You stay here. I'm going to lock the car and have a look around."

Rebecca started to protest. She didn't want to be a sitting duck all by herself if her attacker came back. Plus, the idea of being alone was terrifying right now. She wondered if this was what people meant when they talked about going into shock. It was hard to wrap her mind around what was happening.

Miles squatted, putting them on the same level with each other. Switching the flashlight to his left hand, he continued to sign with his right. "Don't worry. I will wait to canvas your car until help arrives. But I need to make sure he isn't hiding out nearby. I'll stay in sight. Okay?"

It made sense. As long as she could see him, there was no reason to panic.

She nodded. Miles swung the door closed. Placing her hand on the door panel, she felt the vibration of the locking mechanism sliding into place. Only then did she relax. Craning her neck, she watched Miles cautiously approach the alley and inspect it for hidden threats.

Several cars passed them. The flashing lights inside the dark car made her imagine shadows that weren't there. *Hurry, please*, she thought.

Five minutes later, he jogged back to the car and let himself in.

"I didn't see anything suspicious. I still need to examine your car. But I don't want to leave you here by yourself. Let me check on the status of our backup, and we can get this sorted out."

She nodded to show she understood.

Using the button on the dashboard, he placed the call. "They'll be here in a minute," he assured her, then turned off the hazard lights and moved his vehicle over to the side of the street. "I also called for the paramedics. Your throat looks bruised."

She grimaced, but didn't argue. Her throat was hurting.

He reached down for a notebook and a pen. "Okay," he signed. "I need you to tell me everything you can remember. Start at the beginning."

Sitting forward, she closed her eyes as she racked her brain to figure out the sequence of events. It was easier to focus on what had occurred if she wasn't looking at him.

"I work at A Novel Idea. I had agreed to close alone tonight. We stay open late on Wednesday nights. My boss, April Long, was going to visit her parents for a few days, or she would have closed with me, the way she usually does. I walked to my car, got in, looked into the rearview mirror—"

Abruptly, she stopped. The memory of those cold eyes glaring back at her had icy fingers running up and down her spine. She dropped her head into her trembling hands.

A hand tapping her left shoulder jolted her out of her fear. Moving her head so her cheek rested on her clasped hands, she glanced over at the cop.

"It's okay," he signed. "I know this is hard, but we'll figure this out."

Breaking eye contact, he sent a cursory glance down at the notes he had made. "So, did anyone else know what time you were leaving tonight?"

Tilting her head, Rebecca sucked her bottom lip into her mouth and chewed on it.

"I don't know. It's been on the schedule all week. Oh, I did tell one person—I was emailing Jess yesterday about something else, and mentioned that I'd be closing. She offered to have Seth drive me, but I told her I'd be okay." She pushed back her hair and plowed through the rest. "He was waiting for me inside my car. Tried to choke me. I stabbed him in the eye and tried to escape. But he caught me again."

Forcing herself to sign slowly and precisely, she described the attack.

"If you hadn't shown up when you did, he would have gotten me."

She could have died. Been kidnapped. Robbed. Beaten. Any number of horrible things could have happened to her.

Miles shoved away the anger that was burning in

his gut, tamping it down so it wouldn't show on his face. She'd been through a traumatic experience and he didn't want to scare her.

He didn't know the woman sitting next to him that well. She was close to Jess McGrath, now Jess Travis, and he knew that she and her family had helped Jess and Miles's friend Seth when they'd been in danger last spring. Thankfully, the ordeal had had a happy ending, with Jess and Seth managing to unmask their attackers—while falling in love with each other in the process.

They'd gotten married not long ago, and Rebecca had been at the wedding, as had Miles. He had even been asked to interpret for her and several other guests who were deaf or hard of hearing, like Rebecca and Jess. He'd assumed, since her brother was Amish, that Rebecca must have been at one time. But he had never tried to find out more. He'd ignored the initial spark of attraction he had experienced when he'd first met her, when Jess had been under attack. It hadn't been the appropriate time or place. Plus, he couldn't afford to mess up another case with his rash actions.

By the time the case had been closed, he'd convinced himself it was best to keep his distance. Sure, he could have found where she lived, or asked Jess for a way to contact her. But he had let the opportunity slip away. And anyway, she hadn't shown any interest in him.

No, he didn't know her well, but it bothered him when a young woman was victimized. He needed to be careful. He'd let himself act upon his anger once before when involved in a case, and it had almost ruined his career. Even though that time it was personal.

Very personal. Couldn't fall into that trap again. He was still trying to get back into his chief's good graces.

He asked her a few more questions, trying to get most of the details down while they were waiting.

Red and blue flashing lights caught his attention. A second police cruiser pulled up in front of his, then shifted back to parallel-park against the curb. Good. Jackson was here. And he hadn't come in hot. Lights, but no siren. If the attacker was still hanging around, there was nothing to cue him that backup had arrived.

"Okay. Sergeant Jackson is here. I'll have him start looking at your car while we finish this."

Miles opened his door and stepped out. Turning to Rebecca, he paused and took in her wide blue eyes and troubled face. At least her cheeks seemed to have some color, and her trembling had ceased. She looked calmer. Actually, she looked beautiful. If he hadn't met her previously, he would not have guessed her background, growing up Amish. Her skirt was long, but it was rust-colored with gold, brown and orange leaves on it. It was pretty on her. He pressed his lips together when his gaze fell on the rip at her knee. Her gold sweater was simple but elegant. Her pale hair was shorter than he remembered, ending just an inch or two below her shoulders. It made him think of summer, the way it shimmered gold.

What? That kind of thinking would get him nowhere.

"Olsen, what do ya know?" Gavin Jackson sauntered toward him. His voice was casual, friendly, but his gaze was in constant motion, sweeping the area for any threats. Keeping it concise, Miles brought him up to speed.

"Rebecca Miller? Hey, I remember her from Tra-

vis's wedding. Cute little thing." Jackson ducked down
to wave at the girl sitting in the car. Miles frowned,
not sure why it bothered him to see Jackson smiling
at her. But it did.

"Okay, Casanova. Let's process the scene."

Jackson's brows rose, but he made no comment
about Miles telling a higher ranking officer what to
do. Instead, the man shrugged and shifted back into
cop mode.

Between the two of them, they managed to get the
scene processed in a relatively short time. Miles kept
a close eye on Rebecca. She had refused to sit in the
car by herself. To be honest, he preferred having her
where he could keep an eye on her. By herself, she
wouldn't be able to hear the attacker return. And even
though having her accompany them meant she was out
in the open, exposed to another attack, it was hardly
likely that her assailant would come back with two officers so close.

When the paramedics arrived, Miles jogged over
to interpret for her briefly. He knew the paramedic in
charge, a serious blonde woman named Sydney.

Not surprisingly, Rebecca refused to go to the hospital. Sydney didn't push the issue.

"There's no bulging around the area. And your color
looks good," Sydney told her as Miles interpreted. "If
you have any trouble breathing or opening your mouth,
or if swallowing becomes painful, you need to go to
the ER. Immediately."

Rebecca nodded and thanked the woman.

Miles returned to Jackson.

Now they just needed to finish looking over the car,
checking to be sure it hadn't been sabotaged. It was a

possibility. Even in the light of day, the alley behind the store was empty. Only businesses. And most of the businesses closed at five. Chances were good that anyone could damage the car without fear of getting caught.

Inside the car, there were no prints, no clues left behind. The attacker had been careful. Except that the back locks had been jimmied. Something was lying on the floorboard. Flashing a light in that direction, he saw Rebecca's purse. It had been knocked over, the contents spilled everywhere. Why didn't women use bags that zipped? Seeing her phone, he snatched it up and brought it to her.

"Do you have anyone you can call tonight? Someone to stay with you?"

She nodded. It bothered him to see her so pale and worn. Even her signs were lackluster. "My roommate will be home later. She works until ten. She usually arrives home around eleven."

"Maybe send her a text. Let her know what happened so she'll know to come straight home." He handed her the phone, then left her while she composed the text.

"Pop the hood," Jackson called, scooting out from his position under the car.

Miles jogged around to the driver's side and leaned in to pull the lever. The hood released with a small click.

Jackson whistled.

"What?" Miles stepped up beside his colleague.

"Wow."

The engine had been incapacitated, the spark plugs nowhere to be found. One thing was clear—whoever had attacked Rebecca had wanted to be sure she couldn't get away.

"Do you think she was specifically targeted?" He took out his cell phone and snapped pictures of the engine. "Could this be random?"

His gut told him no. This kind of attention to detail took forethought and planning.

Jackson was already shaking his head, frowning.

"I don't think so."

"I don't, either." Miles shoved his hands in his pockets, watching Rebecca as she sat on the cement curb. She looked tuckered out. No wonder. "How does this play for you? I think the perp has been watching her for some time. Maybe a few days, maybe longer. It's possible he picked her because she was deaf. Thought she'd be an easy mark. He knows where she leaves her car, and what hours she works. Chances are he waited here for her."

"But if April hadn't left early, he would have had to contend with two women."

Jackson had a point. He went to Rebecca and posed the question. A minute later he was back.

"Not necessarily. Rebecca said April usually parked in the parking garage across the street. All he would have needed to do was stay down until she was out of sight." He rubbed the back of his neck.

The quiet was broken with a ridiculously raucous ringtone coming from his watch. Jackson's brows rose in amusement. Miles brought up his wrist and fumbled with the buttons, mumbling an apology. He'd left his earpiece in the car, so he moved slightly away from Jackson. It was the chief.

"Olsen here."

"Report, Officer Olsen," the chief of police ordered.

"Sir, the perp is gone and has left no traces we could find. He disabled the car, though. It needs to be towed. Jackson and I think he's been watching Rebecca for a while."

"Rebecca?" There wasn't any censure in the chief's tone, just mild curiosity.

"Sorry, sir. Miss Miller. I know her. Anyhow, we don't yet know why she was targeted."

"Ahh." He could picture the chief nodding as he leaned back in his swivel chair. "Even if the perp was watching her, it might have still been a random attack. Maybe he noticed she drove alone and parked in the alley and thought she looked like an easy mark."

"Sir, I'm going to drive Miss Miller home, and then come in and file paperwork."

"Very well. Does she have someone she could stay with?"

Miles cast a concerned glance toward her. Her arms were crossed on the top of her knees, and her head was down.

"Miles?"

Huh? Oh, right.

"Yes. She has a roommate. I had her text the woman and let her know what was going on."

"Good. I'm glad she'll have someone there for her," the chief responded in a smooth drawl.

Miles thought for a second, deciding his next move. "I also think we should try to get the visual artist in as soon as she's available to see if she can remember any details that might get some hits on the database. Oh, and see if the interpreter is available."

"If not, you could interpret if she waives her right to a certified interpreter."

Miles frowned. "Yes, sir. Although I think it would be better to have someone certified."

People didn't always understand that managing direct communication in sign language and interpreting at a professional level were two totally different skills. Just because someone could speak the language didn't mean they could expertly translate it into English.

"I agree. But interpreters are very hard to come by."

"Yes, sir. I will try to get all that scheduled ASAP."

"Sounds like a good plan." A pause. "Miles, I'm going to put you in charge of this case."

"Sir?" His heart thumped in his chest.

"You've been doing good work since you came back. I want to find this perp. And I think you've proven you can handle the responsibility. Plus, you can communicate directly with our victim, so that makes you the natural candidate."

"Thank you. I will do my best."

He tapped the face of the watch, disconnecting the call, joy bursting through his body. His first case as the lead. The chief trusted him again—he could finally put his past mistakes behind him. This had been a long time coming.

Then he looked at Rebecca, and some of the joy faded. As proud as he was to be lead in the case, he hated the idea that his victory came with the price of her horrible attack.

She was so vulnerable. Just like his stepsister, Sylvie, had been. Suppose this wasn't a one-time attack? Suppose the perp was a stalker, fixated on Rebecca? He would have his work cut out for him, finding the perp before he struck again. Oh, he'd been in on tough investigations before. Chief Paul Kennedy had been slowly giving him more and more responsibility as he had shown he could be relied on.

For some reason, though, this responsibility seemed heavier. Because it was quite likely that the beautiful young woman sitting a few feet away was still in danger.

Chapter Two

The trip to Rebecca's apartment was a quiet one. She'd given him the address, and off they went. Since he was familiar with the area, he didn't need to take the time to plug the address into his GPS.

The trip was silent, but not uncomfortable. Rebecca had calmed down. Once they were ensconced in his vehicle and moving away from the scene, the tension in her shoulders and face seemed to have eased. She wasn't happy, but neither was she panicked. Which was good.

As for Miles, he appreciated the silence. It gave him a chance to process the events of the evening and get a hold of his own emotions. He couldn't help but worry about how she was handling the pressure, though. He turned to look at her—her expression was smooth, unruffled. Could she really be that calm? He would have expected more panic, or at least signs of discomfort. He'd seen the bruises on her neck—they had to be hurting.

Get a grip, Olsen. She's not your sister. She's strong. And now she's your case. Keep it professional.

He was so involved in his own thoughts, he almost

missed the entrance to her apartment complex. Good thing Windy Hill Apartments had a large sign out by the road. Grimacing, he shifted on his blinker and spun the wheel at the last second, swerving hard into the driveway. In his periphery, he saw Rebecca put her hand on the dashboard to brace herself.

Bet that impressed her. Not.

What an awful parking lot to come into at night. It had one light, right in front of the entrance. But the rest was dark, the corners in the lot merging into the shadows and trees. Anyone could hide out in those shadows, and she wouldn't be aware of it until it was too late. Rebecca wouldn't be able to hear any telltale sounds that might warn her of impending danger.

Great. Now he was getting paranoid on her behalf.

He parked the cruiser under the light and switched off the ignition. Turning to face Rebecca, he paused when he saw her pensive glance. Her eyebrows squished together and her lips tightened. She flickered her gaze around the dark edges of the lot. Obviously, he wasn't the only one who found the place unsettling.

He tapped her on the shoulder once, to get her attention.

She glanced nervously at him. She was definitely disturbed by something.

"What's wrong?" he signed, folding his three middle fingers down over his palm while extending his thumb and little finger, then tapping the folded part against his chin.

She pointed to a window on the second floor. The curtains were open, and the lights were out. "That's my apartment. My roommate isn't home yet." Using the one-handed ASL alphabet, she finger-spelled her roommate's name. Holly Fletcher. "I knew she wouldn't be, but—"

"You are nervous about entering an empty apartment?" He raised his eyebrows and crooked the index finger of his right hand in a question mark.

"Yes."

She didn't look happy about admitting it. But at least she wasn't denying it.

"No problem. I will walk up with you and make sure it's all clear."

Nodding, she turned from him to get out of the car. But not before he saw the relieved smile that swept over her face.

Wow, she sure was pretty. Yeah, so not going there. Even though she was.

Back to work, Miles. You have a job to do. And then you need to leave.

Shoving those dangerous thoughts from his mind, he focused on the task at hand. He waited as she tapped in the five-digit entry code. Although not foolproof, the added security measure did make him feel better about her safety here. They climbed the single flight of stairs and walked to her apartment. When Rebecca moved to unlock the door, Miles held out a hand to stop her. Startled, she moved her gaze to his, her brows rising in a question.

"Give me your keys," he signed.

She dropped them in his open palm. He motioned for her to move back. As soon as she was away from the door, he leaned closer to listen for movement inside the apartment. Nothing. He unlocked the door as quietly as he could and signed for her to wait while he checked out the apartment. Her eyes widened as he removed his gun from the holster.

"Just a precaution," he signed.

Keeping his weapon at the ready, he moved through the apartment, checking each room. The kitchen was spotless. No sign of any disturbance. The first bedroom was clear. It was clean, like the kitchen, but he knew at once it was the friend's room rather than Rebecca's. Pictures of the attractive brunette with a hodgepodge of people and in a variety of settings covered the large corkboard on the wall, with some in frames on the desk and dresser.

The next room was obviously Rebecca's. The contrast was startling. The room was clean, but the decor was sparse. There were a couple of pictures. They all looked very recent, none dating back earlier than four or five years ago. And why would there be? The Amish didn't take pictures. Against the far wall, there was a large oil painting. It clearly showed a white farmhouse with a black Amish buggy in the front. It was so realistic, it looked like someone could reach out and open the door of the buggy. He peered closer to see the artist's signature, then whistled softly. Rebecca Miller. Wow. She had some mad talent.

On the desk under the window was an open laptop and several textbooks. A GED certificate was prominently displayed on the wall. That's right, he thought. The Amish only go to school through eighth grade. Right next to that was a college diploma. She had a bachelor's degree in art. It was awarded this past spring.

Giving in to his curiosity, Miles peered closer at the books. They covered topics ranging from the deaf community to the study of ASL and ethics and practices with interpreting for the deaf. Rebecca apparently aspired to get a CDI certificate. He'd only ever met one Certified Deaf Interpreter. They were highly sought after in improving communication with the deaf community in official settings. Good for her.

Returning to the living room, he found Rebecca standing inside the door, her back against the living room wall. Made sense. If you couldn't hear, you didn't want to leave yourself vulnerable to attacks from behind. Again.

"Nothing here. Are you sure you're all right? I can stay until your roommate gets back."

She was shaking her head before his hands stopped moving. "I'm fine. Thank you so much for checking. I feel silly, but I appreciate it."

He stepped closer to her and put his hand on hers to stop the apology, then pulled his hand back at the zing that shot up his arm. Her shocked expression told him all he needed to know. She had felt it, too, and by the look of the frown stamped on her pretty features, wasn't any happier about it than he was. Good. That meant she wouldn't expect anything. He ignored the twinge of disappointment.

He couldn't afford to get emotionally involved with anyone. Emotions had almost cost him his job once. In the end, he had kept his job, but had lost his rank as sergeant. That fact was brought home every time he put on his uniform without the insignia. All he wanted was to earn it back.

"I don't mind checking. I wanted to make sure you were safe." He looked at his watch. "It's almost ten now. Your roommate should be here in an hour. Let's trade numbers, and you can text me if you need anything. I'll text you to let you know if we have any leads."

They exchanged phones. He put in his number, then snapped a selfie so that she'd have a visual in her contacts. Oh, wait. Amish. He flicked a glance in her direction. She was shaking her head at him, a half smirk forming on her lips. Her face had more color in it now, he was glad to note. Her earlier pallor had bothered him.

"Sorry." He shrugged. "I can delete the picture if you want me to. I wasn't thinking."

"It's okay." She snapped a selfie of herself on his phone. "I'm not Amish anymore."

Amused, he chuckled. She was absolutely adorable. He took back his phone and synced it with his watch.

"I have never met anyone who left the Amish community before," he signed. Then he wondered if that statement bordered on rude. Although, bluntness was all part and parcel of deaf culture, so maybe she'd take it in stride.

She shrugged, her face rueful. "Not many do. It was a tough decision, but in the end it was for the best." She shifted her eyes past him, thinking. "I was the only deaf person in my family. My parents are great, but they never really learned to sign fluently. ASL is a hard language to learn, and there weren't that many opportunities for them to learn it in the community. They speak Pennsylvania Dutch and English at home. I was caught between three languages. Out of my family, only my brother Levi and my sister Lizzy can really sign to me. In my classes every day, I'd have a few people I could speak with easily, but then I'd come home and have to struggle to understand and be understood. It grew worse after I left school. There were no interpreters. I think my parents accepted my leaving because they knew that I didn't even understand what was happening at church. In the English world, though, I could be part of the deaf community. I had friends, and I was able to be a full participant."

He nodded. "My grandparents and uncle are deaf. They are very involved with the deaf community."

"So that's why you sign so well! I had wondered."

"Yeah. I grew up with it." He tilted his head. "Do you regret leaving?"

"No. I love my family, and I am grateful to still have a relationship with them. In fact, my oldest brother, Levi, is getting married in a week. On Thursday. I will be there. But someday, I want to get married, and I want my husband to be able to communicate with me. And if I have deaf children, I want them to have full access to the deaf community." She moved away a couple of feet. Restless. "Want to know what was really sad? Until a few years ago, I never even knew that Amish children say '*mam* and *dat*,' instead of 'mom and dad.'" She finger-spelled the Amish versions of the words. "I've never been good at lipreading, and wasn't able to really see the difference when I watched my siblings say the words. In my head, I always see the sign for 'mother and father,' but when I wrote, I wrote 'mom and dad.' Like the other kids at school. Levi read something I had written a few years back and pointed it out to me. He also took the time to teach me the written words and meanings of some of the other Amish words that were used daily, but that I never knew. I have taken pains to try to think of them as *mam* and *dat*, knowing that's how they would prefer to be called, but it wasn't automatic for me."

The urge to touch her hand, to offer comfort, sneaked up on him. He resisted. But it was difficult. The aloneness emanating from her posture as she signed just about killed him.

She's not alone now, he reminded himself. *She has friends in the deaf community. She has her faith. And her family does love her.*

And she has me.

No. She doesn't. I'm temporary. And I have stayed too long.

Lifting his wrist, he eyed the time on his digital watch. And whistled. It was later than he had thought.

"I need to go. Text me if you need anything," he signed with one hand, pocketing the phone. "And lock the door behind you."

She rolled her eyes, but complied without comment.

The second she had closed and locked the door, he was on his way to the station. It would take him twenty minutes to get there. If he worked fast, he should be able to have all his reports filed and all his duties completed by the time his shift ended at midnight. Unless, of course, another call came in. Wednesday nights were usually pretty quiet in LaMar Pond. He should be good.

An hour and a half later, he finished his reports.

With his work completed, his mind turned back to Rebecca. Had her roommate arrived home yet? Maybe he should send her a text to check on her. He quickly shot off a text.

Then he occupied himself while pretending he wasn't watching for a responding text. None came. No doubt her roommate had returned. She was no longer alone. Wilting back against his seat, he let out a sigh. It was after eleven thirty. Chances were good that she was asleep, or that she and her roommate were talking about the night's events and not paying attention to the phone.

Everything was fine.

But it wouldn't hurt to check on her in the morning, just to be sure.

Rebecca came awake with a start, heart pounding. Her hands flew to her throat—she could still feel hands closing around it. But as awareness seeped back in, she realized it was just a dream. No one was attacking her. She sat up, knocking a pillow off the couch in the process. A wave of dizziness attacked her. Closing her eyes, she breathed in deeply until the dizziness passed. When she could open her eyes again, she frowned. She was still in her skirt from work. She had fallen asleep after texting with her brother.

He didn't have a phone, so she had used the videophone to call one of her parents' neighbors who had agreed to let Rebecca's family know what had happened and that she was fine. Which had resulted in a long conversation with her brother. It took some doing, but she finally convinced him that she was okay and didn't need anyone to come to LaMar Pond.

A quick glance at the clock showed it was just past six in the morning.

She hadn't intended to spend the night on the couch. Why had Holly let her sleep? Her roommate usually woke her up if she fell asleep there. The couch was for sitting, not for sleeping. Holly had very definite views about that. So why change?

Rebecca stood and groaned as her back protested. Good grief, she was twenty-five, not seventy-five. She smiled at her silliness, then turned toward the bedrooms.

And every trace of her smile was wiped from her face.

Holly's door was wide open. As if Holly wasn't home.

Fear in her throat, Rebecca moved on leaden feet to the bedroom and flicked on the light.

The bed was made. Not a thing was out of place. The room was perfect. It made Rebecca's blood run cold.

Holly had never come home.

Her phone! There could be a text waiting for her. Maybe Holly had decided to visit her sister again. She had done it before.

Rebecca knew she was reaching. Holly always came home when she had class the next day. She worked so hard to keep her grades up at the small liberal arts college she attended—she wouldn't risk that to go visit her party-all-night sister. Except, sometimes Laurie hit rock bottom and pleaded with Holly until she felt guilty and went over. So there was a small chance. A very small chance, but it was the only hope Rebecca had to hold on to.

She hit the button on her phone and her heart thudded in her chest. One notification. She pressed the text icon. It was from Miles, sent late last night. Any warmth she might have felt that he had checked on her was drowned out by the knowledge that Holly hadn't sent her a text. Holly always sent a text if she would be late. She knew how much Rebecca worried. Holly worried just as much about any situation where Rebecca might be in harm's way. And why shouldn't she? She'd been there. They both had. For days, they had sat together, shackled in the dark, locked in that same small room. Waiting, as terror fogged their minds while hunger gnawed at their bellies.

But Holly and Rebecca had survived. Not all of them had.

Jasmine Winters hadn't made it out in time. She'd been strangled, mere hours before the police had broken through the basement door. They had all wondered who would be next...

No!

Rebecca squeezed her eyes shut and clenched her fists as she pushed that memory out of her mind. The darkness that tried to ooze into her mind didn't belong there. Not anymore. She'd banished that years ago, when she'd testified. When she and the other girls had put away their captor.

The memory of the trial made her shiver more. Would she never forget the face of their tormentor? He had been on his way to prison, and still he had held such control over the women he had terrorized. And he had known it.

He had control over her still—was still the face in her nightmares. What should she do?

Miles! He would probably check to see if she had responded to his earlier text. And he was a police officer. He'd know what to do about Holly.

Unlocking her phone, she pulled up his text. Her fingers trembled as she tapped out a message of her own, explaining the situation. She curled her lip as the auto correct kicked in, messing up a word of her message. She erased the word and started again. Many people would have sent the text anyway, trusting that he would understand. But this was too important. Plus, if she was honest with herself, she knew that people expected mistakes in her English, both because she had been Amish, and because she was deaf. It never failed to gall her. She hit Send.

Then waited.

And worried.

She tried to sit back down on the couch, but couldn't stay still. She bounced back up on her feet. She felt icky. Glancing down at herself, she grimaced. Not only was she still wearing yesterday's clothes, but her skirt was torn and wrinkled. And what if Miles decided to stop by when he got her text? She couldn't be seen this way. Ignoring the part of her that questioned why it mattered how she looked, she showered and dressed in clean jeans and an oversized royal blue sweater.

She checked her phone again. Still no word from Miles.

It was almost seven. She sent him another text, just in case the first hadn't gone through, then dragged out the Crock-Pot and started making chili. After she had the meat, beans and spices simmering, she stepped back and smirked at herself. What had she been thinking? She'd made enough to feed her parents and five sisters and brothers, when it was just she and Holly who lived in the apartment.

Holly.

Immediately, her mind was back in the middle of the current nightmare.

She glanced at her phone. The light was blinking. Maybe it was Miles. She clicked on the message, and his face appeared. The intensity of his blue eyes caught her unawares. Her breath caught in her throat. Those piercing eyes set in his honest face had attracted her from the first time she'd seen him. If only...

But it was no use. A man like him, strong and decent, wouldn't be interested in someone damaged like herself. Some of the members of her own community had been disgusted by what had happened to her all those years ago, even though she hadn't been to blame.

Besides, after what she had gone through, after what she had seen, she needed security in her life. A policeman who put himself in danger every day, no matter how handsome he was or how great he signed, was not on her list of possible mates.

Forcing her mind to accept the reality of her situation, she read his text.

Be there at 7:40. Jackson coming, too.

It was seven fifteen now. The sun was just starting to come up. She had almost half an hour. She'd go crazy just sitting here. To give herself something to do, she set about cleaning her already spotless apartment.

The light in the hall flashed. Someone was at the door. It had to be Miles and Jackson. The cautiousness she'd learned as a teenager wouldn't let her open the door without checking the peephole. Two men dressed in dark blue uniforms stood in the hall. She recognized the LaMar Pond uniforms. Miles and Sergeant Jackson. With a sigh of relief, she swung open the door.

The relief drained out of her when she saw how they looked. The tension emanating from the two men crackled like a live wire. She instinctively stepped back from them. Keeping her distance, she searched for clues in Miles's expression as he entered the apartment. The morning sunlight streaming in from the windows emphasized his serious expression. The downward curve of his mouth. The set of his strong jaw. Both spoke of a man on a mission. And an unpleasant one at that. Something bad had happened.

Fear lay in a leaden ball in her stomach. *Please, Lord, let everything be all right.* Even as she prayed, though, she knew everything was not all right. Something had happened to Holly. What? Sweat slicked her palms. She was about to find out.

Chapter Three

Her throat was dry. "We can talk in the kitchen."

Miles nodded, then turned to say something to Jackson. She was fairly certain he was relaying her message to the other officer. In the kitchen, she grabbed a bottle of water from the refrigerator, then held it up with a questioning look. Did they want one? Both officers shook their heads. Fine. She uncapped it and took a long swallow. It made her throat feel better, but nothing else felt any relief.

Her stomach hurt. Not sick hurt. Scared hurt. The way it always had as a child. The way it had when she'd been held against her will ten years ago.

She scraped back a chair at the table and sat down across from Miles.

"Can you understand okay if I switch to pidgin? That will make it easier to keep Jackson in the loop."

She nodded. Pidgin sign language used mostly ASL signs, but put them in English word order. This way, the signer was able to speak and sign at the same time. Not optimal, but she could follow along.

"Rebecca, I got your text this morning. I drove by the parking lot of the restaurant Holly works at. Her car was in the lot. But she was nowhere to be found. The manager said that she had left after she'd finished her prep work for the morning shift. That was around ten thirty. She never came back in. When he saw her car this morning, he thought she must have had car trouble and had someone pick her up."

What? That was absurd. If she'd left her car, she would have let them know so it wouldn't get towed. How could they not have realized something was wrong?

But she knew she couldn't really blame the manager. Holly's behavior at times was a bit erratic. She had already lost two jobs in the past for being unreliable. Mostly because she'd drop everything if her sister needed her.

"Her car was in disarray. Like someone had been shuffling through her things. Would she have left a mess if she was trying to find something?"

Judging from the skepticism scrawled across his face and seeping into his signs, Miles didn't think so. And Rebecca agreed. Her heart sank.

"Holly would never leave her things cluttered or messy," Rebecca informed him. His mouth was moving as he told Jackson what she said. She continued, "Disorder of any kind bothered her. I sometimes tease her that if there was a fire she'd make her bed before leaving the building."

The joke had made people laugh before. Not anymore.

"I want you to look at this picture," Miles signed. "Is

this the vehicle she would have driven to work yesterday?" He tapped the screen on his phone, then flipped it around so she could see the picture he brought up. It was a white Jeep. He swiped his finger across the screen. A second picture of the back of the vehicle. The familiar vanity license plate came into view.

She swallowed. Nodded. Any hope she'd entertained that there might have been some mistake disintegrated. Something caught her eye.

"Wait, what's that?" She pointed to a large blot of color on the side of the car. It was a dark smear. It hadn't been there the day before. It looked like paint. Or...

A wave of nausea hit her, causing her to sway. "Is that blood?"

Miles hesitated. But the answer was on his face even before he nodded.

Holly wasn't just missing—she was hurt. *Why, Lord? Hadn't she suffered enough?*

She pushed back from the table, stood and moved to the sink. She gripped the counter with both hands, so hard her fingers hurt. Her control was slipping. The trembling started in her insides and worked its way outward. The view out of the window above the sink blurred.

A warm hand settled on her shoulder. Miles's fresh scent washed over her a second later. Without thought, she turned and burrowed into Miles's shoulder, fighting back tears. He patted her awkwardly on the back.

What was she doing?

Stepping away, she wiped at her moist eyes. More to give herself a moment to regain control than because she was crying. As she wiped her sleeve across her eyes, she gathered up the courage to face him. The compassion she saw in his expression was almost her undoing. Almost. But she was made of stronger stuff.

"Sorry," she signed.

He shrugged. "Not a problem. It's a completely natural reaction. Here's what we need to do. I need to bring you into the station to ask—"

"But I've done nothing wrong!"

He raised his hands, made a calm-down motion. "I know. We just have some questions for you, and they should be answered at the station so that we can bring in a certified interpreter to make sure there's no confusion or misinterpretation."

What? she thought. "You sign. Your ASL is beautiful."

She watched, fascinated, as his ears turned bright red. It would have been cute in other circumstances. "Thanks. But it's the law. You need a certified interpreter. Unless you agree to accept me as the interpreter for now."

She sagged back against the counter. "Fine. I accept. I don't want to go to the police station. What do you need to know?"

Miles took his seat back at the table. Reluctantly, she moved to sit down again.

The conversation started very generally. Age, birthday, job. Then it got more specific. Where did Holly grow up? Who did she live with?

"How did you meet Holly?"

"We went to the same school for years. Holly was a year ahead of me."

Jackson said something to Miles, who interpreted,

translating it into sign. "You grew up in Spartansburg, right?" She nodded. "You lived in different districts. How did you go to the same school?"

She cocked her head at the officer. "Holly is hard of hearing. We were both bused out of district so we could attend the deaf program."

"Have either of you had an issue with violent boyfriends, or threats? Anyone hold a grudge against either of you at work?" Miles again.

She paused. "No."

But what about before? Was it relevant?

He waved his hand, drawing her attention back to him.

"If there's something that might be related, we need to know."

She drew a large gulp of oxygen into her lungs. She hated talking about this, and hadn't for years. Not even to Jess. But now she had to. Because Holly was in trouble.

"Ten years ago, when I was fifteen, I went out with Holly and three other girls from her school. Ashley Kline, Brooke Cole and Jasmine Winters. Ashley and Jasmine were older and had just graduated. Ashley was driving her mother's van and pulled over to help some guy who seemed to have broken down on the side of the road."

Abruptly, she stood and moved away from the officers. Memories of that day pulled at her, dragging her under. So much bad had come from one simple act of charity—stopping to help a stranger. Miles slowly got to his feet.

"Maybe we should go to the station."

She shook her head. She could do this. "No, I'm fine. There was just one man. He looked innocent enough. But he wasn't. He hadn't broken down. He was high on drugs and had stolen the car. When we stopped, he pulled out a gun and forced his way into the van and drove us to his house. He kept us locked up in the basement for two days. Until we were found."

She stopped. The memories were hitting hard and fast now. Overwhelming her. She could feel the cement wall against her back, smell the damp moldy basement.

Miles approached her carefully, as if he expected her to bolt. "I'm sorry you went through that," he signed. "And I hate that I have to ask you to relive it, but—"

"I understand," she interrupted. "It's for Holly."

"The man who abducted you, do you remember his name?"

As if she could ever forget. "Terry Gleason."

"Terry as in Terrence?"

She shook her head. "Just plain Terry."

Miles turned his head. Sergeant Jackson must have asked something. Miles nodded and then returned his focus to her. "The other girls, did they know the man?"

"I think some of them might have known him. Jasmine seemed to. She was the oldest. Already eighteen. And possibly Ashley. I don't know about Brooke. But I don't know from where. I didn't really know the other girls. And none of them could sign. Only Holly."

"You said you were fifteen? Did you still go to school together?" Miles pressed his lips together. She could almost see the thoughts running through his mind.

"No. I was still Amish back then so I only went to

school through eighth grade." Regret surfaced, but she pushed away the feeling. Now was not the time. "The deaf program was a small group of students in a public school with a teacher of the deaf. Most of us went to her for Language Arts. The rest of the day, we were in classes with hearing kids and interpreters. Jess, Holly and I were the only three girls in the program. Jess left soon after I did to go back to her home school. That's when Holly started to hang out with the older girls. I met her again a few years later. I was in the middle of my *Rumspringa*." She signed "running around," using the direct translation. That was the only sign for the word she knew.

"Whatever happened to the man who kidnapped you girls? Please tell me he went to jail."

She nodded. "He went to jail. So it probably wasn't him. I testified at the trial. My parents did not want me to. Law enforcement and trials are not something Amish people usually get involved with. But I couldn't not testify."

Miles nodded, sympathy deep in his eyes. "Did all five of you testify?"

The dark hole she kept closed in her mind started to open, letting a few images spill into her brain. She slammed it shut, but some things could never be unseen. "Not all of us. Jasmine was strangled the day we were rescued."

Miles paled. His jaw hardened. Jackson's lip curled and his nostrils flared.

"I had never seen such evil. He left the rest of us after he had killed her. The police came while he was gone. Two officers. He came in behind them and attacked them with a bat. After one fell, the other knocked him down and handcuffed him. I didn't learn until the trial that the other officer had died from a blow to the head."

The officers looked at each other. Some kind of communication went between them. Their expressions darkened.

Miles puffed out his cheeks. She thought he resembled a blond chipmunk. Then he let out the breath and her pulse fluttered. This was no cute little boy. The man who stood before her was all cop, and his eyes were fierce. She trembled at the way his gaze sharpened.

"I need to find out what happened to that man. And if he is still in jail. That was ten years ago, so there is a chance he's free now. Not a very good one, seeing as an officer and one of the girls died. But I'm not comfortable not knowing everything."

Miles asked a few more questions, making sure he had the names of the other girls spelled correctly, and that he had the dates written down both of when they were taken and when they were found. Then he closed his notebook. "Our focus now is finding Holly. We'll pull Holly's driver's license photo from the database. Send it around to see if anyone recognizes her."

"Wait." He raised a questioning eyebrow. "That picture is almost four years old. She's lost weight and changed her hair."

Darting back into Holly's room, she grabbed Holly's tablet and clicked on the photo app. She used her finger to scroll through the pictures until she found the one she wanted. Perfect. It was recent enough that it had Holly's new trendy haircut.

She rejoined Miles and Sergeant Jackson at the table and handed over the tablet.

Miles took the tablet and held it so Jackson could see it, too. "That's Holly," she signed, and pointed at the laughing girl. Miles smiled, but his eyes narrowed. He had something else on his mind.

A second later, he proved her right. He tapped a second picture. When it filled the screen, he pointed to the girl next to Holly and signed, "Who's this?"

"That's Ashley. It must have been taken a few years ago, because she and Holly don't hang out anymore. They had some kind of argument over a man they had both dated."

"Ashley—" he checked his notebook "—Kline? Holly's friend from high school?"

"Yes, that's right."

He handed the device to Sergeant Jackson, continuing to sign as he spoke so that Rebecca would know what he was saying.

"Do you recognize her? I know I have seen her face somewhere, but can't place it."

Sergeant Jackson took the tablet and studied the photo. A frown etched itself into his face as he considered the image.

"Yeah, I have seen her before. But I don't know where. We need to get the pictures to the station, have them compared to the database. Could you email these images to us? Or maybe we could take the tablet, in case there are better images?"

Miles's hands flew as he interpreted. When he

finished, Rebecca nodded. "Will Holly get the tablet back?"

Miles exchanged glances with Jackson. "If it's at all possible, we'll return it," he signed. What he didn't add was that it all depended on if they found Holly alive. It was in their expressions. She shivered. *Please, let Holly be okay.*

"I'm going to send those pics in now, actually," Miles interjected. Jackson raised his eyebrow. "That way they can start looking for Holly, and run a search on Ashley. But we will still need to hold on to the device, just in case."

Rebecca took the tablet back and shared the selected images in a text with Miles.

He pulled out his phone and looked at the images. Then he fiddled with his phone some more. "Done. I sent them in." He put the phone back in his pocket.

His watch lit up. She started. She recognized it as one of those new high-tech watches. It was neon green. Funny. She didn't often see people her age wearing watches. Watching his blond hair flop on his forehead, she decided it fit him.

"Lieutenant Tucker says he got the pictures and will make sure they are processed." His watch lit up again. He tapped it and read the message. "He also says that the visual artist can be there later this morning. You can come in and give her a description of your attacker. Maybe you'll remember something that will help us find him. We should head out. Jackson?"

The other officer nodded once, then got to his feet to head to the door. Miles stood as well, but instead of walking away, he moved toward her. He leaned forward, so close she caught the clean, sharp scent of him. No cologne, just soap, shampoo and Miles. "I can tell you this. I find it doubtful that you and your roommate would be attacked the same night by accident. Someone is after you. We just have to figure out who."

It took some doing, but Miles was finally able to convince Rebecca to come to the police station with him to give a description to the visual artist. It wasn't that she didn't want to help. Turning to the police just seemed to be awkward for her. Growing up, her community didn't go for outside help easily. He understood that. Even though she'd left the Amish community, she was still very close with her family. Those influences would be hard for her to overcome.

He also had a sneaking suspicion that her experiences with the legal system at the age of fifteen didn't help. He knew from watching the trial after his stepsister was murdered that people could be brutal to innocents. Especially the press.

He remembered the agony his father had gone through after his mother had been killed in such a sensational manner. He'd only been four, but some memories stayed with you forever. He shuddered as he remembered the way his father had been hounded by reporters, who wanted to know more about the famous model who'd died in a car crash while running off with another man. Leaving her child behind.

His father had become a broken man. But he'd had the wisdom to send his only child to live with his parents and younger brother. Spending the next two years with his father's deaf relatives had sheltered him from the worst of the drama, and connected him to a community he wouldn't have learned about otherwise.

"Hey, catch you later." Jackson sketched a casual wave and sauntered to his own car. Miles jerked back, grateful to be pulled out of his morbid memories.

"See you." Miles opened the passenger-side door for Rebecca, then jogged around to his own side.

As soon as the door shut, she turned to face him.

"Do you really think someone kidnapped Holly?"

How to answer that? Miles wasn't into giving false hope, but he also didn't want to escalate the situation with unsubstantiated theories. "I think we need to consider all the possibilities." There. How was that for diplomacy?

She wrinkled her nose. "But if it was the same person, why wasn't I kidnapped when that man attacked me last night?"

He twisted his body so he could give her his full attention. "I don't want to scare you. But we have no idea what your attacker would have done if you had not escaped. He may have meant to knock you unconscious and then kidnap you all along." She raised her hands, and he motioned for her to wait. "I don't have the answers yet. I intend to get them. Please, can you trust me a little longer?"

She didn't like it. He could see that, but she relented and let him start the car.

Twenty-five minutes later, he pulled into the station. As he led her into the building, he could see her shoulders stiffen. Her arms were folded in typical closed-off body language. He wished she would look at him, just so that he could send her a comforting look, or try to make small talk. Anything to make the situation easier. But she wouldn't look anywhere but straight ahead.

In the conference room, he saw that the interpreter had already arrived. Miles introduced the two women. Rebecca stared at the brunette with the edgy haircut with something akin to suspicion.

"Olsen!"

Lieutenant Jace Tucker approached, his forehead heavily creased. Uh-oh. Whatever happened, Miles wasn't sure he wanted to know about it. Jace Tucker was known for his no-nonsense attitude. He was also fair-minded. A man who commanded respect. Most of all, he was good at remaining calm and impartial, rarely letting his emotions show while he was working. That he looked visibly upset right now was a very bad sign.

"Yes, sir?"

"Is Miss Miller in there?"

What was this about? "Yes. I just brought her in to meet with the visual artist. She hasn't arrived yet."

Lieutenant Tucker craned his neck toward the room where he'd left the two women. Miles followed his gaze. The women were sitting quietly. Rebecca was staring straight at them. The lieutenant motioned for Miles to follow him. Instincts in high alert, Miles walked with him. They went into Lieutenant Tucker's office and shut the door. It took some effort, but Miles stood at attention, waiting for the other man to begin.

"We might have a witness to the attack on Holly," Lieutenant Tucker began.

Every muscle in Miles's body tightened.

"One of the tenants in the apartment across the

street saw a man approach her as she was getting in her car. She couldn't see his face. He was wearing a mask. But she was able to clearly see that he grabbed the young woman. She struggled, then sagged. He carried her to a van and drove off."

"Did she get a make? Model? Plate number?" The questions burst out of him. He couldn't have stopped them if he tried. Granted, he didn't try.

Lieutenant Tucker shook his head, the regret stamped across his somber face. "Sorry, Olsen. I wish she had. She had just taken out her contacts, and everything was blurry. The only reason she recognized Holly was because she went into the restaurant often and was familiar with all the employees."

He kept a lid on his disappointment. It was more information than they'd had five minutes ago. "So, on the positive side, we know two things. She was abducted and didn't leave under her own power. And, more importantly, we know she may be alive."

"Third," Lieutenant Tucker added, "it solidifies our suspicion that Miss Miller was attacked by the same person, given that the two women were both attacked by a man wearing a dark ski mask. And there's more."

How much more could Rebecca take? His gut tightened as Tucker gave him the rest of the news.

"How much can I tell Rebecca?"

The lieutenant hesitated. "I think we should go ahead and tell her everything. She needs to understand that this is a focused attack so she can stay vigilant."

Miles agreed, though he so didn't want to be the one to tell her and see that lovely face fill with fear. But, the flip side of that was he didn't want her to get the information through an interpreter, whose code of ethics stated she was there only to relay information. That would be such a cold way to learn such hard news.

No, he'd better tell her himself. And he needed to do it now. Waiting wouldn't make the news any easier.

Nodding to the lieutenant, he left the office and made his way back to the conference room. To his surprise, the other officer followed him. Taking in a deep breath outside the door, he hardened his resolve and opened the door.

And found himself looking straight into Rebecca's face. He and Lieutenant Tucker moved into the room. The lieutenant sat at the table. Miles moved to stand next to Rebecca. He nodded briefly at Tara, the visual artist, who'd arrived while he was talking with the lieutenant. Then he moved his gaze back to Rebecca.

Her gaze narrowed as she searched his face. He tried to school his features into a blank expression.

"What happened?" she signed.

He needed to work on his cop face.

"I will sign for myself," he informed the interpreter. "But I would appreciate it if you would voice what I sign for the benefit of the other people in the room." That way he could turn off his voice and switch totally to ASL instead of the pidgin he was using before.

Without displaying a flicker of surprise, she folded her hands into her lap.

"I was just informed we might have a break in the case," he signed, then went on to relate the first part of his conversation with Lieutenant Tucker—the information about the witness—to her. The only sound in the room was the low voice of the interpreter.

"So, she might be alive."

"I'm not going to say yes. I am going to say that I'm almost convinced my original thought was correct. I think your attacker meant to abduct you, as well."

"I concur," Lieutenant Tucker agreed after the interpreter finished voicing Miles's words.

Miles wasn't done. There was no way to soften it. Better to just tell her outright. Sucking in a breath, he prepared to deliver the devastating blow. He then told her the rest of what he and the lieutenant had discussed. "You remember the pictures you sent me? Holly and Ashley? I told you that I recognized Ashley."

Dread shifted into her face. She squirmed slightly in her seat. He thought she looked like she was getting ready to run. Unfortunately, there was no escape from this nightmare.

"We found a match for her in the database. Two weeks ago, a woman matching Ashley's description was found unconscious in Cleveland. She'd been stabbed. The assumption is that either her attacker was interrupted, or he thought she was dead when he abandoned her."

Rebecca swallowed hard. Her lips trembled. She bit them. "Was her attacker the same person? The person who took Holly? And attacked me?"

She looked so forlorn. Tears were tracking down Rebecca's pale cheeks. Otherwise, her slim body was still. Shocked. He wanted to comfort her. But there was nothing he could do for her. Nothing except find whomever was responsible and put him away.

"It's possible, but there's a lot we don't know. We don't even know where exactly she was attacked. The police believe she was moved from the original scene. Until now, they had nothing to go on. No one had reported her missing. I have ordered additional precautions at the hospital, just in case her attacker gets the dumb idea to go after her again. Hopefully, she'll regain consciousness and be able to give us more to go on."

Suddenly, she gasped. "Brooke! Is she safe?"

"I intend to find out. And I will let you know."

"Why? Why is this happening?"

"I don't know yet. But I promise you, I will not give up until you are safe and the man responsible for terrorizing you and your friends is in jail."

Chapter Four

She wasn't happy.

She was scared, mad and moody. And feeling guilty, as she wondered if her escaping from her assailant had led to Holly being abducted. Then she'd remember that Ashley had been attacked, too. So maybe it was all a matter of time before they were each targeted, one by one.

She sat quietly as the car wove smoothly through the winding roads of LaMar Pond back to her apartment. Inside, though, she was anything but quiet. Inside she was a chaotic mess of whirling thoughts. Fear for herself, and for Holly and Brooke, filled her. Miles had already left a message with Brooke's family to contact him immediately.

The one positive thought was that she didn't have to go in to work today—she had already been scheduled to have the day off. Not that she would have gone. It would have been more than she could have borne to have gone back into the bookstore today, knowing that just yesterday someone had sat in her car, waiting to pounce on her. Someone who knew who she was and where she worked. Goose bumps broke out all over her. Tomorrow would be soon enough to face that fear. For now, she had to concentrate on going back to her apartment, knowing Holly wouldn't be there.

She shivered.

The car stopped. Looking up in surprise, she saw they had arrived. She had been so lost in her own mind, she hadn't even noticed how close they were.

Out of the corner of her eye, she watched Miles reach out and shut off the car before removing the key from the ignition. Every movement was quick and decisive.

"Let's go," he signed.

Ready or not, she mentally signed. *Not*. Sighing, she opened her door and followed him to her apartment building. She entered the security code, then they moved inside. They passed Mr. Wilson and his wife on their way up the stairs. The elderly couple moved slowly. Painfully.

All thought of her neighbors fled her mind as they approached her apartment door. The sudden, irrational hope that Holly might have found a way to escape and make her way home sprung up, only to die when she unlocked the door and entered the empty apartment. Holly's coat was not hanging on the hook, nor were her shoes on the mat beside the door.

But…

She shivered.

"Something feels off," she signed to Miles.

He frowned, but didn't mock her, or tell her she was imagining things. Instead, he motioned for her to stand against the wall while he drew out his gun. It still seemed odd to be around someone holding a loaded gun, knowing that he was willing to shoot or stand in front of her to protect her. The Amish didn't believe in violence. While her father and brothers would gladly put themselves at risk for her, she knew they would never consider shooting another person. Even if they or their loved ones were in danger.

But Miles was clearly prepared to do that.

She tracked him as he moved down the hall to the back of the apartment. He turned at Holly's room, sliding along the wall.

A movement broke her focus away from Miles. The closet door beside her was opening. Slowly, slowly. Like a horror movie. A sense of horrible fascination held her captive. She watched, dread building up inside her like a wave about to crest. When a large figure dressed in black slipped out of the closet, she broke from her haze. The figure halted, then charged at her, grabbing her in a viselike grip. His muscular hands squeezed her upper arms until they hurt and attempted to drag her toward the door.

A scream ripped from her throat.

Miles tore around the corner, his gun ready. The man jumped in surprise. He literally threw Rebecca at the policeman. Off balance, she sailed across the room, falling as she did so. Strong arms caught her, then let her go. Miles jumped past her and took off out of the apartment, following after her would-be kidnapper. She ran to the door and followed him down the stairs.

In the parking lot, Miles raised his gun again.

He didn't fire.

The assailant barreled into frail Mrs. Wilson and knocked her to the ground. Agony spread across her wrinkled face. She wouldn't be getting up on her own power. Mr. Wilson sank to his knees beside his injured wife, his face pale.

The attacker never looked back. He hopped into a van that was idling. Into the passenger seat. An instant later, the van took off.

He had an accomplice. There were at least two people who they needed to track down before she could be safe again. Unfortunately, from where she was standing all she could tell about the other person was that he or she was wearing a baseball cap. The grimness that settled over Miles's countenance as his gaze met her eyes made her take a step back.

Miles shoved his gun back into his holster and jogged over to the couple, his hand already at the radio attached to his shoulder. Rebecca didn't need him to sign to know he was calling the 911 dispatcher.

The old man looked up angrily as Miles kneeled down beside the couple. He pointed a harsh, trembling finger in her direction. Uh-oh. She didn't know why, but the man clearly held her responsible for whatever had happened to his wife.

Miles shook his head firmly. He said something to the man. Both his expression and his body language indicated that he had spoken firmly, but not angrily. Like a man in command. The old man scowled, but backed down. Although his glance cut to where Rebecca stood. Even from a distance, she could sense the animosity simmering beneath his skin.

Before long, the ambulance crew and additional police arrived. The woman was put on a stretcher, then both she and her husband were off to the hospital. Rebecca recognized Lieutenant Dan Willis, brother-in-law to Jess's husband, when he hopped in his cruiser and followed the ambulance. No doubt to question the couple about the man who had barreled into them while he fled the scene. The man in the ski mask.

Rebecca waited in the parking lot with another officer while Miles and Jackson went over her apartment again, especially her closet. This time, they were looking for evidence of the man who had hidden inside, awaiting her return.

When Miles returned, she knew they hadn't found much.

"He was waiting for me, wasn't he?" she signed at him. "I don't think he knew you were there. I think he heard someone going back to the bedrooms, and thought it was me."

The smile Miles threw at her almost shocked her. What was there to smile about?

No. She took that back. She had a lot to smile about. *Thank You, Lord, that we are both safe. And please heal Mrs. Wilson.*

"I'm smiling because you're thinking like a cop," Miles signed back, his smile stretching into an infectious grin. Then it winked out. "But you are probably correct. I wasn't speaking, so he wouldn't have heard my voice. And I doubt he would have tried to grab you if he knew I was there. He risked not getting away in time."

She nodded. That's what she had thought.

"So why was Mr. Wilson angry with me? I didn't hurt his wife."

Miles blew out his cheeks and rubbed the back of his neck. Whatever it was, he didn't want to say. But she knew Miles well enough to know that he wouldn't lie. He would respect her right to know.

She braced herself.

* * *

Her skin was so pale, making her blue eyes appear huge. He was reluctant to add any more trouble onto her already overloaded shoulders. But keeping her in the dark would be unfair. It would be taking advantage of the fact that she couldn't hear the rantings of Mr. Wilson. It would be treating her differently just because she was deaf.

He hadn't grown up with deaf grandparents and a deaf uncle for nothing. He understood enough about deaf culture to know that one of the worst insults he could give this sweet, strong woman would be to judge her less than capable because she couldn't hear. His grandmother always told him that the poor communication between the deaf and hearing worlds often led to hearing people underestimating those who were deaf.

He bit the bullet.

"He said it was because of you that his wife was hurt," he signed.

She interrupted before he could go on. "My fault? But how? That's ridiculous."

He shook his head. "I agree. But there's a new development. Apparently, Holly's sister has been posting on Facebook about her sister's abduction. She mentioned you, and that the two of you were kidnapped before. A reporter approached them this morning. About an hour ago. He saw the post and thought it made a great story. Who knows who else has seen it."

Shock flared on her face, had her eyes shooting sparks. If he hadn't known she wasn't mad at him, he might've been tempted to take a step back.

"But how am I to blame? Or any of us. We were the *victims*!"

This was the pits. "I know, I know. But he was angry. His wife had recently had her hip replaced, and now she's hurt again. Angry people tend to lash out."

He was angry himself, right now. Not at the Wilsons, but at the man who had harmed the Wilsons *and* Rebecca, and who had also violated what should have been a safe space for Rebecca. He needed to do something. The feeling that he was going to explode worsened every time he imagined what could have happened to her if he hadn't been there.

But you were there. No sense dwelling on what could have happened.

It was a relief to see the other policeman come out of the building and give him a thumbs-up. She could go back inside. And stay there, alone? Uh-uh. Glancing up at the window of her apartment, he made a decision. Really, the decision had been made the moment that dude had tried to grab her.

"Come on. You can't stay here by yourself."

He waited for her to argue. She didn't. Instead, she lifted her shoulders in a listless shrug. "What are my options?"

"I think an officer should stay here with you. I can stay until this evening. I have my laptop in my car, so I can work from there. And then another officer can replace me. Sergeant Zerosky would be ideal. She goes on duty at eight."

The tension that had started to creep back into her posture bled out when she realized the officer staying overnight would be a woman. Hey, whatever made the intrusion into her life easier was fine with him. It made his job easier, too.

And he could go home and sleep. Not that he imagined he'd be sleeping all that well.

The idea of leaving her here, even with a decorated officer like Sergeant Zee, as they called the tall red-haired officer, left a bitter taste in his mouth. He really didn't like the thought of not being there. But he still had a job to do. And he would be back first thing in the morning.

It didn't help.

He spent the afternoon sitting on the couch, looking up leads on his computer. Rebecca was a very peaceful person to be around. She was a restful companion. Every once in a while, he'd glance over at her to see her reading a textbook or making notes.

Curious, he waved at her.

"Are you studying to earn a CDI certificate?" he signed when she finally looked up.

She nodded. "Yes. I have been working on it for the past two years. I have a bachelor's degree, which is required. I also have all my hours in. I need to take the first part of the test next month."

"Can I ask what inspired that?" It was an admirable goal, but not an easy one.

She grimaced. "The trial. The interpreter they had was wonderful, but there were some concepts that she still had trouble conveying so that I could understand. If she'd been able to work with a deaf interpreter, I think that whatever she'd signed could have been better translated through a person who knew exactly how a deaf mind works."

Wow, did that sound familiar. "My grandmother says the same thing."

Rebecca stood and stretched. The sunlight streaming through the window caught fire in her gold hair. Man, she was pretty. And honest. He had a feeling if she gave her word, she'd bend over backward to keep it. Unlike his mother.

Why had he gone there? His mother had nothing to do with the current situation.

"I'm thirsty. Want anything?" she signed, completely unaware of the dark place he'd gone to in his mind.

He shook it off. "Yeah, I could go for something to drink. What do you have?"

Please say Mountain Dew.

"Coffee, tea, water, lemonade. What's that face for?"

Had he made a face? Oops. He needed to be on guard more. This lady was an expert at reading the nonverbal signals most people were oblivious to. "Sorry. I was hoping you had some kind of soda." When her eyebrows rose to meet her bangs, he grinned and shrugged. "Actually, I really was hoping you kept Mountain Dew."

That cute little nose wrinkled. "No, sorry. I don't drink pop." She turned her left fist upright and smacked her right open hand on top of it in the sign for pop. The sound was strikingly loud in the otherwise silent environment.

He settled for lemonade, and then resumed working.

Twenty minutes later, he got her attention again. "I just received confirmation that Terry Gleason died in prison. So he's not personally responsible for any of this."

Abruptly, she stood, knocking her textbook onto the floor. She ignored it. He doubted if she even realized she had dropped it. She crossed her arms across her chest and rubbed her hands up and down her arms. Walked to the window. Came back. She continued pacing the room like a caged tiger for a minute or two.

He let her pace, recognizing the need to move while she digested the new information.

After a couple of minutes, she seemed to calm down a notch, although she still appeared disturbed. She didn't try to talk to him. Instead, she walked to the flat-screen television and swiped the remote control off the shelf. With a quick jab, she turned on the TV. The local news filled the screen. Huh. He hadn't realized it was already six in the evening. Closed captioning scrolled across the bottom of the screen.

The first story was a burglary in Erie. He grunted and nodded when the anchorwoman related that the suspect was in custody. Good.

The second story began. He sat up straight, his eyes flaring wide. Rebecca gasped and sank down into her seat. A picture of Terry Gleason filled the screen. Next were two side-by-side images of Holly and Ashley. Then a picture of Jasmine Winters. It was her senior picture, probably from the yearbook. A picture of Rebecca was last. Only Brooke's picture was missing. Did they not know about her yet?

Miles was barely aware of the story. All he knew was that their timeline had just moved up. Whoever was after these women had been moving relatively slowly, seeing how Ashley had been kidnapped weeks ago. Now, however, the perp knew that they were onto him, and had made the connection between the victims. A connection that would hopefully lead them to the identity of the attacker. Or attackers, since the man in the apartment earlier had clearly had an accomplice driving his getaway van.

Would the publicity and public scrutiny stop his vendetta? Or would this new development cause his attacks to escalate and become even more violent?

A hollow sensation took hold of his gut. The level of danger to Rebecca had just increased.

Miles immediately called in for more backup to watch over Ashley in the hospital. He'd also make sure Rebecca was never without protection. And he needed to find Brooke.

Things were going to get messy.

Chapter Five

Miles knew the news wasn't good the moment he walked into the station the next day. Lieutenant Tucker was waiting for him at his desk.

"What's up, Lieutenant?" He hoped with all his might that his instincts were off. But he knew, just from the troubled expression on the senior officer's face, that his gut was spot on. Something bad had happened. Real bad.

"A body was found early this morning. It had been dumped in the pond. Some fishermen found it. It was Holly."

Oh, man. He closed his eyes briefly. Poor girl. And poor Rebecca. He had to be the one to tell her.

"You sure, Lieutenant?" Of course Tucker was sure. Miles was grasping at straws.

"Yeah, I'm sure. The ME has already confirmed it and called her parents. It was her. She'd been beaten pretty badly before she was dumped in the pond. My guess is the perp kidnapped her so that he could take his time."

It made sense. The timing of disposing of her made

sense, too—in a sick sort of way. "I think that news report last night might have been the reason she was killed now, rather than him running the risk of keeping her alive longer."

Lieutenant Tucker's eyes tightened. "I'm inclined to agree with you. I called Sergeant Zee. She's bringing Miss Miller in to give a full description of the man from the apartment yesterday. To see if there were any distinguishable marks on the man. Or on the vehicle. Anything to shed some light on this."

Miles nodded. "What about the couple who he ran into? They had said a reporter questioned them about Rebecca. Was it really a reporter?"

"It was. We confirmed that this morning. The reporter, however, had gotten an anonymous tip. Someone's been talking."

Great.

"What about the last girl? Brooke?" Tucker asked.

"I finally got a hold of her parents this morning. She's out of the country on a mission trip. They will call if anything suspicious happens."

Tucker nodded. "Very well. I'm going to go make some calls. I especially want to know what on earth made Holly's sister post about the kidnappings on social media."

Not long after, Sergeant Zee arrived with Rebecca, and escorted her into an interview room. Miles made his way back to Rebecca reluctantly. The last thing he wanted to do was to give her the bad news. But there wasn't any choice. Either she found out from him, or she found out from someone else. And he couldn't bear the thought of her having to hear the tragic news from someone she didn't know.

He'd wasted enough time. If he was going to protect her, he needed to get moving.

Setting his jaw, he shoved open the door and entered the room. Rebecca's head shot up, her blue eyes searching his face. The fear he saw there just about broke his heart before he pushed the emotion away. He couldn't let himself get distracted. Not now, when there was so much at stake.

He sat at the table across from Rebecca. The move was deliberate. He needed distance between them. The interpreter smoothly stood and moved beside him. He didn't even spare her a glance. Lieutenant Tucker shut the door and sat at the head of the table. He gave Miles a nod to go ahead.

Taking a deep breath, he began. "I have bad news. Holly's dead. She was murdered early this morning."

All the blood leeched from her face. Tears pooled in her blue eyes.

He hated this.

"She was killed after the news reported her missing," she signed, her hands shaking. "And reported her connection to Terry Gleason."

He knew she'd pick up on that fact. "Yes. We believe the man is in a hurry to finish his attacks before he can get caught now that a connection has been made."

"Why wasn't Brooke's name mentioned?"

Lieutenant Tucker broke in. "Probably because she was a minor when it happened. I talked with Holly's sister this morning. She started this by posting about it on social media. But she never had Brooke's name.

Even during the trial, Laurie wasn't there, and the names of the minors involved were not released."

Now for the new plan. Miles took over when the lieutenant stopped talking. "You can relax about Brooke. She's safe." For the moment. He quickly relayed what he'd learned that morning. "I don't think you should stay at your apartment tonight. It's just not safe."

She cocked her head at him, her brow crinkling. "But I thought I would have Claire with me again."

Claire? Oh! Sergeant Zee. He almost chuckled. There was so much innocence in her, even after all she had been through. She never tried to keep people at arm's length. Everyone was a friend. The amusement faded. As much as he hated the thought, it would be better for her if she stopped trusting so easily.

"Your apartment is too well-known now. Obviously, your attacker is aware of it. And the security code wasn't enough to keep him out. I don't think the place is secure. You'll be safer somewhere else altogether."

"Where will I go?"

"We'll think of that. First, let's go back to the apartment and you can pack a bag. Grab whatever you need to last you several days."

The moment the lieutenant gave him leave to go, they departed for her home. Jackson met them there. He waved at the other officer, who was on his phone. Jackson had come to add another layer of protection as Miles moved Rebecca. He followed her into the apartment and waited while she gathered her things. She came out of her room sooner than he expected.

"All done?"

"Almost. But I'm worried. My brother's getting married in less than a week. I can't miss his wedding."

Great. One more problem to work around. Part of him considered telling her he couldn't guarantee that she'd be able to go. If her attacker was still at large, then even a special family event wasn't worth the risk. But looking at her weary face, he found he couldn't do it. He compromised.

"I can't make any promises, but if it's at all possible, I will get you to the wedding."

She wasn't completely satisfied with his answer, he could see that. But it was the best he could do under the circumstances. A frown pulled down the corners of her mouth. He had to give her credit, though. She dealt with her disappointment calmly and returned to her room to complete her packing.

He made a few phone calls while he waited. He had just ended a call when she returned, a large duffel bag slung over one shoulder. Her hair had been pulled up under a baseball cap. A backpack was on her back.

"Got your laptop? Your textbooks?"

She jerked a thumb at the backpack. "All in there."

He smothered a grin. She might not appreciate the sentiment, but she was adorable. And the image of the typical all-American girl. No one seeing her would have any clue that until a handful of years ago, she'd been part of the Amish community.

How difficult it must have been growing up unable to share more than the most basic communication with her family. It wasn't just that her family was Amish. He knew that many hearing families struggled learning how to communicate with their deaf children. But being Amish would have limited the opportunities and resources available to them. He was grateful that he could be there for her now, help her through this ordeal. Be her protector...

Mentally, he backpedaled. He was getting too involved. Too close to her. Experience had taught him that he made mistakes when his emotions were involved. Mistakes that had almost cost him his job. And could cost Rebecca her life.

He needed to distance himself. That was the only way he could keep her safe.

She was in the middle of a nightmare. Holly dead. Ashley in a coma. Who would be next? Her? Brooke? She was on the edge of a gigantic black hole, just waiting for it to suck her back into the vortex. Only this time, how would she get out?

Or would she be able to escape at all?

The last time had cost her so much. And not just the innocence stolen by the abuse the girls had endured. She'd been forced to make the decision that ultimately led to her leaving her Amish community. She didn't know if she had it in her to survive the terror a second time. Especially now that she was alone.

Alone. How was she going to be able to handle living in the apartment without Holly, knowing that her friend was never coming home? When Miles had decreed she couldn't stay there for the next few nights, she'd worried about where she would go—but she'd also been so relieved that she'd be able to get away. That she wouldn't have to stay somewhere where every corner reminded her of the friend she'd never see again. Where she couldn't block out the memory of her attacker grabbing hold of her, trying to drag her away.

Relief and confusion warred for her attention. She wanted nothing more than to follow blindly if it meant that she would not have to step foot back in that apartment. But that wouldn't be smart. She needed to be responsible. Which meant not letting Miles, as sweet as he was, make decisions for her.

Rebecca held her breath. If he suggested that the department would put her up in a hotel for the night, she would have to shut that idea down fast. That would put her way too far into debt. Not that they would ever expect her to pay them back. It was the principle behind the idea that mattered, though.

She shot a covert glance his way. He was standing, talking into his watch. She could see a piece of plastic in his ear. A Bluetooth. It seemed odd to her, but it fit him. He was obviously into gadgets. Miles shook his head. His bangs flopped across his forehead. My, he was adorable.

Which meant nothing, she reprimanded herself, ignoring the way her breathing hitched in her chest.

Sergeant Jackson entered the apartment as Miles finished his conversation and went to stand near him. Every now and then he would nod at something Miles said. A few minutes later, Jackson moved outside again and Miles made another call.

Rebecca hated to be petty, but the fact that she hadn't been in on the conversation really bothered her. Because she knew what they were discussing revolved around her. She and Holly and what had happened so long ago.

Don't be silly, she admonished herself. Even if she had been involved, she knew that it was also police business. Even if she had hearing, she wouldn't have been let in on those discussions. Anyway, she was used to being excluded from conversations. Growing up, neither of her parents had been able to become fluent signers. They had tried. She knew that. But Pennsylvania Dutch and ASL weren't exactly compatible. Her parents spoke English, it was true, but they always preferred their native tongue.

It wasn't all bad. Levi and Lizzy had learned ASL very well. Out of all her siblings, he and Lizzy were the ones she was closest too. At least emotionally. Thomas and Joseph were between her and Lizzy chronologically, but the boys had been too busy to learn more than rudimentary signs. The youngest, Ruth, had been just a toddler when she'd left the community.

"I have a plan," Miles announced, reverting back to ASL now that his phone call was done. "I was just on the phone with Jess. I'm going to drop you off at her house. She and Seth have agreed to let you stay with them. I've also cleared it for a cruiser to be placed on watch."

She shook her head. It wasn't that she didn't appreciate her friends, and the kindness of their gesture. She loved Jess, and Seth was great. But without warning, a deep longing for her mother filled the empty cavity in her chest.

"Can't I go stay with my family?" She put as much pleading into her facial expression as possible as she signed to him.

"Your family is Amish."

"I know that."

"We wouldn't be allowed to put a cruiser in front of their house. You'd be an open target. Especially with the renewed interest in the case."

"Would they even know that I grew up Amish?"

"I'm sorry." She believed him. Those deep blue eyes were pools of remorse. "I looked over the information from the trial yesterday while I was on my laptop. Your name wasn't released then, but the fact that one of the girls was Amish was. I can't take the chance. You'd be putting yourself, and your family, at risk."

He was right. As much as she wanted to argue, she had to accept it. She couldn't bear to bring this danger into her parents' home. Disappointment filled her. Lowering her eyes, she tried to conceal her feelings. A pair of spit-shined shoes entered her line of vision. Miles had moved to stand directly in front of her. She had to raise her eyes, tilting her head back so she could look into his face and see his hands moving.

"I wish I could let you go to your family. But you know it wouldn't be safe. At least at Jess's house, I can protect you."

And with that, she had to be satisfied. She followed Miles out to his car. Jackson was outside, standing guard. Rebecca turned and took one last look at her apartment building. Because there was no way she would ever be able to go back there now. She could return long enough to pack up her things for good, but she'd never live there again. Even while she had packed, goose bumps had popped out all over her skin. She had constantly looked over her shoulder. It was the quickest packing job ever as she threw her clothes in helter-skelter. She could only hope she had actually packed the clothes and toiletries needed to last several days.

One thing was certain. The moment this nightmare

was over, she was looking for a new place to live. Even if she had to break her lease.

Within fifteen minutes, they were speeding on their way toward Jess and Seth's house. The darkness inside the car enveloped her like a cocoon. Her head started to nod. Leaning back against the headrest, she allowed herself to drift, thinking about the day's events.

A hand on her shoulder awakened her. Blinking, she pushed herself upright in her seat just as they passed the sign for River Road Stables. Jess had originally run the training and boarding stables with her brother, Cody. After he had died last year, she'd taken over the business. Seth and she now resided in the large white ranch house, which was adjacent to the stables.

The comforting scent of the recently mowed grass and dust mingled with the smell of horses drifted in through Miles's partially open window. She inhaled deeply, feeling soothed by the aromas that had surrounded her as a child in the Amish community. She tapped the button on her door panel to roll down her own window. A cool fall breeze tickled her cheeks, but she didn't mind.

The car swept past the stables and continued up the well-lit driveway. Jess had married a prince of a man. Seth had state-of-the-art security lights installed almost the minute they returned from their honeymoon. He knew how much his wife hated the dark—the result of a childhood trauma. The lights she'd had previously had been seriously outdated.

A pretty woman with a medium-brown ponytail moved onto the front porch as the car came to a halt. Jess. Rebecca hopped out of the car and ran up the steps to greet her friend. And to get into the familiar environment of the house.

She knew Miles was right behind her. She could feel his presence on the stairs behind her. His solid presence steadied her and brought her comfort. That worried her. She didn't want to start to depend too much on him. Yes, he could sign, and he was very protective. That didn't mean anything. He was a police officer. She was a case. That was all.

It had to be.

"Stay for dinner, Miles?" Jess signed and spoke simultaneously.

He flashed a brief smile, making Rebecca's pulse spike. "Thanks. But I need to get back to the station. Continue working the leads. I know Seth is working tonight, so you ladies lock the doors and set the alarm as soon as I go. A police car will be stationed here overnight. An officer should be here within the hour."

He waited for them to agree, then departed.

Rebecca watched his car turn around and start down the drive.

"You okay?" Jess signed.

Rebecca nodded her head.

"Okay. I left the phone in the kitchen. Seth wants me to call to let him know you arrived safely."

Touched, Rebecca hugged her friend. Pulling back, she signed, "Thank him for me, please. It really means a lot that you and he are letting me stay."

As she expected, Jess laughed and shook her head, making her ponytail bounce. "Silly. You're my oldest friend. Of course you can stay."

Rebecca watched Jess amble to the kitchen, taking all the cheer with her. Returning her gaze to the window, she sighed. Miles was gone. She hadn't expected him to stay. He had a job to do. And a killer to catch.

She had never felt so alone.

Chapter Six

What kind of person kidnapped young women and murdered them?

Rebecca tried to study, but finally had to concede defeat. The events of the past couple of days weighed too heavily on her mind to allow her to concentrate on anything else. Setting her books and laptop aside, she went to her bag and pulled out her Bible.

Under the Bible was an old quilt her mother had made for her when she was younger. She pulled that out as well, then wrapped it securely around her shoulders. The blanket soothed her with the memories that were stitched into it. Martha Miller had made quilts for each of her children when they were young. A necessity when living in Pennsylvania where the winters were cold. She'd used the quilts as a way to teach her three daughters the fine art of quilting. Warmth mingled with disappointment in those moments.

Rebecca had sat at her mother's side, watching her hands carefully. She'd learned by watching how to form the stitches. Whatever words Martha had said, however, were wasted. She'd needed both hands for the sewing and could not use even the limited sign language she'd mastered to sign to her daughter. How could one feel so loved and so isolated at the same time?

She did, though. For most of her life.

Sighing, Rebecca turned to God for comfort, glad that she had really gotten to know Him through her friend Jess. Especially now, when she needed to be strong, and wasn't sure if she had enough courage to stand on her own.

Miles will protect you.

Would he? Had God sent Miles in His Providence? A protector who could communicate with her without needing to take the time to write everything down or go through an interpreter?

These questions were still swirling around in her mind when she went to bed an hour later. She had worried that she would be too wound up to sleep, but exhaustion soon caught up with her.

She woke up suddenly. Confusion and disorientation dazed her mind for a moment, until she remembered where she was. Jess's house.

The clock beside her bed said four thirteen. She had hoped to be able to sleep in this morning. She sighed. It would have been great to snuggle back down under the covers, but she was wide-awake now. It would have been nice to talk with someone. No one else in the house would be up for at least an hour. If it was later, she could have used Jess's videophone to call someone. She'd used it to call the bookstore last night and talk with Tracy to let her know she might not be in today. Something she wouldn't have been able to do without the device. Tracy didn't sign. That wasn't an issue though. The videophone connected directly with the Pennsylvania Relay System. She'd been able to sign to the interpreter on her screen. The interpreter voiced what she signed to Tracy on the other end. It didn't even matter that Tracy was using a regular phone.

I wonder what Miles is doing?

She snorted. What did she think he was doing? Sleeping. The odds that he would answer a text or a call were not in her favor. Did he even own a videophone? He had to. Didn't he say once he had deaf grandparents? And the way he liked his gadgets, she couldn't see that not being one of them.

Antsy, she sat up and tapped the touch lamp near the bed once. The low light glowed like a night-light, making the room just light enough for her to see the shapes of the furniture throughout the room. Through a broken slat in the blinds, she could barely make out little pinpricks of light. She loved stars. They were like a connection to God. The window beckoned to her.

Turning the light off, she rose from the bed and made her way to the window. Easing herself down on the window seat, she rearranged and plumped the cushions behind her back before settling into the seat. Then she twisted the rod to open the blinds. The Pennsylvania night sky was awash with stars. They both filled her with awe and humbled her. She'd always loved watching the stars. She and her sister Lizzy used to crawl out their bedroom window and onto the back porch roof at night to watch the sky. They could sit there, silent, for hours. It had always been Lizzy she was with. Besides Levi, Lizzy was the best signer in the family.

Rebecca sighed, content for the moment.

But then all feelings of contentment disappeared.

What was that light she saw? Something was flashing up in the trees. Or was there? Straining her eyes, she leaned forward, her nose almost touching the glass, trying to see if anything was up there.

Nothing.

She sat for another half hour, watching intently, arguing with herself about whether she had seen anything or was being paranoid.

What was she doing? Anyone looking toward the house might be able to see her with her nose pressed against the glass. Stumbling off the window seat, she hurriedly shut the blinds. Then she ran to the opposite side of the room.

Heart thumping, she stood in the dark, rubbing her hand over her heart as if she could slow it down.

What to do?

More cautious now that the possibility of a threat was there, she crept back to the window and moved the blinds slightly so she could look out. Nothing. Again. The only thing moving was the officer stationed outside the house. She'd forgotten about him. She must be losing her mind.

A few minutes later, the floor under her vibrated. The front door had slammed. She leaned closer to see that Jess was headed to the stables.

She tensed. If someone really was out there, would Jess be in danger?

Lights swept up the driveway. The morning help had arrived. She sighed in relief, sure that the threat was ended. The burly young man who exited his truck and followed Jess into the stables would surely deter anyone from coming any closer.

The moment Miles arrived, though, she'd make sure

to tell him about her suspicions. No doubt, he'd search and find nothing. After all, who even knew she was here?

She just had to wait for Miles.

He couldn't sleep.

Flipping over onto his left side, Miles glared at the digital alarm clock as if it was to blame. Five after five. As in a.m. Unreal. It had been past eleven before he had managed to unwind enough to fall asleep. He was edgy about leaving Rebecca at Seth's, even with Thompson stationed right outside.

Why? It was secure. She was fine. He needed to stop worrying about her and get some sleep so he could find the lowlifes who had it in for her.

Flopping back onto his back, he resolutely closed his eyes. His alarm wasn't set to go off until seven. If he couldn't fall back asleep then he'd think about the situation. Images of Rebecca's face swam behind his closed lids. *Think of something else.* Mentally, he ran through the latest saxophone solo he had been working on.

Tossing and turning, he would doze off, only to wake suddenly. Minutes later, he was still thinking. He gave up. Throwing back the covers, he heaved himself to a sitting position. If he couldn't sleep, he might as well be productive. Hefting himself out of bed, he went through the motions of his morning routine.

He changed into his sweatpants and a police academy T-shirt. Then he got down to business. Stretching, sit-ups and push-ups got his blood pumping. Fully awake, he left his apartment for his morning run. Pacing himself, he kept his rhythm smooth. The sound of his feet hitting the pavement echoed in the air. While he ran, he allowed his thoughts to return back to the previous day.

Rebecca.

How was she holding up at Seth's house? Was she really safe there? He mentally squashed that worry as his foot hit a puddle and splashed water up his leg. Of course she was safe. Seth and Jess were both with her. They had installed a top-of-the-line alarm system after the attacks on Jess last spring. And he knew that Thompson took his duty very seriously.

Swerving around in the cul-de-sac at the end of the block, he began the return home. The sun was higher in the sky as he entered his apartment. He took a quick shower, changed and then grabbed a can of Mountain Dew and the pizza he had left over from the night before. He downed half the can while waiting for his breakfast to heat up in the microwave. Hearing it ding, he set the plate and the can on the counter and pulled his worn-out Bible off the shelf.

Best way to start the morning. Eating pizza and drinking Mountain Dew with Jesus.

Twenty-five minutes later, he set the plate in the dishwasher and made a basket into the recycle bin with the can. It clanked against the other cans. He'd have to empty that soon.

Now what?

His peace was interrupted as restlessness crawled through his bones. What he wanted to do was check on Rebecca, but he knew he couldn't. It was too early. And she was fine. *Stop worrying about her.*

Not happening.

He glanced at the clock. If he left now, it would be

eight thirty when he arrived at the Travis home. Surely, that wasn't too early to stop by. She should be up. And if she wasn't, he knew Seth and Jess would be. Then he figured he'd get a head start on the business of the day. The sooner he found out who was targeting the sweet former Amish girl, the sooner she'd be safe. And off his mind.

Grabbing another Mountain Dew from the refrigerator, he bounded down the steps and out to his car, singing a song that he'd heard on the radio recently. He bopped his head to the music in his mind, causing his blond hair to flop on his forehead. Belatedly, he remembered that his neighbors might still be sleeping. A sheepish glance around showed the parking lot was empty, and there were no angry faces glaring out the windows. Shrugging his shoulders, he unlocked his door and slid into the driver's seat.

The drive was slow this morning. A thick layer of fog had fallen over LaMar Pond. Visibility was low. Taking his time, Miles bit back his frustration. It wasn't like he had to hurry to go to check on Rebecca. He had his pager on. And if there was an emergency, he would have heard the call come over the radio.

The emergency system had just hired a brand-new dispatcher. He hadn't met her yet, but she sounded young. Jackson thought she sounded pretty. But then, Jackson did like to flirt with the ladies. He never meant anything serious by it. Miles doubted he ever took any woman seriously. He frowned, as the image of Jackson flashing his charming smile at Rebecca hijacked his brain.

Maybe he should warn her about him. Make sure she knew the score.

Wait a minute. This wasn't any of his concern. And besides, Rebecca seemed far too reserved to put up with his jokester coworker.

And her roommate had just been murdered.

And she might be next.

All thoughts of Jackson fled as the reality of the situation again came to the forefront. Tightening his grip on the steering wheel and on his wayward thoughts, Miles maneuvered the sleek cruiser off the smooth paved road and onto the dirt back road that led to the stables. Immediately, the car bounced as his front tire hit a pothole in the road. It was more like a crater. He grimaced. Too many bumps like that and he'd do some real damage to the car. Just what he needed when he was trying to convince the chief that he was responsible.

Up ahead, he could make out the sign to River Road Stables. A surge of adrenaline caught him off guard. Straightening in his seat, his eyes shifted in every direction as he pulled up the driveway and looked for any signs of trouble. His tension didn't let up as he passed the lower barns. As he drove by the upper barn, he noticed the brand-new horse trailer parked out front. That wasn't worrying—in fact, it was probably good news. Business was doing better for Jess, now that her late brother had been cleared of all the charges that had been brought against him last year.

Miles headed up the lane to the house. His heartbeat quickened. He swung the car into the space behind Seth's pickup truck and stepped out of the car, waving at Thompson. The other man grinned and gave him a thumbs-up before heading out. That was fine. Miles didn't mind staying until the next shift arrived.

The hair on the back of his neck prickled. He swiveled his head around, eyes narrowed as he looked for threats. Nothing. But he couldn't rid himself of the feeling that someone was watching him.

His right hand settled on his revolver as he stepped away from the vehicle. The feeling of the gun was reassuring, but he quickened his pace as he strode up the walk.

A movement in the front window caught his attention. He turned his head. And forgot how to breathe.

Rebecca had pushed back the blue drapes and stood watching him, the lace sheer covering her but not hiding her. Like a wedding veil.

Whoa, buddy. Don't even go there.

He waved at her. She waved back and offered him a smile so radiant, it made his chest tight.

Then she whirled and vanished from sight.

Less than a minute later, he heard the click and twists of the locks and bolts being undone. The door swung open, and Rebecca stepped out to greet him. Her hair was pulled back in a French braid. Without the hair framing her face, her cheekbones seemed impossibly high and fine. Delicate.

Abruptly, he realized he was staring at her. His face heated as he lowered his head. His bangs flopped over his forehead. He brushed them aside as he brought his head back up...and his eyes caught on something glinting in the trees.

Fully alert, he motioned Rebecca back. Then he saw it, the muzzle of a gun. The picture window she'd stood in front of a minute before shattered. Without thinking about it, Miles jumped toward Rebecca, pushing her to the ground and covering her shaking body with his. A second slug hit the porch, sending wood chips flying in every direction.

Miles raised his head and looked at the damaged area. His blood froze.

If the gunman had been two seconds faster, Rebecca would be dead.

Chapter Seven

Miles shot to his feet, his hand pulling his gun from the holster in the same movement. A motor roaring to life beyond the trees caught his attention.

Whoever it was, they were getting away.

"Are you hurt?" he signed, checking her pale face for signs of pain. He saw fear and more than a little shock, but no injuries. As soon as she shook her head, some of the pressure in his chest eased up.

Stepping in front of Rebecca, he motioned for her to stay down. Just in case the car he had heard wasn't the shooter. *Or,* his mind whispered, *if there was more than one person up there.*

Seth burst into the hall. "Was that a gunshot? What's going on?"

"Get her in the house and stay away from the windows."

Miles risked a brief glance to see that his orders were being obeyed. They were. Rebecca had already been hustled into the house and out of his sight. Out of the sniper's sight, too.

Gun ready, Miles edged behind the column on the

porch and peered toward the hillside. Nothing visible. Which meant absolutely nothing.

Not taking his eyes off the line of trees where the shots had come from, he used his left hand to find his radio and called for backup.

The wait for help to arrive seemed to last forever. In reality it was only about ten minutes. Lieutenant Jace Tucker was the first to arrive, followed shortly by Lieutenant Dan Willis and Jackson. He did a double take when he saw Jackson. Jackson wasn't on the clock until noon. Same time as him.

Being a cop, though, meant you were always prepared to answer a call.

"Shooter, up in the trees," he said to the men. "It appeared the shots were intended for Miss Miller."

Lieutenant Tucker nodded, his own blue eyes squinting toward the hillside. "How many shots, Olsen?"

"Two, Lieutenant. One hit the window, and the other the porch." He indicated the damaged area behind him. The other officers all whistled at the hole in the porch. Miles tried to hide a shudder as he recalled how close it had come to Rebecca. He was completely sure it was God's protection that had saved her. Saved them both.

"And Miss Miller?"

"She's fine. In the house with Seth."

"How do you want to play it?"

That gave him a start. Then he remembered. He was in charge of this case. The chief must have passed the word along.

"We need to sweep the trees for evidence. I doubt the shooter stuck around. I heard a motor revving up in that direction right after the shots were taken."

"You joining in the search?" Lieutenant Willis

pulled his sunglasses down over his eyes. He suddenly looked every bit the former soldier that he was.

Miles hesitated. But only for a moment. The urge to stay with Rebecca was strong. But he didn't need to. Seth was present to interpret—he wasn't completely fluent but he was good enough to handle just about anything conversational. Moreover, Seth was a paramedic, and would make sure that Rebecca hadn't been injured. Yes, she'd be well taken care of inside—she didn't need him there. His place was with the team, to make sure the area was safe. That she was safe.

"Yeah, I'm coming. Jackson?"

"I'll remain on guard," Jackson responded.

Wow. He'd expected a bit of an attitude. Jackson was a sergeant. As Jackson joined him on the deck, he clapped a hand on Miles's shoulder.

"Don't worry, Olsen. I'll take care of your girl," Jackson said in a low voice before heading inside.

A leaden ball settled in Miles's gut. Apparently, he hadn't been able to hide his growing attraction to the former Amish girl.

No matter. He had a job to do.

The search didn't take long. Within the space of an hour, they had found the place where the shooter had hidden. It wasn't difficult to spot. Branches had been sawed off trees and left in a pile. From the resulting hole, Miles had a clear view of Seth's porch. How did the perp know that Rebecca would be here? She really didn't have time to tell anyone. Unless she had contacted her family after the fact so they wouldn't worry? Still, Miles had a hard time envisioning her family giving out information about her. She might have left the community, but they were still Amish and tended to keep to themselves. No. It had to have been something else. He'd kept a close eye on the rearview mirror the whole time they'd driven here the previous night and he was sure they hadn't been followed. So what had given her hiding place away?

What was that on the ground?

Miles kneeled down beside the tree. There, on the ground, was a small, pink blob with tooth marks in it. Of all the stupid, careless mistakes for a wannabe killer to make!

"Lieutenant Tucker!" Miles was careful not to touch the object or the area around it. "I have some evidence to bag."

Tucker trotted over and peered over Miles's shoulder. His exclamation made Miles smirk. "Of all the dumb things…is that chewing gum?"

"Yep. Sure is, Lieutenant. Freshly chewed and loaded with DNA."

"Oh, yuck." Dan Willis stopped by to check out the discovery. "Well, isn't that disgusting? But sure is a nifty clue."

"Yeah." Miles carefully bagged the evidence. "Who knows how long it will take to process, though. LaMar Pond is hardly like one of those shows on prime-time television. And when it comes to the district's crime labs, we always have to wait our turn."

Tucker grimaced. "Ask the chief if he could try to put a rush on it."

Miles nodded, although secretly he wondered what good that would do. There was only so much pull a small-town chief had, especially surrounded by bigger departments with higher crime rates.

"You know, even if the results come back and you

find the chewer of that gum, that won't be enough to prove anything."

Miles ducked his head in acknowledgment of the fact.

"I know. This gum is just circumstantial evidence, but it is a place to start."

"That it is."

The officers completed processing the scene. Miles was antsy to get back to Rebecca. He needed to reassure himself that everything was well. He also needed to get into the office so he could continue hunting whomever it was who was attacking women and now had Rebecca in his sights.

Even though Ashley and Holly had not been shot, Miles was convinced Rebecca's attacker and the one who had attacked the other girls were one and the same. It would be too much of a coincidence otherwise. He needed to find the connection to the kidnapping ten years ago. Fast.

Rebecca was sitting in the kitchen with Jess when he returned to the house. A cup of tea was cradled between her hands, but he doubted if she was truly drinking it. It was more likely just a prop to keep her hands busy.

Miles grabbed the chair across from her and pulled it next to her, angling it so that he could look directly into her face. Into those blue, blue eyes. He blinked, and refocused. "I'm sorry that you have to deal with all this. I will do my best to get you some answers as quickly as I can. I want to catch the person who is after you."

"I'm scared," she signed back. His heart ached at

the sorrow he saw in her hunched shoulders. "Not just for me, but for Brooke. And Ashley."

Understandable.

Lieutenant Tucker and Jackson joined them. Jess rose and left them, telling Rebecca she'd be there if she needed her. Miles switched back to pidgin, interpreting for Rebecca with her consent.

"I was wondering about the night you were attacked in your car. You said that your boss had asked you to close for her. Is there any way anyone could have known this?"

She cast her gaze down to her folded hands for a moment. He wondered if she was going to answer when she looked up again. "I suppose it's possible. April had been planning to go out of town this weekend to see her parents. Her mother had asked her to go a day early. She asked me a week ago if I could take the closing shift alone."

Which meant anyone who talked to April could have gotten that information.

"Did closing by yourself bother you? Please don't take this the wrong way, but most customers can't sign."

A brief smile lit her face. "Most of the people are fine using paper and pen to talk with me. Besides, I was only alone an hour before the store closed. We don't usually have many customers at that hour anyway. Most of the work I did was closing out the drawer and getting things put away."

"Is April still at her parents' house?"

She nodded, and Miles made a note to himself to confirm it. That was easy enough to check out.

"Rebecca..." He paused, trying to figure out how

to phrase the question. Then he decided to just put it out there. She wouldn't hesitate to ask the same question if their positions were reversed. "Did you tell anyone where you were staying last night? That we had moved you here?"

A blank look. Then slowly, like the dawn rising, he could see the comprehension and consternation moving into her face. He liked the way he could tell what she was feeling at a glance. No secret motives there. He doubted if she could pull off hiding her emotions.

"Yeah," she signed, bobbing her right hand at the wrist like a nodding head, the thumb and pinky spread out while the other digits were folded over against her palm. "Tracy, the other girl who works at the bookstore. I'm supposed to work with her today. I told her there was an incident and that I was staying with a friend. I also told her that I'd call her later to let her know if I would be able to come into work today."

Miles's first instinct was to give her a resounding *no.* She couldn't go into work today. He wanted her to stay safe. But where was safe? She ought to have been safe at the Travis home. Now that her location was known, he'd have to see about extra patrols here.

And, he needed to check on some leads so he could solve this case.

But in the meantime, was it really that dangerous for her to go to work? If she was at the bookstore with an officer, she should be okay. Obviously, he would drive her to and from the store. As much as he wanted to stay with her, he had a job to do.

A red flag went up as he realized how much he wanted to stay with her. But he needed to be the one working the case. Chief Kennedy was counting on him.

Even more than that, he was aware that he wouldn't rest easy unless he knew for sure every rock was being overturned to find the culprits. And that meant he was getting too close, too involved.

He needed to get this done so he could step away.

No good would come from entanglement. Hadn't his mother's betrayal and death taught him that? Even though his father had later remarried a wonderful woman, the betrayal of his first wife had led to the mistrust that had ultimately destroyed that second marriage. Miles wouldn't become the fool his dad had been. Even being alone was preferable to that.

The words sounded good. But the hollow pang in his heart mocked him.

She didn't like the way Miles's expression had darkened. His face was neutral enough, but the pain in his eyes overwhelmed her. She wanted to reach out and grab his hand, shake him out of his black thoughts. Offer him some of the comfort he had so generously given to her over the past few days.

Instead, she placed her hands firmly on her lap while she waited for him to speak. The effort to not interrupt his thoughts and argue that she should go to work turned her knuckles white. A quick burst of pain shot through her palms. When had she fisted her hands? Her fingernails were digging in deep. *Mam* frowned on her longer nails. Her pretty pink painted nails. Nails that weren't practical at all, but fancy for no reason other than that she liked them that way. Right at the moment they were causing her more discomfort than they were worth. She intentionally unclenched her hands, stretching them wide.

"You okay?" Miles was looking at her, his brow wrinkled in concern.

He was just a tad too observant. It was useless to try and control her facial expressions. They were too ingrained in her, and were as natural as breathing.

"Fine," she signed back, tapping the thumb of her right hand into the center of her chest, keeping her fingers spread wide. "I just scratched myself with my fingernails."

He nodded, accepting her excuse.

No wonder. There were other things to consider.

"Here's my thoughts." They weren't happy thoughts, judging by the frown on his face. He switched back to pidgin. "I think you should go into work. I need to check out the leads we have. I will ask Chief Kennedy to have an officer meet us at the shop so you won't be alone."

Rebecca chided herself for the spurt of disappointment that his words evoked. Well, of course he couldn't stay with her. He had a job to do. It wasn't like she was anything more than his latest case. Anyway, it would be better for them to spend some time apart. She was far too attracted to him as it was.

"Let me call Tracy. Let her know I'm coming in later. What time? I work from ten to four every Saturday."

Miles brought his arm up to glance at the watch on it.

"It's ten thirty now. Tell her you'll be in before noon. I will drop you off before I go into work. That will give the chief time to find coverage to stay with you while you're there. Which means I should call him now. Excuse me."

Before she could respond, he turned and left the room, tapping on his watch and talking. Why did the room feel so empty without him? Weird. She really needed to stop staring at him. Especially since two of his colleagues were sitting at the table with her. Face burning, she tried to be nonchalant as she met their gazes. Fortunately, both men were professional in their demeanor.

Awkwardness set in. They couldn't speak with her, not with Miles out of the room, and they appeared to be unsure if it would be impolite to carry on a conversation that would exclude her. She had to appreciate the sensitivity. Many people would have been completely unaware of how left out and alone she felt while they conversed. Even her parents had not been aware of how abandoned she often felt, sitting alone in silence at mealtimes while the flow of conversation and activity moved around her. When her throat grew hot and tight and her eyes burned, she realized she had let her past take control. Again.

When, Lord? When will I learn to control my emotions? To let go of these feelings?

Tired of feeling useless and sorry for herself, she stalked to the stove. Nothing soothed her like cooking or painting did. Since she had left all her art supplies at the apartment, cooking was her best option. Jess hadn't started lunch yet, and Rebecca really needed to eat before she went into work. With all the excitement that morning, she had forgotten all about breakfast. But now she was remembering with a vengeance. Her stomach was starting to churn, as hunger rippled through her.

Bending down, she dragged a pot out of the cupboard and filled it with tap water. Water sloshed out of it as she set it on the burner. She felt the handle vibrating in her hand from the force with which she'd slammed it down. Wow. She hadn't meant to be so aggressive. She shrugged. No harm done.

Footsteps vibrated behind her. She whirled around as Miles burst through the door. His gaze darted back and forth, searching for something. What was wrong with him? There was a wild glint in his eyes. Lieutenant Tucker and Sergeant Jackson both came half out of their seats, their hands flying to the guns strapped into their holsters.

"What's going on?" Miles demanded, his signs abrupt. "What crashed in here?"

Sergeant Jackson settled back in his seat and crossed his arms, a mocking grin on his face. He uncrossed his left arm long enough to jerk a thumb in her direction. Miles started to sign to her what he said, hesitated, then continued, flicking a concerned glance her way.

"Jackson says you were banging the pots around. Are you angry? I'm sure your boss would understand if you didn't go to work today given the circumstances."

Lieutenant Tucker rolled his eyes. Sergeant Jackson's smirk widened. What? She looked closer. Miles's ears were turning red. Apparently, that wasn't all Jackson had said. Her lips tightened.

"I want to go to work. And I was feeling frustrated by the situation. Which I think is normal."

He nodded and interpreted.

Her eyes narrowed, and she fixed a hard stare on Sergeant Jackson while she continued to sign. "Please inform Sergeant Jackson that it is rude to say things

in front of me that you would not feel comfortable interpreting."

Jackson's mouth dropped open, making him resem-
ble a fish. A tide of red surged up his neck and face,
melding with his hairline under his dark hair. Miles
smirked and slapped him on the back. She could see
Jackson's lip curling up in a mock snarl. Then he gave
Miles a playful shove. And Miles shoved back. Within
seconds, they were both grinning.

They were like children. Full-grown men with difficult jobs and important responsibilities…goofing off
like children on a playground. Shaking her head, she
turned around and grabbed up one of Jess's magazines
to leaf through while she waited. After a few minutes,
she switched her attention back to her pot of water,
now boiling on the stove. She measured out two cups
of macaroni. Stopped. Measured out two more. None
of these men were small. They all were tall and muscular. And they had worked hard combing the woods.
She shuddered, remembering why. No! She would not
dwell on that. God was in control. She needed to give
Him the fear. Still, her stomach turned and quaked. The
fear in her was so strong, she knew it would choke her
if she didn't control it. Forcing herself to concentrate
on fixing the meal, she measured two more cups of
macaroni, ignoring the way her hand shook.

Someone entered the room. She froze, then relaxed
as another officer entered the room. It was Claire. Rebecca smiled at the red-headed officer who had stayed
with her two nights earlier. The woman had so much
responsibility on her plate, but seemed to be handling
it well.

She tracked the young officer's path across the floor

to the table where the men sat. They all looked up at her arrival. Their faces showed varied levels of expectation and dread. Why dread? With a grimace, the woman slapped a crinkled picture in the center of the table. Rebecca wrinkled her nose. She could see the mud stuck to the picture from where she sat.

Miles shot to his feet, jerking his head in her direction. Lieutenant Tucker said something to the woman, and she responded. Both faces were grim.

Rebecca clenched her jaw. Lipreading had never been her forte. As many times as she had insisted she didn't care, she wished she could just this once.

What was in that picture that had Miles so shook up?

Curiosity burned in her mind. Without making a deliberate decision to do so, she stepped toward the table to get a better look. And felt her world tilting.

Bile surged in her throat. She was choking. She couldn't breathe. The picture lay there, mocking her. The glass measuring cup slipped from her numb fingers, shattering on the immaculate kitchen floor. Macaroni and glass flew in every direction.

Footsteps. Miles was there, his big hands warm on her shoulders. Every other part of her was so cold. The panicky thought flitted through her mind that she'd never be warm again.

She could feel his gentle breath on her ear. She shivered. He was talking. She felt more footsteps. Police were on every side of her. And Jess was there, taking her arm. No doubt she'd heard the crash. Jess could hear quite a bit with her hearing aids in.

She shook off Jess. Her friend didn't understand. She hadn't seen it. She didn't know. Her arm weighed a ton as she pointed at the offending picture on the table. Miles's hands tightened on her shoulders before he turned her away from it and pulled her head against his chest, shielding her. She burrowed in, squeezing her eyes closed. She felt Jess grab her hand again. This time she didn't shake her off, but held on tight. Raising eyes that burned, she caught sight of Jess's ashen complexion.

Feeling like her right arm was coated in cement, she raised it, signing to Jess and Miles, "That picture was in a frame on my desk. I didn't notice it was missing before. It was taken last year."

Jess rubbed Rebecca's cold hand briskly between her own two warm hands. The masculine arm around her shoulders tightened. But no matter how much they comforted her, she didn't think she'd ever rid herself of the image of her, Jess and Holly, laughing at the camera. Or the big red *X* slashed through Holly's face.

Chapter Eight

Rebecca pulled away from Miles. His arm moved from her shoulders, but he kept the palm of his hand firmly on one. The warmth sank in, sending a flow of comfort coursing through her. Lieutenant Tucker took his place on her left side. She allowed the two officers to lead her around the debris and back to the table. Miles let her go long enough to sweep the disturbing picture off the table and hand it to Jackson, who neatly shoved it inside his jacket.

Lieutenant Tucker left her side once she was situated. He said something to Jess, who gave a jerky nod before disappearing. A moment later, she came to the door of the kitchen and handed him a broom and dustpan.

Her eyes met Rebecca's. Years of friendship trickled through that glance, and Rebecca read her concern and fear in an instant. "I'm fine," she signed to her friend. "I have two cops right here with me."

Some of the worry left Jess's expression. But her face was still shadowed. "Okay. I'm not abandoning you. Jace has asked Seth and me to remain in the other part of the house while the police investigate this situation."

Jace? She was confused for a moment before a lightbulb switched on in her brain. Lieutenant Tucker. She couldn't bring herself to think of the man so casually. Although she did remember seeing him and his pretty wife at Jess's wedding.

The wedding. A happy time so far removed from all that was happening now.

Miles pulled a chair close to her and sank onto it, about a foot away from her. If she stretched out her hand...

Wait. What? Relying on a man was not something she wanted to do. But it was Miles, her mind argued. He was sweet. And protective. And she trusted him. Didn't she?

Without warning, another face shot into her mind. A smile that had seemed innocent at first. Only later did she see the menace behind it. Shackles on the wall stood in stark relief in her memory. She rubbed her wrists as if she could still feel them cutting into her skin. The total darkness of the room. The complete lack of sight and vision had preyed on her senses, on her emotions, for what felt like much longer than the two days until she was rescued.

A face appeared in her line of vision, and a hand tapped her arm. Instinctively she recoiled. Then regretted it as hurt flashed in the blue eyes before her.

When would she ever learn to control her reactions? Was she destined to live in fear of men because of one man's actions? Not all men were cruel. And not all touches were bad. Forcing her breathing to slow, she worked her mouth into what she hoped was an apologetic smile. "Sorry," she signed. "I'm freaked out right now. Didn't mean to react so much."

A streak of warmth returned to his face. "I understand."

Before he could continue, she broke in. The questions were fizzing up inside her like a bottle of soda that had been shaken. She could feel the pressure.

"Where did Claire get that picture?" She swiveled her head around. The female officer had taken off. As had Jackson.

Miles intercepted the next question. "Jackson and Sergeant Zerosky are headed back out to the station. The picture was found on the road near where we think the shooter parked his vehicle."

"Why would he need it? Was it to terrorize me more? To taunt me?" A single tear escaped and ran down her cheek. She swiped it off with her fist. Now was not the time to cry. She wanted answers. Correction—she wanted her life back. Now.

Miles let out a sigh. It was hard enough to ruffle the bangs on her forehead.

"It wouldn't make sense for him to taunt you. That doesn't seem to be his method." His signs paused. He tilted his head and tapped one long forefinger against his chin.

Rebecca sucked in a breath. Held it. He was debating how much to tell her. She didn't want him to clam up now. And too much of a reaction might convince him she could not handle the truth. Which, if she was honest with herself, she was not sure she could. But to be left in the dark was not something she was willing to accept.

It felt like forever as she waited. Finally, he seemed

to come to a decision and raised his hands to resume signing. She let out her breath. "My best guess is that someone gave him the picture so that he would recognize his targets. The lieutenant agrees with me."

Rebecca raised her hands then dropped them again. There were just no words. She went numb. A helpless shrug was all she could muster to convey her complete sense of discombobulation.

"I will figure it out," Miles signed, an earnest frown wrinkling his brow. His hair almost covered it. In normal circumstances it would have been adorable.

The need to escape was strong. Overpowering.

"I need to get ready for work."

Rebecca bolted from the room and raced down the hall. Diving into the guest room Jess had prepared for her, she shoved the door closed behind her. All at once, her burst of energy drained out of her. She felt shaky and weak. Leaning against the door, she pressed her forehead against the wood. As if the pressure could erase everything she'd been through in the past few days.

If only. She squeezed her eyes and lips tightly shut, straining to hold in the tears that wanted to break free, but they couldn't be repressed. Her levee was broken. Hot tears cascaded down her face. Turning from the door, she crashed down onto the bed and pulled the pillow to her. Held it to her mouth to bury whatever sound she made while weeping. She'd learned early on that hearing people could hear her when she sobbed. Muffling the sobs as best she could, she allowed herself the luxury of her tears. For herself. For Ashley. And especially for Holly.

Half an hour later, she presented herself to Miles,

outwardly calm and ready to go to work. If Miles noticed her red, puffy eyes, he was kind enough to ignore them.

When they arrived at the bookstore, he spent a few minutes questioning Tracy. Rebecca wasn't privy to the conversation, but judging by the way Miles tightened his lips, he wasn't happy with her answers.

He stalked over to Rebecca, blue eyes shooting sparks. "Sergeant Parker just pulled up. He will remain on the premises until your shift is done and then drive you back to the Travis's home. I am heading into the station, but I will call you tomorrow morning."

"Wait!" She pulled at his sleeve as he made to leave. "What did you ask Tracy? I could see that her answers annoyed you."

He shrugged, his lips twisting. *He's not going to tell me*, she thought.

"Please. I need to know. Do you think I will be safe here? Has she noticed something suspicious?"

Miles turned his blue eyes directly on her, and she felt her face warm. Inside her stomach, she had a fluttery, squirmy feeling. What was it about him that disturbed her equilibrium so bad? She had never felt this way around any man. In fact, since she'd been kidnapped, she avoided men. Feared them. She had learned firsthand what her mother had tried for years to instill in her. A handsome face sometimes hid an evil heart.

But Miles didn't inspire fear. She wasn't afraid that he would try to control her, to overpower her. Instead, she felt safe and protected when in his care.

Which probably wasn't good. It meant she was dropping her guard.

Lifting her gaze back to his face, she saw his face had softened. "I asked Tracy if anyone had been in asking about you, or if she had told anyone that you were staying at Jess's house."

A lead ball of anxiety dropped into her stomach. She had told Tracy where she was staying and hadn't thought to mention that the girl should keep it to herself, so if that was how the man today had found her, then that meant it was her fault it had happened. Her fault Jess and Seth's home had been damaged. Her fault that Miles had nearly gotten shot protecting her. "You're telling me that she did tell someone?"

Please say no.

He nodded. She wasn't surprised, but her mouth suddenly felt as if she had swallowed cotton. "She claims a man came in late last night, right before she closed, claiming to be a friend of your brother's," he signed. "He asked if you were working, and said he had stopped by your apartment to see you, but you weren't there. He was worried. She told him you were fine, but staying at Jess's. She didn't think anything of it, because he didn't ask for the address, just smiled and left."

"If she gave Jess's last name, he could have looked it up," she signed, feeling hollow inside.

He brushed her shoulder. "If he was working with someone who knows you—knows where you live and who your friends are—he wouldn't need to have her last name."

Working with someone who knows her? That would make sense. Although the idea that someone she knew could be helping the man targeting her was terrifying.

Questions bubbled to the surface. She welcomed

them, as they replaced the panic that was circling, waiting for the opportunity to pounce. Before she could ask them, another officer arrived. Miles introduced him as Sergeant Ryan Parker. He seemed like a nice enough man. Certainly, there was nothing alarming about the handsome officer, with his brown eyes, friendly grin and close-cut auburn hair.

But he wasn't Miles. As Miles left her in the sergeant's care, she straightened her shoulders and went to work, stocking shelves and filling online orders. She couldn't shake the feeling that something bad was about to happen.

Lord, I surrender this day to Your care, she prayed.

Miles dropped the phone back onto the holder, then sat back in his chair. Pushing off with his feet, he tipped back his chair, bringing the front legs off the floor. He swept his hands through his hair.

His suspicions had been confirmed. Somehow, it brought very little comfort.

He rocked his chair, ignoring the sharp squeaks of protest the chair emitted. What did he know? Mentally, he began adding up the facts and events from the past few days.

"Olsen? You planning on buying a new chair when that one breaks?" The smooth drawl slammed into his consciousness, breaking him off midthought. The wheels of his chair crashed against the floor with a hard clatter.

Chief Kennedy stood before him, a quizzical half smile on his face. Miles felt like a kid caught with his hand in the cookie jar. Or possibly a kid who'd been caught trying to sneak a snake into his bedroom. Which he'd done. To his grandmother's horror.

"Sir!" He faced his chief. "Just thinking about the case. I had a few suspicions. And I'm just about positive that they just got confirmed. I got a little wrapped up in my thoughts."

The chief dipped his chin. "It happens. Want to tell me what you've come up with so far?"

Glad that he wasn't going to hear more about the chair, Miles proceeded to give the chief an overview of the events of the case.

"And we are sure that Gleason had nothing to do with any of these attacks?"

Something in the chief's voice made Miles sit up straighter. The chief wasn't doubting him. He was seriously wanting to hear Miles's thoughts and conclusions. As if he valued them.

"I just got off the phone with the warden of the prison where he was being held. He passed away almost a year ago. Cancer. The first attack—on Ashley—happened recently."

"What're you figurin'?"

Miles leaned back again and swiveled his chair slightly, back and forth, as he collected his thoughts. "Well, it's definitely not playing out as a copycat situation. The attacks and murders aren't following any pattern. At least not that I can tell. The only connection is the fact the people attacked were all survivors from Gleason's final binge. The ones who sent him to jail. This is personal. It feels like vengeance. But by who?" Unable to keep still, he got up and paced a few feet from the desk before turning to face the chief again. In his mind, he was ticking through the facts he knew.

"Does Gleason have any kin? Or did he have a significant other? Someone who could be carrying a grudge?" the chief asked.

Miles shook his head. He'd wondered the same thing. "No, sir. No hint of any relationships. Nor any kin that would want to hurt these girls. He was an only child of two only children. He was three when they adopted him. His conviction devastated them, but they never denied his guilt. Or theirs. I spoke with them just a few minutes before you arrived. They said he was in and out of trouble all his life, filled with anger and a sense of having been wronged. In their words, he felt the world owed him something." Sighing, he ran a hand through his hair. "He was almost nineteen. They decided to take a cruise, so they left him on his own for three weeks. His mother didn't want to. Didn't trust him. But they thought if they gave him some responsibility, it would force him to mature a bit."

Miles popped back down into his chair and scooted to his desk. Where had he put the paper? Yep. That's the one. He snatched up the notes he'd taken and read through.

"These are my notes from the prison warden. Gleason insisted until the day he died that the girls were at fault for what happened. It turns out he did know them. At least he knew Ashley and Jasmine."

"Check in to that. Also, let's widen our search. Do we know who visited him in prison?"

"The list is being sent to me, sir."

Chief Kennedy pursed his lips, deep in thought. "So out of the five young women Gleason abducted, two are dead and one is unconscious. You are keeping watch over Miss Miller. What do we know of the last girl?"

He was ready for that one. "Brooke Cole. Out of the country right now. Her family knows to beware."

The chief nodded, his dark eyes shadowed. "Good plan. If everything works out, we can catch this guy before she comes home. You're doing a fine job, Olsen. A fine job."

Miles felt his eyes widening. Something tight in him relaxed. He had been waiting a long time to hear those words. Words he had feared would never come his way after his gaffe. Even now, almost three years later, he couldn't believe that he had allowed his grief and anger to sap him of his self-control and good sense.

When his stepsister, Sylvie, had been killed, his stepmother had been devastated. The trial and conviction of the woman they all believed to be guilty had brought some closure—but that closure was shattered when Melanie Swanson was released from prison just a few years later. The public hadn't been happy with her release and there were threats and vandalism—even an attack on Melanie's aunt. Enough violent activity to get her police protection, which had included Miles.

Driven by his worry for his stepmother, and his anger over his stepsister's death, he'd taken the opportunity to sneak in some anonymous harassment of his own, hoping that Melanie would get fed up and decide to leave LaMar Pond once and for all, letting them all finally put Sylvie's death behind them. He hadn't known—none of them had—that Sylvie's death hadn't been Melanie's fault at all. That she'd been framed, and that the same people who had ruined her life and gotten her thrown in jail were also trying to kill her once she was released.

Everything had ended well. The real criminals

had been caught and imprisoned. Melanie had gotten through her ordeal and had fallen in love with one of her police officer protectors. They were happily married now. But the knowledge that everything worked out didn't take away Miles's feelings of guilt over what he'd done. He was reminded of it every time he saw Lieutenant Tucker. How that man tolerated him after what he had done to his wife was beyond Miles's comprehension.

Clearing his throat, he swiveled to face the chief again. "Thank you, sir."

The chief glanced at the clock on the wall. "Why don't you finish up and go get Miss Miller? Her shift is almost done. I think you are the best man for the job of protecting her right now."

"Okay. Give me about twenty minutes to finish up here, then I'll head out."

"Keep me posted." Whistling, the chief strolled away. Why was it always *The Andy Griffith Show* theme song? He'd be hearing it in his mind all day now.

He grabbed the bottle of Mountain Dew sitting on his desk and took a long swig. He put down the bottle and wiped his mouth, then set about making some more phone calls. Half an hour later, he felt he had accomplished all he could do there.

Flipping his wrist over to see the time, he noted he still had time to get to the bookstore before Rebecca's shift ended. He gathered up his keys and finished off the Mountain Dew before tossing the bottle in the recyclables can. He tapped his watch, bringing up Rebecca's contact information, and sent her a text to let her know he was on his way. It was only polite. Plus, he didn't want her to worry if she saw him pull up when he'd said he would talk with her tomorrow.

He was in his vehicle two minutes later, and there was still no response. Which could mean nothing, he told himself. Not everyone was attached to their phones. When he sent a text to Parker and got no response, though, he couldn't ignore the voice that told him the situation was off.

His pager crackled. The dispatcher's voice broke through the static. "Suspected high-level carbon-monoxide event at 309 Main Street, A Novel Idea Bookstore, with multiple victims."

Fear clenched his heart like a fist. Rebecca was there! Miles flipped on his siren, and peeled away from the curb. Cars pulled to the side as he whizzed past. He switched on his own radio and yelled, "LaMar Pond PD unit six en route to the scene."

Why didn't Parker respond? As a police officer, he should have been aware of the situation before it became critical and started to evacuate the premises. Unless there was more going on than just a carbon-monoxide poisoning.

There was no way this was accidental.

The dispatcher acknowledged his call. Then repeated the call for the local volunteer fire departments to respond. It was the middle of the day. On a beautiful Saturday. He knew from experience that in the rural areas responses might be slower. And he also knew it would take twenty minutes for the local ambulance to arrive. He was Rebecca's best hope.

Please, Lord Jesus, help me be on time.

There was an empty parking space across the street from the store. He parallel-parked, then leaped from his car, running across the street as soon as it was clear. A couple of older customers milled around outside of the store, concern etched on their wrinkled faces. A cursory glance into the window made his heart rate spike. No one was in view. And he knew that there was a minimum of three people who were supposed to be in that store and who were unaccounted for.

"Ladies! Is anyone in there?"

"Yes, officer." One of the women stepped forward. "We were in there and saw the girl at the counter fall down. She didn't move. Then Margie here said she felt funny." She pointed to the other woman.

Miles switched his gaze to Margie. "Are you all right, ma'am?"

"Yes. My son is an EMT for East Mead township. I know the signs of carbon-monoxide poisoning, so we came out and called 911. There were two other people in the store, but I didn't see them when we left."

"We tried to move the lady behind the counter," the other woman interrupted her. "She was too heavy for us."

Miles thanked them and ran to the entrance. He grabbed the door handle and swung the door open, flipping the mechanism at the top of the door to hold it open.

"Ladies," he said to the women outside, "I need to go into the store and start bringing people out. When the paramedics arrive, you need to let them know that there are at least three people inside, four including me. This door needs to remain open so the fumes can begin to air out."

He waited just long enough to receive a nod of agreement, then dashed inside. As he passed the checkout counter, he could see a pale arm stretched out behind the edge of the counter. He recognized the charm bracelet on the slim wrist as the one that Tracy had been wearing earlier that day. Still no sign of Rebecca. Panic rocketed inside him, but he forced himself to push it down. Unfortunately, there was a book cart jammed up against the counter. Not a very safe place for it. Jumping over the counter, he stepped to Tracy's head, and bent down to hook his hands under her armpits. Moving backward, he pulled the unconscious woman out from behind the counter, shoving the book cart out of his way with his hip until he could pick her up. He paused long enough to take the decorative scarf off Tracy's neck and wrap it over his face. He knew it wouldn't provide that much protection, but maybe it would provide just enough for him to do the job.

All the while, Rebecca and Parker were still unaccounted for. *Dear Lord*, he prayed. *Guide me. Help me find them before it's too late.*

What if it was already too late? He couldn't go there. He just could not face the sense of failure he would experience if he let her down. Why did he agree to let her go to work?

A wail split the air. An ambulance was parking up against the curb, its siren wailing. The two paramedics exited, one of them immediately going to Tracy and the customers to check on their condition and start them on oxygen. The other one was holding a handheld carbon-monoxide tester. As soon as he stepped into the building, the tester started beeping. Paling, the young man read the results. "Over eight hundred parts per million! That's almost impossible. Anyone inside is in immediate danger. This level of poisoning acts quickly. Unconsciousness within two hours, death within three!"

"There are still two more people inside, but I couldn't see them! One of them is deaf, so calling out for her won't do any good, even if she's still conscious."

A second emergency vehicle pulled in across the street. Good. But they were still not exiting quickly enough for his peace of mind.

Miles bolted back through the door, ignoring the paramedic who bellowed after him to stop. He should wait, let someone else go in who had protective gear and hadn't already been exposed. But he couldn't be sure there was time, not with two people missing.

This was life and death.

Chapter Nine

Miles ran through the bookstore, searching every nook and cranny. He peered around every case as he passed it. Nothing. He began to cough. He knew that the scarf wouldn't provide that much protection. He had hoped it would give him a little more time, though. Reaching the back of the store, he took hold of the doorknob and turned it, pushing the door open with more force than was required. The door slammed against the back wall and bounced back, hitting his shoulder as he charged through it. He barely noticed. All his attention was focused on the scene before him.

Parker was unconscious against the wall, blood dripping from a wound on his head. Given the angle he was at, it was highly unlikely his injury had happened as a result of a fall. More likely, he had interrupted the attacker and had been bludgeoned into unconsciousness. Beyond him lay Rebecca. For one terrifying second, he thought she had stopped breathing. No. Her breaths were erratic and shallow, but he could see her chest rising and falling.

A paramedic burst through the door, followed by

an EMT. They nodded as Miles went to Rebecca. Between the two men, they managed to get Parker off the floor and carry him out, going through the back door instead of retracing their steps through the gas-filled store. Good idea.

Muttering a prayer of thanksgiving under his breath, he bent down and lifted the unconscious woman in his arms. Her face was so pale. *Do your job*, he reminded himself.

Miles followed the paramedic and EMT out the back door into the alley. The ambulance was being moved to the back. He stood by as Parker, Tracy and Rebecca were checked and hooked to oxygen. They were all breathing, although none of them regained consciousness.

The paramedic insisted on checking him out, too. He endured the examination as patiently as he could, but all he wanted was to make sure Rebecca, Tracy and Parker were safe.

Within minutes, the three victims were all loaded into ambulances and carried off to the hospital. Miles waited only long enough to see the ambulance carrying Rebecca pull out into traffic on Main Street, sirens blaring, before putting a call into Chief Kennedy to tell him what had been found. Not that that's what he wanted to do. No, indeed. Every instinct inside of him was screaming for him to hop in his car and follow the ambulance to the hospital. But he knew he had to contact his chief first. It made it easier knowing that Jackson had responded to his 911 call and was already en route to the hospital. He would look out for Rebecca until Miles arrived.

"Has a cause been determined?" Chief Kennedy's voice was quiet, but it ran deep with concern.

"Yes, Chief. This was no accident. The furnace had been sabotaged, and the carbon-monoxide alarm was discarded on the ground near where Parker was found. Which is right next to the basement stairs. My guess is Parker had heard the intruder as he attempted to leave through the back door."

"Not a very skilled assassin. He left a witness."

Miles winced. He had thought the same thing. "From the angle of the blow, it's possible that Parker never saw the attacker. And I highly doubt he thought anyone would survive. The level of toxin in the air was shocking. The paramedics said that level of gas could kill within a short time. This was definitely premeditated. I also think it's suspicious that both attacks happened as the owner is conveniently out of the way."

"In your opinion, she's a link. Or a suspect."

Miles nodded, then realized the chief couldn't see him. "Yeah. I'm leaning more toward the idea that our attacker knows her. From the description Rebecca gave me the other day, she's not big enough to have been the attacker herself. Nor did Rebecca know anything of her before she opened the bookstore. Chief, I would like to request that both Tracy and Parker be guarded. At least until they are capable of looking out for themselves."

A heavy sigh drifted over the connection. "I figured. Of course, we'll do what we can to provide protection. Still, it's always sad to hear about such evil, to willingly kill innocent people like that. This makes the fourth attempt on Miss Miller's life."

As if he could forget it.

"Miles, I think as soon as she is released we need to get her into protective custody."

"I would love to see that happen. But somehow, I don't think she'll go for it."

"Not even with everything that's happened?"

Miles took a moment to consider everything that had happened and what he knew about Rebecca. She had been attacked and was aware of the danger, but he also knew she believed that God was looking out for her. And he also had figured out that her family was of utmost importance to her. She worked so hard to keep those ties, it would devastate her to miss Levi's wedding.

"Sir, her brother's wedding is in five days, on Thursday. I'm pretty sure she will be in the hospital until Monday, so it would be easier to keep an eye on her for now. We can up the security at Seth's for when she gets out. Make sure she is never alone. On the day of the wedding, I will be with her the entire time. I will talk with her about the ceremony. It's important to her, so I will ask her to invite me as her guest." He waited while the chief thought about it.

"I agree that you should be there. Also, I think it would be better for her if she dressed Amish for the wedding."

Was that even allowed, since she had chosen to leave that world behind? He would have to see what could be done. Would she agree? He knew her reasons for leaving the Amish community were very personal.

"Will she go along with that?" Chief Kennedy's voice was filled with skepticism as he echoed Miles's thoughts.

"Does she really have a choice?" Miles shook his

head, knowing his words came out a bit stronger and more sarcastic than he had meant them to when speaking to his boss. "Anyway, I think she will do whatever she can to be there. And then afterward, I think we will have a better shot at convincing her to go into hiding. Hopefully, we will find the attacker before too long. And before anyone else gets hurt."

Oh, wait. "Chief, I think it would be safe to say that I won't be able to openly carry a gun at the wedding."

A lengthy pause filled the silence. Miles imagined the chief closing his eyes and pinching the bridge of his nose. "I don't like the sound of that. We'll have to think about it. I would prefer you have a weapon on you, even if it's concealed. You will be on duty, even if you're dressed as a guest. If the killer shows up, we need to be prepared."

Yeah, that could get awkward. Although if the attacker was close enough, Miles felt confident he'd be able to take him down in hand-to-hand combat. He was a black belt in karate, thanks to the need to prove himself capable. One more thing he owed to his parents' dysfunctional relationship.

"Okay, Miles. I think you have a good handle on this. I will put all personnel on notice that they may be called upon for a security detail."

Miles disconnected the call. For a couple of minutes, he stood where he was, running over the conversation and his options in his mind. And realized he really didn't have any. He had to protect Rebecca. And unless she decided to accept his recommendation that she place herself in protective custody, that meant he had to attend an Amish wedding. Why was he so nervous about that? He'd attended lots of weddings before. Lieutenant Willis had gotten married a year and a half ago and Seth had gotten married just a couple of months ago.

But he knew why this one was different. He was going there, as an outsider, as Rebecca's guest. Even if it was for protective purposes, he would be viewed as if he had a more personal connection with Rebecca. And the worst of it was, there was a connection. He liked her. She was smart and funny, and her strength and sorrow-filled eyes touched his heart.

Which was precisely what worried him.

None of that was important, though. All that mattered was that he would be there to protect Rebecca and those she loved from a killer.

Where was she?

Rebecca opened her eyes, squinting as her head ached in protest. She was connected to a machine. For someone raised in a small Amish community with no electricity or modern technology, the sight should have been unusual, maybe even upsetting all on its own. Unfortunately, Rebecca had very clear memories of waking up in a hospital before, surrounded by far more frightening-looking machines and monitors, and a crowd of people looking down at her.

Reflexively, she glanced down at her wrists. No rub burns from restraints this time. And though her head hurt, her back and legs didn't feel as though they were on fire. Because no one had been beating her this time, or cutting her. No one had physically assaulted her at all this time…but that didn't mean no one was hurt.

Sergeant Parker.

She needed to find out if he was alive. She had

walked into the back room to get something and found him bleeding on the floor. She remembered helping him to sit up—feeling a little woozy and sick herself as she crouched down beside him. He'd tried to tell her something. Maybe some kind of warning, but he had been too weak to make his point understood. She must have blacked out. Or had she been attacked, too?

No. She would have remembered that. Instead, all she remembered was a searing headache before absolute nothing.

The door opened. A nurse entered the room with a cart and smiled. Miles followed her in. The tightness that had begun to bunch in her shoulders loosened at the sight of his familiar face. He approached the bed and waited as the nurse busied herself with the machine and checking on Rebecca's vitals.

Then she started speaking. Miles positioned himself near the nurse's shoulder and interpreted, reciting the information the nurse offered about how her vitals had stabilized nicely.

"Okay, the doctor should be in shortly," Miles concluded.

One of her hands was still connected to a machine. Rebecca used her free hand to ask what was wrong with her.

"The doctor will explain everything. Don't worry. You're in good hands here."

The nurse wheeled her cart over to the door. Miles beat her there and held the door open. As soon as she left, he closed the door again.

She tried to push herself up to a sitting position, but he placed a firm hand on her shoulder and shook his head. Fine. It was embarrassing talking to him lying down. She felt vulnerable and weak. That didn't matter, though. "Is your friend all right? The officer named Parker?"

Miles leaned in closer. "I just left his room. He will be fine. Probably needs to take a few days off work. But no permanent damage has been done."

Her bones dissolved. At least that's how she felt as she melted back into the mattress, the anxiety festering inside her evaporating. The officer would be well—he hadn't been seriously injured because he'd been protecting her.

"Will you tell me what happened?" She was not in the mood to be placated while she waited for the doctor to make an appearance. All this avoidance of the issue only made her feel worse.

"What do you remember?" Miles moved the lone chair so that they could see each other without being hampered by the tubes and wires. She appreciated the thoughtfulness.

What did she remember? Not enough, that was a fact.

"Not much. I was supposed to change the window display today. I went into the back room to gather what I would need. But I found Sergeant Parker on the floor. He was bleeding, here…" She touched her head with her free hand. "When I knelt beside him, he opened his eyes and tried to sit up. I didn't think he should, but I couldn't get him to stay still, so I helped him. He seemed agitated, upset. I think he was trying to tell me something. Maybe he thought I could read his lips. I'm sorry. I tried to learn, but I never mastered it…"

Would things have been different if she could?

She noticed Miles looking at her arm. The scars

from when Terry Gleason had cut her for his amusement were thick scarlet slashes on her pale skin.

Would he be repelled by them? She was afraid to look at him.

Miles touched her hand, then caught her gaze as she looked up. His eyes were soft. She could see no sign of disgust. "You can't blame yourself for any of this. What happened next?"

Closing her eyes briefly, she let the images from earlier fill her mind. What happened next? She signed the question in her mind, thinking through the answer.

"I had started to feel sick earlier. And my head was aching. I was getting sleepy. I think my headache got bad really fast. And then, I must have fainted or something. Because the next thing I was aware of was waking up here."

He nodded and leaned back. His normally expressive face was nearly blank. The ultracontrolled expression scared her more than anything else could. It stated without words that the situation had escalated even more. And that there was nothing random about what had happened at the bookstore.

Not that she'd thought there was. Not even for a second.

Miles waved his hand slightly. When she looked at him, he touched his index finger to his chin and made a twisting motion. "Serious." She tensed again. It was a definite statement that something important was coming. "This was no accident. I'm sure you already know that. Someone sabotaged the furnace so that the store was flooded with carbon-monoxide gas. I have to think that Sergeant Parker somehow interrupted the person responsible and that was why he was hit. There was a fire extinguisher on the floor. It had blood on it. That's most likely what the attacker used."

Her breath exploded out of her. Thinking back, she vaguely remembered stepping past the extinguisher. She'd been so worried about Parker that she hadn't given it a second thought.

"He says he went to the back room to do a routine check of the premises, and didn't see anyone. The person must have hidden behind the door leading to the basement stairs until Parker was already in the room. Then *bam*!"

She jumped as he slammed his fist into his palm. She wasn't offended at the graphic description, but her nerves were so strained that any little thing made her jumpy. Miles continued. "He'll be able to leave here tomorrow or Monday so that's good news. Although, that means there will be one less police officer on the job." His brow furrowed as he considered that. Poor Miles. He looked exhausted. "When you are released, I will bring you back to the Travis house. We've increased police protection."

Suddenly, her mind took a detour.

"Wait! Thursday is my brother's wedding! What am I supposed to do about that?" It was unbearable, thinking of missing Levi's special day.

Miles ducked his head slightly, and his shaggy blond hair bobbed on his forehead. "I've been thinking of that. I know that non-Amish people sometimes are guests at weddings. How about if I go with you? To protect you and your family."

She blinked. That was an interesting idea. But a police officer…

"You can't go dressed in your uniform."

He responded with an elaborate eye roll. "Please. Give me some credit. I do own some church clothes. I will do my best not to stand out."

"But you will."

She watched his eyes widen and realized she had probably been too blunt. She hurried to explain. "Sorry. But I have seen you while you work. Your eyes never stop moving. You are constantly looking around for danger. Even while you are laughing, your eyes are moving. The only time they don't is when you are signing to me." She pursed her lips and tilted her head, examining his surprised face.

Miles smiled, an open smile showing straight white teeth. Lovely.

"I won't apologize for that. I plan to keep on my guard to keep you and your family safe." His smile widened even more, becoming a grin, with a touch of smugness to it. "And I think spending a full day in your company will be very enjoyable."

Oh, my. She was aware of something shifting inside of her heart. Keeping a step ahead of a vicious killer wasn't her only problem. No. Now it seemed she also had to keep her heart safe from the man she believed God had sent to protect her.

A short while later, Miles stood and stretched. She averted her eyes when she realized she was watching the play of his biceps under his T-shirt. *Not appropriate, Rebecca.* He yawned, but to her mind it looked exaggerated.

"I need to head out. You okay if I go?" he signed.

No, no, please stay.

"Of course, I will be fine. You go work. Or whatever."

He grinned, his blond hair flopping over his forehead. Her fingers itched to brush the soft hair back. Why was she letting herself get so distracted? Her eyes met his, and the smile slipped from his face. His blue eyes grew intense, and the air between them sizzled. For a moment, she felt breathless, as if the air had grown thin.

He backed up, and the moment faded.

Sketching a brief wave, he sauntered out of the room, though he did turn back and catch her gaze one last time before he left. She had a feeling she'd be reliving that weighted glance and trying to dissect it for the rest of the evening. It was going to be a long sleepless night.

Chapter Ten

The next morning, the nurse was just carrying away Rebecca's half-eaten breakfast tray when the door opened. Rebecca's eyes shot wide when her boss, April, entered the room, her face pale and drawn. Normally, April was very well put together. This morning, she was without makeup and her hair had been slapped up in a messy bun. She approached the bed, taking in Rebecca and her surroundings. As she stopped at the bed, she pulled out her phone and tapped a message, then showed it to Rebecca.

R U ok? I just saw Tracy. She'll be fine.

Rebecca took the phone and tapped a message back. I'm fine. I will be going home soon.

April's lips firmed as she read the message. And then she typed a response. I heard about your roommate. I'm so sorry. And Tracy said you were attacked the other night after closing the store. What's going on?

Good question. How to answer it.

She could see Miles's image in her mind, signing to her to be careful, not to give away too much information. It wasn't that she didn't trust April, but her innocent conversation with Tracy, revealing that she was staying with Jess, had shown her it was safer to be vague. The police are looking into it. I don't know too much more than that.

Well, that was true, wasn't it? She really didn't know too much more. Other than the same group of girls she'd been abducted with years before were being hunted down, one by one. But April didn't know anything about that event. And, she realized, she didn't want her to. Didn't want to see her boss start to view her as a victim, to look at her with pity.

Rebecca kept the past to herself. And when April finally left after a few awkward moments, she was relieved.

The rest of the day dragged on. Rebecca hated not being able to get to church, so she comforted herself with watching a service on the TV and praying.

The next morning, she was informed that she was being released.

Rebecca should have been overjoyed. After all, she hated hospitals. She'd been stuck in one for three days after the abduction, needing constant medical care after being dehydrated and brutally beaten. It wasn't a pleasant memory.

She wasn't happy to be leaving the hospital this time, though. In fact, she was terrified.

She had expected Miles to be here when she was released. But he wasn't. She had no idea where he was. And that made her feel distinctly uneasy. In her mind, she replayed the conversation they had had the night before. He hadn't mentioned being here when she was released. She'd just assumed. Although, they didn't know she would be sprung so quickly.

The nurse entered the room pushing a VRI, a video remote interpreting system. It was a portable device used by hospitals and legal offices to connect with certified interpreters. Personally, Rebecca preferred to have an interpreter physically in the same room. If she needed to go to the doctor or the audiologist, she always made the appointment and scheduled an interpreter well in advance. Clearly, an interpreter wasn't available currently. She sighed, but didn't complain.

The nurse began to explain the release procedures while the interpreter relayed the information to Rebecca.

It was amazing. Brilliant. Incredibly helpful. And yet she felt so alone.

No one was here that she knew. How would she get home? Text Miles? But he was either working, or home enjoying his time off shift, and either way she felt hesitant to disturb whatever it was that he was up to. Because she hated the idea of relying too much on him.

Finally, the efficient nurse shoved some papers under her nose. She was to sign to show she understood. And then she could go.

Great.

As she was finishing up her signature, the door opened. A familiar head popped in, shaggy blond hair flopping to the side due to the angle he was holding his head. Her mood lightened instantly. Caution stirred inside, as well. The nurse smiled at Miles as she left the room.

"Hey." Miles grinned and pulled the rest of himself inside the room. "Your guard outside let me know that you were being released. I was taking a trip today. Thought you might want to come along."

Interest stirred.

"Where?" she signed.

He sauntered closer to her. "The visitor log from the prison arrived this morning. It seems Terry Gleason had only three visitors the entire time he was in prison. His parents and a man by the name of Declan Winters."

"Winters? The same last name as Jasmine?"

He bobbed his head up and down in a slow, exaggerated motion. Even his signs were exaggerated, emphasizing that this was very unusual. "Exactly like Jasmine's. In fact, Declan is her older brother. I want to know why this man was visiting the man who killed his sister on a weekly basis."

Wow. She didn't even know what to say to that.

"So, you want to go? Or should I drop you off at Jess's house? There's someone on guard there at all times now."

"Are you kidding me? Obviously, I'm going with you."

The smirk that graced his face told her he expected her to say that. She didn't care. The idea of going back to the house was unappealing. And going with him would be interesting. Plus, she'd hopefully find out more about what was going on.

But, wasn't there some kind of rule against taking her along on police business? She asked him.

"The chief gave his approval. We're short-staffed at the moment with Parker out of commission. Plus, he thinks that as I am the only one who can sign, it might be beneficial for you to stay with me."

Sounded like a good idea to her.

* * *

This was probably the dumbest idea he'd ever had. Taking Rebecca on a police visit? It had made so much sense when he had broached the subject with the chief that morning. But now? Not so much. Not when she was so charming and funny. And her blunt honesty really struck a chord with him.

Seeking something else to focus on, his eyes flicked to the rearview mirror and he noticed that the car behind them had gotten a little too close.

Not again. He tapped on the brakes, and the car fell back. It took a lot of guts or arrogance to tailgate a police car. Was it deliberate? He sped up to see if the car would follow them.

It stayed back, and soon two other cars were between them. Maybe he should consider going on vacation when this case was over. He smirked to himself. He was getting paranoid. But better paranoid than careless. He stopped at a stop sign.

A hand tapped on his arm. He glanced over briefly. Rebecca signed the word *funny*, scrunching her eyebrows down in a motion that signaled a "wh" question, meaning "What's so funny?"

He slid his eyes back to the road and answered one-handed as he continued through the intersection. "I'm starting to see things. I thought we were being followed, but it was only my imagination."

He hoped.

Once more he flicked his gaze to the mirror. The car was out of sight. Yep. He needed a vacation.

Between the attraction that simmered between them and the always present concern of being followed, the car ride to Warren, where Declan Winters resided, was rife with enough tension that he half expected the air to start crackling with it. He rather suspected that was why their arrival at Winters's house seemed so anti-climactic.

No need to wonder if Winters was home. The man himself stood outside in his driveway, his expression intent as he used a circular saw on a two-by-four laid across two sawhorses. He stopped sawing as they pulled in. When he bent down and unplugged the tool before removing his safety glasses, Miles silently approved. You never left equipment plugged in when it wasn't in use.

"Declan Winters?" Miles asked as he left his vehicle. Rebecca remained in the car, as he'd instructed. He didn't want her out in the open until he knew it was safe. She was better off where he could keep an eye on her and keep her out of harm's way at the same time.

"Yeah? That's me." The tall man standing behind his makeshift workplace narrowed his gaze, letting it drift to the badge and the name. "What can I do for you, Officer Olsen? Do you have more information about my sister?"

Miles quirked an eyebrow. "Your sister?"

The man waved, like he was swatting a fly. "Yeah. I assumed this was about Jazzy again."

"Because?"

"Some reporter left a message on my machine, wanting to discuss her kidnapping and murder. I never responded." Now the man grew cautious. "If you're not here about my sister, what's this about?"

Give a little. Maybe he'll open up more about his sister.

"Mr. Winters, are you aware that the women who

were abducted with your sister ten years ago have recently been targeted?"

"Targeted?" Declan paled. He shook his head. "Targeted how?"

"Targeted as in abducted and beaten. One of them is in a coma in the hospital. Another is dead. A third has been attacked, but escaped."

"It's not Terry Gleason. He's dead. I know because I visited him every week for years."

Miles smiled. His instinct told him the man was on the level. "I know. Why? He killed your sister."

Declan straightened, hands behind his back, a fierce scowl appearing. Not at Miles. He appeared to be struggling with himself. Miles had a sudden picture in his mind of Dan Willis, standing in a similar posture. Dan was ex-military. The file had mentioned that Declan had been in the navy.

Following his instincts, Miles suggested they move to a more secure location, less in the open. Like the garage. When Declan agreed, he moved to the cruiser to get Rebecca. She exited the vehicle, her posture tight. She seemed ready to bolt, and he waved her ahead of himself, using his body as a buffer for whatever dangers might be out there.

His shoulder blades twitched. He ignored it, just motioned her to move faster. She didn't ask questions, just quickened her gentle gait until she was inside the relative safety of the garage walls. He pushed past her to grab the large door and pull it closed. Well, that wasn't helpful. The door was cut into three sections, and almost the entire top section consisted of three rectangular windows. He found himself as close to growling as he had ever come. How was he supposed to keep Rebecca safe in these conditions?

No one knew she was here, he reasoned. Still, caution was the word of the day. He signed to her to move to the side of the garage for safety, voicing it aloud for Declan's benefit.

Declan shrugged, and got his first clear look at Rebecca. His jaw dropped.

"Hey! I remember you! You were at the trial!"

Funny how some things stayed in your mind.

Miles quickly signed introductions. He made sure to sign everything in pidgin. "We were discussing why you went to visit your sister's murderer in prison. I would have expected you to be angry at him."

Declan rubbed the back of his neck with one hand, the other hand set loosely on his hip. "It's odd, I know. After the trial, I was bitter. Yeah, Gleason went to jail, but my baby sister was still dead. My parents couldn't handle the stress. They split. Both of them have remarried. My mom still can't celebrate Mother's Day. It practically destroyed my family. So yeah, I was angry. Beyond angry. I was at rock bottom. And then I met someone who taught me to see it all through faith. It didn't happen overnight. It took a good year for me to get to a place of forgiveness."

"Forgiveness?" Miles jerked a little at that. He was a Christian, and he still felt hostility rearing in his soul whenever his stepsister's murderer was mentioned. Yet this guy was talking about forgiveness.

"Yeah, forgiveness. It's not easy. But it was necessary. You gotta understand—bitterness was eating me alive. I could feel it destroying me from the inside out."

Miles nodded. He had experienced the same feeling.

"I forgave Gleason, not because he needed it, but because I did. And then I became an outreach minister at my church. When the program moved into the prison system, I knew I was being called to go there."

A gentle nudge pushed at his conscience. He knew he was supposed to forgive those who wronged him, but did that really extend to murderers?

Father, forgive them, for they know not what they do. How many times had he heard that Scripture? It had always made him faintly uncomfortable. Yes, he knew he needed to forgive. Allowing the bitterness inside him to fester had almost cost him his job once. By letting it remain, he was risking letting it cost him even more.

A warm hand crept into his, squeezing gently. Rebecca. "Are you okay?" she signed one-handed. *No. But I'm gonna be. Father, help me to forgive and move on.*

"I'm fine. Thanks," he signed back. And returned his attention to Declan.

"Was Gleason receptive?"

Declan shook his head. "Not really. He was very angry. Apparently, he knew a few of the girls from school. He was a year behind, so he graduated when he was almost nineteen. From what he said, they were pretty and popular and took delight in tormenting him. At least, that's his side of the story. I think he tolerated my visits because they gave him an outlet to vent his anger. That, and no one else came to visit him."

"I know he had no family aside from his parents," Miles began, but stopped short when Declan shook his head.

"He had an older brother."

What? He quickly signed the statement to Rebecca.

"A brother!" Rebecca signed, jumping into the conversation for the first time, eyes opened wide.

Miles knew just how she felt. "His file lists him as an only child."

"An *adopted* only child," Declan amended. "He had a biological half brother somewhere that he lived with until he was three. The brother was five. When his birth mother was killed, the brother was sent to live with his birth father, who refused to take Terry because Terry was no relation to him. Terry was adopted by a well-meaning couple who thought it was cruel that the brothers were separated. So they made sure Terry knew about him. I know Terry always intended on finding his brother someday. But he died before he could."

"He never met him after they were separated as kids?" Miles tapped all the information into his notes app. Later, he'd email it to himself so he could make out a report and a list of details he needed to check. Just to give himself a clear picture of all the connections in the case.

"Not that I'm aware of."

It was enough to make a man crazy.

"Do you have a name for this brother? A physical description? Anything?"

Declan shook his head. "Sorry. All I know is that he was two years older."

Just when he'd thought they were getting somewhere. Was it possible that his brother had come looking for Terry—or for revenge on the people who had put Terry away? Miles's mind whirled at the implications. He needed to start looking for this brother. Because he had the feeling the brother had already found them.

Miles opened his mouth to thank Declan for his time. But never got the chance. The window next to him blew apart, showering all three of them with glass. Almost immediately, the sound of more glass breaking echoed from outside. A car window. Miles dove for Rebecca. So did Declan. Between the two men, she was hidden from view of whoever was shooting.

Miles wasn't. He was well aware that he had just made himself a breathing target.

Chapter Eleven

Hunched between two muscular men, Rebecca couldn't even get enough air to scream. The middle window blew apart. She flinched. Miles pulled her in closer to him. Her forehead was pressed up against his neck. She could feel his pulse racing.

She drew in a deep breath—his clean scent came with it, bringing comfort. And security.

And fear.

What was he doing? If she raised her head to look over his shoulder, she knew she'd have a clear view of the windows. Which meant someone looking in could see her. And would literally have to go through Miles to get her. And maybe Declan, too, she realized. Whoever was after her was relentless, and seemed to be growing braver by the hour, so she had little doubt that he would shoot other people to get to her.

She did her best to pull back from Miles, so he could find shelter, too. But he wouldn't let her. Instead, those strong arms tightened, drawing her closer. There was nothing to do but wait it out.

And pray.

Rebecca lifted her mind to God, and in her mind, she signed to Him, asking for safety, for all three of them, and for Brooke and Ashley. She prayed that the killer would be found. And then, she paused. Slowly, she sent another prayer, asking for her attacker's redemption. It felt strange, but she knew, after learning Declan's story, that it was the right thing to do. The memory of Miles's shattered expression as he'd listened to Declan burst into her mind.

There was a story there. An anguish that he kept hidden. If they got out of this alive... No. *When* they escaped this situation, she'd ask him. He knew her history. She wanted to know what haunted him.

Her right leg was starting to go numb from being crouched in an awkward position for so long. Abruptly, Miles released her, catching her again as she started to stumble back.

"Sorry," he signed. "I can hear sirens outside. One of the neighbors must have called the police."

She nodded and straightened painfully. Standing was difficult, as pins and needles attacked her right leg. "My leg went to sleep," she signed in apology, clutching at Miles's arm for balance.

He grinned, the unexpected expression sending her heartbeat skittering, but the look was gone in a flash, replaced by his cop face. Which was probably why she nearly fell over as he leaned in quickly and kissed her forehead. "You're okay, right? Anything hurt?"

"Fine," she signed, wishing she could stem the tide of warmth spreading through her face. The man was making her melt like a gooey marshmallow. Not good.

"You okay?" He addressed Declan.

She melted some more. Except for police business,

even when he wasn't talking to her, he remembered to sign, to include her in the conversation. Her own family didn't do that. Couldn't, she reminded herself.

She broke out of her thoughts when Miles jerked back. "Police are at the door." He strode to the main door and looked through the broken windows, then yelled out, continuing to sign for her benefit, "Hold up your badge, please." She could see his body relax slightly before he opened the door.

"Could you two remain here, please?" he asked Declan and Rebecca. They both nodded.

She understood. He wanted to make sure everything was safe. As much as she hated not being able to see him, she knew he had a job to do. And she couldn't keep him from it.

It struck her just how dangerous his job was. Her heart was becoming attached to him, but she didn't know if she was happy with that. After the abduction ten years ago, she'd wanted safety. She had lived through enough fear. She didn't know if she was strong enough to go through more. Giving her heart to a policeman meant watching that heart walk into danger every day. Could she live with that?

But then, wasn't she living through it now? She'd been surrounded by danger ever since the attacks had begun. And she wasn't falling apart. God would help her through whatever situation she was in.

He'd done it before.

It felt like forever until Miles returned. The tension inside her escalated. What if it was a trick? What if he was out there in danger? The thought that she would be next also popped up, but she shoved that aside. Because right at the moment, Miles was what mattered.

The one thing that helped was that Declan was so calm, knowing that he could hear some of what was happening outside. She could see him cock his head several times, listening. He sent her a small smile. It didn't send her heart racing like Miles's did, but it comforted her. Surely, the man wouldn't be smiling if he thought a murderer was about to charge through the door and finish them off. Right?

Just when she thought she could not stand the strain one more minute, Miles popped his head back through the door. His shaggy hair was going in all directions, as if he'd been running a frustrated hand through it. Many times. She tucked the corners of her mouth in, hoping to keep her smile from peeping through. Judging by the way he squinted at her, she wasn't totally successful. He shrugged, and waved at them to come out.

Two police cars were in front of Declan's driveway. At least fifteen people dotted the street, craning their necks to get a full view of everything. It was probably the most excitement this small town had seen in a while. It was natural that they would be curious. Still, she ducked her head, uncomfortable with the scrutiny. Miles, she noted, did his best to keep himself between the crowd and her, shielding her from prying eyes and any dangers that might come flying at them.

Again, a smile threatened. It died completely when she saw Miles's cruiser. She gasped. The side passenger window and the windshield were shattered. Another bullet had gone through the driver's door. She knew without being told that they wouldn't be driving back to LaMar Pond like that. It was going to be a long day.

"Why shoot the car?" she signed to Miles, having trouble processing what she was seeing.

"It was in the way." He kept his face blank, but she sensed there was rage beneath the surface. She shivered. "He must have been over there—" he waved vaguely to the left "—and was trying to get to us in the garage. I assume he didn't care who or what he hit."

The local police were questioning a woman about her mother's age. The woman motioned down the street, then swung her arm in an outward arc toward the other side. When her finger was pointing at Declan's house, she acted like she was aiming a gun at the garage. Then she jerked it back. *Bang, bang.* Rebecca could see it clearly in her head. Then the woman moved her arm and pointed toward the opposite end of the street.

Miles moved to stand beside her. Uh-oh. His jaw was cranked so tight, she thought it would shatter if she touched it. A muscle jumped on the right side. Something the woman said was eating at him. What?

Finally, the officer nodded and the woman drifted off. Miles turned to her. "The gist of that conversation is that the woman noticed a car driving down the street. Three, four times. Each time it got to this house, the driver would slow down. All she could see for sure was that he was wearing a dark hoodie, and the hood was up. The last time he went past, he opened fire."

"Why would he risk firing with witnesses around?" It didn't make any sense.

"There were no witnesses outside. She was upstairs in her sewing room, and just happened to be facing the window. He probably didn't realize she could see him."

Okay. That made sense. "So, what else is wrong? You're a lot more upset than you were ten minutes ago." And that was saying something, because he was plenty upset then.

He started.

Yeah, busted, she thought, but kept it to herself.

"I'm mad at myself mostly. You and Declan are in more danger, because of me."

She tilted her head, trying to make sense of that. "I don't see that. You didn't shoot at us."

He paced away, then turned and faced her. The torment in his blue eyes just about ripped her heart out. "But I should have trusted my gut more. I am almost one-hundred-percent sure the shooter was in that car I thought was following us earlier."

How to handle this? She was beginning to realize that her protector had a very sensitive soul. One that had been wounded before. He was also the kind of man to shoulder the blame for everything himself. She didn't want to add to the guilt she could see weighing him down.

"How could you have known?" she signed. "Once he realized he'd been spotted, he turned off before we could get a good look at him. You can't see the future. Only God can. I think instead of blaming yourself, you should be praising Him. I am. He knew that there would be danger today, and sent me someone who would know how to keep me safe when it happened."

He shrugged. But his lips curled upward. She sighed, some of the ache dissipating.

"I feel bad about him, though." Miles jerked a thumb over his shoulder at Declan, who was still talking to the police. "He is going to take a leave of absence from work and go out of town. He's in danger now. I think our interest in him has put him on the hit list."

Another person in harm's way.

"He might have been in danger anyway," she argued. "Didn't you say he was Terry Gleason's last visitor? Maybe that's why the shooter was so willing to kill him."

The lips that were still curled bloomed into a full smile, filled with wonder. Her breath caught in her throat. Stunning.

"You are amazing, do you know that?"

"Thanks," she signed, flushing. Accepting praise was not her strong point. Deflection, however, was. "Do you think it was Gleason's brother?"

He cast her a glance that clearly said she wasn't fooling him.

After a moment, he nodded. "I do. I can't prove it yet. But I need to find out as much as I can about the brother. Which means we need to get back to LaMar Pond."

She prayed with all her might that he would find the brother. Too many people were in danger. And she knew life wouldn't get back to normal, for any of them, until whoever was responsible was stopped.

Would this nightmare ever end?

This was getting out of control.

Miles tightened his grip on the steering wheel and clenched his teeth until his jaw ached. He forced himself to relax. No sense letting himself get riled up. He couldn't afford to let his judgment get clouded.

Speaking of that...

He angled his head until he had a clear view of Rebecca, fast asleep in the passenger seat. Poor woman. She was exhausted. They'd had to wait around for two hours until the glass repair people had come and fixed the broken windows. He'd have to wait to get the damage done to the actual door repaired, but at least the car was drivable again.

Rebecca had conked out soon after they had left, giving him time to think.

And worry. He was getting too attached to Rebecca. He knew it. Had known it as soon as he realized how anxious he was at leaving her alone inside the garage to talk to the other police officers. Okay, so Declan was there, and the man looked like he knew how to take care of himself. But Miles hated trusting Rebecca's safety to anyone else.

Getting emotionally involved was a bad thing. Hadn't he learned his lesson when his mom left, nearly destroying his dad? Or, even more recently, when he'd let his judgment get skewed enough to act like some vigilante?

Reflexively, he moved one hand to his shoulder, where his sergeant insignia had once been. He shouldn't complain. It was his own fault he'd been reduced in rank. It could have been worse. The chief would have been justified in firing him altogether. Miles knew that. He was humbled and grateful for the opportunity to prove himself.

An opportunity he could easily mess up again if he allowed his feelings to interfere.

Not just that, he realized. If his feelings got in the way, it could keep him from seeing a threat or a clue. Someone could get hurt because of him. Rebecca could get hurt.

Or worse.

Time to man up, Miles. This isn't the time for a relationship.

They were almost back to LaMar Pond. He hated to disturb her, but knew he needed to. He waited until the last minute, though. Finally, as he parked the car outside of Seth's house, he had to wake her.

He reached out a hand and gently shook her.

Screeching like a scalded cat, she shot up in her seat, hands out in front as if she was ready to fight. The seat belt pulled her up short. He watched the realization of where she was sink in. And grinned as she slumped back into her seat, glaring.

Trying to wipe the grin from his face, he leaned up against the door, hands raised. He started to sign. A laugh spluttered from him. Her glare intensified, lids lowering until her eyes were almost slits. She was adorable.

"Sorry! You're back at Seth and Jess's house. It was time for you to wake up." No matter how hard he tried, he couldn't squelch the chuckles that kept coming. His shoulders shook with the effort to hold them back. It was most likely the stress of the past few days catching up with him.

He was about to issue another apology, worried that he'd really offended her, when her lips started to twitch.

"Fine. Whatever. Do you want to come in for a cup of coffee?"

He shouldn't. He really shouldn't. "Yeah, sure."

So, of course he did. He rolled his eyes at himself when she got out of the car.

He looked around and frowned. "Is anyone else here?" She swiveled her head around in surprise. All the cars were gone.

Raising his watch, he saw he had missed several messages. And an alert. He must have switched it to mute by accident. Of all the times for that to happen.

"Hold on," he signed. "I have several messages."

"Let's go inside, I will fix coffee, and you can check your messages."

Made sense. He nodded and followed her inside the house, then did a walk-through to make sure everything was secure. Then he joined her in the kitchen. While she busied herself making coffee, he read through his messages. His alarm grew with each message.

By the time she sat down across from him with two mugs, his nerves were buzzing, making sitting still difficult.

"What's wrong?" she signed.

Of course, she'd pick up on the body language. One thing was for sure, he'd never be able to lie to her. Not that he ever would—he'd learned that deception was a very poor choice.

"I have messages from Seth, the chief, Jackson... everyone! There was a fire at the LaMar Pond Senior Center. Residents need to be evacuated. Seth is there. He says he dropped Jess off at his sister Maggie's house."

"Oh, no!" she signed. "Was anyone injured?"

He tapped his watch to view the message that was just coming in. And grimaced. "Yes. Multiple injuries, from mild to severe. And two residents died. One of the residents who died was Sergeant Zee's grandmother. She's going to need to help her family deal with this situation."

"You need to go." It wasn't a question. Her signs were calm, rational, giving him permission to go do his job.

But he could sense the fear. She couldn't lie to him, either.

"I need to go, but I won't leave you unattended. Seth won't be back until all the residents have been checked over. Nor do we have an extra police officer to spare to guard you right now. Let me think."

She waited, sipping her coffee. He paced the room. Where would she be safe until this crisis was over? Then it hit him.

"Come on. I'm taking you to stay with my family. My grandparents and uncle live less than half an hour from here."

"Will I be safe there?"

A valid question. "I believe you will. No one will know you're there except for those I tell. And my uncle and grandfather both know how to handle a gun. Plus, I know they have a security system in place. It made sense, because they're all deaf."

Some of the fear seemed to melt away. He got it. The possibility of being unable to communicate was part of what scared her. That would not be a problem at his grandparents' house. Even the majority of their guests were skilled signers.

It took her only a few minutes to gather together her things and get ready. Within forty-five minutes they were pulling into his grandparents' driveway.

As he'd expected, his family and grandparents were delighted to have her stay with them. Sally and Bruce Olsen were the kind of people who never turned anyone out. And his uncle Greg lived to entertain others. The fact that he was completely deaf had never stood in his way.

For a moment, Miles was struck by how different

the rest of his family was from him and his father. And not just in the fact that they couldn't hear, either. The rest of the family was open and embraced life and people. Miles's father, on the other hand, had allowed bitterness to taint everything he did. And Miles? He didn't think he was bitter, but he sure wasn't as accepting as the others.

"I will come back later. Is it okay if I take the couch for the night?"

"Of course!" his gran signed. The smile she beamed at him was the best guilt trip ever. It was filled with joy. And gratitude. As if him coming to stay with them was an unexpected gift. He needed to stop by more often. When had he become too busy to visit his family? Before the guilt could swamp him too much, she continued. "I will leave the front porch light on. And something to eat in the refrigerator."

Where was Rebecca? She had disappeared with his uncle while he had talked with his grandparents. He should say goodbye.

Why? She knew where he was going. It wasn't like she was his girl.

He wished she was. That rocked him off balance. When had she become so important to him? The emotional tug he felt toward her had sneaked up and sunk its claws into his heart without his even being aware just how deep he was falling.

But he didn't have to act on it. Everyone would be better off if he stopped thinking about Rebecca and refocused on the job. Because that was what he was good at.

Giving his gran a kiss, he walked out the door without seeking out Rebecca.

* * *

Hours later, Miles let himself back into the house. It was dark outside. He had expected to find everyone asleep. So he was astounded to find Rebecca sitting up waiting for him at the kitchen table.

The moment she spotted him, she stood and yawned. Then she walked over to him and wrapped her arms around him. He enfolded her in his arms before recalling he was going to keep his distance. Now that he held her, though, he was powerless to let her go. The scent of her shampoo was just what he needed to soothe his frazzled nerves.

Finally, he pulled back and allowed himself to drink in her tired face. Wow, those eyes were the bluest he'd ever seen. Had she slept at all? Dark circles bruised the delicate skin beneath them.

"Everything okay?" he signed, wondering why his grandparents hadn't contacted him if something was amiss.

"Fine. But I was worried. You were gone for so long. All I could think of is what if my attacker went after you because of me."

She moved back. He let his arms drop, immediately missing her.

So he took a step back, too.

They had no future. He had to remember that. The turmoil that gnawed at him made him want to yell. He needed a workout. A bout with his karate sensei. Anything to relieve his anguish.

"Your grandma and uncle showed me some pictures."

His heart dropped. Instinctively, he knew what pictures she was talking about.

"Sylvie?"

She nodded, her face shadowed. Yes, she understood it was a painful memory.

Rubbing his hands across his face, he tried to erase the image of Sylvie lying in a coffin from his brain. It made no difference. He figured that image was burned into his soul forever.

She reached out and took his hand with her left one, leaving the right one free to sign. "Want to tell me about it?"

No, no.

But he stopped. Actually, he did. The words he'd kept in for so long were ready to burst from him. But only to her.

"Did my grandmother tell you that Sylvie was my stepsister?" He waited. She bobbed her fist quickly, up and down. *Yes.* "When I was a kid, my mom never had time for me. Or my dad. She was a former model, used to living well and being the center of attention. Being stuck in small-town Pennsylvania didn't appeal to her. When she left us to go back to that life, it broke my dad's heart. Then she was killed in a scandalous way, and the tabloid frenzy nearly killed him, too. My grandparents took me in, because he wasn't capable of caring for me."

Once he got started, the words erupted from him, like lava from a volcano. They burned. She didn't interrupt. And her presence was an anchor, helping him continue.

"After several years, he managed to stop drinking. And he married again. Louise, his new wife, was great. I loved her more than the mother I barely remembered. Isn't that terrible?"

Her head moved back and forth. No. But she didn't say anything, even when a tear slipped down her cheek.

"She had a daughter. Sylvie. Several years younger than me. I adored that kid. She was such a brat at times, but she was my sister, even though we weren't related by blood."

He paced to the bookshelf, looked at the pictures. The hardest part was yet to come. "My mom, though, she'd destroyed my dad's ability to trust. Louise tried to help him heal, but she eventually divorced him because she couldn't deal with the constant badgering. The lack of trust. I tried to keep in touch. And I saw Sylvie as much as I could. Then she got murdered while she was in college. And I thought I knew who did it. The woman who was convicted was released after four years. I made her life miserable. Because I knew her presence in town, walking around free after killing Sylvie, hurt Louise. You want to know the worst thing?"

He laughed. There was no humor in it.

"Turned out the woman convicted wasn't the murderer. She was innocent. My cruel, dangerous actions seriously upset a woman who had done nothing wrong. They almost cost me my job. And my self-respect. They did cost me my rank as sergeant. I decided then and there I would prove myself. Get my rank back. Which means I can't ever let my emotions get the better of me. Not again."

Chapter Twelve

And there it was.

Dawn was breaking, and Rebecca was still tossing and turning in her bed in the guest room, unable to stop reliving the conversation she'd had with Miles several hours ago. She'd left the kitchen struggling not to show just how shattered his revelation had left her. And not just the matter of his stepsister's murder. Or his stepping out of his role as a protector and admitting his mistakes in the past. Because she knew God was merciful, and redemption was possible. Hadn't she seen for herself what an honorable man he was?

Rebecca had been telling herself from the moment she'd met him that the attraction she felt for the sincere police officer was useless. Her past had left her damaged, and with unsightly scars. When Miles had seen her scars and not been repulsed, she had allowed herself to believe that maybe, just maybe, there was hope.

But he was a police officer. A man who would always put himself in danger to help others. She had gone back and forth with herself over whether or not she could deal with his choice of career. Because it was obvious to her that being a policeman was his God-given calling. Which was something she could never challenge.

Now, it seemed, she wasn't going to have a chance to decide if she could accept it. He had told her point-blank that he didn't do relationships. Which meant that he, too, had experienced attraction on some level. Experienced it and decided against it.

How dare he make that decision for both of them? The heat of the blush on her face wasn't just caused by anger. She remembered the way she had embraced him when he'd come in. The warmth of his arms had made her feel so safe. Cared for. Had she imagined it?

No! He'd hugged her back, just as fiercely. But he insisted on acting like it didn't matter.

Well, she definitely wasn't going to be able to sleep. Swinging her legs over the side of the bed, she slid forward until her feet touched the wooden floor. And immediately snatched them up again. It had been a long time since she'd set her bare feet on cold wooden floors. Not since she'd left home. Her parents' plain house didn't have a single inch of carpeting in it. Her *mam* and *dat* believed that was too fancy. She was used to that once, but had long since developed a liking for warm, soft rugs protecting her feet from cold floors first thing in the morning.

Feeling foolish for letting such a silly thing stop her, she slapped her feet down again and ignored the discomfort. But only until she'd snagged a clean pair of socks from her bag.

Next, she grabbed her laptop. Hurrying back to the bed, she booted it up and logged on to the *Erie Times News*. Nothing interesting on the front page of the paper's website. It was all election news. People were still in shock that Seth's dad was retiring from his job as a senator. The opponents for the open seat were vicious in their attacks of each other.

Bored, she logged on to her Facebook account and started to scroll down the news feed. After a few minutes, she stopped. Stared.

Time stood still. For a few moments, she couldn't take it in. There had to be a mistake.

But there it was in full color. Brooke's picture. She was smiling and carefree. Someone had posted an article. *Local Missionary Vanishes Upon Return.*

A sick churning started in her stomach as she read the story carefully. Brooke had returned from her mission trip. There were witnesses that she had been picked up from the airport by her mother. For the next day, her parents had organized a welcome-home party for her. She never showed up.

But the connection had been made. The article went into detail about the abduction from years earlier, and the fate and whereabouts of each of the other girls today.

Horrified, she started to read the comments. Some were sympathetic, some not so much. And one made her blood turn to ice.

Someone had written "I hope the last girl is ok. I saw her. She was dropped off at my neighbor's house. They're deaf, too."

How hard would it be to find out where the woman lived and who was deaf on her street?

She couldn't stay here! Miles's uncle and grandparents weren't safe with her around!

Without conscious thought, she grabbed the laptop

and flew through the empty hallway and down the stairs. She tripped on the last stair. Pain seared through her foot as her big toe was bent back. She didn't even slow down.

Miles was asleep on the couch, his arm flung over his eyes as he slept.

Halting beside the couch, she yelled out.

Miles jackknifed up off the couch, his eyes wild. His left hand was at his waist, about where his gun usually was. He sank back down when he saw her, his head falling to lean against the back of the couch. She could see his chest rise as he drew in a deep breath.

"Rebecca." His greeting was remarkably calm, considering she'd just terrified him. "Is something wrong?"

Instead of answering, she thrust the open computer into his arms. The screen was blank, so she toggled the mouse button to bring the article back up.

She pointed at the post, then yanked her arm back when her finger trembled. Even as she watched, another comment popped up.

Miles reached out and grabbed her hand before she could tuck it behind her back. He pulled her down to sit beside him, looping his arm around her shoulders, and hauled her closer so she was snuggled up against his side. She dropped her head on his shoulder, drained. He set the computer on the coffee table in front of him.

He was just comforting her, she reminded herself. She shouldn't read anything into this. Yet she couldn't stop herself from snuggling just a little closer. Nor did she complain when his arm squeezed her shoulders briefly in response.

He scoured the post, never removing his protective

hold from her. She didn't complain, but angled her head up so she could see his face. The hair that always seemed to need a haircut was once again flopped on his forehead. In contrast, the rest of face had tightened. As his gaze skimmed down the post to read the growing list of comments, she could feel the clasp around her shoulder grow taut. In fact, Miles practically vibrated with tension.

She finally had to protest as his grip around her shoulders became unbearable. Shifting in his hold, she brought his attention back to her.

His arm loosened, although it didn't move away completely. His mouth softened. "Sorry. I didn't mean to squeeze so hard," he signed one-handed.

Her chest tightened when his gaze roamed her face, then landed on her lips. Her breathing hitched. Could he hear her heartbeat race? The hard *thud, thud* of her pulse vibrated in her throat.

"I don't think I need to tell you that this isn't a safe place for you anymore," he signed.

"I know. But what about your grandparents? Your uncle? If the killer thinks I'm staying here, they'll still be at risk, even if I leave." She would never forgive herself if something happened to these kind people because of their generosity to her.

"I am going to encourage them to go stay with friends for a few days. Not that I think they're in trouble. So far no one has been hurt if you weren't around." She winced at that. Ouch. "I think our man's too smart for that. After all, he's avoided being caught up to now."

"Where will I go?"

It broke her heart, but she knew he'd probably put her in some safe place far away. Which meant her brother would get married without her being there. And, she jolted at the thought, she'd be left in someone else's care, away from Miles.

She wasn't ready to part with him. The emotional twang she experienced was almost a physical pain. She might never be ready to part with him. Policeman or not.

She braced herself.

Man, she was getting tense. Miles thought she'd break apart if she grew any stiffer.

"You're going to stay with me." Her posture drooped. Had she been worried he'd push her off onto someone else? Even if he'd wanted to, which he didn't, he knew the department was stretched to its full capacity right now. The chief was planning on hiring two new officers, but had not been able to yet. So until further notice, he was on Rebecca detail.

The fact that he wanted to smile at the thought worried him, but he pushed it aside. Right now, she was only one step away from being captured and killed.

He prayed urgently that it wasn't too late for Brooke.

"I need to talk with Brooke's family again, and I can't leave you here. We'll go as soon as you are packed and we eat. And I need to talk with my family."

An hour later, she was packed and ready to go. Miles had talked with his grandparents and uncle and explained the situation. Gran was unruffled, and entirely unwilling to impose on any of their friends. When he'd tried to convince her, she'd simply shrugged, then signed, "The Lord will protect us. He always has."

Miles scratched his head. The urge to kick something was very strong. Until he saw Rebecca smile, her face soft and amused.

"What's so funny?" he signed, curiosity getting the better of him.

"Your grandmother. She reminds me of my *mam*." She signed *mother*. He automatically translated it to *mam* in his head, remembering her explanation of the Amish word for *mother*. "*Mam* and *Dat* never let anything shake their trust in God."

"Would your parents let you convince them to move to a safe house?" he asked, his signs sharper than intended.

"No. They would not. They would consider this all part of the fancy world, and wouldn't let it bother them."

Great. Now his girl was encouraging them.

His girl? No way did he just think that. But he did.

His uncle surprised them. "I texted my brother. He is going to let us stay with him for as long we need to."

His jaw dropped. He couldn't help it. "What? My dad is letting you stay with him?"

His dad was a bit of a recluse. He didn't appreciate others in his private space. Even when Miles visited him, he was tolerated for only a day before his dad started making hints that it was time for him to leave.

"I can be persuasive when I need to be," his uncle signed back, a satisfied smirk settling over his features.

They couldn't afford to waste more time on idle chitchat. Miles hugged his family and then signed to Rebecca that it was time to go. It was just past eight fifteen when they finally hit the road.

Just in time to hit rush hour, he fumed an hour later.

Still, they managed to arrive at Brooke's parents'

house by ten. Brooke's teenage brother answered the door, the pale cast to his skin proof of the horror the family was living through. Poor kid. No one should have to deal with this sort of anguish. No one.

The family wasn't alone. A woman in her forties with graying red hair sat next to Brooke's mother on the sofa, an arm around the weeping woman, and standing off to the side...

"That's April! My boss!" Rebecca signed.

April's face went ashen as she saw Miles in his police uniform. "Have they found her?" she gasped out, clearly expecting the worst.

All talking ceased. Brooke's parents, two brothers and both women focused on Miles. His heart broke a little for the mother, who was staring at him, hope and dread fighting for dominance on her face. He hoped he never had to give her the information she feared, his stepmother's ravaged expression in his mind.

He sent Rebecca an apologetic glance. She nodded. He had told her in the car that he wouldn't be able to sign to her. Technically, she shouldn't even be in the room.

"No, Mrs. Cole. I have no new information. We are still searching for your daughter. I hate to bother you at this difficult time. But I may have a lead that is connected to Brooke's disappearance. If I might have a few minutes of your time?"

"Officer, anything you need to help us get our daughter back, just name it," Brooke's father said. Harold Cole. That was his name. And his wife was Susan.

When invited, Miles sat on the empty chair near the window, ignoring the dog hairs that were sure to stick like glue to his spotless uniform. He was aware of Rebecca remaining out of the way in the doorway. Brooke's parents looked her way, but didn't say anything about her.

"When I talked with you several days ago, you never mentioned Brooke was coming home."

"We didn't know," Susan Cole replied. "She called us to say there was some sort of unrest where she was, and she was being sent home. She called us from her layover at Cleveland. We barely had time to get her."

"Do you have any idea who could be responsible?" Harold asked.

"Yes, sir. We have reason to believe Terry Gleason had a half brother he was separated from when they were children—a man who might want revenge in his brother's honor. Have you noticed any strange men around lately?"

He could tell they were trying their best to think of anything that could help, but no one seemed to have noticed anything. After a few minutes, he concluded that there didn't seem to be anything new to be gained.

Before he left, he turned to April. "Miss Long?"

She startled. "Yes, officer?"

"I know that Rebecca works for you. May I ask how you are related to the family here?"

April didn't answer. The woman on the couch did. She looked like April. "Susan and I are stepsisters. Brooke and April are cousins."

His former suspicions regarding April returned. It was too much of a coincidence that she knew two of the victims. He wondered if she had anything else to hide. It wasn't something he wanted to get into now, not in front of the devastated family, but he intended to talk with her.

A few minutes later, he rose from his seat. "Mr. Cole. Mrs. Cole. Thank you for your time today. I give you my word that I will do everything possible to get your daughter back to you." *Hopefully, alive.* No need to say that part aloud. Nor did he deem it necessary to admit that he had a personal reason for wanting to catch this fellow immediately. Or that his personal reason was the beautiful blonde standing in the doorway, waiting for him.

He followed her back to his car, his hand on her shoulder as his gaze darted around the street in a continuous sweep. Arriving at the car, he opened the passenger-side door and waited while she stepped into the car.

Nearby, he heard an engine rev. An orange car sped around the corner. Miles pushed Rebecca's head down. The car approached. A gun was in the driver's hand. Miles had his gun out and was aiming for the tires.

Without warning, the driver dropped his arm and sped away.

What? Why hadn't he shot?

Miles caught the first four characters of the license plate. Punching the button on his radio, he reported the details to the dispatcher. He also was able to tell her the make and model of the car. "The driver is armed and dangerous."

It shouldn't take them that long to identify the plate, if it belonged to that car.

"Who was that? Was he holding a gun?"

Miles spun around. April was standing five feet away, her face drawn and ashen. Did she think she was going to get hurt? Or did she have another reason for being so upset?

Whatever her reason was, he now thought he knew what had sent the driver racing away without finishing his quest. Given his prior behavior, Miles would have expected the man to kill him and take Rebecca. Although if she had died, the perp probably wouldn't have cared. Miles figured that he was expendable because he was obviously searching for the attacker's identity.

Well, he wasn't going to stop now. He would keep searching, looking under every possible rock, in order to protect Rebecca. And if he ended up getting hurt saving her, it would be worth it.

His radio crackled back to life. "Officer Olsen? We have the make and model of the car. It is registered to a Nicole Weller."

Nicole Weller. Looks like he'd just found his next rock to overturn.

"Great job. Where is this Nicole Weller located?"

Chapter Thirteen

You know something's wrong when you see an Amish man at the police station.

Miles took a swig of Mountain Dew and screwed the cap back on without taking his eyes off the man. Levi Miller—Rebecca's brother. He remembered him well. It had only been four months since Miles had last seen him. He still remembered Levi's petrified expression as he had sat beside Rebecca while she drove. Well, to be fair, she was driving very fast at the time.

What was he doing at the station? The Amish community didn't go seeking outside help. Unless it was an emergency.

Levi saw him and made a beeline for Miles's desk. Miles raised his eyebrows before he managed to hide his response. One of these days he'd learn to control his features. It was just natural to let his face and body language speak for him. That's what happened when one was partially raised by deaf grandparents.

"Officer Olsen." The Amish man halted in front of his desk.

"Mr. Miller. How can I help you?"

"My sister Rebecca is missing."

"Missing?" Oh, wait. He'd never even thought of the fact that there would be no phone at the Miller home, no way to send them a message to let them know she was all right, short of going there to tell them in person. "She's not missing. She's here at the moment."

Levi let out a loud sigh. Miles knew relief when he heard it, and felt his own guilt grow in response. He should have contacted them to let them know they didn't need to be worried about her. "That is *gut*. I was worried about her. She hasn't contacted the family since Wednesday. I went over to see her at her apartment. She wasn't there. I went to where she works, and the store was closed. Not even Jess could tell me where she was. Only that she was fine, and I needed to come and see you."

Miles smiled at the man. The family might have trouble communicating with her sometimes, but it was very clear that they loved her dearly.

"She's here, in the conference room. I'll take you to her." Miles tossed down the pen he'd been fiddling with and stood, indicating that Levi should come with him. "I moved her to a safe location. Until the situation is under control, I don't want her to be alone." As concisely as possible, Miles explained what had happened over the past several days.

"She is all right, *jah*?" Levi asked when he was finished. "She was not seriously hurt?"

"She's fine." He hastened to reassure the man. "A little shook up, and I'd say impatient to get back to her normal schedule, but I'm doing all I can to find the guy responsible and keep her safe. We all are."

"That is *gut*," the Amish man said simply, his calm demeanor firmly back in place.

This was his chance, Miles realized. He rubbed the back of his neck, grimacing as he realized how warm it was. Great. He probably looked like a blond lobster. But he couldn't waste the opportunity. He looked across at the other man. Levi was scrutinizing him. Yep. His nerves were showing.

Get it over with.

Clearing his throat, he plunged in. "Mr. Miller, Rebecca is determined to go to your wedding on Thursday."

The man's face fell. "It is too dangerous?"

Aw, man. "No. I mean, there are precautions we can take so she can still be there. She was going to ask if I could go with her. Just to keep watch over her, and get her out of there if it seemed necessary. I hope nothing will happen, but I don't want to take a chance."

Why did he feel like a teenager asking a father if he could date his daughter? This was police business. He was doing his job. That was all. Except, it was Rebecca. And he'd never thought of any of the other people he'd helped in the same light as he did her.

Levi was thinking, bobbing his head. "*Jah.* That could work. If you protect my little sister." Here the man cast as stern a glance as any father ever had at the police officer. As if he knew Miles was developing stronger feelings for his sister. Which could be awkward.

It was a relief to finally reach the conference room. He swung open the door, then stepped back to let Levi precede him into the room. Rebecca was flipping through one of the books she'd stuffed in her backpack.

Miles rapped on the table and Rebecca looked up. Then, beaming, she launched herself into her brother's arms. Levi returned her embrace, although he seemed a little uncomfortable. Probably wasn't used to being demonstrative.

"What are you doing here? I wasn't expecting to see you before the wedding!" she signed. She repeated her signs, slower, when Levi didn't understand her the first time around.

"I was worried about you. I went to your apartment this morning. The door was open, so I went in." The man hesitated.

A wordless whimper escaped Rebecca's throat.

Levi made a calming gesture. "I didn't see anything broken. Drawers and cupboards open." He made a final sign, giving his hands one quick shake. "That's all."

What? Why hadn't he said something earlier about the break-in? Instead, they'd talked about his wedding.

Miles said as much to him.

The Amish man swallowed. "It is not easy for me to come to the police with my troubles, to report crimes like break-ins and robbery. When I came to see you, my worry was for my sister's safety. I did not care about the break-in, I only wanted to know she was safe."

Rebecca backed up and shook her head, face ashen. Was she going to pass out? Miles took three quick steps to her side. She slumped back into her chair before he could touch her. He settled a hand on her shoulder, gave a gentle squeeze.

"I'm here," he signed when her eyes met his. "I promise I won't let anything happen to you."

"Someone was in my apartment, going through my things. How long can this continue?"

He couldn't ignore her distress. Nor could he follow his instincts and pull her into his arms. Not while standing in the police station in full uniform. And definitely not in front of her older brother. Especially knowing how strict the Amish community was about public displays of affection except between family members. He'd done some research once he knew there was a possibility that he'd be traveling into Amish territory for the wedding. It was pretty much what he'd expected. Except that the bride and groom would not kiss.

The unbidden image of Rebecca's face close enough to his to kiss blindsided him. He blinked. Shook his head. Can't go there.

Rebecca and Levi were both watching him.

Great.

He remembered Rebecca's fear. That, he could deal with. "I think the person was just trying to find where you went. Now that the story about you being at my grandparents' house has broken, we can't go back there. But the chief told me an hour ago that Parker is out of the hospital. And the emergency at the center is about over. So we will have the manpower to protect you and anyone else involved wherever you decide to stay."

He brushed a strand of hair from her face. Her gaze found his and stayed.

The phone rang, breaking the spell.

Backing away from her, he answered the phone. "Officer Olsen."

"Olsen," the chief said, his normal drawl a terse bark. Miles instinctively straightened and threw back his shoulders. That tone of voice never boded well. "Your DNA from the bubble gum at the crime scene came back. It belongs to a young man named Chad

Weller. Details and a picture are being faxed to you right now."

"Weller? The license plates and car I reported today were licensed to a Nicole Weller."

"His ex-wife. He has a record of domestic abuse, but charges were always dropped before he could be brought to trial."

"Figures. Did he steal the car? And if he did, could the ex-wife be convinced to testify against him?"

"That's what I need you to find out."

"I'm on it."

He hung up the phone and turned to find Rebecca and Levi watching him. "That was the chief." He related the pertinent details.

"You could maybe find this man now, *jah*?"

Miles sighed, rubbing his neck. He could really use a Mountain Dew right about now. "Maybe, but I don't think it will be easy."

"I can bring Rebecca home with me. Then she could just stay for the wedding. That would be *gut*."

Uh, no, it wouldn't. He might like Levi and all, but to trust him to take Rebecca forty-five minutes away in an unprotected buggy? Yeah, not happening.

"I think I will bring her with me. I will bring her to your house tomorrow night before the wedding and we'll both plan to stay. How about that?"

Miles could tell Levi wasn't happy about it, but he didn't argue. Neither did Rebecca, which surprised him. He'd expected her to want to go and stay with her family right away. That's what she had originally wanted. But that was before she was shot at and so ruthlessly targeted. He imagined she was worried about putting her family in danger with her presence.

Lord, I don't want to fail this woman. Please guide me. Help me to protect her.

It was almost four in the afternoon when Miles parked the cruiser in the driveway of the house belonging to Nicole Weller. Rebecca sat quietly, apparently lost in her own thoughts. He frowned. Something felt off. He couldn't quite put his finger on it.

Then he realized the house looked abandoned. The full garbage can was still up near the garage. The other houses on the street had their cans near the curb, empty. It seemed to be garbage day, but she hadn't brought hers down. From where he sat, he could see at least three newspapers in the paper box at the side of the road. If he had a warrant to look, he'd probably find several days' worth of mail in the box.

"I don't like this," he signed. "Stay close, and do whatever I tell you without asking questions."

"I will."

They went up the three steps to the house. His hand slid to his waist and he removed his gun. Better to be safe.

Nerves jangling, he rang the doorbell. No answer. Leaning to the side, he peered into a dark window. Was that movement?

"Mrs. Weller, LaMar Pond Police Department. Do you need assistance?"

A muffled crash. Followed by a low groan. Someone was in pain.

"Mrs. Weller, I'm coming in."

The door was unlocked. Shoving it open, he went in first, gun ready as he checked every direction for danger. Seeing none, he continued in, aware of Rebecca behind him. Nicole Weller was lying on the floor in her own blood. She was alive. Badly beaten. But alive.

A quick prayer of thanksgiving. He used his shoulder radio to call 911. Then he kneeled by her side. Her lashes fluttered.

"Mrs. Weller, can you hear me?" A groan answered him. "Mrs. Weller, can you tell me who did this to you?"

He knew, but he needed confirmation.

She sucked in a shallow raspy breath. When she spoke, he leaned closer so he could hear her. "Chad... so angry...tried to kill me."

In the silence that descended the harsh breathing of the injured woman was amplified. He closed his eyes as a wave of gratitude surged through his veins. This could have been Rebecca. But it wasn't. And if he had his way, neither Rebecca, nor Nicole Weller, nor any other woman, would die at the hands of Chad Weller ever again.

The image of the injured woman stayed with Rebecca for the remainder of the day. She had returned to the Travis house, and as Miles had said, Parker was there to guard her. He seemed embarrassed at having failed her before, and was doubly determined to protect Rebecca at every moment.

By Wednesday morning, she was ready to climb the walls.

Miles was busy making sure Ashley and Nicole were both safe. It was both good and bad that they were in cities run by different departments, he'd explained to her. Good because LaMar Pond was a small-town force, and didn't have the manpower to protect all those different women around the clock at the same time. But also bad, because it meant that they were more difficult to keep track of.

Finally, it was time to go to her family's house. Normally, she would have enjoyed the trip. This time she couldn't. As she got into Miles's car, the hair on the back of her neck stood on end.

"What's wrong?" he signed.

"I keep waiting for someone to jump out at us with a gun."

He nodded. "I'm going to take a roundabout way to make us harder to follow. And I have alerted the local police in that area of the issue, plus sent them what we have on Weller. Which isn't much. If he got into any trouble in high school, those files are sealed. There's nothing from the time he turned eighteen until he married Nicole and she filed domestic abuse charges. He kept to himself. His last known address was near Cleveland. At present, no one seems to know where he is."

It seemed like he had thought of everything. But she still couldn't shake the feeling dogging her that something bad was coming their way.

They made it to her parents' house without any mishaps. She should have been relieved. The large white farmhouse was bursting with joy and activity as her parents and her five siblings worked. And yet the ache in her stomach wouldn't go away. She had to keep reminding herself to unwrap her arms from around her waist. When her mother asked her if she was fine in her halting sign language, Rebecca forced herself to paste a smile on her face and nod. *Mam* frowned, but let it go.

Soon, the entire family was involved in wedding

preparations. Most of the cooking would happen the next morning. But her family still had much to do to get ready for all the guests that would soon descend on them. Rebecca found herself doing whatever jobs she could that required very little communication.

At one point, Levi asked Miles if he could help moving benches. She could tell he was going to refuse so he could stay near her.

"I'm fine," she signed to him. "I will be in here, with my family."

He didn't look convinced, but finally agreed.

Every few minutes, she'd go to the window to search for a mop of floppy blond hair. Once, she looked out and saw him standing with Levi, laughing. He glanced up and caught her eyes. The laughter stopped. Immediately, he signed, "Are you all right?"

She nodded. "Just checking." Her cheeks grew warm. Now he'd know how much she was relying on him. Knowing how he avoided emotional attachments, she wasn't anxious to see his reaction. He surprised her, though. A warm glance caressed her face. Her face grew even warmer, although not with trepidation. "I won't leave," he signed. "I promise."

She nodded, then returned her focus to the room. Her sister Lizzy watched her, brows raised high. Great. Lizzy could never stand to be kept out of any secret. Her little sister was only sixteen, but looked so much more mature. Actually, now that she thought about it, Lizzy looked exactly like Rebecca had several years before.

"What are you working on?" her sister signed to her.

She looked over to where she had been doing some

mending and noticed that her aunt had stepped in and taken it over.

"Nothing."

Lizzy's eyes lit up immediately. "Perfect! You can come with me. I need to take the buggy to Aunt Lavinia's to pick up some things. We haven't had time alone together in so long."

Rebecca bit her lip. The urge to go with her sister was strong. But for the two of them to go off alone, well, that wouldn't be smart.

Some of what she was feeling must have shown on her face. Lizzy sidled over to her gave her a pleading look, her sister's blue eyes huge. She even batted her lashes for good measure. Rebecca held a hand over her mouth to cover lips that quivered with the urge to smile.

"Please? You can dress in one of your old dresses and *kapps*. The person after you has never seen you in Amish dress. I doubt he knows where you're from. And we are only going a mile away from here. We should be back in less than thirty minutes."

It would be nice to get away from the fear for a bit. And Lizzy was right. Chad Weller had never seen her in her Amish attire. Even his brother hadn't—she'd been in Englisch clothes when she'd gone out that night with Holly and her friends.

Holly. A hollow pang hit her in the chest.

Unable to stand thinking about her dead friend, she nodded to her sister. "Just let me go change." She ran up to her old room and found one of her old dresses and a *kapp*.

"Are you ready?" Lizzy signed when she tripped back down the stairs.

Reluctantly, she nodded. But her heart was heavy.

Outside, she peered around for Miles. She could let him know where she was going. But she couldn't spot him, and her sister was grabbing her arm and pulling.

"Come on. I told Ruth to tell your friend where we were going."

Good. Their youngest sister could be trusted to do what Lizzy told her to.

They hitched up the horse to the buggy. "I want to drive," Lizzy signed. Naturally. It had been so long since Rebecca had driven one, she preferred that her sister take charge of the vehicle.

The hairs on the back of her neck stood on end. Was someone watching her? Moving her head from side to side, she tried to see if anyone stood out. She didn't even try to act nonchalant. What was the point? But she saw nothing suspicious. She was letting her fears get the better of her.

Still, she clambered up into the buggy quickly.

Lizzy climbed up beside her and gathered the reins in her hands. It was almost all Rebecca could do to keep from yanking the reins from her sister and making the single horse move faster. Not that they would be able to pick up any speed until they reached the paved road at the intersection. Suddenly, the half hour her sister had quoted seemed like a very long time.

They arrived at the intersection without incident. The road was clear, so her sister moved the buggy out onto the paved road. That was when a car roared up behind them. It pulled into the left lane, as if to pass, then slowed to keep pace with them. Lizzy threw an irritated glance over her shoulder, then the color drained from her face. Rebecca followed her line of vision. The white car beside them was nothing out of the ordinary.

Rebecca had never seen it before. But she had seen the man in the ski mask behind the wheel. She screamed as she saw the rifle being held in one hand. Pointing right at them.

Rebecca reached out and jerked on the reins. The horse, startled, reared. Lizzy let go of the reins and covered her face, letting her older sister take control. Rebecca steered the buggy into the yard beside them. The car moved as if to slam into them.

A semitruck crested the hill, heading toward them. The car shot ahead.

The semi flew past.

The brief feeling of respite ended as the car slammed on its brakes. A second car passed them and slowed, giving them a buffer. But a very small one. They only had a moment before the driver could reach them.

Rebecca didn't even bother signing. She clutched her sister's sleeve and literally yanked her out of the buggy. Chances of outrunning the man were slim, but they would give it their best try. Giving up was not an option.

Oh, why hadn't she told Miles where they were going?

You didn't want him to tell you not to go. It was true. She had allowed her desire for a peaceful interlude with her sister to overcome her common sense.

Out of the corner of her eye, she saw the car door open, and a figure in black charged from the car. She froze briefly, terror taking hold. Only for a second. Then she grabbed her sister's sweaty hand and hauled her as fast as she could toward the woods.

A chunk of dirt flying up a foot in front of her made her stumble. He was shooting at them! She righted herself and flashed her eyes to her sister. Please…oh, please, let her be okay.

She was. Terrified, but uninjured.

Rebecca sent up a prayer to keep it that way.

A tug on her hand pulled her to a stop. What was Lizzy thinking? Some madman was trying to kill them. They needed to run.

She tried to pull her sister with her, but Lizzy dug in her heels and yanked on Rebecca's hand until she was forced to turn. That's when she noticed the blue and red flashing strobe lights reflecting on the trees.

She nearly fainted from relief. Hot tears burned in her eyes. She didn't even try to hold back the sobs. Miles had arrived. And the man shooting at them was speeding away. Blinking, she saw that the blond cop was holding his watch up to his mouth and talking fast, even as he charged toward them. Most likely telling the police where he was and what had happened.

He took a small leap to bridge the shallow ditch and reach the girls. She launched herself at him and found herself caught up against his chest. Burying her face in his neck, she continued to shake and cry. Eventually, she became aware that he was rubbing her back in soothing circles with unsteady hands. Every few seconds, she felt him kiss her hair.

Lifting her face, she blinked away the remainder of her tears. She needed to tell him they were fine. And to apologize for her poor judgment, which could have ended disastrously.

She never got the chance. He kissed her the moment she looked up. The feel of his lips touching hers made everything else fade.

The sweet kiss ended. He lifted his face away from

hers, searched her face and then kissed her a second time. Her fists held on to his shirt as she breathed in his clean sent.

Lizzy! She'd totally forgotten her sister. Breaking away, she blushed as she cut her eyes to her sister. Lizzy rolled her eyes and grinned. Shyly, Rebecca looked through her lashes at Miles.

"Are you two hurt?" he signed. When they shook their heads, he sighed and gave Rebecca another quick hug.

"Aren't you going to lecture us?" Rebecca asked, wrinkling her nose.

He quirked a grin. "You know it. When you are safely inside the house again. Never do that to me again. Promise?"

For the first time, she noticed the shadow in his eyes. His sister had been murdered, she remembered. And here she was putting herself in danger when she knew he felt responsible for her safety. She couldn't believe how selfish she had been. Moving up on her tiptoes, she kissed him softly. A kiss of apology.

"I promise. I won't put you through that again."

He ran his fingers down her cheek. "Let's go. I have the local police searching for the car. But let's not take any chances. I have a feeling that he won't give up until we stop him."

Or until he finishes what he started, she thought.

Chapter Fourteen

The morning of the wedding dawned clear, although there was a definite nip in the air. Miles finished dressing for the day and went to find Rebecca. He'd tossed and turned late into the night, the image of Rebecca dragging her sister across the field while being shot at seared into his brain.

Whether he was aware of it before or not, the killer now knew that Rebecca had Amish roots. And that she was in town for a wedding.

Jackson had called later to let him know that the car had been found, abandoned. As expected, it had been a stolen vehicle. Jackson would be arriving soon, as would Parker. When informed of the almost tragic incident less than a mile away, Mr. Miller had agreed to allow Miles to put extra security precautions in place. Which included more police at the house during the reception.

The problem was that the actual ceremony wouldn't be at the Millers' house. Miles had wanted to pull his hair out when he'd learned this little tidbit. Apparently, weddings were so much work, that the wedding often happened at a relative's house. In this case, Mr. Miller's brother was hosting the wedding. So all the benches they had loaded onto the tractor last night were set up at the uncle's house.

Jackson and Parker would be relegated to strolling the perimeter of the property. Which was fine. Miles would be at the wedding itself. They could keep the threat at bay from the outside. The officers would not be in uniform so as not to distress the guests or disturb the ceremony, but all Miles cared about was that they would be there and he would be able to protect his Rebecca.

He stopped. His Rebecca. How he wished it was true. The kisses last night had come from the strong emotions arising from seeing her in danger. Yet he couldn't help thinking they would have happened sooner or later.

He needed to focus on keeping her safe. Maybe later, after all the danger had passed, he could figure out a way to meld his career and his personal desires. He refused to consider that maybe he would fail to keep her safe. But the fear lurked in shadows, and it wore Sylvie's face, reminding him that he had failed once before.

Enough! He had a wedding to attend and a woman to protect.

He had decided to wear his gun after all. It was well disguised under his jacket, so none of the guests needed to even know of its presence.

Clomping down to the kitchen, he paused at the doorway. And forgot to breathe.

Rebecca was already there at the table. She wasn't dressed plain. Instead, she was wearing a simple A-line dress of cobalt blue. Her shoulder-length golden blond hair was swept up into a simple bun at the back of her head and held in place by some sort of clip.

She took his breath away.

One of her brothers asked him a question. Which one was it? He knew her two brothers were Thomas and Joseph, both in their late teens. Problem was, they looked like twins. He answered the questions and watched as the morning wore on and guests arrived. He was pleased to note that Seth and Jess were there, not just because he liked the couple immensely, but also because he was glad that Rebecca would have other proficient signers around to keep her company. He really liked her family. They were down-to-earth, kind, generous people. But it grieved him to think of Rebecca growing up with communication barriers putting distance between her and her loved ones. Having never been to an Amish wedding, he was amazed at the magnitude of the event. Almost three hundred people were there. In a barn. The benches he had helped the men to move the night before were facing each other. The men sat on one side and the women on the other.

As a non-Amish guest, he sat outside the barn on metal bleachers with Rebecca, Seth, Jess and the few other Englischers who were at the wedding. He had pulled the metal bleacher in as close to the barn as possible. And had gained permission to put it under a tent. That way they wouldn't be sitting there with invisible targets on their backs. Still, he was unable to relax and enjoy the wedding. Even knowing that Parker and Jackson were both on duty, making rounds and keeping track of everything going on around them, his teeth were on edge. Every thirty seconds or so, he let his gaze drift to the trees and the outskirts of the property. The one negative thing about the tent was that even though it limited the killer's view of them, Miles's vision was also cut off.

Was that a movement? Near the north end? He couldn't be sure, but he wouldn't relax until he knew. As discreetly as possible, he tapped out a text to the two cops roaming the grounds. Then he tapped his fingers anxiously on his knee while he waited, his body tense and ready to move. Another movement in that area and he would grab Rebecca and...

A warm hand smoothed over on top of his. Rebecca. He drew in a deep breath.

His watch vibrated. Finally. Jackson. He had scoured the area that Miles had indicated. There were footprints. But they were much too small to have belonged to Weller.

That was a small relief. But he didn't let his guard down. He was convinced that Weller was escalating his attacks. They were getting closer and deadlier, as if the man had realized he had to work fast to achieve his goal. Miles shuddered. His goal was to eliminate the woman Miles lov—

No.

Yes. He briefly closed his eyes. Everything he had done to stay unattached had failed. His heart belonged to the slender woman seated so peacefully at his side. He opened his eyes, and they immediately slid to Rebecca. And found her gaze on him, questioning, her forehead wrinkled in concern.

The urge to run his hand over those lines and smooth them out did nothing to lessen his inner anguish. He couldn't let himself give in to emotion. Not when his future, and hers, depended on it.

But would he be able to walk away from her when the case was over? And say he did manage to walk away…

The pain that hit him stole his breath. He rubbed a hand over his chest. He was in deep. And he wasn't sure if there was anything he could do to change it.

By the time the ceremony ended, he had a roaring headache. And a stiff neck. No doubt from the constant strain of watching in all directions for a threat to emerge. The guests emerged from the barn and started to walk toward the road. The reception would be held at the Millers' house. Fortunately, that was only two houses down the road.

How long would they have to stay? He was anxious to get Rebecca back to where he was more familiar with the layout. And where there weren't so many people around. It was almost noon. Rebecca had said the reception could last for a few hours, but should break up by midafternoon.

As they walked, a car drove up beside them. Miles moved quickly, putting himself on the outside and Rebecca closer to the edge of the road. His hand moved to his gun. The car pulled up beside them. A young man in a baseball cap. Too young to be Weller. He relaxed. The car continued on ahead of them, turning at the intersection.

They arrived at the Miller house. He had never been so happy to see a house in his life. The yard was full of buggies, and soon the air was thick with laughter.

Miles had a brief word with Jackson and Parker about the possible threats and hiding places for an attacker, then he returned to the reception. The feast provided by the family looked fantastic. His stomach grumbled loudly, reminding him that it had been hours since breakfast. He watched Rebecca pick at her food.

An hour into the reception, Jackson came to find him. He moved outside to talk with his colleague, leaving Rebecca safe inside with her family.

"We have a problem. The dogs chained up outside? It looks like they've been drugged. They're breathing, and appear to be fine, but they won't wake up. I found Benadryl tablets mixed in with their food."

He was here. The killer was here. "Keep searching for him. He's here."

Miles made it back into the house in half the time it had taken to leave.

His heart slammed against his ribs.

Rebecca was gone.

Rebecca was getting worried. After lunch, Lizzy had left to go ask their mother something and hadn't returned. Remembering the way the driver had gone after them in the buggy yesterday, her stomach cramped, as she worried that Lizzy was in danger. Being in the Amish community was not the haven she had thought it would be. Yesterday had proven that. And the killer was getting desperate. He didn't even care that others were getting hurt. She remembered something that Jess had said when she'd arrived and seen Lizzy and Rebecca standing together.

"She looks just like you, Rebecca."

Jess had meant it as a compliment, and had smiled as she had signed it. And Rebecca had rolled her eyes and laughed.

She wasn't laughing now.

She was being targeted. And the sister that could be easily mistaken for her was outside on her own. She tried to remind herself that the whole day had gone so smoothly. And there were so many friends and relatives about. This was probably the safest place she could be.

But no arguments would calm her nerves. The trembling hands and the agitation would not stop until she knew that Lizzy was safe and sound.

She had to find her sister. She wished she could tell Miles, but when she had slipped out the front door, he was in an intense conversation on his phone. She had left a message with her brother Joseph to have Miles find her as soon as he was off the phone.

He had nodded. She watched him approach the newlyweds and sighed. She had watched Levi and Laura, and realized, more than ever, that she wanted that with the man she married someday. Their communication was visible in every look and expression.

She'd never find that in her parents' community.

That's not important now—find Lizzy. Get her back inside and out of danger.

Where had Lizzy gone?

Rebecca had been searching for her sister for almost twenty minutes. No one seemed to have seen her. Of course, there was always the possibility that they hadn't quite understood what she was asking. But she was fairly sure she'd gotten her point across. Her family might not all sign well, but they did all know the basics. Such as name signs.

Mam had shaken her head then made the sign for *barn.* So Rebecca had walked in the direction of the barn.

No Lizzy.

She'd trekked through the fields behind the barn, and into the other buildings. The silo. The second barn, where the animals were kept. She'd even walked down to the neighbor's house.

Nothing.

Finally, she headed home. Maybe Lizzy had shown up while she was away.

Wait a second. She stopped. That was Lizzy's bonnet.

Her heart ceased beating, then took off like a freight train. Beside the bonnet, the grass and dirt were scuffed up. Almost as if her sister had been struggling with someone.

Her chest clenched tight, cutting off air to her lungs. It felt like she was trying to breathe through a straw. Her baby sister was in the clutches of a madman!

Calm down. You don't know for sure what happened. But she couldn't shake the image of her sister being dragged away, the discarded bonnet a symbol of the evil that had once again entered their lives.

Without giving herself time to talk herself out of it, she followed the trail. Behind the outbuilding. Toward the pond.

The pond! Was the sadistic monster planning on drowning her sweet sister?

Miles. If Miles was here he'd know what to do. Oh, why hadn't she waited for him to be free to come with her? Her urgency to track down her sister may have very well cost Lizzy her life.

Rounding the corner, she gasped. Lizzy was struggling with a man in a ski mask.

He looked smaller than before. And not as strong. Because Lizzy was holding her own. Fortunately, there wasn't a gun in sight. There was a rather large stick on the ground. Perfect. Rebecca hefted it in her hands and grasped it like a baseball bat. Then, giving a yell that scratched her throat raw, she rushed the man holding her sister.

He reacted immediately, dropping the Amish girl and whirling to face this new threat, his arms out to defend himself. Rebecca plowed into him, arm swinging the branch. It connected soundly with his left side. She felt the impact all the way through her. He must have felt it, too, for he doubled over.

Rebecca became aware of others racing toward them. Miles was in the lead. Uh-oh. She'd have some explaining to do later.

But at least both she and Lizzy would be alive for it.

Miles reached them. Instead of the lecture she expected, he pulled her into his arms and squeezed. She could feel his heart racing through his shirt. Guess she wasn't the only one who was scared.

Abruptly, Miles released her and turned his police stare on the man still crouched in front of them, holding his gut. Lizzy scooted around them, giving the man a wide berth, and stood shoulder-to-shoulder with Rebecca.

She was pale. Though her eyes were furious. Rebecca placed an arm around her and directed her toward their parents. Once she was in *Mam*'s arms, Rebecca moved back to where she could see Miles. And the man who had caused her such misery.

Miles reached out and removed the ski mask. Rebecca felt as though the ground had fallen out from under her. She knew the man in front of her.

She waved her hand, getting Miles's attention.

"I know him," she signed when he looked her way. "That's Wyatt. He makes deliveries to our store."

Miles's expression hardened. Suddenly the young man she often thought looked too fresh-faced to be a policeman looked every inch an officer. She shivered, and chanced another look at the miserable young man before them. He certainly didn't look like a hardened criminal. Nor could she imagine those thin arms reaching out and strangling her in her car...

That was it! She knew what was missing.

The tattoo.

"Miles...this is not the man who attacked me before," she signed frantically.

"Are you sure?" he signed back. But the look on his face said he had already come to the same conclusion. They were still looking for Chad Weller.

"Absolutely. Remember? The man who attacked me before had a tattoo on his wrist."

Both of them looked at Wyatt's wrists. Neither of them sported a tattoo. Miles nodded. "Okay, but that doesn't explain this fellow attacking your sister." He leveled a glare at the now cringing man before them. "I need to question him. I can do it easier if I don't sign. I will share any pertinent facts later."

She nodded, understanding. Police business was different.

Reaching out, he surprised her by squeezing her hand and giving her a smile. Then he retracted his smile, and froze Wyatt with the ice in his eyes. She could see Wyatt's Adam's apple bob as he gulped.

By the time Miles was finished barking questions at him, rapid-fire, Rebecca's anger was starting to be replaced by sympathy. Wyatt seemed to be shrinking with each question that hit him.

Finally, Miles pulled a piece of paper from his pocket and showed him. It was a picture. It looked like a driver's license photo. A young man with longish black hair and a beard. Was that the picture he'd been sent of Chad? The brown eyes and bushy eyebrows were familiar. Had she met him before?

Wyatt was jabbering fast, his hands gesturing wildly at the picture.

Miles finally turned to Rebecca, disgust on his face. He switched to ASL. "He was in jail with Terry Gleason the last six months of Terry's life. Grew to admire him. Terry told him how he'd been framed by you girls. When Wyatt was released, Chad approached him. He," he pointed a finger at Wyatt, "agreed to help him get even. He drove the vehicle at your apartment. And he broke into your apartment and stole the picture. He's not very loyal. He's agreed to help the forensic artist create a more accurate image of Weller."

Rebecca understood. The killer was getting desperate. And more dangerous by the moment. They were running out of time.

Chapter Fifteen

They returned to LaMar Pond that afternoon in two cars. Jackson and Parker had Wyatt with them in a cruiser. Miles followed behind with Rebecca and Lizzy in his Jeep. He'd changed into his uniform, and his suit was packed away again.

He hadn't intended on having both sisters with him. In fact, he had fully expected Mr. and Mrs. Miller to refuse to allow their younger daughter to come to the station to give a statement. Mr. Miller, however, had surprised him.

"Two of my daughters have been attacked," he'd informed Miles. "These children were given to me by *Got* to protect and raise. I will let her make a statement so I can do *Got*'s will and protect them."

So, the teenager now sat calmly in his back seat. Although, he suspected neither of his passengers were truly calm. He'd seen Rebecca twisting her fingers. It wouldn't surprise him if Lizzy was doing the same in the back.

The small group arrived at the station and hurried inside. He had both women precede him and kept his right hand on his gun. The left he placed on Rebecca's back. Partly to keep her moving, and partly, he admitted to himself, to assure himself of her continued presence. That she was well. All the smiles from the wedding had faded.

They were dealing with a killer who was determined to kill again.

They had to wait for another forty-five minutes for the sketch artist to arrive. Miles stopped at the vending machine on the way to the conference room and got some bottles of water and a Mountain Dew. It looked like this could take a long time. He figured he would need the caffeine before the day was done.

When the sketch was finally done, Miles ordered Wyatt to be booked and then went to find the Miller girls. They were in the conference room with Jackson, who had replenished their drinks and found them some snacks. The feast at the reception had been amazing, but he knew Rebecca had been unable to eat much. And who could blame her with all she'd been through?

He came into the room and sat down beside her, touching her hand on the table briefly in the guise of getting her attention. The truth, though, was that he needed to touch her, to tell her silently that he was there. And because that small touch reassured him that she was fine.

He was a mess.

But he would do anything, put himself in front of any danger, to see that she was safe. He might not have anything else to offer her. But he could do that.

Please, Lord. You know I love her. Please help me keep her safe. Even if she isn't meant to be mine.

Right. Back to business.

He laid a picture on the table in front of her.

"This is how Chad Weller looks now. Do you recognize him?" he signed.

Rebecca gasped, her hand flying out to grab the picture and bring it closer. "I know this man!" she signed. "That's April's boyfriend!"

"April Long? Your boss?" How many Aprils could there be? But he had to be sure.

"Yes. But I don't understand. She is Brooke's cousin. Isn't that what her mother said?"

His gut twisted at the pain on her face. "Yes, that's what she said."

"Then how can she be dating the man who killed Holly? Who abducted her own cousin and may have killed her, too?" Her eyes grew damp at the last thought.

He reached out and squeezed her hand. "Let's not think about that yet. We don't know what has happened to Brooke. And we don't know the extent of April's connection."

"Do you think she knew he was waiting in my car that night?"

He shrugged, helpless. He wished he had the answers for her questions. "I have no idea. But I will get answers for you. I promise."

She stared up at him. Then the corners of her mouth lifted. It broke his heart. She was trying to be brave, while he could tell she was being torn apart.

The door flew open.

Miles and Jackson both jumped to their feet.

"Sorry, sorry!" Parker raised both hands. "I know better than to charge in like that."

Yeah, he did. Something big must have happened.

"Spit it out, Parker!"

Wow, had he just barked like that? Parker's grimace was all the answer he needed.

"Didn't mean to yell."

"No prob, Olsen. But the girl in the coma? She's awake. And she remembers everything."

"We're on our way."

It was close to six in the evening when they arrived in Cleveland. Miles hadn't taken any chances. He'd insisted on bringing Rebecca and Lizzy along. Parker had followed in his own car. It made sense, even if it wasn't the most efficient plan. If one of them needed to go after a suspect or chase a lead, they wouldn't have to drive all the way back to LaMar Pond and get an extra car.

Ashley was just finishing her dinner when they arrived. Her head turned sharply as they entered the room, her short, dark hair brushing her chin. The bruising that had been visible in the crime-scene photos had healed, but she still had a haunted look about her. She flinched as he stepped into the room. He was glad that Parker and Lizzy stayed in the waiting room. She was jumpy enough without a crowd of strangers descending upon her. Miles held out his badge as he approached to question Ashley. He brought Rebecca along because she had known Ashley a little, and was very much a part of the investigation. Plus, he was reluctant to let her out of his sight again. She slipped away far too often for his peace of mind.

Approaching the hospital bed, he saw the way Ashley's fists clenched.

"Miss Kline, I'm Officer Olsen from LaMar Pond. I have some pictures to show you. One is of the man

I believe to be responsible for hurting you. If you're up to it?"

What would he say if she said no?

"Yes, I can look."

She pushed herself into a sitting position. Then she turned her focus on Rebecca for the first time. And gasped. "I remember her! She's the deaf girl that was taken with us. Rebecca."

Miles interpreted for Rebecca. "Yes. And it appears that the man who attacked you is going after the others who were with you that day."

Ashley's stiff posture deflated. "The others? Are they okay?"

He hadn't meant to open that can of worms. But since he had, he quickly related the events up to this point. Ashley's ashen complexion was wet with tears when he had finished.

"Let me see those pictures." She wiped the tears from her face.

He showed her Weller's image. "He did this?" She jabbed the picture with a long finger. "I know him! Brooke's cousin April is dating him!"

That gave him pause. "How do you know April?"

"Brooke and I have been in contact off and on since school. Last summer we were both invited to a former classmate's wedding. April was friends with the bride, too, so she was there, and he was her date."

Interesting.

"Was Holly there?"

She shook her head, and then her brow furrowed. She leaned her head to the side, thinking. "Now that I think of it, he was asking a lot of questions. But it was all done in a joking manner. It didn't feel like he was being nosy. But he was, wasn't he? He was getting info so he could grab us."

The real question was, did April know he was digging for information, or had she been duped, too? Chad could have targeted her deliberately, knowing she was close to Brooke, to give himself that connection and insight into their circle of friends. As for finding Rebecca...that would have been easy once April hired her. How had Rebecca ended up working at April's bookstore? That was a question he intended to find answers for.

"Why would he do this?"

The soft whisper brought him back to the conversation at hand.

"I don't have all the answers yet, but I do know that this man is Terry Gleason's half brother."

Ashley bit her knuckle. The pain in her gaze seared him. Rebecca brushed past him and held the other woman's hand. To his surprise, Ashley held tight. Or maybe it wasn't surprising. These two went through something devastating together.

He continued. "Jasmine's brother said that you and Jasmine had bullied and mocked Gleason in high school."

She snorted. "Yeah, he told the jury that, too. We never bullied him. He had asked both of us to a dance. We both said no, we had dates. His friends were the ones who teased him about it. They always made fun of him. Not us."

They didn't get too much more information out of her, but that was fine. It was enough to have a definite identification of who the killer was.

"I need to find out if April was involved in this."

* * *

Had April lured her into a trap?

She hated to think it was true, but had to admit it was a definite possibility. But April had always seemed so sincere. They hadn't been friends, but she had liked the woman.

"How did you start to work at the bookstore?" Miles. Dear Miles. He was fast becoming a steady rock in a crumbling world.

"April had asked Brooke if any of her friends needed a job, and Brooke had passed the information on to Holly, knowing that Holly sometimes had trouble holding down a job. She had something at that time, though, and knew I was job hunting, so she had asked if I could come and interview. She went in as my interpreter. April didn't want to hire me at first. She never said so, but I think the idea of working with a deaf woman intimidated her. But then later she called back and said the job was mine if I still wanted it. I did, so I started the next week."

"She probably had told Weller about you, and he realized who you were. In fact, it was probably his idea for her to ask Brooke to approach her old friends from school." He paused, rubbing his neck as he thought. "I think it's possible that he targeted April for information. She may not have had any idea what was happening. Or maybe she did. I have to find out."

When they entered the waiting room, Rebecca went to sit with her sister while the police officers made their plans. The whole situation was unreal. The planning that Chad Weller had done to carry out his vicious crimes was something she couldn't wrap her mind around. To plan the abductions and murders of four complete strangers! Even the thought of so much darkness made her shudder, as if she, too, had been tainted.

Lord, keep us safe. Keep us free from malice. Protect Miles as he goes after this man.

For he would go after him. She'd seen that expression. Miles would do whatever he could to keep the evil from touching her. Even if it meant he himself would be hurt.

And she loved him.

When had that happened?

She didn't like it, but accepted the truth. She was in love with Miles Olsen. And he wanted no part of any long-term relationship. Oh, sure, he'd kissed her. Her nerves buzzed thinking about that kiss. But that had been an emotional reaction to a narrow escape.

She longed for some gesture of affection now. Something to comfort her. She hadn't realized how much she had enjoyed those casual touches. But she feared he was going to start drawing away from her now. He didn't want any kind of emotional attachment.

The men approached them. She straightened, preparing herself for the next move in this dangerous game.

"You're both going to ride back with Parker." She clenched her hands to keep her protest in. "I will follow, then go and see if I can chat with April. Parker will take you and your sister back to Jess's house. You can stay there until I return. Please don't leave without me or Parker."

She nodded. A cold ache had started to grow inside her. Was this it?

Miles hesitated. Then, so quickly she had no time to respond, he leaned in and kissed her. "Let's go."

She blinked. He'd kissed her. In front of his colleague and her sister. She bit the inside of her cheek, but the grin that started in her soul wouldn't be stopped. It stretched itself on her lips even as she pressed them together to keep it in.

Parker smirked after his colleague, but said nothing. Lizzy nudged her with an elbow. Rebecca felt her face heating up, but was too pleased to mind their teasing too much.

The drive back to LaMar Pond was uneventful. Rebecca fell asleep, and woke up in time to look back and see Miles turn toward the police station. Refusing to let fear gain control, she prayed the rest of the way back to Jess's house for his safety.

Parker pushed a button on the dashboard. Miles's name was there. He must have called. Was he okay? Every nerve stretched taut. She relaxed as she saw Parker laugh. He wouldn't laugh if Miles was hurt. But why had he called?

Lizzy was motioning to her in the mirror. Rebecca shifted in order to see her sister more clearly.

"It's your policeman." Rebecca blushed at that. She wished Miles was her policeman. "He called to check and see if we are fine. Mostly he wanted to know if you are fine."

She sat back, smiling. Miles was checking on her. Maybe he was missing her as much as she was missing him. That had to mean something, didn't it?

Her phone vibrated. April's number had come up on display. The text sent ice churning in her. Run as far as you can. Chad after you. He's a killer. I'm sorry. I didn't know. She showed it to Parker. He nodded and pulled off the road so he could read the text.

Parker said something. Lizzy tapped Rebecca's shoulder. "He said send it to Miles."

Rebecca nodded. But before she could forward the message, the windshield burst. Shocked, she dropped the phone on the floorboard. Parker slumped next to her, a red stain seeping over his shoulder. He'd been shot!

He was still awake, though. He reached for his gun, hitting the switch on the door as the face she'd now recognize anywhere loped toward them, a rifle in his hands.

He wasn't bothering with the ski mask. Which meant he knew they had his identity and he didn't care about hiding. None of them was safe anymore.

Lizzy pushed open the back passenger door as Parker forced himself to stand and face the man coming toward them, his gun ready.

"He said run!" Lizzy signed to her.

Rebecca watched as Parker was thrown back against the car and slid to the ground.

Please don't be dead.

The killer was almost there. And there was no one to protect them.

Chapter Sixteen

Rebecca pushed open the door on her side. Parker had risked his life to save theirs, maybe he was already dead. She couldn't waste the chance.

She didn't expect to make it to safety. But maybe she could save her sister. She would willingly accept death if Lizzy could be saved. Her feet hit the pavement and she grabbed on to her sister's hand. Pulling the younger girl with her, they ran along the side of the road. If only there were woods to go to for cover!

But there were wide-open fields on both sides, a few cows and horses scattered in them. And now that they were out of the main center of LaMar Pond, there wasn't much by way of traffic or houses nearby, either.

A burning sensation stung her hip, causing her to stumble. Tears blurred her vision. She blinked them away. Now was not the time. She couldn't fall. Couldn't stop. Sucking in her breath and trying to ignore the agony, she continued pulling Lizzy along. Her hip burned with every step she took.

A chunk of gravel exploded in front of them. Another shot. She sidestepped the spot and kept moving.

Another chunk flew up inches from them, showering gravel fragments on their dresses. She swerved to miss the new hole.

Lizzy tripped and fell, ripping her hand from Rebecca's grip.

Rebecca turned and reached out to Lizzy. It was too late. Chad Weller was already there, hauling her sister to her feet. He had thrown down the rifle. Was it empty? She didn't know. Either way, it didn't give her any peace. He drew a long, sharp knife from his belt and pushed the blade against the soft skin of Lizzy's throat. A small drop of blood appeared.

Rebecca understood the message. If she attempted to run, or made any wrong move, her sister would pay the price.

How could she save her now?

She couldn't. But God could. She prayed. Even as her breath grew shallow and her palms grew sweaty. Nausea struck her as they passed the police car. How she wanted to look and see if Parker was okay! But he was on the other side of the vehicle.

Weller continued to push the girls to his car, parked farther up along the side of the road. He opened the back door, still holding the knife to Lizzy, and leaned in, emerging with a revolver.

A car was passing them. It slowed, faces gawking at the man holding a gun on two young women, one in an Amish dress. He scowled and aimed the revolver at the car. They got the message and raced away. Still scowling, he forced both girls into the back seat and tied their hands together. Slamming the door behind them, he got into the driver's seat and pulled away with enough force to make the sisters crash into each other. But where were they going?

It was all she could do not to vomit when they arrived at their destination.

Terry Gleason's old house. Chad Weller had bought his brother's old home. The memories flooded her panic-stricken mind. Images of being beaten, slapped, cut…all branded in her mind, impossible to forget.

She shook her head. Tried to focus on prayer. But her mind was too overwhelmed.

Please. Please.

Contradicting thoughts raced through her head. *Miles will come. But Miles is far away. The text from April had never been forwarded. It didn't matter. Miles always comes.*

She held on to her hope though it was as thin as a thread. But it helped her stay sane as her attacker pulled behind the house and parked near the back door. He didn't undo their hands. He hauled a dazed and terrified Lizzy out first then jerked his head at Rebecca. She climbed out on legs that felt like jelly, trembling so hard she could barely stand.

He sneered at her and said something. His sneer widened when she didn't answer. And with her hands bound, Lizzy couldn't tell her what he said.

Jerking his head again, he indicated that she needed to walk into the house. She did as she was told, her hope of being seen by a neighbor weakening with every step. She couldn't scream, either. Because there was a knife against her sister's throat again.

Opening the back door, she stepped into her own private nightmare. The house was clean but sparsely decorated. There were no personal touches like pictures or knickknacks.

Chad had bought the place only to torment his victims. He had no plans of making it his home. The cold-blooded way he'd gone about setting everything in its place chilled her.

Finally, he pushed them to a door. She froze. And shook her head vehemently. She was no longer seeing Chad Weller in front of her. She was seeing Terry Gleason, forcing them down the stairs into the basement. Chaining them up. Strangling Jasmine.

Something inside her broke as the image took control of her mind. She backed up and turned. Not to leave and abandon her sister. But in desperation to flee from her own memory.

A movement to her side. Lizzy had fallen, or had she been pushed? Her eyes were wide as she opened her mouth. Rebecca could tell she was screaming. A warning?

Chad stood with fury vibrating in every muscle of his body. He lashed out, his large fist catching Rebecca on the side of the face. She saw that she was falling toward the counter but couldn't move out of its way.

She was going to hit her head.

The pain lanced through her, then everything went black.

Miles wanted to call Parker, to check on Rebecca again. But he knew he couldn't. Not a second time. Parker had given him a hard time with the last call. But he couldn't shake the unease that had been brewing ever since he'd parted from the others.

Well, he knew what he needed to do. He needed to

talk with Miss April Long and see if she could lead him to her boyfriend.

He really hoped she wasn't involved in all this. His gut said no. Her concern over Brooke's disappearance struck him as genuine. And the car...

He tapped his hands on the steering wheel as he remembered the car driving by the Coles' house. Something had stopped the driver from shooting at them. April had walked outside to talk with them. And the driver had gone past.

Maybe Chad hadn't realized she'd be there? It was pretty bold for him to attack at the girl's home. But then, he had to have been feeling the cage closing in around him. Had to have known that his window of opportunity to fulfill his evil plan was closing.

Which was what scared Miles. The man was now acting out of desperation. Which meant he would be willing to take any opportunity to kill his victims.

Miles saw April's road and pulled in, quickly finding her house and parking. He radioed in that he had arrived at his destination. He got out of the car and strode up the path to the door, double time. He didn't have any time to waste.

Knocking briskly on the door, he blinked as the door swung in. It hadn't been shut. He called for backup, then drew his weapon and stepped inside. From where he stood, the place was a mess.

Someone had left in a hurry. Or had been taken. Things were overturned, as if there had been a struggle, and there was blood on the floor.

Dialing the chief's number, he gave him a rundown. When the chief gave him permission to proceed with caution, he stepped carefully inside, hoping he wouldn't find a body.

He didn't. He did find a suitcase, half-packed in a haphazard fashion and abandoned, open, on the bed.

She'd been leaving. Running away, from the look of it.

And she'd been caught before she could finish.

Voices outside. Backup had arrived.

The scene was processed, pictures taken. There was a picture taken at a wedding. Brooke, Ashley and April all smiling, arms around each other. Brooke was in the center. It was heartbreaking, the joy on all three young faces.

And a man with revenge on his mind had deliberately set out to use one of them to get to the other two—and two others, as well. They needed to find Brooke and April fast.

He was heading back to the station to do the paperwork when Parker texted. Weller attacked. I'm shot, ambulance on the way. He has girls.

Miles stopped breathing. No! How had this happened? If anything happened to Rebecca...

What could he do? He arrived at the station, ran into Chief Kennedy's office and showed him the text, not trusting himself to speak. The chief didn't mess around. Every available officer was brought in and a search began.

"Olsen." It was Lieutenant Tucker.

"Sir." He didn't have time to chat now. He had a woman to save. Some of his struggle must have shown on his face, because Tucker's own face softened. Which freaked him out a little.

"Miles." And that freaked him out more. Because

the lieutenant never called him by his first name at work. "I know what you're going through. We have all seen how hard you've fallen for Miss Miller. And we're behind you. We won't leave any lead unchecked. And we'll help you bring her back."

Miles looked away until his eyes stopped stinging. "I appreciate it, Jace."

And he meant it. The officer had clearly forgiven him for his past actions. And now he was offering more than support. This was friendship. And he needed it, was happy to accept it. Jace nodded and left him. Miles headed back out to his own car to begin the search. But where to begin?

His ringtone went off. It was the chief. He tapped his watch. "Olsen here."

"Someone just called the station. They heard what sounded like screaming at the house that Terry Gleason's family used to own. It had been sold again recently. They said the new owner is a young man who keeps to himself, so they called it in."

"I'm on my way. Have all available officers and an ambulance meet me at that location. Tell them not to go in hot. We don't want to lose the advantage of surprise. Who knows what he'll do if he hears us coming."

"Take care, Olsen. Wait for backup before you go in."

"I'll be careful, Chief. And if I can wait, I will."

Chapter Seventeen

Consciousness slowly returned.

With it, came pain. Rebecca forced her swollen eyelids open, blinking against the grainy texture that scratched her eyes. Was she on the floor? Yes, her cheek was resting on cold cement, and the scent of dust filled her nostrils and coated her throat.

Gingerly, she sat up. The room swayed briefly. It was dim, and cold, but there was enough light coming in from a single light bulb attached to the ceiling to get a vague impression of her surroundings. Half a dozen cement posts ran from the floor to the ceiling, each about six inches in diameter. She remembered the half-circle windows around the ceiling. Terry Gleason's basement. The furniture was restricted to one couch against a wall and two end tables.

Memory came rushing back. Lizzy! Where was her sister? She scrabbled up on her hands and knees and tried to stand. That's when she noticed the shackles. Her left leg was shackled, and the chain was bolted to one of the posts. Just like before. At least her hands were free this time. Or were they left this way to taunt her?

The ability to breathe was getting difficult. Fear and anxiety were clawing their way up her throat, working against her lungs, blocking out the air. She couldn't pass out! She had to find her sister!

A movement to her left caught her eye. Someone was sitting against the wall, shackled to a post just like she was. It was Lizzy. Relief coursed through her, allowing her to breathe again. Lizzy was dazed, but she didn't appear to have been hurt. She stared at Rebecca, and tears started to flow down her smooth cheeks.

"It's okay, Lizzy. God knows we are here. And Miles will search for us."

"How will he find us? No one knows where we are."

Rebecca did her best to reassure Lizzy. "It doesn't matter. Miles has been working very hard finding answers. He won't give up. You don't know him like I do. He will keep looking."

Her heart ached at the thought. Miles. Sweet Miles. He would search relentlessly until she was found. She knew that. What would happen to him if she was hurt? Would he carry that burden in his heart the way he did with his sister?

Dear Lord, help Miles find us. And help him let go of his remorse. Lord, I love him. Let me have the chance to tell him that.

Had her brother's wedding only been this morning?

Doubt crept into her mind. The idea that Chad would buy this house had never occurred to them. How was Miles supposed to find her?

Have faith, she reminded herself. *God is in control. No matter how dark or hopeless the situation, He is in control.*

"Someone else is here," Lizzy signed. "Another woman."

Rebecca glanced around carefully. Too much movement made her head throb. She hadn't even noticed the third woman, chained on the opposite side of the room. Even without seeing the woman's face, she knew who it was under the curtain of short, curly blond hair. Brooke. And Brooke was obviously hurt. Her arm hung at an odd angle, and there was blood on it.

She had disappeared several days before Rebecca and Lizzy were taken. Chad seemed to be changing his pattern. Was she still alive? And why had he taken all three of them? He'd taken Ashley and Holly one at a time.

A bright light flared to life. Rebecca and Lizzy both shrank bank, blinking their eyes as the brightness struck them. It took a few minutes for her gaze to focus on the figures coming toward her. Figures?

For there were two people. One seemed to be pushing the other. Her vision cleared. She watched, heart thudding in her throat, as Chad pushed April into the room ahead of him, and shoved her down on the couch. The force of the shove caused her to fall, her ankle wrenching. Her face twisted, and she opened her mouth as if she was speaking. No. Not speaking. Crying out. Although Rebecca wasn't sure if it was in fear or pain. Probably both. But why had Chad taken her? She wasn't part of the original group. Nor had she been with either Brooke or Rebecca, as Lizzy had been. Something wasn't making sense.

Chad scowled down at the weeping woman on the couch, disgust crawling across his face. When he abruptly switched his attention to Rebecca, she froze.

The pure malice she encountered made her want to crawl out of her own skin. She shivered and inched away from him as far as the chain around her ankle would allow.

Until he turned and fixed that horrible gaze on Lizzy.

Hot, liquid rage burned through her chest, hazing over in her mind and burning away the fear as he kicked the young Amish girl. Pain flashed across Lizzy's face. Her mouth opened, her cry of pain a silent dart into Rebecca's heart. Rebecca lunged forward. That chain stopped her before she could get anywhere near the monster standing in the middle of the room. He sneered, and snarled at Lizzy. She shook her head fiercely. Until he said something else. It didn't seem possible but Lizzy paled even more. Tears streamed down her checks as she signed to her sister.

"He says he will kill you if I don't tell you what he is saying."

He will kill us anyway, if he can. Rebecca didn't say the words. This was hard enough without scaring her little sister even more. *Please, Lord. Save us. Send Miles.*

Chad continued hurling words at Lizzy, watching their effect on Rebecca as the younger girl silently, haltingly, signed them to her sister.

"He says this is all your fault. I will die, and it is your fault. You and your friends. He knows because he found where his brother had been after he died. He had been looking for him for a long time. Terry had told people that Jasmine and Ashley had been part of a group that had bullied him in high school. That was why they needed to be taught a lesson. Then at the trial, you and your friends continued to torment him. Terry went to jail, and died there. Because of you and your friends this man was denied a real reunion with the only family he had left."

"But Holly and I were never part of the group that made fun of his brother."

Lizzy interpreted, and got another kick from Chad.

Rebecca held in the protests gurgling up inside her. The pressure was intense. The last thing she wanted was for this man to turn his vitriol on her sister.

He continued talking.

"He says to stop lying—that he knows better than to believe anything you'd say. He says that he has been planning this for a long time. He met April, and realized that she had gone to high school with the other girls. When she mentioned her cousin Brooke, he knew she was his link to all of you. He dated April for two months before it paid off. She was invited to a wedding and brought him as her date—he met Ashley and Brooke there. He convinced April to hire someone at the store so they could spend more time together. He convinced her to hire you when…" Lizzy's signs slowed, and then paused. Rebecca understood. She didn't want to tell her what April had really thought about her when she'd applied for the job. It didn't matter. She knew.

But why was he going after April now? Rebecca glanced at the woman on the couch without thinking, then whipped her eyes back to the man towering before her. He sneered again. It seemed that whatever affection he'd had for April was gone.

"She is weak," he said, pointing to April. Lizzy's hands trembled as she continued to sign. "I thought I had found someone I could trust. But she found out what I was doing. She tried to break it off with me, and I knew she planned on going to the police. That's your fault, too."

He advanced three steps toward Rebecca. Shrinking back was instinctive. "If you had died in the store like you were supposed to, she would never have known. You have cost me my brother and my girlfriend. And now, the police even have my picture broadcast on the news. You don't deserve an easy death. None of you do. Not after all you have cost me."

April suddenly moved, jumping up from the couch and leaping toward him, her hands curled like claws. She was no match for him. Enraged, he caught her and slammed her back against the wall, inches away from where Rebecca was chained, his hands at his former girlfriend's throat.

He was choking her!

He was focused on April, not paying attention to Rebecca's movements. And Rebecca was close enough to reach him now. With a strength she never knew she possessed, Rebecca hurtled herself at his unprotected back and grabbed on to him, her hands clawing and scratching at his face, at his neck.

Chad released April and swiped Rebecca from his back. April fell in a heap to the ground. All his rage was fixed on Rebecca now. He dragged her up by her hair and pressed her back against the wall. He leaned his face in close. His breath washed over her. Stomach turning, she struggled. He was too strong. His hands reached up and closed around her neck. She scratched at his hands. Remembered how she had escaped before and tried to gouge out his eyes. He dodged out of the way.

She was going to die. Her mind grew blurry. Miles. He was going to be too late.

Miles pushed his way past the broken gate blocking the path and raced up the creaky stairs to the front porch, his gun in his hand. He prayed that backup would get there fast. Somewhere inside the house, he could hear a young girl screaming. Lizzy. Which could mean that Rebecca was in dire straits even as he opened the battered door.

Lord, protect her. Shield her.

His mind wasn't capable of stringing together more than that. So he repeated it, knowing that the God of all would understand what was in his heart.

He probably should have waited for another cruiser to arrive. That would have been the safe, responsible thing to do. Moreover, it was what his chief had directly ordered him to do, and doing otherwise could have serious consequences for his career. But he couldn't take the chance of being too late. Not when Rebecca's life was at risk. Nothing was more important than getting to the woman he loved right now. Not even his job. If he saved her, but lost his job, he would consider himself blessed.

Crashing through the front door, he followed the screaming and noises. They were coming from below. The basement. He attempted to be cautious as he hurried down the basement stairs, trying to keep his noise to a minimum. Not that anyone would be able to hear him over Lizzy's screaming. And another woman was groaning. Brooke?

Jumping down the last three steps, he burst in on a horrific scene. Lizzy and a blonde woman he recognized as Brooke were both chained to posts. Lizzy had pulled herself as close to Chad as she could, screaming and trying to reach him, tears pouring down her face. The woman moaning on the floor was barely recognizable as April. Her neck was bruising. As if she had been strangled.

And Rebecca!

A red haze of rage misted over his brain as he saw Chad's long fingers around her throat. With a roar, Miles charged at him and knocked him away from the woman he loved. She toppled to the floor. Was she alive?

For a suspended moment, his heart stopped beating, and he couldn't breathe. Until she started to move and cough. It was a weak, wheezy sound. But it meant his Rebecca was alive. He hadn't lost her.

He'd turned his back on Chad too long. The other man charged at him, a knife in his hand. He sliced at Miles's arm. Miles jumped back out of the way just in time.

The two men circled in the traditional fighting stance. Miles knew he couldn't risk shooting. Not with all the women in the room.

The other man grinned, an angry leer filled with malice. He probably assumed that without his gun, Miles was weak. His face grew cocky. He maneuvered closer and closer, swinging the sharp knife in front of him. He was taunting Miles.

Miles let him.

The anger settled, cooling and hardening into fierce determination. Calmness filled him. He sent up a prayer of gratitude. God had prepared him for this day, although he hadn't understood at the time. God had given him skills that made him capable of defending himself, and the four helpless women, from the man dancing before him.

His fear vanished. He was, after all, a black belt.

Chad lunged, knife swinging.

Miles was ready. He stepped into the charge, and kicked. The knife dropped and skidded across the cement floor. For the briefest instant, Chad was still, speechless. Then he howled and charged again, his head low and arms out. He intended to tackle Miles to the floor. Miles bent and scooped his arms under Chad's, bringing his hands behind the other man's back. Chad squirmed, but couldn't break loose. One, two times Miles thrust his knee into the other man's stomach.

Chad buckled.

In an instant, Miles had him on his stomach and was clapping handcuffs on him, reciting his Miranda rights.

The front door slammed.

"Olsen!"

"In the basement, Jackson! I have four women down here who require medical care."

The rush of footsteps thumping down the stairs was one of the best sounds he had ever heard.

As the paramedics and police swarmed into the basement, Miles went over and kneeled by Rebecca. Her eyes were open. She blinked, then narrowed her eyes on his face.

"You came," she signed, a tear trickling down her dusty cheek. "I knew you would come. I was afraid it wouldn't be in time."

A sobbing to his left made him pause. April was having a meltdown as the paramedic checked her over. "I didn't mean to help him! I didn't know what he was doing until it was too late!"

What?

Rebecca patted his knee. He switched his attention back to her instantly. "She was his girlfriend. He used her to get to us. When she found out, she tried to break up with him. She sent me a warning text before, when Sergeant Parker was driving us home. It just came too late—we were attacked before I could send it to you."

He wiped the tear from her face, then realized he was fighting back his own tears. "I don't know what I would have down if I had lost you."

She smiled. He sucked in a breath. And sat down, hard, shaking. "I love you. You know that, right? When I knew you were in trouble, nothing else mattered. Not my job, my past, nothing. Only you."

"I love you, too. I am so grateful that God created a man so special, and let me have him in my life." She stopped signing, a frown touching her face. "Your job? Will you lose your job? Why?"

Miles had been aware on some level of Seth, who was part of the team of paramedics, telling the chief the less personal details of the signed conversation, including the part about April.

"He's worried he might lose his job because he didn't follow protocol today when he learned you were in danger. He put you first." Seth signed the answer to Rebecca for Miles. It was a good thing, because she was clinging to his hands. The chief looked at Miles. Not, Miles was glad to see, with anger or disappointment.

"Officer Olsen, I am rather proud of your deportment on this case." Miles couldn't help the way his jaw dropped. The shock nearly knocked him over.

The ambulance crew started to load up the women on stretchers. Lizzy insisted on walking, as soon as they had freed her. April and Brooke were in no shape to walk, though. Neither was Rebecca. All he wanted was to go with her. The chief motioned for him to stay back. He obeyed, but wasn't happy about it.

Chief Kennedy chuckled. "Easy, officer. This will only take a moment. Then you can go to the hospital and be with your girl."

Miles felt himself flushing. He'd been pretty obvious about his feelings, he guessed.

"Officer Olsen, I want you to know that I believe you did the correct thing."

His head shot up. "Sir? I disobeyed a direct order. You told me to wait for backup. And I didn't."

"I know. And normally I'd be furious with you. But if you hadn't, at least one of those women, if not more, would have died. Your actions and quick thinking saved the lives of four women. And you managed to capture a vicious killer, alive. He will go to jail, and those women will be able to go on with their lives, instead of constantly looking over their shoulders. Well done."

"Thank you, sir!" He couldn't wait to go to the hospital and tell Rebecca!

"Oh, and Miles—" the chief paused at the base of the stairs "—I think it's time we reviewed your record. I think you've earned a promotion. Don't you?"

Whistling that same TV show theme song, the chief started up the stairs. Miles stared after him a moment, unable to believe his ears. Then a grin split his face. He all but ran out to his car to go see Rebecca.

Of course, once he arrived at the hospital, he had to wait for her to be seen by a doctor. When he was finally able to see her, she was getting ready to go.

"They aren't keeping you overnight?" he signed, surprised.

"No." She grinned and winked. "I can go anytime."

"Where will you go?"

"I can't go back to my apartment. I'm going to move out of there. But Seth invited me back to his place."

That was a relief. Even with the danger gone, he hated to think of her in that apartment she had shared with Holly, knowing the sad memories it would bring back. "Can I give you a ride?"

She hesitated. "Maybe. First, did you mean what you said in the basement?"

"Yes," he signed without missing a beat. "I love you."

She sighed. A sigh that seemed to come from deep in her soul. Her eyes closed. But only for a moment. When she opened them again, she graced him with a mischievous smirk, one that took his breath away. "Then why haven't you kissed me yet?"

He could do nothing about the grin that spread from his heart and across his face. Or about the way his entire being hummed with love for this bright woman. "I have no idea."

And because there was no good reason not to, and being the intelligent man that he was, he pulled her gently into his arms and kissed her.

Epilogue

One month later

It had started to snow while she was inside. Fluffy white flakes drifted down. Already, the layer on the ground was two inches deep. She grinned and stuck out her tongue to catch a cold flake. She loved winter. Thanksgiving was next week. Miles had invited her to spend the evening with him at his grandparents' house. His father would even be there. Rebecca was nervous to meet him, but she knew Miles would be there to support her. As he always did.

Rebecca cast a glance at her watch as she made her way to where her car was parked. She felt confident that she had done well on the test. She'd get her scores back sometime after Christmas. If all went well, she would be able to take the performance portion of the exam in the spring or summer.

Right now, though, she was running late for her dinner date with Miles. Just thinking of the love of her life brought a smile to her face. They'd been dating for a month now. Maybe it was too soon by society standards, but she knew he was the man she wanted to spend the rest of her life with. When would she ever find another man who understood her so well, who made her heart race and loved God as much as she did?

She was going to see Miles tonight, in fact. Her parents had invited them over to their house for dinner. At first, she'd been tempted to reschedule. She and Miles had a lot to celebrate. His chief had been very pleased with Miles's work on her case. In fact, he had just been reinstated as a sergeant. But, like the sensitive man he was, he had convinced her to accept the invitation. It would mean so much to them.

Sending a prayer of thanksgiving to her Father in Heaven, she searched through her overlarge purse for her cell phone to send Miles a text. Behind schedule. Leaving now.

A moment later, her phone vibrated. That's ok. I'm behind schedule 2. Meet you at your parents' house? Love u.

Fine. Love u 2.

It took her almost an hour to go home, shower and change, and get ready to leave. As she was finishing getting ready, her gaze in the mirror caught on the small earrings in her ears. She'd gotten her ears pierced soon after she and Lizzy had been rescued. Miles had gone with her and had held her hand as they put the piercing gun to her ears.

It was more than jewelry to her. It was a physical sign that she knew who she was and which world she belonged in.

She hesitated. Should she take them out before going

to her parents' house? She pondered, then pressed her lips together. No. Her parents knew her choices. And they accepted them and loved her. They were generous people who wouldn't let this effect their relationship.

The earrings stayed in.

She drove to the farmhouse near Spartansburg, her excitement growing with every turn in the road. Soon, she'd see Miles. They hadn't been able to see each other for two days because of work schedules. Funny how long two days could be!

Pulling into the driveway, she noted his Jeep was already there. She bounced out of her car and nearly ran up the stairs. He met her at the door. She knew why. Once inside, there would be no hello kiss. Not with her parents watching. But here, out of their sight…

Miles let the door close behind him and pulled her gently into his arms. She snuggled closer, feeling like everything was right in her world again. He bent and kissed her slowly, letting her know how much he'd missed her the past few days.

"I missed you," he signed when the kiss ended.

She sighed. Bliss. "Missed you, back. Two days is a very long time."

"Forever," he agreed.

In sync, they moved into the house. Her *mam* hugged her, the sparkle in her eyes letting them know she wasn't fooled. She knew why they'd met outside.

Rebecca was too happy to be embarrassed.

It was a perfect evening. Her *mam* and *dat* were pleased to see their oldest daughter. They didn't so much sign as gesture, letting Miles take care of facilitating the communication. She didn't mind. They were trying, and they were showing their care and love in every gesture.

It wasn't until the meal was almost finished that Rebecca got the hint that something else was going on. Her normally calm father seemed a little flustered, and her mother's smile grew more pronounced, even though she kept putting her napkin to her mouth to hide it.

And Miles? Since when had he become clumsy? He'd dropped his fork twice. The second time he picked it up, he gave her *dat* a small nod. Like a signal.

Uh-oh.

What was going on?

Her father reached over and patted her hand. She looked at him, suspicion growing.

He started to gesture, then stopped. He rose and went to grab some paper and a pencil. And began to write.

Rebecca, my daughter. I want to tell you this myself. I do not sign, so I will write. Miles came to talk to us. He said it was an Englisch custom. He asked us for our blessing to marry our beautiful daughter.

Her breath stalled and her heart quickened. Was this really happening?

Her *dat* continued.

We love you, and would be very happy to have him as our son. We told him yes. He has our blessing. So do you.

She stopped fighting the tears and let them fall. Miles stood up from his chair and moved to her side. He kneeled down on one knee before her, and began to sign. Straight ASL. She understood the message. This moment was just for her. They could repeat it for her family later.

"Rebecca, I love you with all my heart. You are strong, and beautiful in every way. You make my life complete. We have not been dating long, but these past two days without you have been very lonely. Please, marry me?"

Her heart was full. "Yes. I love you so much. I will marry you!"

His eyes glinted. He blinked. Then reached into his pocket to pull out a ring. It was simplicity itself.

This man truly understood her.

Holding out her left hand, she didn't care that it trembled. It should tremble. With joy and hope. Her life was changing forever.

She'd spent too much time holding her heart back. Now, she was giving it freely to this man.

He slid the ring on her hand. Then, even with her parents watching, he leaned in and kissed her softly. She smiled against his lips, the promise of the future bright in her heart.

* * * * *

If you loved this book, don't miss the first heart-stopping Amish adventure from Dana R. Lynn's AMISH COUNTRY JUSTICE *series:*

PLAIN TARGET

Find more great reads at www.LoveInspired.com

Love Inspired®

Save $1.00

on the purchase of any
Love Inspired® or Love Inspired®
Suspense book.

Available wherever books are sold,
including most bookstores, supermarkets,
drugstores and discount stores.

- ✂

Save $1.00

on the purchase of any Love Inspired® or
Love Inspired® Suspense book.

Coupon valid until September 30, 2018. Redeemable at participating retail outlets
in the U.S. and Canada only. Limit one coupon per customer.

52615870

Canadian Retailers: Harlequin Enterprises Limited will pay the face value of this coupon plus 10.25¢ if submitted by customer for this product only. Any other use constitutes fraud. Coupon is nonassignable. Void if taxed, prohibited or restricted by law. Consumer must pay any government taxes. Void if copied. Inmar Promotional Services ("IPS") customers submit coupons and proof of sales to Harlequin Enterprises Limited, P.O. Box 31000, Scarborough, ON M1R 0E7, Canada. Non-IPS retailer—for reimbursement submit coupons and proof of sales directly to Harlequin Enterprises Limited, Retail Marketing Department, Bay Adelaide Centre, East Tower, 22 Adelaide Street West, 40th Floor, Toronto, Ontario M5H 4E3, Canada.

5 65373 00076 2   (8100)0 12377

U.S. Retailers: Harlequin Enterprises Limited will pay the face value of this coupon plus 8¢ if submitted by customer for this product only. Any other use constitutes fraud. Coupon is nonassignable. Void if taxed, prohibited or restricted by law. Consumer must pay any government taxes. Void if copied. For reimbursement submit coupons and proof of sales directly to Harlequin Enterprises, Ltd 482, NCH Marketing Services, P.O. Box 880001, El Paso, TX 88588-0001, U.S.A. Cash value 1/100 cents.

® and ™ are trademarks owned and used by the trademark owner and/or its licensee.

© 2018 Harlequin Enterprises Limited

LIINC1COUP0718

*When a former sweetheart reappears in this widow's
life, could it mean a second chance at love?*

*Read on for a sneak preview of
A Widow's Hope,
the first book in the series Indiana Amish Brides.*

He knocked, and stood there staring when a young, beautiful woman opened the door. Chestnut-colored hair peeked out from her *kapp*. It matched her warm brown eyes and the sprinkling of freckles on her cheeks.

There was something familiar about her. He nearly smacked himself on the forehead. Of course she looked familiar, though it had been years since he'd seen her.

"Hannah? Hannah Beiler?"

"Hannah King." She quickly scanned him head to toe. She frowned and said, "I'm Hannah King."

"But...isn't this the Beiler home?"

"*Ya.* Wait. Aren't you Jacob? Jacob Schrock?"

He nearly laughed.

"The same, and I'm looking for the Beiler place."

"*Ya,* this is my parents' home, but why are you here?"

"To work." He stared down at the work order as if he could make sense of seeing the first girl he'd ever kissed standing on the doorstep of the place he was supposed to be working.

"I don't understand," he said.

"Neither do I. Who are you looking for?"

"Alton Beiler."

"But that's my father. Why—"

At that point Mr. Beiler joined them. "You're at the right house, Jacob. Please, come inside."

He'd never have guessed when he put on his suspenders that morning that he would be seeing Hannah Beiler before the sun was properly up. The same Hannah Beiler he had once kissed behind the playground.

Alton Beiler ushered Jacob into the kitchen.

"Claire, maybe you remember Jacob Schrock. Apparently he took our Hannah on a buggy ride once."

Jacob heard them, but his attention was on the young boy sitting at the table. He sat in a regular kitchen chair, which was slightly higher than the wheelchair parked behind him.

The boy cocked his head to the side, as if trying to puzzle through what he saw of Jacob. Then he said, *"Gudemariye."*

"And to you," Jacob replied.

"Who are you?" he asked.

"I'm Jacob. What's your name?"

"Matthew. This is Mamm, and that's Mammi and Daddi. We're a family now." Matthew grinned.

Hannah glanced at him and blushed.

"It's really nice to meet you, Matthew. I'm going to be working here for a few days."

"Working on what?"

Jacob glanced at Alton, who nodded once. "I'm going to build you a playhouse."

Don't miss
A Widow's Hope *by Vannetta Chapman,*
available August 2018 wherever
Love Inspired® *books and ebooks are sold.*

www.LoveInspired.com

LIEXP0718

Love Inspired®

Inspirational Romance to Warm Your Heart and Soul

Join our social communities to connect with other readers who share your love!

Sign up for the Love Inspired newsletter at **www.LoveInspired.com** to be the first to find out about upcoming titles, special promotions and exclusive content.

CONNECT WITH US AT:

Harlequin.com/Community

 Facebook.com/LoveInspiredBooks

 Twitter.com/LoveInspiredBks

SPECIAL EXCERPT FROM

*With a child missing and a killer on the loose,
Ava Esposito and Oliver Davidson team up to
save a life and hunt a killer.*

Read on for a sneak preview of
Rescue Operation *by Lenora Worth,*
the next book in the Military K-9 Unit miniseries,
available August 2018 from Love Inspired Suspense.

Ignoring the tilt and rumble of the HH-60G Pave Hawk
helicopter about to hoist her down below, Senior Airman
Ava Esposito adjusted the sturdy harness sleeves around
the black nylon sling holding the sixty-five-pound yellow
Lab that was about to rappel with her. Roscoe's trusting
eyes followed her while he hovered close to her chest.

"That's right. It's showtime. We've got to find that little
boy."

Roscoe wouldn't understand, but they were armed and
ready for anything or anyone they might confront in the
dense woods that belonged to Canyon Air Force Base.
This reserve covered hundreds of acres and could hide
a person for weeks if not months. Right now, she had to
find a lost little boy and watch her back for a serial killer
who'd escaped from prison in the spring and was reported
to be back in these woods.

Her focus humming on high alert, Ava checked her weapons and equipment one more time. Then she patted the alert K-9 on his furry head. "Ready?"

Roscoe woofed his reply.

Nodding, she scooted to the open side of the chopper and let her booted feet dangle out, Roscoe's warm breath hitting the inch or so of skin she had showing outside of her heavy camo uniform, protective combat vest, knapsack and M16 rifle.

Above her, a crew member adjusted the carabiner holding the pulleys that would hoist both Ava and Roscoe so they could rappel down, each with their own pulley to hold them securely together.

Nothing but heavy woods, scattered rocks and hills. But somewhere out there was a lost, scared little boy.

Something whizzed past her. But even with the chopper's bellowing roar all around her, she heard the ding of metal hitting metal.

And then she saw it. The ricochet of a bullet hitting the fuselage. Someone was shooting at them!

Don't miss
Rescue Operation *by Lenora Worth,*
available August 2018 wherever
Love Inspired® Suspense books and ebooks are sold.

www.LoveInspired.com